ECLIPSE

by

DALTON TRUMBO

MESA COUNTY PUBLIC LIBRARY FOUNDATION
GRAND JUNCTION, COLORADO
2005

Lovat Dickson & Thompson Ltd., Publisher, London, 1935
Published with new introduction, foreword, maps and supplementary
material, Mesa County Public Library Foundation, 2005

Cover design by Erik Lincoln
Interior design by Tami Jo Russell and Katherine Lopez

ISBN 0-9772015-0-3
ISBN 0-9772015-1-1 (trade paperback)

10 9 8 7 6 5 4 3 2 1

DEDICATION

" . . . Because my grandfather took a vigorous part in the building of the portion of Colorado which the story deals with, I should like to add a dedication to the book. He is a grand old man who cleared the land, fought in the cattle-sheep wars, put in twelve years as a sheriff when fast shooting and hard riding were essential, and is still hale enough to enjoy any slight triumph his grandson might render him. Hence I should like the dedication to read:

To
My pioneer Grandparents
Millard and Hulda Tillery

Will you please notify Mr. Dickson of this alteration, and also any subsequent publisher? . . .

Cordially,
Dalton Trumbo"

— From a December 15, 1934, letter to Dalton Trumbo's agent, Elsie McKeogh. The dedication was not included in the original 1935 printing of Eclipse, *an omission happily corrected by this subsequent publisher.*

FOREWORD

My father, called "Trumbo" by my mother Cleo and his friends, was born in Montrose, Colorado, on December 9, 1905, and moved to Grand Junction, Colorado, with his parents in 1908. There his parents, Maud Tillery and Orus Trumbo, had two more children, Catherine and Elizabeth. Orus was a hard-working man who had little material success. After working several different jobs, he became a shoe salesman in Benge's Shoe Store until he was let go in 1924. He also had a large vegetable garden, which supplied the family with food year-round and brought in extra money as my father peddled vegetables around town.

My father was energetic and industrious. In addition to selling vegetables, he had a paper route, and during his high school years, he worked on *The Daily Sentinel* as a cub reporter, which gave him an intimate knowledge of the workings of the town as he covered the courts, the mortuary, the high school, and the various civic organizations. This familiarity with the town's institutions no doubt contributed to the creation of many of the characters in *Eclipse*.

He considered Grand Junction his hometown. In a letter to his mother written from Boulder when he was at the University of Colorado, after his parents moved to Los Angeles, he wrote, "Yes, I am still in the notion of going to Grand Junction Xmas if possible. If I can't be near my parents on Christmas, I would at least love to be near the scenes where we spent so many happy Christmases together."

In 1924 Trumbo left Grand Junction to attend the University of Colorado in Boulder. Known in Grand Junction as a young man with potential because of his oratory and debating talents, he was also known as a hell-raiser whose high school grades were mediocre at best, and he was determined to do well at the University. He wrote his mother, "I seem to feel the anticipation of my high school teachers that I will flunk, the confidence of my friends that I won't, and above all the strong backing of my parents and sisters, and their confidence that I will make good." His expenses, as he outlined them to his parents, were $30 board, $14 room, and $4 fraternity dues. He pledged the Delta Tau Delta fraternity. He believed it was the best fraternity at the University and hoped that he would benefit from the friends he would make there. His parents were contributing $15 each month, and his aunt, Elsie Tillery, had agreed to provide another $5. It was up to him to make up the difference, which he did with a reporting job with the *Boulder Camera*, typing other students' papers and doing various odd jobs. Nonetheless he was always in need of more money. Unanticipated expenses such as laundry bills, books, carfare, and additional clothes ("I bought a pair of hot pants the rah rah boys wear"), and his family's inability to maintain their level of financial support ended his college career in the summer of 1925.

His father lost his job with Benge's Shoe Store shortly after Trumbo left for Boulder in the fall, and the family moved to Los Angeles with the hope of better prospects. He joined his parents and sisters in Los Angeles that summer. His father, who had been ill in Grand Junction, grew worse and became unable to work. Maud went to work as a bookkeeper in a car dealership and later worked out of their small apartment as a seamstress. Trumbo took a night job at the Davis Perfection Bakery and also worked days when he could, repossessing motorcycles and even trying bootlegging until he found it too dangerous. Orus died in 1926 of pernicious anemia, and Trumbo became the primary provider for a family of four at the age of twenty-one. Ironically it was but a few months later that three doctors in Cambridge, Massachusetts, developed a cure for the disease—regular intake of liver—for which they won the Nobel Prize the same year that *Eclipse* was published.

While he was at the University of Colorado, it became clear to my father that writing was his passion, and he determined to become a writer. He worked on the campus humor magazine, the yearbook, and the campus newspaper in addition to the Boulder newspaper, and when he moved to Los Angeles he kept on writing in every spare moment. He said that he wrote six novels before *Eclipse* was published, all while he was working nights and often days as well.

When my father began working in the bakery, he told himself he'd be leaving it any day, that he was going back to college. In fact he enrolled at the University of Southern California but wasn't able to complete his classes there. As the years wore on, he became desperate to be out of the bakery, fearing that he would spend the rest of his life there, day after day, never becoming the person he and his family believed he was destined to be. He worked there for ten years, supporting his mother and sisters.

The years in the bakery changed my father. In Grand Junction and in Boulder he was an energetic, talented, brash, determined young man. He believed that with hard work and his natural talent he would succeed. Just a few years later, fortunate enough to be employed at all in the midst of the Great Depression, he found himself in a job he hated, fearing that he was trapped. His determination to succeed took on a driven edge. As much as he hated the job, he developed friendships in the bakery and compassion for the people he worked with and respect for the quiet, difficult lives they lived. He also became keenly aware of social class differences. He watched bakery workers hand out day-old bread to people lined up three deep, for more than a block. The generally conservative views of his upbringing (Maud was a Republican) slowly transformed to a more radical understanding of differences in class and privilege, of poverty and wealth. In Grand Junction his family had struggled, but there was always food on the table, and if other distinctions of class existed, they didn't seem to be particularly noticeable or troubling to him. In Los Angeles he saw the differences and experienced hardship first-hand.

Like Sinclair Lewis's *Main Street*, *Eclipse* is a novel about a town and its people in the style of the social realists. The social realist school was born out of a reaction to the excesses of romanticism and classicism and aimed to describe everyday life as realistically as possible without sentiment or flowery language. This approach included a frank look at people's ethnicity, social class, the work they did, how they did it, their desires for power, sex, status and money.

Reading *Eclipse*, one gets a true sense of how life in a small American town in the West was lived in the 1920s. Men got up in the morning and walked to work, children went to school, mothers washed and cooked and cleaned, summers were hot and lazy, winters cold and deep with snow. A frequent tool of the social realists was satire, and in *Eclipse* it is harsh, particularly in the first third of the book. Perhaps Trumbo blamed the town for his family's difficulties and for his father's early death. In the biography *Dalton Trumbo*, the author, Bruce Cook, quotes Trumbo as saying of his father, "Being fired, as he was, from Benge's Shoe Store after working there for so many years, well, it came to him like a bolt out of the blue—this was the end! Now I perhaps reacted to this more unfairly than I should have." Trumbo goes on to explain that the John Abbott character is a substitute for his father. This character, who is based on the real-life Grand Junction citizen W. J. Moyer, was also destroyed (as his father had been) by the depression. He says, "And that, possibly, accounted for some of my passion against the town itself, which actually had been quite good to me."

The premature loss of his father froze their relationship in time, depriving my father of the deepening shared knowledge and understanding that growing older with a parent makes possible. My father loved his father and also was troubled that his father was a failure. In *Johnny Got His Gun*, Joe Bonham says, "His father couldn't make any money. Sometimes his father and mother talked together in the evenings about it . . . It was hard to understand how his father could be such a big failure, when you stopped to think about the thing. He was a good man and an honest man . . . Even rich people in the cities couldn't get vegetables as fresh or as crisp . . . Those things you had to raise for yourself . . . even the honey they used on the hot biscuits his mother made. His father had managed to produce all these things on two city lots and yet his father was a failure."

The John Abbott character is sympathetically drawn. He is a thoughtful, generous, moral, kind man who dislikes public displays of appreciation. He extends credit in his store, he gives generously to various charities, he facilitates loans for townspeople who are short of ready cash, he quietly helps several boys with college tuition, and he is as helpful to Stumpy Telsa, the town Madam, as he is to Harry Twinge, his immediate competitor. His caring and concern for Shale City is almost fatherly. "When a business house failed, John Abbott felt that in some fashion he had been negligent."

Abbott also has a mischievous sense of humor. When Stumpy Telsa asks him if he can help find a job for a girl who came to her for help, and who chased a patron with a hairbrush when he mistook her for one of Stumpy's girls, Abbott suggests she work for Violet Budd, who is looking for a housekeeper. Mrs. Budd regularly launches morality campaigns to run Stumpy out of town, and the man the girl ran off turns out to be Mrs. Budd's husband, so the girl will certainly be protected from discovery if she works there since Clem Budd won't say a word for fear of disclosing his own patronage of Stumpy's. So Violet employs, unbeknownst to her, an object of her unbridled scorn and her husband's passion. Stumpy and Abbott share a spontaneous laugh as they think over this situation. This humor is distinctly Dalton Trumbo. He delighted in exposing hypocrisy and relished the opportunity whenever it presented itself.

Hermann Vogel, a teacher in the high school, is the antithesis of John Abbott. He has open love affairs, he terrorizes the faculty at the high school, he behaves as though he is John Abbott's equal, he ridicules even John Abbott, and despite, or perhaps because of, their differences, the two are good friends. John Abbott vicariously enjoys

Vogel's exploits and irreverence, and through the friendship "escaped the shackles of respectability and became a creature of Mephisto." Vogel's moody lectures often leave John Abbott feeling strangely uncomfortable. On one occasion he tells Abbott, "They may turn against you some day, these organizers, these praters, these ex-Loyalty Leaguers. And when they do—God pity you."

Vogel makes his last appearance in the book when the depression has taken hold. He has worked out a theory which he tells Abbott. It is that the depression is a necessary cleansing. "I foresee an era of pleasant, graceful living ahead," says Vogel. "It will endure only so long as we keep the moralists hungry . . . let them, therefore, labour fourteen hours a day at extremely low wages and they will have little urge to thrust their snouts beyond their own doorsteps. They will have no time to dictate what their neighbour may read, what he may see in the theatre, what he may wear, what he may think, what he may eat, what he may smoke, whom he may love."

At my father's memorial service in 1976, Ring Lardner, Jr., a long-time close friend, said of him: "At rare intervals, there appears among us a person whose virtues are so manifest to all, who has such a capacity for relating to every sort of human being, who so subordinates his own ego drive to the concerns of others, who lives his whole life in such harmony with the surrounding community that he is revered and loved by everyone with whom he comes in contact. Such a man Dalton Trumbo was not." That might, however, be a description of John Abbott. My father was more clearly like a very successful Hermann Vogel—a brilliant, ambitious, contentious man who enjoyed exposing the hypocrisy and lies that he observed, a man whose drive, determination, humor and powerful personality generally got him what he wanted. He won a National Book Award for *Johnny Got His Gun* and two Oscars while blacklisted in Hollywood for refusing to testify before the House Un-American Activities Committee. He went on to break the blacklist with *Spartacus* and *Exodus* and wrote twelve more screenplays and one more novel before his death in 1976.

Yet John Abbott and Hermann Vogel both reside in my father. His written works are often stories of kindness and love (*The Brave One*), fairy tale romance, (*Roman Holiday*), of honesty and dreams (*Our Vines Have Tender Grapes*). Others are stories of individuals acting on their ethical beliefs (*Spartacus, Lonely Are the Brave, The Fixer*). His interpersonal relationships were almost always conflicted. Yet he loved animals without reservation, and it was in his relationships with the birds he owned or rescued in later life that I saw in him a tenderness and consuming love. He had a large screened-in area built for a fledgling mockingbird he had raised from babyhood so it could experience the outdoors in safety before it was freed. On another occasion I witnessed his anguish when a pet parakeet died in his cradled hands on a frantic trip to the vet. It was difficult for him to expose his vulnerability. Satire is self-protective. It serves to keep deeper, more tender feelings safely hidden. Trumbo satirized Grand Junction rather than expose the pain he felt upon the loss of his father, rather than expose the love he felt for the town and the childhood he left there.

—Nikola Trumbo
2005

L: Dalton Trumbo in 1915 as a newspaper carrier at age 10.

R: High school yearbook, 1924.

L: Trumbo with his father, Orus, 1924.

R: Trumbo's other famous office, 1967.

INTRODUCTION AND ACKNOWLEDGMENTS

The rest of the world associates Dalton Trumbo with two places: Hollywood, California, and Washington, D.C.

In Hollywood, Trumbo won two Academy Awards during his five-decade screenwriting career. In Washington, D.C., he and the other writers and directors of the Hollywood Ten were blacklisted in 1947 in the first killing frost of the cold war.

But here in Grand Junction, Colorado, Trumbo is forever associated with Shale City, the fictitious name given to his hometown in screenplays, novels and a play.

After leaving Grand Junction in 1924, the city's most successful artistic export went on to write dozens of films and win a National Book Award for *Johnny Got His Gun*, but it was his first published novel, *Eclipse*, that assured Trumbo's fame—and infamy—back home.

Some Grand Junction readers were offended by the fiction in the book—others by the truth. Whether through vanity or reality, readers in 1935 (and, even later, their descendants) saw enough similarities between themselves and the characters to take grave offense at being cast in Trumbo's early experiment with social satire.

Mildred Hart Shaw of *The Grand Junction Daily Sentinel,* in a February 6, 1977, book review of a Trumbo biography, described the town's reaction to *Eclipse* this way: "It was (and is) a human reaction to an unexpected, unjustified attack: Bewilderment, pain and anger, at least from those directly affected, and they were many."

Trumbo jabbed the hatpin in the parade balloons of civic boosterism. He insulted the town, his own town, in the eyes of many residents. But with time and seven decades' distance, most now understand that he was not composing chamber of commerce pamphlets or drafting documents into the historical record. He was writing fiction, with all its latitude of borrowing, combining and fabricating to best effect.

Grand Junction's reaction to *Eclipse* is now part of the local lore, probably second only to the Ute Curse in terms of recognition. Many believe as fact the tales that copies of *Eclipse* were burned by mobs, tossed to a watery grave over the Fifth Street Bridge, or smuggled regularly from the library in order to keep the book's contents a secret.

In fact, there likely never were many copies of *Eclipse* to begin with, and those who were angered enough to destroy books and put down efforts to fund a memorial to Trumbo in Grand Junction were a vociferous minority.

Enter this reprint.

Over the years, discussion came from various quarters to reprint *Eclipse*. Finally in 2005, those individuals and groups combined to a critical mass to get the job done. The year 2005 has double significance: It marks 70 years since the publication of *Eclipse*, and December 9, 2005, is the 100th anniversary of Trumbo's birth.

Dalton Trumbo was a man of strong convictions, a wordsmith of no small mastery and a bootstraps kind of success story. We are proud to say he was from Grand Junction—from Shale City.

With the generous support of Trumbo's wife, Cleo, and his children, Nikola, Christopher and Mitzi, the copyright for *Eclipse* was passed from the family to the Mesa County Public Library Foundation.

All profits from the sale of the book will benefit the library.

Several people's efforts stand out, though everyone on the reprint committee contributed. Ken Johnson spearheaded the committee. Bernie Buescher provided inspiration and support. Jim Spehar and Lois Becker secured underwriting. Miffie Blozvich coordinated and organized the steering committee. Priscilla Rupp-Mangnall and Gordon Rhodes planned the 100th birthday celebration. Jacquie Chappell-Reid took the lead on marketing. Jeanine Howe of the Mesa State College Theater Department oversaw the staging of Trumbo's play *The Biggest Thief in Town*.

As for the book itself, Pat Gormley, Dale Williams, and Judy Prosser-Armstrong of the Museum of Western Colorado provided materials. Dave Fishell shared historical insight. Tami Jo Russell and Katherine Lopez completed layout. Suzie Garner drew the Shale City map. Christina Ovalle retyped the book. Donna Bettencourt and Bob Kretschman painstakingly proofread and handled copyright logistics. Erik Lincoln designed the cover. Mitzi Trumbo generously shared the family photographs.

—*Laurena Mayne Davis*

Eclipse reprint committee:

Lois Becker, Donna Bettencourt, Tillie Bishop, Miffie Blozvich, Bernie Buescher, Tess Carmichael, Jacquie Chappell-Reid, Doug Clary, Laurena Mayne Davis, Dave Fishell, Pat Gormley, Dale Hollingsworth, Judy Jepson, Ken Johnson, Gregg Kampf, Jeff Kirtland, Bob Kretschman, Gordon Rhodes, Priscilla Rupp-Mangnall, Allison Sarmo, Diane Schwenke, Jim Spehar, and Christopher Trumbo.

WHO'S WHO IN SHALE CITY?

Eclipse may be a work of fiction, but Grand Junction readers made a true sport of speculating on characters' real-life inspirations. A number of lists exist—jotted down quickly, penned in delicate script or typed on stationery tucked between *Eclipse's* pages.

On a handful of characters various lists agree: Abbott for Moyer, Twinge for Benge and Brown for Walker. But from there, it was anybody's guess who Trumbo had in mind when he created his characters. Some list-makers went so far as to weigh in on the veracity of events in *Eclipse* and betrayed a bit of their own sleuthing in the process. Partial contents of a half-dozen lists are compiled here, with recent editing and research by the Mesa County Historical Society.

Mrs. Alloway's Cafeteria	Mrs. Glessner's Cafeteria *(Brink's jewelry store on North 5th)*
Bradford Creek	Kannah Creek
The Emporium	The Fair Store
Ferber's Shoes	Lowe's
Moffat Ranch	Lincoln Park
Sawtooth Mesa	Grand Mesa or Bookcliffs
Shale City	Grand Junction, Colorado
Shale City B&L	Composite of Mesa and Mutual
Gerald Abbott	Wm. Weiser *(nephew of Moyer)*
John Abbott	W. J. Moyer *(While on the blacklist, Trumbo took the name John Abbott as one of his pseudonyms under which to write.)*
Fred Best	Harold Wolverton
George Boone	Mr. Bill McGuire *(assistant manager, Fair Store, dress shop owner later)*
Stanley Brown	Walter Walker *(The Daily Sentinel)*
Violet Budd	Emma Budilier *(Story is true . . . WCTU . . . Probationer . . . Very bossy woman who tried to run G.J.*
Henry Crooks	Frank Winfield *(Stationer & Music 500 Block of Main St.) or Chapman stationer (blind—wife still here)*
Mrs. Art Frank	Mrs. Ottman
Art French	Sterling D. Lacy

Jerry Gorba	Jim Golden, pool hall *(grandfather, lawyer)*
Walter Goode	D. B. Wright *(real estate)*
Phil Haley	Bernard Woolverton *(dress shop)*
William Harwood	George Parsons *(jewelry store)*
Mrs. Delmor Hayes	Biggs, Kurtz or C.D. Smith
Karwin	Krohn
Freddy Kilner	Dalton Trumbo
Dr. Lawrence	Dr. Day
Donna Long	Belle Lay *(W.B. Johnson's sister-in-law . . . lived on First Fruitridge)* *(No one knows that I have talked to who she could be . . . Some people seem to think she was true. As Mrs. Trumbo and Mrs. Moyer were the closest of friends. Mrs. Trumbo is the mother of the author.*
Richard Maesfield	J. Talbott *(Lived in Goodwin house)*
Claudia McQuaid	Merle McClintock *(society editor of Sentinel)*
Me-catch Me-kill	Old Santa Claus Smith
Frank Packton	Charlie Lumley
Bill Robinson	Clarence A. Harris *(Ladies' dress store owner)*
Hermann Schonk	A. E. Carleton
Miss Septimus	Julia Taylor *(Latin teacher)* or Miss Wilson *(owned home with Belle Lay at 1158 White)* *Watson (Lay & Watson, 1138 White)*
Slocum	Rev. Forsythe
Stumpy (Maria) Telsa	"Broken Jaw Nell" Paige *(Story not all true—had broken jaw from gun shot—came from Leadville—don't know about Moyer & money but know she gave lots to charity)*
Harry Twinge	B. M. Benge *(shoe store owner—buxom wife)*
Hermann Vogel	History teacher Hydle

Miss Weems	Ethel Cox (*story true*)
Mildred Wessingham	Edith Wickersham (*social climber in the 400 set with Mrs. Lacey etc . . . True, and really did blackmail him*)
Henry Wilhelm	H. Webber
Williams	Carl Hillyer (*music professor*)
Henry Wilmer	Mr. House (*good Methodist*)
Sam Wilmer	Bill Rhone

And for those a little less savvy of the makings of Shale City, here is one last comment included with an identifying list of names:

No nice woman walks on the South Side of Main . . . because of proximity of barber shops and cigar stores and pool rooms . . .

TRUMBO/WALKER LETTERS

"... As for 'Eclipse,' I hope you will not be angry if you find characters whom you recognize in it. I am convinced that all novels are based in fact, and distorted for fiction purposes to suit the author's particular talent. I do not pretend that any of the portraits in 'Eclipse' are real, yet you will, I am sure, see at least some characteristics of their counterparts in real life. I have no apologies although I do confess to some qualms. But the job is done, and it took a long time in the doing, and since I understand that one or two copies have already hit Grand Junction, there is no use trying to keep the book a secret. . . ."

— From a letter Dalton Trumbo sent to Walter Walker, his former boss at The Grand Junction Daily Sentinel. *Trumbo included an inscribed copy of the recently published* Eclipse.

"My dear Dalton:
. . . It goes without saying that 'Eclipse' has caused a great deal of local comment. While in your letter you say you do not pretend that any of the portraits in 'Eclipse' are real, nevertheless people in a town that is used as the locale for a story or a novel are prone to accept as real any characters which they think they recognize.

Walter Walker,
Museum of Western CO Photo

Naturally, I have no feeling of anger toward you concerning the book. After all, it was your privilege to utilize your old home town in demonstrating your talents as a writer if you wanted to do so. Furthermore, I might say, in looking at it from a selfish standpoint, that I have no cause to complain because you treat me very decently in the book. Frankly, however, with the personal regard and affection I have for you and the admiration I hold for your talent, I do regret that you saw fit to release this story at this time. The only personality involved in the book that actuates me in saying this is that of W. J. Moyer. Had not misfortunes piled up on him quite so heavily and so frequently, and if he were not alive, this regret of mine would be considerably reduced in volume. . ."

— Walter Walker's reply a month later.

Dalton and Cleo Trumbo at the House Un-American Activities Committee hearings in 1947.

Dalton Trumbo with his father and sister Catherine at their Grand Junction home.

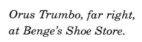

Orus Trumbo, far right, at Benge's Shoe Store.

Trumbo family at their California ranch in 1948.

*A family group
(Tillery side)
photograph taken
in 1908.
Left, M.F. Tillery,
Dalton's grandfather
at age 51, his mother,
then 23, and
great-grandmother
Tillery at age 86.*

*Trumbo kids—Nikola,
Mitzi and Chris, 1947.*

*Trumbo and sister
Catherine sitting
on top of their
father's workshed.*

*Trumbo and Cleo
at the Academy
Awards, 1945.*

CONTENTS

Book I

John Abbott: a Day in his Life
August 6th, 1926
Page 2

Book II

John Abbott and the Town
1928-1929
Page 87

Book III

John Abbott and the World
1930-1933
Page 149

BOOK I

JOHN ABBOTT
A DAY IN HIS LIFE
AUGUST 6, 1926

I

IT was eight o'clock that morning when John Abbott awakened
from a dreamless sleep and squinted at the timepiece which stood
on a table beside his bed. Each day for more than twenty years he
had awakened at this precise hour, taken through half-closed eyes the
same oblique glance at the clock. If it were two or three minutes
before eight, he never failed to experience a pleasant sensation of triumph, as though he had managed in some fashion to swindle fate.
But if it were even a few seconds after the hour he felt sharply
annoyed, and was blighted throughout the day with a premonition of
small adversities to come. Every clerk entering his service at the
Emporium had heard at some time or other the story of John Abbott's
fabulous ability to pull himself promptly out of the deepest slumber.

This morning it was neither before nor after the hour: it was eight
o'clock to the second. John Abbott raised himself on his elbow and
scratched his chest meditatively. He swung his feet to the floor and
sat on the edge of his bed for a little period, staring at the clock and
considering how narrowly he had escaped missing his mark. Then he
walked to the window in his wrinkled muslin nightshirt for a look at
the world.

From this exalted position he surveyed the smooth expanse of his
front lawn, close-clipped, intensely green, descending to the sidewalk
of North Fifth Avenue in a prim little slope. The shadow of the house
cut sharply across it, with the clear brilliance of sunlight crowding in
at the borderline. Beds of nasturtiums and zinnias on either side
marched in two flaming columns straight to the sidewalk. Beyond the
shaded area a hose burst into a misty spectrum. John Abbott
breathed deeply. The air was fresh, invigorating, unusually warm. In
his opinion the day was going to be a scorcher.

Staring thus at the sparkling morning, completely refreshed from
a night of untroubled slumber, greeted on all sides by omens of order
and tranquility, a feeling of profound contentment took possession of
him. He sighed and turned from the window, a faint little smile curving his lips. He padded over to a little writing-desk which stood
against the wall, sat down before it and thumbed for the proper page
of his diary. It was his custom each morning to record the events of

the preceding day. He paused, pen in hand, gazing for a moment at an old photograph of the Emporium which faced him from the wall. Then his pen scratched across the leaf of the open book.

"Had a good day and night. Nothing happened. What more could I ask?"

He read the notation carefully, paused as though considering some addition, and then closed the book. Still conscious of the placid ecstasy which filled his mind, he sat down again on the edge of his bed. If he had been a boy of twelve he would have shouted at the top of his voice. If he had been a young man he would have burst into song. But he was sixty, so he contended himself with little grunts of satisfaction as he thrust bony toes into bedroom slippers and prepared for his bath.

After a cool shower he set himself to the grave task of shaving. He used a straight-edged razor that once had belonged to his father. In the course of this operation he discovered a curious anomaly. The left side of his face was marred by a little scab which—now that he thought of it—had been there for months. He remembered that it had started one day with a tiny eruption which he carelessly had sliced off. Every day thereafter he had shaved away a fresh scab, causing the wound to bleed anew. He had, after a fashion, come to accept the diurnal fleck on his cheek as an inescapable circumstance of his existence. Now he understood that it was merely an example of malignant thoughtlessness. Carefully he shaved around the blemish. Give it three days' reprieve from the blade and it would vanish entirely. A great many of life's inconveniences, he mused, could be vanquished as easily provided one took the trouble.

He went downstairs in his shirt sleeves. At the landing he paused for a moment to drink in the beauty of his favourite gew-gaw—a stained-glass window which caught the sunlight each morning and spilled it through the hallway in a gorgeous mottling of blues and yellows and purples. Coffee aroma wafting through the hall lured him from this spectacle to the dining-room, where Nora, the housekeeper, awaited his pleasure. He ate a dish of sliced peaches drowned in yellow cream, and four buttered griddle cakes floating in maple syrup and wreathed with crisply fried bacon. After his second cup of coffee he bit the end off of the cigar he had brought with him, lighted it thoughtfully, and sent a cloud of pale blue smoke curling into the shafted sunlight from the east window. Then he walked slowly upstairs.

As he passed his wife's bedroom he heard her call to him.

"John—" her voice came faintly from behind the closed door, "I want to see you before you go to the store. I have something to tell you."

"In a minute," he called back to her.

He went into his room and put on his coat and vest, which were of a silky material reputed to be very cool in the summer time. Coming out once again, he paused in the hallway before Ann Abbott's door. He wondered what on earth she could have to tell him. Then, with a little gesture of resignation, he opened it and entered.

Nora, who had come upstairs with a tray containing Mrs. Abbott's breakfast, heard them speaking and waited at the end of the hall. She was too honest a person to approach closely enough to eavesdrop, but she knew the conversation was not pleasant. She could hear their voices rising sharply in anger, then subsiding to sullen undertones. Presently John Abbott burst out of the room and went downstairs without looking at her. When she took the tray in to the bedside, her mistress was weeping . . .

John Abbott walked slowly toward Main Street looking straight ahead all the way. The intense morning sunlight beat down upon him feverishly. Perspiration beaded his forehead, but he paid no attention to it. His face was taut, and his stricken eyes were filled with bewilderment.

II

BY noon Shale City lay exhausted and panting beneath the grilling incandescence from above. The seasons did not deal kindly with the Colorado Valley, of which it was the metropolis. Summer suns arose early from behind the level rim of Shale Mountain, crept slowly and mercilessly across the face of heaven, and disappeared reluctantly into the immense aridity of eastern Utah, leaving the country beneath a parched desolation from June to September. A faint breeze from the west sprang up every afternoon, choked with quivering heat from the Utah Desert. Out on Sawtooth Mesa the dry-farmers cultivated their fields endlessly, drooling mud from the corners of their mouths, damning the fate which had tempted them to wean crops from so fierce a land.

The Colorado River meandered through the valley, a treacherous sluggard intent upon its rendezvous with the Green beyond the state border. In August it was yellow oil fringed with pale cottonwoods, willows, sweet clover—all its majesty turned sickly from the spending of turbulent spring passions. North of it lay green fields and pleasant orchards laved with ditch water, fading fifty or sixty miles beyond into lofty mountain pastures. But to the south of the river stretched an empty desolation contested only by hard-bitten squatters, serried with canyons and fantastic horrors in rock, tinted with red from decayed sandstone, thirsting for moisture which never came.

In an elbow of the stream, at the dividing line between cultivation and aridity, the town of Shale City encroached bravely upon the natural domain of sage brush and desert. There was something magnificent in the spectacle of the town with its adjacent farmlands rising in green vigour to challenge the wilderness which extended so far in every direction. The very fact of its existence seemed almost an impertinence. Yet there it was, four hundred miles from Denver to the east, three hundred miles from Salt Lake to the west, dependent almost entirely upon its own resources for food and drink, for comfort and security, for business and wealth—a huger metropolis in view of its surrounding terrain than London ever was.

It fastened its great water mains like a greedy vampire to the throat of Bradford Creek twenty miles into the mountains. At one point the stream was a surging flood; farther down it was scarcely a trickle. Shale City, burning with thirst, had sucked it nearly dry. The water was stored in two artificial lakes concerning which periodic scandals arose. It was a popular rumour in Shale City that each time the reservoirs were drained the bodies of unwanted infants were found. No one ever verified such reports, yet every two or three years they popped up to cause a little stir of indignation.

Water was the most important single item in the life of Shale City. Without it the town would wither, burn up, return to dust within a single season. For all the care taken to preserve it, the supply frequently ran low during the summer. Whenever this occurred the fire insurance companies sent scolding letters which threatened a rate increase. Sprinkling hours were inaugurated to keep the pressure even throughout the day. Citizens arose at three or four o'clock in the mornings to appease their thirsty lawns and gardens. Despite the inconvenience, they never neglected this duty, for green things vaguely symbolized the civilization they had wrested with such toil from the desert.

Just as the river divided the valley between fertility and desolation, so Main Street in Shale City was the boundary between respectability to the north and poverty to the south. Below Main Street lay the industrial district. There were the railroad shops and the great square icehouses which disgorged their contents into refrigerator cars during the harvest; there was the flour mill, the beet sugar factory, the canning factory, the broom factory, the chemical factory, the ice cream factory, the gas plant, and the chain of wholesale grocery warehouses.

In this section, inhabited by labourers and their fruitful wives, also flourished the less pretentious but equally vigorous business of prostitution. The addresses of the three on Lower Street—526, 532, and 538—were known to every person in town. When schoolboys wanted to be extremely *risqué* they had only to mention the numbers knowingly. Sometimes the very young boys scrawled them on sidewalks and fences as though they were lewd words to be flung defiantly in the teeth of their elders. Women and girls of the town beholding them there were constantly reminded of the threat of professional competition. Though there were sporadic crusades against them, the houses had been standing as long as the town, and there appeared to be little prospect of getting rid of them. The girls were pretty and the madames ugly. The girls came from the east, and floated on to Salt

Lake and eventually to California when their popularity waned. The madames stayed on. Stumpy Telsa, or Maria Telsa, as she signed her name to legal documents, was the dowager of Lower Street. The girls of Shale City, prizing their virtue above riches, had enabled her to become the wealthiest woman in town.

North Shale City was something very different. It contained two paved residential streets with green parks extending through the centres. They were lined with good solid houses—square, wide-windowed, comfortable and as resolutely defiant of the elements as the people who inhabited them. There were broad lawns and many trees. There were gardens and spacious screened porches. There was shade in the summer and warmth in the winter. One had little need for more. It was the ambition of a boy in Shale City one day to build his home on East Main Street or on North Fifth Avenue. But if fortune did not smile upon such schemes, any location in the northern half of the town was acceptable.

Farther to the north, after one passed through the residential district, stood the Shale City Country Club, stoutly constructed of stone and white mortar. High on a little mesa, it had nine holes of golf, two tennis courts and locker rooms which were always cool. Its ballroom opened with great arches on to a sweep of terrace, from which one could view the whole valley in panorama. The spectacle at night, when the earth was slowly cooling and there was no sound, seemed all velvet and diamonds with the silver ribbon of the Colorado winding off into the darkness. The young people of Shale City loved to dance at the Country Club, and to steal from the ballroom on to the terrace, or even into the sparse foliage of the grounds, there to enjoy the warm splendour of the night and of each other.

III

JOHN ABBOTT devoted the morning to small affairs, exaggerating their importance in order to divert his mind from the shocking things Ann had told him. After a spartan lunch at Mrs. Alloway's Cafeteria, he returned to his desk in the glass-enclosed office overlooking the Emporium.

The room was situated somewhat above the level of the store, so that its occupant could view the whole place without himself being seen. This arrangement afforded John Abbott privacy, yet permitted him to be constantly in the midst of the business he loved.

He sat down in his leather-upholstered chair, squinted over the store briefly and then sank into the torpor of his siesta. He had slept for over an hour when the sound of a motor backfiring on Main Street awakened him. He drew himself slowly together. His collar was wilted and his coat was wrinkle-stained with perspiration. Heat flooded over him like a fever dream.

He sat upright at his desk, a short man, moderately thin, with a permanent attitude of deprecating modesty. The top of his head was greasily bald, fringed with greying hair of which a few wisps were long enough to brush over the bare expanse above. Despite a close-cropped moustache, his features were not impressive. His chin did not jut, and his lips were neither coarse nor fine. He was the sort of man one might expect to find as a bookkeeper, or perhaps a retired clergyman. His eyes were blue with corner wrinkles partly concealed by gold-rimmed spectacles. Notwithstanding his mild, almost milkish appearance, success had conferred a benevolent dignity upon him, and power had blessed him with an indefinable air of authority.

He gazed down over the store. Fatigued by the heat and lacking customers, the clerks lolled behind their counters. He nodded in bemused approval. It was well enough for them to have this rest period in the afternoon. They were always busy in the mornings, and around five o'clock, when the heat had subsided somewhat, the women of the town would venture outdoors for a last-minute spurt of shopping. He listened approvingly to the whirr of little conveyors as they brought the money of stray customers to the cashier's booth. He heard the ring of silver as change was made, and the hum again as it was sped unerringly to its destination.

He glanced out of the window upon Main Street. It was three o'clock —that time of day when the blazing torch overhead seemed to marshal all its fury before entering upon a sullen descent. Main Street's length caught the heat on white pavement and hurled it upward again. Almost no one braved its glare. The few automobiles which drifted through the business section were driven by young people—high-school students killing the vacation lethargy of a dull afternoon.

At this time of day the drug stores would be crowded with listless boys drinking uncounted glasses of sweet syrups, reading magazines from the racks. In the stuffiness of his office he could almost smell the antiseptic odour, almost hear the hypnotic hum of drug store fans. He noticed the boys as they idled before the soda fountain, beheld the intense glaze of day dreams over their eyes as they stared toward the sun-swept sidewalk. Only the passage of a girl could distract their attention. The girls wore the thinnest sort of dresses, lacy and transparent. The boys scrutinized them with faintly enthusiastic approval, then resumed their dreams.

Seized with a sudden restlessness, he arose from his desk and went to the window. He could see the river, and Sawtooth Mesa's slate-grey expanse beyond. He could see the factories below Main Street, stopping short at the row of business buildings which quivered in heat waves near at hand. He could see the network of northern streets—green trees and wide-eaved houses where once an Indian encampment had stood. This town was his—every foot and stick of it: for he had built it out of nothing at all . . .

He had started with only four hundred dollars and his seventeen-year-old wife, Ann. That was in 1886, when he deserted Pennsylvania for a more spacious country. He had journeyed slowly through Kansas and Nebraska, and finally into Colorado, alert for a suitable spot. Denver and Pueblo were too civilized, and Leadville was too barbarous, but when he beheld the indiscriminate row of shacks which was to become Shale City, he knew that he had reached the end of his quest. He thrilled to the natural advantages of the place: a central location isolated between two larger cities, an abundance of cheap land which might be made to bloom, a great river to furnish water for irrigation. He had wanted to find a new place in which he might establish himself for ever, a country in which he might grow to be a power. Shale City fulfilled all of his requirements. He rented a frame building twelve by twenty-four feet, stocked it with two hundred dollars' worth of merchandise, and named it the Emporium.

It was he who named the town also. When he came it was known only as "the Junction", because a railroad just nosing its way through the wilderness had selected it for a minor division point. Great mountains of shale extended in all directions from it: one could throw a slab of shale on a camp-fire and watch the oil ooze from it, and see the slow flame which consumed the oil.

"Some day the oil wells are going to run dry," John Abbott declared. "Then there will be no other source but this shale. We have whole mountains of it. One day Western Colorado will lubricate the world. It will be the centre of a great industry. We will name the place Shale City."

So it was done.

Shale City became an incorporated town, and the barren country around it slowly quickened with life. The government built canals, and the farmers planted orchards. The fruit soaked up sunlight and mountain water, and throve. In the upper reaches of the valley settlers carved out vast ranches with fields lush in alfalfa, timothy, wheat, oats. Great herds of cattle roamed in mountain meadows, and later the sheep came too. Slowly the whole empire assumed form before John Abbott's eyes. There were other towns. There was an organization, a unity of purpose. A barren, lonely country took on fertility for the seeds of civilization.

In all of this John Abbott played a vital part. He yearned for the smokestacks of industry to confirm and perpetuate this triumph over wilderness. The Emporium constantly outgrew its quarters. There was need for a bank, and he organized the Shale City National. He induced the sugar company to put up its factory in Shale City, bringing a new industry to the valley. He donated the land upon which the flour mill and the grain elevators stood. He organized the Shale City Building and Loan Association. He distributed credit, financing hard-pressed ranchers and business men through his bank while he assisted their employees to build homes through his building and loan association. He trusted the people of Shale City at the Emporium, and they seldom imposed upon his trust. In the end he grew wealthy, and no one begrudged him his eminence.

Although he was chairman of the board of the Shale City National and president of the building and loan, it was the Emporium which claimed his deepest affection, for he was a born merchant and the Emporium was a fine store. It had grown until now it boasted three aisles, a men's department and a basement wherein toys and notions and hardware were sold. Its huge plate-glass windows were decorated by a Shale City boy whom John Abbott had long ago sent to Chicago especially to learn the work.

There were travelling men who maintained that no store in Denver offered a better stock of merchandise than that which might be purchased at the Emporium. National trade magazines praised its management and published photographs of its window displays. Often they printed interviews with John Abbott, relating how he had built the business from a shack into an institution. It was rated as one of the first three small-town department stores in the country. John Abbott took more pride in its standing than in the strength of his bank or the services rendered by his building and loan.

But the Emporium was more than just a store: it was a vital thing in the life of half the state. It is doubtful whether even the schools and churches were more important factors in the cultural growth of Shale City than John Abbott's store; although they attended to the intellectual and spiritual life of the town, the Emporium supplied those refinements which the cultivated mind and spirit inevitably require of existence. It was a fabulous international bazaar, looting the far countries of the earth, supplying the housewives of Shale City with silk from Japan, perfume from France, porcelain from Bavaria, linen from Ireland, furs from Siberia, rugs from Persia—all of these treasures gathered in a place which was less than a generation removed from the frontier!

The store had a social significance, too, for its large sales staff included nearly every impoverished widow in Shale City. It was almost axiomatic that if a man died leaving his wife inadequately supplied with money, she would clerk at the Emporium whether there was actual need for her or no. Some of the store executives murmured against this policy, but their protests were unavailing. John Abbott distributed stock bonuses among his older employees each year, and gave parties at the Country Club for them all. The women had their own social organization—The Emporium Women's Club—and it was almost as important as the Shale City Women's Club itself. Working in the Emporium, one almost attained the dignity of a doctor or lawyer. The job was institutional rather than commercial. One was engaged in furthering the public welfare.

It was not strange, therefore, that John Abbott enjoyed the actual affection of the town. Business associates complained of his leniency,

but the citizens found only goodness in him. There was no air of righteousness about him, just as there was no taint of sin. He shrank from
gratitude and was faintly terrorized before acclaim, yet his benefactions
had touched so many people that canonization as a local saint had crept
upon him unawares. Since he had worked hard and dealt honestly,
since public applause was the incidental dividend of his labours rather
than an end toward which he consciously had striven, he derived a
sound pleasure from it—pleasure which he could not, of course, admit
to anyone. There were but two things he would have arranged differ-
ently, given the opportunity to start over again, and they were circumstances which had been almost beyond his power to alter.

IV

THESE matters were not a conscious part of John Abbott's thoughts as he stared over the rooftops of the town he had built. They existed as absolute facts, fragments of his life history, so undeniably a part of him that they flashed swiftly and effortlessly through his mind in a single instant, a series of passing contingencies, the importance of which dwarfed beside the larger considerations which had been thrust suddenly upon him.

For he found himself confronted with a crisis which reached to the very foundations of his existence, and, like a hungry wanderer through time and space, he was groping his way backward to its intimate beginnings. He stared into the glare of the sun until his eyes watered faintly behind his spectacles. He pressed the bridge of his nose between thumb and forefinger in a characteristic gesture, while netted wrinkles of concentration spread along his forehead. And then slowly, eerily, as a strain of music one has almost forgotten, as a thought one has entertained in some remote and innocent childhood, it began to come back to him . . .

The bank and the building and loan, the factory smokestacks and the Main Street stores, the fine square homes and the office in which he stood—all of them withered and vanished, dissolved like a whimsical dream into the Shale City of thirty years ago: the Shale City of straggling frame houses and rutted roads, of scrawny trees and reluctant fields, of a blacksmith shop, a livery barn, a sheriff's shack and a weather-scarred Emporium—a knotty, gnarled, tough little town with its tough little aspirations. Long-gone voices spoke into his ears, and the dead seemed to parade before his eyes.

Gently the heat of summer passed away; the cottonwoods shed their leaves; white frost lingered on after sunrise; snow fell softly and still more softly until there was none of it left in the sky; the night became brilliant with cold stars freezing in the midst of their immaculate splendour. He was sitting in the old Emporium on a winter's night thirty years ago . . .

Sharp, nostalgic odours filled the air. He caught the scent of new leather and earth-crusted potatoes; of perfumed soap and cans of kerosene; of stinging white peppermint drops nestled beneath a curved glass case alongside plug tobacco, writing tablets, cotton gauntlets; of woollen blankets, stiff blue overalls, fresh bolts of gingham, Stetson hats, lisle stockings, fleece-lined drawers—all these latter impregnated with dyes and chemicals to provide a cool, hygienic overtone for the prevailing medley.

A stove in the centre of the store roared with contentment, the lower reaches of its pot-belly glowing redly. Its jewelled draughts sent little moats of green and blue and purple playing over the room. One could see yellow flames through cracks around the vents. Outside it was white and still and bitterly cold. Frost crept over the knob of the front door, and the window was a fantasy in frozen steam.

John Abbott was a young man once more, seated at a roll-top desk beneath the hissing glare of a patented kerosene lamp. All day long they had been taking inventory, and now he was suddenly tired. He yawned, took a silver watch from his pocket, snapped it open and stared at its face in surprise. It was half-past nine. He dimmed the light to a bare glow, tossed his eye-shade upon the desk, and turned deliberately in his swivel chair.

On a horsehair sofa ten feet across the room Donna Long was fast asleep. She had been working with him steadily since six-thirty in the morning, counting nails and rubber boots, halters and pounds of coffee. No wonder she was exhausted! He had been thoughtless to stay on so long. He walked over to her on tiptoe.

Her face, framed between corn-coloured hair and the prim yoke of her dress, was smooth and childishly relaxed. He could see the lobe of her ear and observe for the first time the lovely curve of her eyelids in repose. One arm was thrown above her head, bare to the elbow, soft and deliciously round. For a moment there seemed to be no motion in the room save the rise and fall of her breasts, no sound save that of her breathing.

A little spasm of desire quivered through him. It was a bitter, inconsolable desire that had been with him from the first moment he had seen her; from that first day when Ann had been too ill to come down to the Emporium, and he had engaged Donna Long to take his wife's place. He had battled it with a sickening foreknowledge of defeat. But he knew there was no more battling it now.

Donna Long, lying before him in her deep exhaustion, was the most glorious sight he had ever beheld. Never, even in his adolescent dreams, had he thought he would find her. Yet she was with him, and no one existed anywhere in the world but the two of them. Outside there was timeless night and endless winter, with mountains bowed down beneath the snow. Here it was warm and he knew that he loved her.

His heart beat painfully as he bent over to touch her arm; his throat was so choked with anticipation that the musical elision by which he always called her came scarcely above a whisper.

"Donnalong!"

And then he was kissing her lips and eyes and temples—even the tip of her nose and the little curve of throat beneath her chin. Her arms reached out for his shoulders. It seemed that he was drinking from a well that had been close at hand all the while, but which he had never dared approach before. There was no doubt mirrored in the calmness of her eyes, nor any timid, nasty fear. Beneath a billowing eternity of muslin—of tucks and lace and shy, hand-made medallions—she was a drowsy white nymph, trembling, eager, delicately strong.

Oh, it was good enough to be young! Good enough to be young in a young place; to be young on a cold night in a warm place; to be safe and adored in the midst of a wilderness. No storm that ever blew could disturb them here, for a frail little wall that a man had made kept out the storm, sheltered something that heat nor cold nor wind nor rain nor any other thing could ever vanquish.

There were no recriminations, no tearful silences or thoughts of sacrifice, for she was fine and strong, full of life and courageously defiant of everything else. She had given herself to him not one jot more than he had given to her. The primitively divine equality of their bargain bewildered him, bound him to her all the more closely. It would be this way for ever and ever.

He banked the fire for the night and blotted out the lamp. He threw his coat tenderly over her shoulders. Outside it was much warmer than they had expected. The stars had given way to a universal whiteness. Snow was falling with that faint crush which is even more lonely than silence. She was close to him, his arm drawing her closer as they walked. Past the little row of buildings, past a dim house and then another, on into the still white immensity, with only the hushed music of their feet treading together upon new snow . . .

A wave of intolerable heat swept over him. Strange air roared through his head as the years whisked him back. He heard a voice speaking distantly. Someone had entered his office. He whirled about to face Donna Long.

He scarcely recognized her.

V

J OHN!" she exclaimed in a frightened voice; "John! What's the matter?"

He brushed his forehead, and brought the open hand down over his mouth and chin, his eyes staring dazedly at her all the while.

"Nothing," he said finally. "Only the heat, I guess. I felt a little sick for a minute."

"Sit down," she commanded. "You musn't stand in the sunlight on a day like this. Mrs. Britton just fainted in the rest room. The heat—I never knew it to be so bad. I wish it would rain. How I wish it would only rain!"

He nodded and sat down.

"Is someone taking her home?" he asked.

"Me-catch Me-kill is taking a delivery truck. She'll be all right."

Me-catch Me-kill was the swarthy Sicilian janitor whom the boys in the stock-room had christened twelve years ago in mimicry of his threats against an invasion of rats.

John Abbott nodded absently. He couldn't take his eyes from Donna Long.

"Donnalong!" he blurted awkwardly, "I have something to tell you. Something—nasty."

She had taken a chair opposite of him at the desk, and was writing something on a little pad. Now she paused, pencil upraised, to look inquiringly at him.

"Yes?"

"Something that is—well, something that's pretty bad."

She knew. He looked across the desk, and saw the muscles in her throat standing out in little cords as she braced herself, and he understood that without being told she knew.

"Ann knows." Her voice betrayed neither surprise nor complaint. Rather it seemed to call his attention to a fact as natural as a bank statement or an inventory sheet.

He nodded.

For a moment the office was isolated in silence. Then they both heard the buzz of a bluebottle fly as it beat out its life against the burning window screen. The heat and brightness of the day seemed suddenly to have centred upon them as the twin focal points of a hot, tortured world. Donna Long half rose from her seat, and then sank back again. John Abbott couldn't bear to look at her. Instead he stared off intently into the third aisle. He could hear her fingers drumming against the note-pad. Then her heels clicked as she walked around the desk toward him.

He looked up at her, and beheld only a plain woman who had defied the ravages of forty-nine summers to pillage her calm self-assurance. Thirty years she had spent in the Emporium, until now she was its vice-president and most efficient employee. She knew more about the business than he did himself, and he trusted her above all living persons. And during all that time, unknown to anyone, she had been his tower of strength, his mistress, his most dearly beloved. She stood before him now, both hands outspread on his desk to support her bended weight. He saw her nails, cleanly unpolished, white to the quick from pressure above.

"Of course," she said in a dull voice. "Of course. Of course . . ."

She covered her eyes with a stubby hand. John Abbott could see tears entrapped in little pools above each finger. Then, breaking over those small dams, they splashed down her cheeks. She was the only woman in the world, he thought, who could weep with dignity. Her emotions were so clear and faultless that tears gushed from her eyes with something approaching beauty. Watching her now caused little twitches of anguish to stir his bowels. It seemed to him that the August suffocation had suddenly invaded their privacy, leaving both of them parched and a little ugly. Something was ripping at the illusions of thirty years, trying to strip them before each other's eyes, to reveal them one to the other as commonplace people instead of the serene and gentle lovers they had always thought themselves.

Suddenly Donna Long did a surprising thing. She dropped to her knees, folded her arms in his lap, cradled her head against them, and by the simplicity of the gesture added her complete existence to the gift of her body which had been his for so many years. He looked down at the even parting in her hair, and dropped his hand gently over it. Instead of sobbing, as he might have expected, she sighed just once, and then, the resistance gone out of her utterly, she relaxed against him. John Abbott had never thought that love could be so terrible.

"We might have known," came her muffled voice. "How could we expect—?"

That had been the strange part of it. No one had ever suspected.

Who would have dared connect Donna Long—so brisk and efficient, so utterly flawless—with a romantic interest in John Abbott? And as far as he was concerned, it would have been blasphemy to suspect the town's only authentic oracle of an illicit affair. It was a thought which simply did not warrant consideration. And they had been careful, too. Very careful.

He stroked her hair.

"We just made a mistake, John." She lifted her face upward so that she could look into his. "We shouldn't have compromised. You should have divorced her, or I should have gone away. Out of this heat and dryness. Maybe that's it. This terrible hotness, where people are so frightened in the face of the sun that they cling to each other like scared things. I guess it's this town, maybe, and the dust and dryness and dirt and the hot, hot pavements. I'm not sure . . . but from now on it will seem like walking down Main Street everyday of my life, naked and dirty . . ."

"Sh-h-h!"

Her face was sallow clay, and John Abbott knew there was no beauty in it. Yet she had always seemed beautiful to him—even more beautiful than Ann as a bride. Even as she sat before him now she was more beautiful that anything he could imagine.

". . . it seems like such a waste," she murmured. "Such a waste, because I wanted children. I—I guess I was made to have children . . ."

There was the deeper thing, cutting into him with every word. She was made to have children. She was genuine and fine. She was strong. Her hips were wide and curving. Even the virginal leanness of her breasts seemed to cry out for an infant . . . But did she suppose *he* hadn't wanted children too? Did she think he had gone childless all these years from choice?

Of course she didn't. Like everyone else—if they considered it at all—she thought Ann Abbott was to blame for that. But if Donna Long, wanting children as she did, knew what Ann Abbott had known for so many years, would she still love him? It was hard enough to endure the scorn of one woman. To feel Donna Long's contempt fastened upon him as well—that would be too much. But for the shameful secret of his own sterility, he would have divorced Ann long ago, and married Donna Long, and lived the sort of life after which he had always hungered. They would have had children, he and Donna Long. They would have founded a dynasty, a regnant line of strong children to take over this country they had pioneered together.

There was no use even to think about it. This question of not having divorced Ann and married her had come up before. It had been the one phase of their relationship which Donna Long could never understand—and the one which he could never explain to her for fear her knowledge of it would drive him mad.

His mind went back desperately, searching out reasons, looking as always into the past. Perhaps if he and Ann could have had children, Donna Long would never have entered his life. When he had discovered the real reason for his barren marriage, it had seemed to him that Ann's feeling toward him changed mysteriously. Perhaps it had been only his imagination—or perhaps it had been a reflection of his personal reaction to the discovery. Whatever the reason, he had never since been wholly at ease with his wife. He knew that physically he was mild and inoffensive. But to be sterile as well—how could he expect Ann to love him? What, indeed, was more insignificant than a man without the germ of life?

Driven by his own shame and what he imagined to be Ann's reproach, he had found solace in Donna Long: Donna Long with her quiet sympathy and her splendid grasp of living. He had taken the fine rapture of her love under the false pretense of being a man. She had always been so careful, too. It was almost comical. She attributed their successful relationship to this passion of hers for avoiding all pitfalls. But how would she feel if she had known all along that he was harmless as a child?—that fundamentally, basically, he was hollow? That because of this hollowness he had rushed into her arms, and that later it had become the principal obstacle to any steps he might have taken to marry her? It seemed preposterous that the same cause could produce two such opposite effects. Now—no matter what they did—they couldn't recapture that which he knew never could have been captured. And besides, Ann's health was failing. He had to think of Ann, too.

He knew well enough that Donna Long had had the worst of their bargain. He knew it, and damned himself for it, and in the end always exerted every effort to continue the relationship which had been so unkind to her. For thirty years she had been his life: without her he could not have attained the puzzling heights from which he now surveyed his little portion of the earth. She was everything he had . . .

"I love you, Donnalong," he muttered. "That isn't very much, but I do. I love you."

"Don't talk nonsense, John." She sprang suddenly to her feet and smiled wryly at him. She had the knack of puncturing his romanticism, of making him believe that she understood him better than he understood himself. She was moving back to her chair now. "It's rotten for both of us. There's nothing to do. It will be hard to face Ann. But that's part of it. Please bolster me when I feel a little whorish, won't you? Please give me a little encouragement!"

"Oh, Donnalong!" He walked swiftly to her and tried to kiss her lips; but she averted him, and his caress fell on her cheek instead. She was a little taller than he. "You're—wonderful!"

It sounded vaguely foolish to him, yet he meant it.

She was suddenly busy.

"I think Mr. Twinge is coming over to see you in about five minutes," she said briskly. "He called and I told him to come along. He would be goggle-eyed to see two old animals kissing each other on such a hot afternoon. Go away. You'll muss my hair." She laughed shortly. "But you're sweet, John Abbott. I love you well enough. Too well."

Her heels clicked out of the office. He sat down and mopped the top of his head with a large linen handkerchief. Harry Twinge was coming over to ask his advice about something or other. He would come into the office, and John Abbott would gravely tell him what to do. Harry Twinge would go away with his problem solved. But all the time John Abbott would be far more confused than his visitor. It seemed that all his life had been spent in just such confusion. He couldn't make any sense out of it. Excepting, of course, that he loved one woman and was married to another, and deserved none at all. No wonder he loved Shale City. It was his only hope for immortality.

VI

HARRY TWINGE was a lean man with ferret eyes and a permanent expression of baffled perturbation. His movements betrayed a conviction that some esoteric peril lay in wait to make sport of his slightest error. His high collar set off to unflattering advantage an extremely large Adam's apple that rode well up under his chin. Whenever he spoke the cartilage leaped into a curious series of gyrations which continued for several seconds after he had ceased, diverting attention to the fact that his collar, wilted at the edge and tinted a delicate greyish yellow, should have been discarded the day before. He shaved each morning, yet by eleven o'clock a black stubble had arisen to confound his efforts. He wore dark suits—hard-woven, square-cut and extremely durable; his shoes dwindled to a point.

He was the proprietor of Twinge's Bootery, from which he extracted a modest livelihood for a fat French wife whose vulgar joviality, even after twenty-four years of marriage, still embarrassed the nervous shoe merchant. There were, in addition, two female Twinges of marriageable age. It was a decided problem for Harry Twinge to keep a young man clerk in the store, for Mrs. Twinge constantly intrigued against the youth with one of her daughters. The clerks endured her little stratagems for a time, but in the end they preferred idleness to the horrid risk of being snared into matrimony with one of the young Twinges. Mrs. Twinge came to the Bootery every afternoon, coaxed her lardy thighs between the arms of a chair reserved for her near the front of the store, and remained until six o'clock. There she gossiped with all who approached, roared hilariously at her own doubtful witticisms, and passed scurrilous remarks about the private lives of departing customers. Poor Twinge's haggard demeanour was not wholly without reason.

Twinge hadn't made an independent business decision for eighteen years. As regularly as the seasons he walked across the street to the Emporium and deposited his problems in John Abbott's lap. The soundness of such a procedure was attested by the fact that Twinge owed no bills, held title to a good house and car, and maintained an excellent credit rating at the Shale City National Bank. John Abbott sold shoes, too, but that didn't prevent him from giving Twinge advice. He merely revealed to Twinge what he was going to do with the Emporium's shoe department, and Twinge followed suit. If the idea was valid, they both profited; if not, they lost. Twinge, along with every other business man in Shale City, knew that John Abbott wouldn't offer advice unless he was willing to stake his own money on it.

On this afternoon Twinge entered John Abbott's office with an air of extreme gravity. He snapped a handkerchief across his forehead and jerked himself on to the edge of a chair, where he sat as if poised for flight at the first hint of danger.

"I'm worried about the fall and winter business," he burst out to the owner of the Emporium. "I just can't figure it."

John Abbott smiled benevolently. He knew that in four or five months Twinge would be worried about the spring and summer business. Twinge was never able to figure it.

"If I go ahead and put in a style line for winter, and things go bad, why then I'm stuck, and would've been better off with a medium line," argued Twinge. "But if I put in ordinary stuff, and things look up, why then I'll miss a lot of quality sales. Brownstein-Faberman have their line down at the Shale House, and it's mighty pretty stuff. But it's gin-gerbready, and I'm a little afraid of that, Mr. Abbott. That is," he qualified with the air of a man who is always amendable to reason, "that is if I can't sell it."

He cleared his throat twice, agitated his Adam's apple, and gazed earnestly across the desk.

John Abbott made a sympathetic noise with his lips. "Fruit's going to be pretty good this year," he murmured sagely. "The trees are weighted down with peaches, Twinge. Apples are fair, and the pears are heavier than I've ever seen them. If we don't have a car shortage this fall, things are going to hum. And the railroad tells me we're going to have the cars."

Harry Twinge nodded and pursed his eyebrows thoughtfully.

"I'd say off hand that it'll be a good fall all the way around," continued John Abbott. "I'm putting in three lines of ladies' shoes—all style specials. You know—higher heels, shorter vamps, two-tone combinations. Not a whole lot, you understand, but a good variety."

Harry Twinge nodded again. "This Brownstein-Faberman line," he mourned, "is pretty high. Eight-fifty is what I'll have to get for their cheapest number. But it's pretty stuff, Mr. Abbott. It's real nice."

"Eight-fifty isn't too much," said John Abbott. "I'm even going to have one or two numbers up to twelve. But not too radical. People who buy twelve dollar stuff have pretty good taste. I have a rule around here: the lower the price the showier the style. As a matter of fact, I'm getting two hundred pairs of six-dollar shoes that would turn your stummick. But the six-dollar people want that sort of stuff—that is, in a good season. People who can't buy as often as they'd like usually want a little flash for their money."

"That's right," declared Twinge firmly.

"Then I'm going to push Christmas stuff. We should have a very good Christmas this year. I'm going to stock up on gift house-slippers, and push them out cheap. Not ordinary slippers, but something with a little pepper. Colours and furs, and satin mules at a dollar and a quarter."

"That's just what I've been thinking," maintained Twinge. "Although I can't see why the women want those mules. No warmth to 'em, and the floors are going to be just as cold this winter as ever. I always liked a good heavy bedroom number." John Abbott smiled, thinking, perhaps of Mrs. Twinge. "But I've been thinking about those mules," continued Twinge. "Brownstein-Faberman have some with pom-poms. What d'you think of that?"

"Good!" said John Abbott. "Get some, Twinge. Figure a short profit and turn 'em fast."

Harry Twinge sighed. John Abbott felt a little envious of a man whose difficulties were so easily dissipated. "This sure had me worried, Mr. Abbott," he declared. "I feel a lot better. It's mighty fine of you—this telling me what you're going to do. Helps out a lot. And you a competitor, too."

John Abbott smiled. "There's a lot of room, Twinge. We'll make this town style conscious, once those peaches and pears—'specially the pears—get to the eastern market."

A shrewd mask slid over Twinge's face. "I've been hearing," he probed slyly, "that Ferber's are having a little tough luck. You know how things like that get around."

John Abbott looked surprised. Ferber's Shoe Company was Twinge's hardiest competitor. Twinge realized that John Abbott would know at once if Ferber's found the going too rough. John Abbott smiled inwardly. Twinge was trying to milk him.

As a matter of fact, he knew the report was true. Ferber's was overdue at the bank, and had a burden of dead stock on hand. On John Abbott's advice, however, the store was going to hold a clearance

sale at the end of the month, hereby unloading its slow lines in anticipation of new fall shipments. Abbott was carrying the firm at the
bank. He was going to see that Ferber pulled through until fall,
after which a good season would save him. When a business house
in Shale City failed, John Abbott felt that in some fashion he had
been negligent.

"Hm-m," murmured John Abbott. "Haven't seen Ferber for a long
time. How's he looking? You know he had jaundice in the spring, or
something like that. Maybe that's the bad luck you heard about. At
least I don't know of any other."

Harry Twinge performed tricks with his Adam's apple and mois-
tened his lips with quick little tongue-darts of disappointment.

"By the way," he ventured delicately, "I'll be needing about six
hundred to discount my bills before the tenth. I thought maybe we
could arrange a sixty-day note."

"I think we can," agreed John Abbott. "I'll give Gerald a ring,
and you can drop over to the bank in the morning. Glad to accom-
modate you."

It was not unusual for Shale City merchants to be hard pressed
during the summer. Fall was their one big season. Gerald was John
Abbott's nephew. He was president of Shale City National Bank.

Harry Twinge thanked John Abbott profusely, leaped out of
his chair, and a moment later was knifing through the middle
aisle on his way to the street. He tarried for a moment in the
shoe department to offer chill salutations to Mrs. Stanley Brown,
who was buying a very dressy pair of pumps. Mrs. Brown was
one of Twinge's best customers. He did not look kindly upon her
apostasy. Watching the little tableau from his office, John Abbott
smiled. Then he telephoned Gerald at the bank to advance
Twinge six hundred in the morning.

VII

AS Harry Twinge scuttled from the store, Mrs. Violet Budd lumbered in. John Abbott, seeing her squeeze through the Main Street entrance, grew faintly panicky. He knew that she would plough straight through the middle aisle, ascend the stairs, and ensconce herself in his office before he could devise any means of escape.

Mrs. Budd was one of the three largest women in Shale City. The very fattest, by long odds, was Claudia McQuaid, literary lady of *The Shale City Daily Monitor*. Mrs. Budd was second, robbing Mrs. Harry Twinge of that honour by a full forty pounds. Claudia McQuaid's corpulence was rock-solid and formidable. Mrs. Harry Twinge's was a water fat, giving the impression that if a pin were inserted beneath her shining skin she would drain to normal weight. Mrs. Budd's obesity was very soft and flabby and pious.

Violet Budd's love of virtue was matched only by her hatred of sin—a term she considered synonymous with pleasure. Whenever the forces of heaven seemed to be having a bad time of it, Violet Budd could be relied upon to give a hand at the right moment and send the enemy screaming to its sties. During the prohibition campaign she had earned her position as the town's number one showman by dressing the Sunday School children of Shale City in white, equipping each with an enormous bouquet of chrysanthemums and thrusting them on hayracks to participate in the stirring battle. On election day a long procession of the hayracks passed along Main Street. The children chanted a war cry, waving their flowers rhythmically to a verse which, once heard, never could be forgotten. John Abbott thought of it while its author approached his sanctum.

Chrysanthemums up! Chrysanthemums down!
We want—we want—a good dry town!

He could still recall the shrill voices and the horrified surprise of local tipplers as they assembled to regard the spectacle. Violet Budd won the election hands down, and Shale City went dry long before Colorado and the nation.

The dry campaign had been only one of a long string of wallops which Violet Budd had delivered for righteousness' sake. She was always flapping her enormous breasts in some new cause. This illusion was induced partly by the hypnosis of her splendid bulk, partly by the looseness of her flesh, and partly by the beribboned waists which she affected. Genuinely aroused, she was an odious sight. She hissed through her nostrils, swelling and contracting rhythmically while her whole body quivered with devout agitation.

She dressed in voluminous greys, whites, and lavenders, and always exuded a faint stench of cologne which blended curiously on hot days with fumes of unctuous perspiration.

In addition to her church work and extra-curricular reform activities, she was County Probation Officer, an office which lent the dignity of authority to her pronouncements. Clem Budd, her husband, was a thin, stoop-shouldered cadaver of a man who worked for the railroad. He had many chances to serve the Shale City division, but he seemed always to prefer some more distant place. Sometimes he worked in Eastern Colorado; and when he grew tired of the country, he secured a transfer to Western Utah. Once when the railroad company insisted that he remain for a short period in Shale City, he drank rat poison in a fruitless effort to save himself. He awakened reluctantly in a company hospital, after which the superintendent respected his horror of home town employment.

The Budds had two grown sons. One of them drank discreetly and seduced the local debutantes. The other taught a Sunday School class and stayed home at night. Neither was married.

Violet Budd burst into John Abbott's office with a "God bless you, Mr. Abbott!" and eased herself into a chair across from him, panting, wheezing, smiling in her most amiable fashion.

John Abbott had always been fascinated by the woman. Her lips, thickly moist and colourless, reminded him of boiled liver, and seemed always on the verge of kissing someone. He watched them obliquely, as a bird is reputed to watch the eyes of a snake. On one occasion, when he had given money to her favourite charity, she actually *had* kissed him—right on the top of his head. He had never forgotten the spongy-wet pressure against his naked pate, and ever since had been alertly on the defensive.

"Well, how are you, Mrs. Budd?" he inquired, hastening with some concern to answer his question—"but you don't look well at all. Tch! Tch! Tch! You're overdoing yourself this summer, Mrs. Budd."

He knew she would be delicately offended if it were intimated that she looked as robust as a span of mules. She preferred to be regarded as one who places personal health in jeopardy for the common good, and beamed at John Abbott's recognition of this simple truth.

"I know it, Mr. Abbott," she agreed tremulously. "But there seems to be so much to do—and so few people willing to do it. The Lord's business comes last in so many cases—*so* many cases. My hired girl quit on me last week, and for the life of me I can't find another. If you happen to hear of a good one, do let me know, won't you, dear Mr. Abbott?"

"Of course I will." He nodded in deep sympathy. "It's too much— this hot summer and your regular work, and the things you always do besides. I don't see how you stand it."

She dropped slightly and nodded a weary assent. Then, remembering her mission, her eyes lighted and she cast her indolence.

"I came to see you about the Perkinses out on Sawtooth Mesa," she declared. "Their house and barn burned down Friday. It would break your heart, Mr. Abbott, to see that poor brave little mother taking care of her flock, while that fine father starts in all over again."

He made a queer clucking noise deep in his throat.

"I've been gathering things to take out to them. You know—bedding and clothes and furnishings and food. I thought perhaps you'd like to share in the work."

John Abbott was relieved. He had feared that she might want to enlist him in her newest cause, about which a great deal of controversy had reached his ears. If he could credit these reports, Violet Budd had set out to get the girls on Lower Street. Stumpy Telsa, it was intimated, had declared she would see Violet in hell first. Violet had gone to her pastor, old Reverend Slocum, urging him to lead a crusade against scarlet women. But Reverend Slocum had taken to his heels under cover of an absurd misinterpretation of the parable about the woman found in adultery, leaving Violet Budd the delightful task of hurling the first brick.

This had offered the opportunity for a minor skirmish before the general engagement, an emergency to which Mrs. Budd had arisen heroically. She was presently leading a rousing insurrection to oust Reverend Slocum in favour of a fighting preacher who would not hesitate to smite the Shale City jezebels. Over at Sid Hapwell's barber shop they were betting on Violet against the preacher. It was pretty funny, Sid Hapwell said, to think of the preacher praying to God he would hold his job, while Violet and her gang were praying to God he wouldn't. Reverend Slocum was over sixty, and of an exceedingly gentle disposition. Hap predicted that Violet—placing less confidence than Slocum in prayer—would slip in a few wallops on her own account, thereby winning the struggle. As a result of this turbulence, the embittered hosts of the righteous were potshotting at each other, while the girls on Lower Street, with nothing but *esprit de corps* in their favour, were offering a united professional front to the enemy. Stumpy Telsa boasted openly that she would remain in Shale City long enough to spit upon, or even more effectively to desecrate Violet Budd's grave.

"You go through the store," said John Abbott, "and select anything you need. Have it billed to me. And tell the Perkinses that I'd be glad for them to come in and see me any time they want to."

"That is splendid of you, dear Mr. Abbott!" replied Mrs. Budd. "God remembers things like this—He can't possibly overlook them, Mr. Abbott."

As a matter of truth, Mrs. Budd already had collected enough second-hand articles to care for the Perkins's needs. But she had a nephew in Utah who had settled down in a one-room cabin with a new wife, and stood in need of a few good blankets and other necessaries. Her nephew would receive the nice new merchandise from the Emporium, and the Perkinses would get the used things. Everybody would be satisfied, and no one would know the difference. Charity, after all, began at home.

Mrs. Budd leaned across toward John Abbott. Her expression changed ominously.

"I'm starting out once more to clean up Lower Street," she hissed as though this information could have escaped his knowledge. "The women of this town, Mr. Abbott, are going to run these prostitutes out of Shale City for ever."

Oh dear! John Abbott felt the blood rushing to his face. He had often noted that women were less delicate than men, once their feelings on a subject were aroused. He had heard them make the most surprising statements, advocate the most preposterous ideas, analyze the most painful subjects—all in the presence of their embarrassed, wriggling men. Even Donna Long startled him occasionally with her frankness, and Ann Abbott had always been accustomed, with sturdy vigour, to call a spade a spade. He had never grown accustomed to it. It seemed incongruous to the point of vulgarity for a lady to burst into conversation about prostitutes.

"Oh," he said after a little pause, "are you?"

"Yes indeed," replied Mrs. Budd stoutly. "This Maria Telsa, Mr. Abbott, has got to go. She's a menace to the purity of every boy in Shale City—her and her lewd women! I can tell you"—a faint wash of tears scummed her eyes—"I can tell you, Mr. Abbott, that only a mother of two fine sons can know and appreciate the menace of a condition like that one on Lower Street!"

"Oh, I'm sorry, Mrs. Budd!" he exclaimed. "I didn't think that Ellsworth and Ralph—" Quickly perceiving his mistake, he snapped his lips together miserably.

"Ellsworth and Ralph—! Why—why Mr. Abbott!" Her bosom stirred with honest indignation. "Why—you didn't mean that. Most emphatically not! They're fine clean boys. Those girls down there aren't even a temptation to them. I have raised my boys before God, Mr. Abbott. They have been brought up to respect all womanhood. But it's the others—all those boys who run around and are likely to be ensnared. Oh, it's them my heart bleeds for!"

He pooh-poohed commiseratingly, and wished that Mrs. Budd would go away. It was turning into a very distressing interview.

"The trouble is," continued the probation officer, "that these women have protection of some sort. I can't find out exactly where it comes from, but I'm getting a good idea. I had their places watched for several nights, and d'you know, Mr. Abbott, that the automobiles of two of our most prominent business men were parked all night in front of their dives."

"No!" he exclaimed. Goodness, how he wished she would leave him alone! He didn't want to hear any more. What did she expect him to do? He wished he were larger. This woman dominated him completely.

"Art French and Walter Goode!" she hissed.

"M-m-m!"

"A fine example for the town boys!"

"Tch! Tch! Tch!"

"And with the help of God"—she pronounced it quaveringly—"the Christian women of Shale City are going to cleanse the town of them and their foul diseases once and for all!"

His face was flaming scarlet now. Would the woman stop at nothing? Diseases, indeed! Why, he never discussed such things even with men. He was a little timid about them. Yet this woman could mention them to him without blushing. He told himself now that which he had told himself a thousand times before—and which he believed to be completely original: you can never tell what a woman is going to do or say!

Mrs. Budd was regarding him closely. She perceived his acute distress, and decided to spare him. She knew John Abbott well enough to understand that he could be disgustingly non-committal. He might be successfully solicited for any philanthropic enterprise, but when it came to something really important like the problem on Lower Street or the morals of Shale City youngsters, he always refused to choose sides. He was neither for nor against.

Such apathy was exasperating in a man who possessed so many splendid qualities, but he was too generous a person to be pushed. Each year she extracted several thousands from him for her various good works, and she had no intention to risk his ill-favour by forcing a stand on Lower Street.

Instead of persisting, she beamed affectionately upon him and arose from her chair.

"I'll tell the Perkinses how kind you've been," she said. "You are a fine man, John Abbott."

He mumbled an unhappy farewell, and watched her impressive side-sway as she waddled from his office. Downstairs she headed straight for the bedding department. He studied her with a shade of irritation. There was something about Mrs. Violet Budd which didn't ring true. He couldn't put his finger on it, and she was too valorously virtuous for him to condemn her for it. But none the less, it was there. He frowned thoughtfully. A disturbing idea skipped through his mind.

"I hope she never finds out about—Donnalong and me."

VIII

HE was still shuddering slightly at the prospect of Mrs. Violet Budd discovering the relationship between the president and vice-president of the Emporium when Phil Haley tip-toed into his office. Phil Haley worked at the Shale City National Bank. John Abbott glanced up at the clock. It was four-fifteen. Phil had come away from the bank early. Usually they did not finish over there until five or after.

He liked the boy who stood before him. Phil Haley was nineteen. He lived with his mother, who had been suffering from some obscure nervous disorder ever since Mr. Haley's death in a roundhouse accident. Phil, after being graduated from high school, had attended the Colorado Business College in Shale City, and John Abbott was glad to have him start in at the bank. He was a fine tall boy, with curling hair and a careless eye. Often at the bank John Abbott paused to watch him. Phil Haley, seated on his stool at the adding machine, was a beautiful sight to the merchant. His shirt sleeves were always rolled to his armpits, and he pumped furiously at the machine, as if the whole business were a game. John Abbott's heart warmed to him. He wished Phil Haley might have been his own son.

"Hello, Phil," he said kindly. "Sit down."

It was a relief to have this boy in the office after so formidable a visitor as Mrs. Budd. He felt his self-respect flowing back.

Phil Haley seated himself hesitantly. For the first time John Abbott noticed the strange pallor of the boy's face. He seemed ill. He stared at John Abbott as though he were facing his executioner.

"Why Phil!" he exclaimed. "What's the matter?"

Phil stared at him and through him. He turned a shade paler, if possible. His lips stirred without any accompanying movement from the rest of his face. His voice was dull.

"I came over here to make a confession, Mr. Abbott," he said. "I stole some money from the bank."

John Abbott started. This was the sort of thing he dreaded even more than Mrs. Budd. Once before there had been a theft at the bank. He would never forget it. It had left an indelible impression on his mind. For a moment he couldn't say anything. He merely sat and stared at Phil Haley. He hoped the boy hadn't taken too much.

"How much, Phil?"

"One hundred and eighty-seven dollars."

Relief surged through him, but he gave no hint of it. He nodded his head gravely.

"Suppose," he said after a little pause, "suppose you tell me all about it."

Phil Haley was prepared for such a request. He filled his lungs like a diver about to plunge into strange waters. He spoke rapidly. It seemed almost as though he were reciting from memory.

"About three months ago I had to have some money. I—well, I just had to have it. The only way I could think of was to mis-send cheques. You understand how that can be done? . . . Well, it is like this: when a cheque comes into our bank for deposit, say from Denver, why it's my job to send it to the bank on which it was drawn, to be honoured in the regular way. But if I sent the cheque to a bank in Miami, Florida, for instance, it would take about fourteen days for it to pass through the clearing house there, and be returned to Shale City with the notation 'Sent to wrong bank'. You see how that would let somebody in the bank at this end use the amount of cash involved in the cheque until it came back?"

John Abbott nodded. He was constantly amazed at the methods people devised to appropriate money that didn't belong to them. They were, it seemed, always at their best when engaged in such perilous enterprises. He listened intently while Phil Haley continued.

"Well, it just happened that at the time I needed this money, a cheque for a hundred and eighty dollars came in. It was on the Denver Exchange Bank. So I took it and sent it to the Miami First National, and used the money." The boy was trembling now. He gulped, and plunged on with his story. "When it came back, I didn't have the money to cover it. But I had to, you see? So I mis-routed other checks. It isn't often that we have a cheque amounting to just a hundred and eighty dollars, so I had to send out whatever smaller ones came in. And naturally I had to send 'em to other banks."

He paused and stared for an instant at an inkwell on John Abbott's desk.

"I've been doing that for three months, Mr. Abbott!" he finally burst out. "Three months I've been sending those cheques out, and trying to keep 'em straight in my head. I didn't mean to steal. You don't know how easy it is, Mr. Abbott, to do something wrong like this, without ever wanting to do it, and thinking you can get away with it! Whatever you do to me, Mr. Abbott, I just want you please to know that I'm not really dishonest. I—I just got caught with something I couldn't stop. Now—" he made a desperate gesture with both hands, "now I'm so mixed up I don't know where the cheques are, or when they'll be back or anything. Why, I've got cheques coming in and out every day, now, with different dates and different amounts and everything so mixed up I'm crazy! I just had to tell! *I couldn't stand it any longer!*"

John Abbott felt pangs of pity running through him so strongly that there was physical pain somewhere below his chest. It seemed almost as though he himself were being exposed. Phil Haley had said that John Abbott couldn't understand how a person might do something wrong, without ever wanting to do it, and thinking he could get away with it. He thought again of Mrs. Budd. How would she deal with John Abbott, if he were to confess that he had been leading an adulterous life for three decades? Yes, he could understand Phil Haley's fear.

He had to say something; had to do something. The boy was working himself up to a frightful pitch. If he didn't break the tension, Phil Haley would snap to pieces.

"When do you have to have the money?" he asked quietly.

"To-morrow morning."

"Well . . . don't worry. I'll see that you have it."

For an instant Phil Haley swayed uncertainly. Then he brought his head into his arms on the desk, and began to cry. His broad shoulders twitched, and the room was filled with the sound of his sobs, harsh and uncontrollable.

"Oh God, Mr. Abbott—*Oh God!* I—what can I—say?"

John Abbott reached across the desk and patted the boy's head.

"Just try to get hold of yourself," he soothed, "and then we'll talk this over."

It was several minutes before Phil Haley was in a condition to resume the conversation. When he finally looked up there was nothing but honest shame in his eyes.

"In the first place, Phil, can you tell me what you needed this money for so badly?"

The boy hesitated. "I—I'd rather not—oh yes, I'll tell you. That's the least I can do. I—I got a girl in trouble. She was a nice little kid, and I liked her, and I couldn't bear to think of what would happen to her, and I couldn't marry her either. You wouldn't understand, I guess. When you're in a fix like that without any money, why you feel like going all to pieces and—well, killing somebody. Or anything. I had to get the money, no matter what happened to me."

"That's a better reason than most people have."

A wan smile came over the boy's face, and disappeared quickly.

"I'm trying to think, Phil. Trying to figure out how to deal with this. The money part is simple. It's already taken care of. But it's you I'm worried about. There are so many sides to a thing like this. For example, it shouldn't have been possible for you to do this. We'll have to arrange it so that one of the officers over there will watch every cheque and be responsible for its routing. That will remove the temptation. Besides, Phil, you should have come to me. Everybody comes to me when they need money." There was no braggadocio in the remark. It was a simple statement of fact. Phil Haley nodded.

"But still we've got to decide about you. Because I understand what you've done, and am going to help you get out of it, is no reason that you should think I excuse your dishonesty. You must remember that. No forgiveness can quite nullify a dishonest action. On the other hand, I want you to keep your self-respect. You simply mustn't get to thinking of yourself as a thief. Otherwise you're lost. Somewhere between those two points lies your salvation. You must take this as a horrible lesson, but you must not let it destroy you. Understand?"

"I think so, Mr. Abbott."

"Then again, the bank isn't mine. It belongs to the stockholders, who are responsible for the money. The money belongs to people who have worked for it, and have put it in the bank because that is the safest place they know of. If I keep you over there, knowing what you've done, then I'm not treating the stockholders and the depositors fairly. You can see that part of it too, can't you?"

"Yes, sir." Phil Haley was taking it like a man.

"On the other hand, if I discharge you, there'll be talk. There always is, when a man leaves a bank in a town this size. A lot of vicious rumours are spread around, and the man is pretty well smeared by the time they've died away. I can't let that happen to you. You agree with me?"

"That part of it isn't for me to say."

John Abbott nodded approvingly. This Phil Haley had stamina. The situation was rounding out so well that John Abbott took actual pleasure in it. He supposed it was selfish and contemptible—this immeasurable satisfaction he found in solving other people's problems. But it was his talent, and he enjoyed it as a musician enjoys the mastery of a new and difficult score. He loved to talk to people, to sympathize with them, to inspire their confidence, to bring them slowly around to his point of view. There was no use denying that the gratitude which rewarded his efforts was pleasant. He enjoyed being thanked. It appeased his chronic spiritual malnutrition. It seemed to vindicate his existence.

When he dealt with a boy his interest was redoubled, for boys were his weakness and greatest extravagance. It was, he presumed, his deep desire for a son which accounted for the strange tug he felt whenever he looked at a healthy male youngster. It cost him about five thousand dollars a year to pay the educational bills of various Shale City boys. No one knew the names of those who benefited by these expenditures. He didn't like such benefactions to become matters of public knowledge. But he enjoyed bestowing them as completely as though the giving were a vice.

"I think the best thing for everybody concerned"—he spoke with the feeling of an artist who has delicately reserved perfection for the climax—"is for you to come to work in the Emporium. I can use you around the office, checking up. You can become familiar with the books. I—I need someone like you around here—badly. Will you help me out?"

"Will I—? Why, Mr. Abbott!"

"That's fine. No one will know a thing about this except you and me. Not even anybody at the bank. It is something which has happened, and now it is definitely finished. There are probably opportunities here to steal as much as you could have at the bank—and I know you won't steal a penny. You can pay me the hundred and eighty-seven dollars as you go—a little each week." He paused and gazed keenly across at Phil Haley. "Now I think you'd better go home and get some rest. You look pretty bad. On your way out, stop in at the candy counter. Tell Miss Harmes there to let you have a box of chocolates. Give it to your mother, and tell her I hope she's feeling better."

Phil Haley arose from his chair, and started to say something. His face twitched dangerously. Then, without a word, he turned and walked softly from the office. John Abbott saw him at the candy counter, making his selection. He almost bolted out of the Fifth Street door. Considering everything, John Abbott believed he had got a pretty good man for the Emporium.

ECLIPSE

IX

BILL HITCHCOCK entered the office without being announced, an expression of placid contentment resting like a benediction upon his face. Bill Hitchcock was a salesman for the Gluckman Rubber Company of St. Louis. For the past seventeen years John Abbott had been one of his five best customers. Although he hated to do it, Bill Hitchcock had put over rather a fast deal upon John Abbott last night in the display room of the Shale House. The Gluckman Rubber Company had been overstocked the previous year on Jumbo Brand rubbers. Orders had gone out to all salesmen in the field to slough off the surplus stale merchandise at fifty-five cents a pair less the regular discount.

Jumbo rubbers were a bargain at such a price; but this particular lot had been in the warehouse for over a year, and rubber deteriorated swiftly under such conditions. Bill Hitchcock hadn't mentioned to John Abbott that he was selling him year-old merchandise. He merely had explained that the Gluckman Rubber Company had got a good buy on raw rubber and was handing it on to the trade. John Abbott, delighted at this news, had instructed Bill Hitchcock to come to his office the next day and sign him for five hundred pairs . . .

"Jeez, it's hot!" greeted Bill Hitchcock. Then he glanced across at John Abbott uneasily. He was never able to remember whether or not the owner of the Emporium approved of profanity. "I mean it's hot," he compromised.

John Abbott smiled amiably. "If it was like this all year 'round, I'm afraid the Gluckman Rubber Company'd have to close down."

Bill Hitchcock grinned at this banality: it was his job to grin at banalities. He flicked his cigarette ashes delicately into John Abbott's tray and pulled out his order book.

"That was five hundred pair, wasn't it, Mr. Abbott?"

"Um-m. Jumbo Brand at fifty-five less the regular discount."

Bill Hitchcock nodded happily, and began scratching on his pad.

"I was just thinking I might be able to use a few more at that price," murmured John Abbott. "How you lined up?"

"All you want, Mr. Abbott," declared Bill Hitchcock, scarcely able to conceal his elation.

"I guess I'll just double that order then," said the merchant lazily. "Make it a thousand pair—same size assortment."

"A thousand it is. You'll never regret it, Mr. Abbott. Best buy I ever offered you."

He finished the order and handed the pad to John Abbott for his signature. John Abbott studied the bill for a moment.

"Um-m—by the way, this's all fresh rubber, isn't it? Strictly 1926 stock? But pshaw—of course it is! You wouldn't dump old stuff on me."

"I guess I'd be pretty much of a fool to, after having done business with you all these years," evaded Bill Hitchcock, observing his customer with a certain wariness.

"Yes. That's so too. Ah—better make a note of it here, I guess, Bill. 'Guaranteed 1926 stock, fresh rubber.' Something like that, I guess. Not that I'd mistrust you for a minute. But just for the factory shipping department." He made a deprecating gesture. "They pull mistakes sometimes, you know."

Bill Hitchcock gulped. For a moment it seemed to John Abbott that the salesman was choking. His face grew red, and his expression of surprise as he stared across the desk could have been no greater had the owner of the Emporium suddenly pulled a rattlesnake out of his ear.

"Yeh, of course," he muttered.

John Abbott shoved the pad across the desk. Bill Hitchcock's hand trembled as he made the additional notation. When he completed it, he knew that he had signed away a full month's commissions. No—nearer two months'. Damn John Abbott! This was the first time in seventeen years that any stipulations had been made between them—and the first time they could have affected the transaction. Almost with admiration he watched John Abbott affix his signature to the order and carefully tear out his duplicated copy. Slowly Bill Hitchcock replaced the pad in his pocket, still gazing at the merchant, whose smile was bland and expansive. Then he arose as if to leave.

"Keep your seat," urged John Abbott. "I've nothing to do. Tell me, how's business up and down the line?"

"Fair," said Bill Hitchcock listlessly, without sitting down. "I'd better go. I don't feel so good to-day. The heat."

John Abbott nodded commiseratingly. "'Tis hot," he admitted philosophically. "But it's just like a lot of other things—you have to learn to bear it."

Bill Hitchcock agreed with a jerk of his head. He hung momentarily above John Abbott's desk, still dazed by the foul thing which had happened to him.

"You got a real good buy there, Mr. Abbott," he declared reverently.

"That's what I think," agreed the merchant after a little pause. "So good I telephoned George Tate at Mycope to be sure and snap up a few pair for himself when you called."

Bill Hitchcock gasped. This was rape! Dimly he recalled a yarn some underwear drummer had told him years ago about the owner of the Emporium. At the time he had discredited it. Now, with deep bitterness, he realized that the underwear drummer had not exaggerated. He walked to the door like a cuckold aware for the first time of his betrayal. There, remembering the ancient obligations of his guild, he turned gallantly.

"Won't you have dinner with me to-night at the hotel?"

"Matter of fact, I've got an engagement," murmured John Abbott regretfully. "Mighty nice of you though, Bill. Come to think of it, I feel almost like I owed *you* a dinner."

Bill Hitchcock pursed his lips at this, muttered something about seeing John Abbott around the first of the year, and departed. John Abbott watched him hurrying through the middle aisle. Bill Hitchcock walked as though the devil were snapping at his heels. The owner of the Emporium chuckled. It was too bad the rubber salesman had thought him an easy mark. Perhaps it was just as well though. He stood to make a nice profit on those Jumbos. And all because he had taken the precaution to make telegraphic inquiries of Ed Robinson, who handled Duckbacks, the opposition line out of St. Louis.

X

FTER the rout of Bill Hitchcock, John Abbott idled through a
sheaf of papers in a futile pretence at being engaged in important work. Then, encompassed by the grilling warmth, he
leaned back frankly in his chair and allowed himself to drift off into
endless, meaningless thought-circles. He noticed that Donna Long
had kept out of the office most of the afternoon. This morning's conversation had been a brutal thing. He wished he could have thought
of a better way to broach it. He must be very kind, very gentle to
Donna Long. She had talked hysterically about the dryness, the sense
of imminent suffocation. Perhaps he would install an air-conditioning
system in the store. It seemed to him that he could hear the heat
waves as they pounded through the open window on to the floor. The
sun seemed to hum in his ears.

About a half-hour before closing time, Donna Long appeared in the
doorway.

"You have a visitor waiting at the foot of the stairs," she said.

He detected a note of mockery on her voice.

"Who?"

"I'll send her up," said Donna Long, without asking whether or not the
visitor would be welcome. "It's Stumpy Telsa."

She paused long enough to smile oddly at him. He saw that she found
the situation amusing. Donna Long could appreciate the humour of Violet
Budd and Stumpy Telsa calling on John Abbott the same afternoon.

In a moment the door re-opened, and Maria Telsa, the acknowledged
queen of Shale City's modest underworld, hobbled into the room. John
Abbott always felt confused when it was necessary for him to speak to
her. He couldn't decide whether he should call her Miss Telsa or Mrs.
Telsa. It seemed to him that it would be much simpler to call her
Stumpy, but he was far too polite for that. There should, he thought, be
some neuter designation for such women as Maria Telsa: some term
which would impute no unnecessary stigma, and yet would be adequate
for social usage. But he knew, of course, that she really was a widow.

Everyone in Shale City was familiar with her history. Mike Telsa had
taken her out of a house in Leadville, and together they had operated The
Gadfly there for the miners. Mike really married her. When they took

over The Gadfly, Maria Telsa gave up active practice of her profession, excepting, of course, during those times when there was an extraordinary rush of business. She managed the girls while Mike dominated the bar. He was a great swarthy Italian, who had prospected unsuccessfully around Leadville for years. They did very well in The Gadfly.

Mike was a tempestuous fellow who numbered his enemies by the dozens. When he didn't fancy the conduct of a Gadfly patron, Mike reached out, gathered the ill-doer under his arm, and thrust him violently through the front door. This was not calculated to increase his popularity in town which had small esteem for repressive measures. One night he threw out a shrivelled little fellow who had tried to cotton up to Maria. The injured man returned the same night, nursing a hearty grudge and a Smith and Wesson. He killed Mike outright, and sent two slugs in Maria just for good measure. The bullets lodged in her right leg, necessitating its amputation the next morning. That was how she came to be known as Stumpy.

The amputation practically ruined Stumpy for resumption of her trade. She bought a wooden leg and learned to use it fairly well. But there were so many women in Leadville with two legs that Stumpy found it impossible to buck the competition. Moreover, it was difficult for her to manage The Gadfly without assistance, and she was unable to find a barkeep and bouncer who would keep his fingers out of the cash box. Consequently she sold the place in disgust, and moved to Shale City, which was young and to her liking. She had a good eye for girls, and her place prospered.

Stumpy Telsa was a thrifty woman. She had seen too many ladies of love buried in paupers' graves to risk such a fate for herself. When she had saved her first thousand dollars, she asked one of her customers about investing it. The customer told her that everyone in Shale City went to see John Abbott when he had money to invest: he gave the soundest advice, and didn't charge a penny for it. So Stumpy brought her thousand dollars to the Emporium—then a very small place—and John Abbott bought a lot on Harbin Avenue for her. It trebled in value within five years. During the war, acting on his advice, she invested every surplus penny in Liberty Bonds. It was quite a joke around the town. The houses on Lower Street were close to the depot. Transient soldiers from a hundred different troop trains deposited their dollars in Stumpy Telsa's lap—tainted money which she purified by immediate conversion into Liberty Bonds. Thus the federal payroll speedily returned to its source, while Stumpy became the fourth highest purchaser of patriotic securities in Shale City.

During the accumulation of her comfortable fortune, she had never made an investment without consulting John Abbott. She was as consistent in this respect as Harry Twinge, although of course she never sought advice concerning the actual conduct of her business. She considered herself a specialist in her own field of endeavour. She simply brought her money to him, and he invested it for her. At first it had been very embarrassing to the merchant, but he hadn't the heart or the courage to refuse her. Now she called regularly twice a year.

She walked across his office with a queer, mechanical shuffle caused by the slow recoil of her wooden leg as it caught up with her good one. She smiled, and seated herself. She was between fifty and sixty, John Abbott surmised. She dyed her hair a raven-black, and her face was layered with cosmetics. On a hot day like this, the powder tended to gather in white gullies which were wrinkles, leaving the ridges exposed and shiny. She wasn't pleasant to look at, but her voice was strangely low-pitched and musical.

"Another year, another dollar," she said in a matter-of-fact tone.

John Abbott smiled stiffly. He was still feeling expansive over the Bill Hitchcock incident, but even the association of years couldn't make him quite at ease in this woman's presence. He fished about for something to say.

"Maybe we'd better put the money in ice this year," he suggested, heavily attempting humour.

She flashed a gold-crowned smile at him.

"Beer," she declared. "I'd sooner put it in a brewery. Ice only makes you hotter on a day like this. Good sound beer cools you off."

He nodded doubtfully.

She fumbled with a patent leather hand-bag, and drew out a roll of bills. She never availed herself of the facilities of the Shale City National Bank, nor of the other one, the Farmer's. John Abbott had warned her several times about keeping such large sums in a neighbourhood where there were floaters and prowlers from the railroad yards. But Stumpy grimly maintained that she was a good shot with a gun, even if she wasn't an expert dodger, and that she thought she'd be able to take care of her money until she got it to him.

She placed the bills on the desk before him.

"Thirty-five hundred," she said. "What'll we buy this time?"

It was her custom to have him deduct 10 per cent of whatever sums she brought him. This, she insisted, was for him to disburse to the Red Cross or any other charity he selected. She firmly refused to make donations in her own name. She contended with almost pious severity that it wouldn't look well. So John Abbott carefully recorded his expenditure of the 10 per cent., and sent her regular accountings. Thus the polluted profits of Lower Street reached the arms of sweet charity under John Abbott's name.

"I've been thinking of public utilities stock," he said thoughtfully. "I believe utilities are going to become increasingly important in this western country. Water and power. There'll be a big development. An investment in one of the larger companies should bring good returns. And it would go into the big job of getting more water on this"—he made a circling gesture—"on this desert country."

She nodded approvingly.

"That's what you do, then."

He took the money, counted it carefully, and wrote out a receipt. She put it in her bag without looking at it, and arose to go. John Abbott wanted to say something pleasant by way of farewell. But it was difficult. He couldn't, for example, express his hope that her fall business would be good. He couldn't ask her how everything was at home. He couldn't call to mind a single subject of which he could speak freely with this strange half-human. So he contented himself with smiling vaguely, and tucking the money away in a safe which fitted into a compartment of his desk.

She was half-way to the door when she hesitated, and turned resolutely to face him. "There's something else that bothers me," she said sharply.

His heart sank. He had a fearful premonition that she was going to bring up this subject of Violet Budd's drive on Lower Street. It would be just like a woman. What in heaven's name would he say?

"It's about a girl that's down at my place," she said.

He saw that she, too, was somewhat embarrassed, and he felt better. If she sensed the strain of their being together any longer than necessary, then surely she wasn't going to enlist him in a counter crusade for the defence of Lower Street.

"Sit down," he said kindly.

"I haven't ever said anything to you about my place," said Stumpy Telsa. "But you know well enough what it is. Well, about two weeks ago a girl drifted in and asked for work. She was young and pretty, and said she knew what she was about. So I gave her a room, and let it go at that. New faces always help business. She said she came from Colorado Springs.

Stumpy paused and scratched her nose vigorously. John Abbott masked his confusion behind a glassy smile.

"Well, a couple of days later, after she'd got used to the place, I sent a customer up to her room. He was only up there a minute or two, when I heard the dam—the awfullest racket. And then in a second he came galloping downstairs, half scared to death, hollering that the girl wasn't even civilized. She'd come at him with a hair brush, and da–and pretty near hammered his head in before he got away."

"Well, I went up to see what it was all about, and she was over in a corner on the floor, crying. She said that she'd never done anything like this before, and that she'd lied to me because she was broke, and didn't know anything else to do. Well"—Stumpy Telsa made an eloquent gesture—"there I was. I couldn't throw her out, because she *is* a sweet little thing, and pretty young. I was a fool for taking in any kid so young. So I've been keeping her up in that room ever since. She won't even come out for meals. Everything has to be sent up to her room. And the rest of my girls are getting kind of hot under the collar about it. You see they can't understand how this kid gets away with it—acting so ritzy and everything. I try to explain, but it don't do much good."

Stumpy paused, and gazed earnestly at John Abbott, who wriggled in his chair, and pretended to be thinking very hard. Presently he lifted his eyes to hers and said, "Well?"

"That's just it," said Stumpy hopelessly. "I tried to give her money to go back home, but she says she don't want to go back. She says she wants a job here in town, and she asked me to get one for her. Well you know, Mr. Abbott, what a big help *I'd* be recommending the kid around. I don't mind keeping her, but it's not doing her any good being down there like that. I've got to get her out some time."

"Has anybody down there seen her—anyone who, if they saw her working somewhere in Shale City, might start a lot of talk?"

"There's only one man saw her—the one she chased out of the place. And he's only in town now and then. I haven't let a single other man even look at her."

John Abbott nodded thoughtfully.

"The idea is, you want me to find a job for her," he stated precisely.

"That's just it."

"You're sure there isn't any way it would get out—that is, about where she came from? It would be hard on her."

Stumpy shook her head positively. "I won't say anything," she said. "Nor any of my girls won't. And the only man who saw her, as I said, isn't in town often. I'm dead sure she's safe."

Suddenly a smile crept over John Abbott's face. He rubbed his chin speculatively.

"I know of a place," he said finally. "A girl to do house work—cooking and all that. Think she could do that kind of work?"

"I know she could," declared Stumpy. "That's the kind she wanted me to get her."

"Um-m-m. Tell you what you do. I'll give you a note here"—he scratched at length on a piece of paper, blotted it carefully, folded the note and gave it to Stumpy—"and you tell her to take it this afternoon to Mrs. Violet Budd. She can tell Mrs. Budd she just got into town— friend of mine—anything. You know. Work out some logical story. She'll get the job."

Stumpy's eyes blazed wrathfully. "Sa-a-ay!" she rasped belligerently, "Do you think I'd send a nice kid like this over to that old hex? Why I wouldn't let Violet Budd touch one of my dogs!" Stumpy raised thoroughbred Boston terriers, and took a great deal of pride in them.

"But it's the only job I know of," protested John Abbott. "Besides, Mrs. Budd is a fine woman. The girl'll be in excellent surroundings. She'll have a job as long as she wants it, if this man doesn't see her sometime and give her away."

Stumpy meditated upon this. Then she began to smile, just as John Abbott had a moment before.

"You know," she said with sudden brightness, "I think that's a good idea. I'll do it. And I don't believe that fellow will ever say a word." Her lips formed a thin line, still twisted by the smile. "Know why? Because it was Clem Budd she chased out with the hairbrush!"

Quite suddenly they were laughing together. They must have laughed a full minute before John Abbott, overcome with sudden embarrassment, halted abruptly and assumed a cheerless expression. Stumpy Telsa, noting this change in his demeanor, thanked him and made her departure.

For days John Abbott cherished the thought of the trick he played on Violet Budd. Two months later he felt a twinge of remorse when he heard that young Ellsworth Budd had eloped with the girl. After the feeling of guilt passed, it seemed to him that the whole affair had ended brilliantly. He sent the happy couple a sterling silver set of hairbrushes as a wedding gift.

XI

THE day wore on. The sun imperceptibly dipped toward a ragged western horizon, its blinding white now softened to bloodshot yellows. But still it hung reluctantly above the mountain tops for a period, whirling insanely, spinning out great wheels of colour before its ultimate surrender to evening. Shadows struck mightily toward the east, and Shale City gasped with relief.

Main Street took on a pleasant, neighbourly animation with the six o'clock closing of its stores. Merchants lingered before their stores gossiping with last-minute customers. Shoppers with bags suspended limply over their arms sauntered homeward through a dusty red haze. Boys and girls strolled together or chattered shrilly in little groups. Children on roller skates dodged breathlessly in and out of recessed store entrances, pursued by excited mongrel dogs. The street was filled with automobiles roaring from the kerb, sparring for position in the sudden flow of traffic. Over the scene hovered the odour of cooling tar-paper from store roofs, of gasoline fumes from hot exhaust pipes, of sticky bodies turning dry as the evening carried a faint, cool smell of sweet clover from the river. It was the good time of day, the carnival time of day, the restful time of day: there was no more work to be done, and soon the earth would begin to cool.

John Abbott walked slowly through the middle aisle of the Emporium nodding benignly to right and left as he bade his clerks good night. He had to go to the Y.M.C.A. for a banquet which was scheduled to begin at seven o'clock. That left him an hour to kill. Donna Long had gone home from the store a few minutes early. He wished she had waited to talk with him. He felt a little lonely. But he supposed she was exhausted with the heat, still sickened from their conversation. Poor girl! Poor, tired child! He wished she had stayed.

In the cauterized outer air he paused a moment, trying to think of something to do. Then he walked very slowly along the Main Street and the Fifth Street windows of the Emporium. Fred Best had just completed a new window trim. John Abbott inspected it with careful satisfaction.

He stood at the corner, peacefully aloof from the throng of passers-by, inflamed in the nimbus of a dying sun. He loved this moment of the day. People ceased to be workers and miraculously were transformed into free creatures once again. They were filled with unconscious speculation concerning the idleness of the evening to come. Soon there would be family reunions across supper tables laden with well-done steak and mashed potatoes and garden salad and rich, home-made cake. And afterwards, would they go for a ride through the warm twilight? Would they treat themselves to a movie? Would they walk in that little park which fringed the river near the bridge? Or would they sit on the screen-porch with their shoes off and their throats bare, reading *The Saturday Evening Post*?

He sighed a little enviously, and walked across the street towards Mrs. Alloway's establishment. He was not going to eat, but the old building which housed the cafeteria offered a front veranda with wicker rocking chairs, screened by woodbines to furnish a measure of privacy from the street. He would go over there and sit down for the idle hour, watching the people pass by, soaking himself in the heat which, at this time of day—provided you were in the shade—was tranquil and delicious.

He sank into one of the rocking-chairs. Mrs. Alloway bustled out to chat with him for a minute. She was disappointed when he said he had come only to rest for a while. She offered to bring him a glass of cold lemonade or some fruit punch, but he thanked her and declined. After she had gone he slid down in his chair and closed his eyes for a moment. Then he opened them slowly . . .

Directly across the street from Mrs. Alloway's cafeteria and diagonally across from the Emporium loomed the Shale City National Bank. It had started as a one storey building of red sandstone. Now it raced five floors toward the sky, all creamy brick and gleaming windows and impressive marble entrances. It shaded Mrs. Alloway's veranda from the setting sun. It was the tallest building in Shale City; the tallest building in all of western Colorado and eastern Utah. It represented credit, confidence, strength: it represented John Abbott.

Yet as he gazed at the edifice, an old thought entered his mind; one which had skirted the corners of his conscience for ten years. "You are spattered with blood," he thought, staring at the bank. "Richard Maesfield's blood is mixed with your mortar."

He remembered the first time he had seen Richard Maesfield. Hermann Schonk had sent him over from Colorado Springs. Hermann Schonk had enacted the same role in eastern Colorado's development that John Abbott had played on a smaller scale in the western half of the state. Schonk, however, was far the wealthier, having made millions in mines, and later in Wyoming oil. He was a very good friend of John Abbott. He owned stock in the Shale City National Bank, while John Abbott owned stock in Schonk's Colorado Springs institution. "Richard Maesfield is a good man," Hermann Schonk had written in his letter of introduction. "He is honest as the day, and will be a big help to you."

At first Richard Maesfield served as a teller in the Shale City National—a tall handsome man in his late forties, with a charming wife and two pretty daughters. He spoke so rarely of himself that no one in Shale City could say he really knew him—not even John Abbott. He possessed an air of soothing competence which quickly drew clients to his window at the bank. His punctilious work, combined with his increasing popularity, impelled John Abbott to make him cashier.

About that time a group of Shale City people thought that there was room in the town for a second building and loan company. Naturally they came to see John Abbott about it, and he agreed with them. Inasmuch as he already was president of the Shale City Building and Loan, he thought it would be better if he were not too closely identified with the new venture. He subscribed heavily to its stock, but induced Richard Maesfield to become its president. It was called the Protective Building and Loan. Maesfield, retaining his position in the bank, purchased some stock on his own account, with the agreement that he would take over John Abbott's holdings when he was financially able.

And then the cloud began to hover over Richard Maesfield. At first it was nothing but an unreasoning nervousness. Later it took definite form. Sam Wilmer, the secretary of the Protective Building and Loan, was exposed as a thief. He had stolen twelve thousand dollars from the institution. Richard Maesfield had trusted Wilmer so implicitly that, aside from the semi-annual audit of the books, he had never inquired about details of the business.

There was a great scandal. It was the first time such a thing had happened in Shale City. People came from the whole length of the Colorado Valley to Sam Wilmer's trial and returned to their homes keenly disappointed that he had received no more than a five-year term in the state penitentiary.

It was commonly believed that Richard Maesfield had done everything within his power to lighten Sam Wilmer's sentence. And when it became whispered that Richard Maesfield was supporting Sam's family during his imprisonment, matters looked even worse. There were rumours that the president of the Protective Building and Loan had deliberately sacrificed Sam Wilmer to save himself. Richard Maesfield was too proud to dignify the gossip with denial. Nobody but John Abbott ever knew for certain whether or not Maesfield actually was helping the Wilmers; but the fact remained that Sam's wife and his three children managed to live decently all during his incarceration. "It's the least I can do," Richard Maesfield told John Abbott. "Clara Wilmer isn't to blame for what her husband has done."

In order to confirm his confidence in Richard Maesfield before the whole town, John Abbott made him vice-president of the Shale City National Bank a week after Sam Wilmer was taken to prison. The bank's position was strengthened under his guidance. Although John Abbott was the nominal president, he spent most of his time at the Emporium, leaving the bank in Maesfield's hands as much as possible. Maesfield knew when to be harsh and when to be lenient. He was a good judge of character. He understood property values. There was very little bad paper in the bank during his *régime*.

Shortly after Richard Maesfield's assumption of the vice-presidency, John Abbott's nephew from Pennsylvania finished college and came to live in Shale City. Gerald Abbott was an orphan—an odd young man with a hollow chest and an enormous, booming voice which he had used with great success in college debating societies. John Abbott had financed his education, and although he found Gerald a strangely unaffectionate, passionless young man, he took great pride in his attainments.

Gerald Abbott won instant popularity in Shale City. People referred to him as a stirring orator, a brilliant thinker, a completely fascinating fellow—and wondered what John Abbott was going to have him do. After a year of keeping books in the Emporium, Gerald Abbott solved the problem for himself by announcing his candidacy for the state legislature. Although John Abbott never interfered in local political feuds, the strength of his name was sufficient to assure his nephew's election. Gerald served for two years in the lower house, booming away prodigiously and making friends all over the state. At the conclusion of his term he returned to Shale City permanently. "No man can serve in the state legislature longer than two years and remain honest," he declared in announcing his retirement.

John Abbott, realizing that his nephew's talents were worthy of something more splendid than a position in the Emporium, established him as cashier of the bank. Soon reports sifted through the town that Gerald Abbott and Richard Maesfield found it difficult to agree. Indiscreet clerks whispered of bitter quarrels behind the glass panels of Maesfield's office. Such talk didn't do the bank any good. People expected unity and high perfection in an institution as large as the Shale City National.

And then the cloud hovered again over Richard Maesfield. It overshadowed John Abbott too, and everyone else connected with the bank. Nobody knew what it portended. Even now, ten years later, John Abbott stubbornly refused to think of it. He deliberately had built around it a wall of forgetfulness so perfectly constructed that he could review the whole affair without once considering its real cause.

It ended with Richard Maesfield's resignation; or rather, as it was given to *The Monitor,* with the announcement that Maesfield had requested and been granted a six-months' leave of absence. Gerald Abbott became acting vice-president that same day. As a matter of truth, the cloud had darkened so ominously that it had driven Richard Maesfield insane.

There was a troubled stir in Shale City on the day he left the bank. The lights in his big English house on North Fifth Avenue burned all night and into the early morning. No one except John Abbott, Gerald Abbott and Mrs. Maesfield knew that its owner was insane. John Abbott telegraphed for a specialist and two guards to come over the mountains from Denver to care for the stricken man. They arrived the next evening. Mrs. Maesfield wired the two girls to return from college.

Even now John Abbott could hear the maddening cadence of Richard Maesfield's voice shrieking in his ears: "You've done it! You've done it! You've done it! You've ruined me!" It was in the nature of a chant. Sometimes the demented man introduced variations. "You wanted me to build this house. You and Hermann Schonk made me do it. You made me take the building and loan. My position—a man of my position—my position! That's what you said, all, all, all. You've done it! You've ruined me! I haven't any money! You've done it! You've ruined me!"

John Abbott, living next door to the Maesfields, could never forget those first sleepless, terrifying nights. He lay by an open window, listening for screams from the tightly-closed Maesfield house. And all the while the town thought Maesfield was ill with pneumonia.

John Abbott and Mrs. Maesfield made arrangements for Richard Maesfield to be taken to a private sanatorium near Denver, where he would be given skilled attention. On the morning of the fourth day of his madness, Mrs. Maesfield told her husband that they were going to leave on the midnight train for a vacation. He grew very calm. He even went upstairs accompanied by his two burly nurses and slept for a short while. John Abbott hadn't talked to him since the first day, but when Mrs. Maesfield informed him of the change in her husband's condition, he decided to go over in the evening and say good-bye.

At eight o'clock he crossed the strip of lawn between the two houses. Mrs. Maesfield met him in the hall, whispering that everything was packed and her husband appeared eager for the journey. John Abbott walked softly into the huge living-room with its gracious, shaded lights and its quiet pictures. Richard Maesfield was sitting in a comfortable chair, his head thrown back, his eyes closed. The two guards were reading close by. At the sound of John Abbott's footsteps, Richard Maesfield stiffened in faint confusion, then arose to greet him. They shook hands.

"I'm going away for a little while," Maesfield told his guest.

They talked about casual matters, both of them carefully avoiding any mention of the subject most strongly in their minds. John Abbott decided that Richard Maesfield was as normal a man as he had ever seen. Surely this wasn't the creature which had screamed behind bolted windows for three nights running! The man was faultlessly dressed, cleanly shaven. He was calm almost to the point of lassitude. He talked freely, punctuating their conversation with smiles, even laughing once or twice at remarks in which John Abbott could find no trace of humour. Suddenly he arose from his chair.

"I'm thirsty," he said. "I think I'll get a drink."

As he started for the kitchen, one of the attendants arose to go with him. The Denver specialist had warned them never to leave him alone. Richard Maesfield glanced at the guard and smiled casually.

"I don't need any help," he said. "I'm quite all right."

The guard looked questioningly at John Abbott. "Of course he's all right," said John Abbott. He saw no reason for upsetting a patient who seemed to be progressing so nicely.

The guard slumped back into his seat, and Richard Maesfield left the room. They heard his footsteps going through the dining-room, through the pantry and into the kitchen. The cascading of water in the sink told them that he had turned the tap. Then came a heavy crash.

All three of them reached the kitchen at the same time. Richard Maesfield lay stretched on the floor with blood gushing from his throat. A knife lay not far from him, just as it had fallen from his hand. He was still alive, staring up at them, smiling faintly. His eyes were beginning to glaze. The tap still ran. One of the guards turned it off. The other rushed to the telephone. Mrs. Maesfield entered the kitchen while John Abbott was bending over the stricken man. She ran to her husband and cradled his head in her arms, bringing the lips of his wound more closely together so that the flow of blood was diminished.

She looked up at John Abbott, her lips thin, her face pale, her eyes tearless.

"I have known all along it would come to this," she murmured.

John Abbott cringed before her eyes.

An ambulance came and the wounded man was bundled into it. He died before they reached the hospital, without ever speaking. There they examined him and pronounced him dead. That was how the town discovered the cause of his death: some of the nurses had talked. *The Monitor* in its story of his passing said that he had died at his home of pneumonia.

The town filled with tumultuous rumours. By morning wild tales shuddered through half the state. At ten o'clock a bulletin appeared in *The Monitor* window. It was a signed statement from the board of directors of the Shale City National Bank declaring that the institution was in perfect condition as attested by the fact that an emergency audit of its books revealed no irregularities of any sort.

Mrs. Maesfield took the corpse to Colorado Springs for burial. Richard Maesfield's two daughters arrived there on the day of the funeral. John Abbott wanted to help Mrs. Maesfield and her daughters, for he knew there was no estate. He offered to send the girls back to college; to establish a permanent income for Mrs. Maesfield; at least to assume the funeral expenses. But it was no use: Mrs. Maesfield refused to accept assistance. None of the family returned to Shale City. The big house was sold. There were some who maintained that it really belonged to the bank; that Richard Maesfield had never been even moderately well off. Four or five years later word drifted back that one of the Maesfield girls had died—the pretty one who had been salutatorian of her class in Shale City High School. That was the last the town heard of the family.

And even now, with ten long years to soften the memory, John Abbott stared at the Shale City National Bank Building in the approaching twilight and could not bring himself to think of what had caused the tragedy. He was the only man in Shale City who knew. Anyone looking at him as he sat slumped in Mrs. Alloway's wicker chair would have thought that he suddenly had grown old—a full twenty years older than he really was.

"Richard Maesfield's blood is all over you," he thought, gazing at the bank. Its northern and southern sides were edged with crimson from the last glow of sunset.

XII

HE must have fallen into a doze, for the next thing he knew someone was plucking gently at his coat sleeve. He stirred faintly, pretending that he had been aroused from profound meditation rather than slumber. He heard the musical voice of Hermann Vogel, history teacher at Shale City High School—an arrogant, moustached, Satanic man who mocked everyone, and himself most of all.

"Dining?" inquired Vogel.

Anyone else in Shale City would have asked John Abbott if he were going into Mrs. Alloway's for supper. But Hermann Vogel flavoured his most mundane actions with the spice of ritualistic elegance. His sarcastic comments upon the art of eating kept Mrs. Alloway in a state of permanent frenzy: he delighted to send her into little flurries of consternation by bringing recipes of strange dishes which he wanted her to prepare especially for him.

"No," answered John Abbott. "There's a banquet over at the 'Y' tonight. I'm just waiting here until time for it to start."

Hermann Vogel nodded, and slipped easily into a chair beside the owner of the Emporium. He was the only man in Shale City who treated the town's richest inhabitant without deference. Bullies, merchants, preachers, housewives—they all approached John Abbott with a certain humility engendered by knowledge of his wealth. But Hermann Vogel paid no attention to money at all. He lived expensively on a small salary, and conducted himself as though he were the financial equal of any man on earth.

He was, in a way, the town's leading mystery. He defied the colourless routine of Shale City High School by assuming a mantle of gay self-ridicule which marked him for a superior, and therefore an unpopular person. No one knew why he had elected to live in Shale City. No one knew precisely whence he had come. During his first years in the town—the years of the War—a faint Teutonic accent had established him as a suspicious character: now the accent had almost vanished, and no one remembered the War.

For some inexplicable reason a fast friendship—never to be

mistaken for intimacy—had grown up between the merchant and the school teacher. Perhaps the cause for it lay in the fact that each was an outstanding personage in the town's life. John Abbott was the richest, and Hermann Vogel beyond all doubt was the cleverest. No one dared to match wits with him. He delighted to confound the Shale City intelligentsia led by Mrs. Art French, and to defy the reform group under Mrs. Violet Budd. He held his position in the high school by systematic terrorization of his collegues, and in the town by merciless ridicule of its dearest shibboleths.

John Abbott admired Hermann Vogel's flair for investing monstrous ideas with a glamour which made them seem almost pleasant. Hermann Vogel was always saying things which John Abbott, considering them later, wished he might have said. Moreover, Vogel did not hesitate to practise the doctrines of which he spoke. There was no doubting the fact that he had affairs with women; flaming adventures which he managed with such nicety that no one could discover a tangible excuse for interference. John Abbott envied Hermann Vogel's easy conscience, his tranquil acceptance of women and love. The owner of the Emporium had entered into but one extra-marital attachment in thirty years, yet guilt had festered every moment of its pleasure. By knowing Hermann Vogel, he was enabled to live a dual life; his own and that other mysteriously charming one of easy conquest to the ring of derisive laughter. Hermann Vogel was his emotional safety valve, that 'other face of God' in whose countenance even the most arrogantly conventional find a certain beauty which only fear prevents them from snatching. Through the school teacher, John Abbott escaped the shackles of respectability and became a creature of Mephisto.

There were times, however, when he could not escape the bleak sensation that he was a laboratory subject for Hermann Vogel's subtle research. Occasionally the school teacher heaped abusive ridicule upon him, beneath which John Abbott squirmed resentfully without ever being able to erect an adequate defence. In compensation, there were other moments when the two of them together seemed to be leading a secret existence of placid understanding—the only reasonable creatures in a madhouse world. The fruit of these latter intervals was a feeling of indefinable well-being which stole over John Abbott, a sensation he could place in no exact category.

"So," said Vogel after a while, "the vultures are out for money again."

"Who?"

"The Y.M.C.A., of course."

"I don't see why you say that."

"Because, my good friend, if they weren't after money, they wouldn't be after you!"

John Abbott snorted softly and closed his eyes.

"Do you know what ails you?" Vogel waited for a moment for the answer he knew would not come. "Then I shall tell you, my friend. You suffer from a very malignant disease. It's no disgrace. A lot of great men have had it. Napoleon, for example."

John Abbott stirred uneasily.

"Cancer?" he asked.

"No. More dangerous than cancer. Practically incurable. You are a victim of acute pedestalization."

John Abbott perceived that Hermann Vogel was in one of his difficult moods. The fellow could say things which left him uneasy, discontented, vaguely unnerved for hours afterwards. He wished Hermann Vogel would go inside and eat his dinner. Meanwhile, some answer was required of him.

"Nonsense!" he said sharply, settling further down in his chair. Mrs. Mildred Wessingham was passing along the sidewalk: his eyes followed her until she reached the corner.

"Not quite nonsense. On the contrary, it probably will be fatal. I think you're going to die of pedestalization, old friend, just as your archetype did."

"Just as who did?" Mrs. Wessingham having vanished, he forced his mind back to the discussion.

"Napoleon. He stated the proposition rather clearly at Dresden. 'Your legitimate kings can be beaten twenty times and still return to their thrones. But I am a soldier *parvenu* . . . and my throne rests upon my successes in the battlefields.'"

"I haven't any idea what you're talking about," complained John Abbott irritably.

"I was afraid you wouldn't have," sighed Hermann Vogel. "Tell me, are you going to give the vultures their carcass to-night?"

"What do you mean?"

"Are you going to give the highbinders at the Y.M.C.A. what they need to pull them out of the hole?"

"I suppose so."

"Oh God, what a fool!"

"Why do you say that?"

"Because I think it. Reason enough. And now tell me why you're going to save their hides."

John Abbott turned angrily toward his heckler. "Because of the kids in this town, that's why! Kids who need the 'Y'. Kids who would be playing in alleys if it weren't for the gym over there."

"And a good place for them," agreed Hermann Vogel heartily.

"Where?"

"In alleys, the little savages."

"You've no right to say that. This town has a fine bunch of kids."

"A fine bunch of savages, I say, and I know. I've been trying to beat something into their stupid heads for fourteen years. Brainless little savages—all of them—from savage homes out of savage dams by savage sires!"

John Abbott couldn't think of an apt reply. He fixed his eyes sullenly on the bank building across the street. Some day he was going to rip into Hermann Vogel.

"I know what you think," continued his tormentor cheerfully. "You make the common error of regarding them as human beings. Excusable enough, I suppose. I've seen monkeys just as smart, though. There are little tree monkeys in Central America that are smarter, perhaps. When you come upon a female carrying her infant, and point your rifle at her, she holds the babe toward you in outstretched arms, beseeching you, explaining that as a woman and a mother she is morally immune from your raid. Could your own mother defend her child against a monkey better than they defend themselves against man?"

"Instinct," muttered John Abbott, although Vogel, as usual, was beginning to fascinate him.

"So? I had a plantation once on the coast of East Africa. One evening a foreman rushed into the house with news that mandrils were raiding the agaves. Twenty of us went out with high-powered rifles to give battle to four hundred mandrils. When you hit one of them, he screamed like a soul in hell. If he was dead, his companions let him lie. But if he was only wounded, they picked him up by his arms and legs and carried him back into the jungle, pausing occasionally to turn and shake their fists at you. When they saw that their cause was lost, those nearest to the jungle scooped up all they could carry, and disappeared. But a rear guard covered their retreat systematically, ripping agave plants out of the earth as they withdrew, making sure our victory would be a fruitless one. You've heard, of course, how retreating armies burn bridges, pollute wells, destroy food depots? Instinct, I suppose."

Hermann Vogel yawned, and then was silent for a little period. When he spoke again his voice had taken on a dream-like quality. "Armies . . ." he mused. And then he asked suddenly, "What is the date to-day?"

"The sixth," replied John Abbott.

"August 6th, 1926." Hermann Vogel stared straight ahead of him. "Do you have any idea of what happened twelve years ago to-day?"

John Abbott shook his head.

"Austria-Hungary declared war on the Russian Empire. There was an Emperor in Austria then, you know, and a Hungary too."

"Yes," said John Abbott. "They were getting ready for the fireworks."

"Fireworks!" echoed Hermann Vogel in an awed tone. "They were preparing the world for hell. The maddest thing God ever let happen. Declarations of war crackling back and forth like lightning on a wire fence. Lights in the Foreign Office all night, and the Skoda batteries always where they should not have been. Ten million deaths—you could take your miserable Y.M.C.A. swimming pool, John Abbott, and fill it twice a week for two years with the brains of men who died in that war. So many gallons of brains—and the thoughts that must have been in them. God!—who ever dreamed what would happen?"

"Yes," John Abbott agreed soberly. "All because some little prince or something got shot."

"Archduke Francis Ferdinand?" A queer note entered Hermann Vogel's voice.

"I guess he was the one."

"The heir of the oldest dynasty in Europe—a little prince!" Hermann Vogel chuckled soundlessly. "He was a Habsburg, John Abbott. The first real Habsburg in three generations. That means something. If he had lived he would have accomplished things. Watched out for Prussia, colonized Lower Austria. . . ." Hermann Vogel's voice faded away.

"You think so?" encouraged John Abbott.

"Think so!" Again Hermann Vogel chuckled. "He was the only man in Austria who dared stand up to the Emperor. You could hear him three rooms away in the palace, shouting at old Franz Josef as though——"

Suddenly he broke off. John Abbott waited patiently for him to continue. Finally he could endure the silence with its breathlessly poised question no longer.

"How do you know?" he asked.

"Because—I was—because I'm a history teacher."

John Abbott understood that it was sheer waste of energy to ask further questions. A dozen times they had seemed to stand thus on the brink of some revelation, only to have Vogel hastily draw the veil over his mind. Glancing at him now, John Abbott saw that he had changed. He was stern—arrogantly aloof. His eyes were strange with an expression which might have been grief

"Well, America got into it too," he said finally. "Oh God, what fun! May no one ever forget how we elected Wilson because he kept us out of war. May they never forget, and may the dead forgive them. Teddy Roosevelt roaring through the country bellowing at the poor rustics— 'Neither Washington nor Lincoln kept us out of war! They put righteousness before peace . . . save America from that gross taint of selfishness and cowardice!' What did he think about England? Well, he didn't say. But Hughes swore that if he had been President, he would have avoided the *Lusitania* mess altogether. What a rotten programme for a candidate in that election!—when everybody knew that if the old tub hadn't gone down we would have missed the biggest show on earth. . . ."

Hermann Vogel was gazing steadily at the final glory of a sun which sprayed Shale City's western skyline with pure fire.

"Speaking as a historian," he said finally, "a war is divided into two phases—preparation and participation. I was in Shale City all the time. My history of the thing is different from that which will go down in the books, because I saw only the war at home. They had one on the front too, you know, but it was piffling compared to the stench the arm-chair patriots raised. After Roosevelt came a man called Elliott. He said that Wilson, in keeping us out of war, had shown 'too great caution'. A man by the name of Elihu Root blamed the President for not 'backing up' his 'brave words' about the *Lusitania*. A man by the name of Henry Van Dyke, late of Queen Wilhelmina's Court, wrote a poem. I shall never forget it:

"You dare not say with perjured lips:
'We fight to make the ocean free' . . .
You whose black trail of butchered ships
Bestrews the bed of every sea
Where German submarines have wrought

Their horrors! Have you never thought
What you call freedom men call piracy?"

"After that a man named Cardinal Gibbons went to a prepared-
ness meeting in Baltimore, and urged that 'every boy be 100 per cent
patriotic'. I wonder if some papal prince in Bavaria was urging little
Bavarian boys to be patriotic also? Things happened swiftly from
then on. Congressman Sherwood of Ohio deserted a lifetime of paci-
fism gallantly to offer his services and eighty-two years' experience to
the army. Big Bill Thompson of Chicago endowed with $25,000 a
Chair of American Patriotism at Lincoln Memorial University in the
enlightened Commonwealth of Tennessee. You see, I'm a good historian. Better than most."

"When the school children of Altoona, Pennsylvania, telegraphed
the President assuring their 'undivided loyalty . . . and united support
in any action you may find it necessary to take', the last obstacle was
removed. The war was on. Mayor Curley of Boston urged his
Brahmins to fly the national banner until 'peace with honour is the lot
of America'. Simultaneously the United States Senate ordered an
investigation of the flag octopus. Old Glory, it seemed, was costing
patriots some 300 per cent more than a few days before. Kipling
piously celebrated the return of the colonies by applauding 'the Lord
on high whose strength has made us whole'.

"The rush to the colours was immediate and gratifying. William
Howard Taft joined the New Haven Home Guards; William Jennings
Bryan telegraphed the President—'Please enroll me as a private
whenever I am needed'. The ladies of Bayonne, N.J., organized a
Women's Revolver League; the ladies of New York formed a female
cavalry troop; the ladies of Washington, D.C., sponsored a Military
Camp for Women. American womanhood was preparing to sell its honour dearly, you see. Joffre came to us, and was smothered beneath
fried chicken and carnations; the poisoning of a hundred and nine
army mules at Buffalo indicated the strength of the enemy within;
Liberia pitted her youth against the Imperial Assassin; and we sang
*Good-bye Maw, Johnny Get Your Gun, Just a Baby's Prayer at
Twilight, America I Love You.* We read Arthur Guy Empey, damned
profiteers, shuddered over casualty lists, cut down on sugar, listened
to Barney Baruch—oh, it was wonderful. Remember? The butchers
of Shale City even imported half a whale as a substitute for beef. The
taste—ugh!"

Hermann Vogel shivered at the revolting memory. John Abbott sat motionless, waiting for him to resume.

"You know," he finally continued, "I wouldn't have minded all that. I really wouldn't have. But then you got busy here in Shale City. You formed a Loyalty League. Remember? You were its secretary until you resigned after they tarred and feathered old Professor Fuchs. That Loyalty League did something to this town, John Abbott. Something that will never be overcome. It wasn't the fact that they wrecked little Johann Tiller's photograph studio hunting messages from the Kaiser, or that they ripped up Henry Rechstein's ironing-board in the dead of night seeking the code of the German Secret Service. It was something more than that. For the first time, Shale City felt the pulse of the world. For the first time Art French and Walter Goode and Stanley Brown and William Harwood—yes, and even you for a while—discovered that you were participating in the history of nations. Power—that was it. It was power over the Johann Tillers and Henry Rechsteins—the power of snoopery, persecution, investigation. And no one dared oppose the snoopery and persecution, because no one dared risk the charge of treason.

"Then came the Armistice, and with it the end of power. The Loyalty League didn't matter any more, because its cause was won. And the Loyalty Leaguers couldn't stand their loss of power. Once tasted, it is never relinquished. You can remember that not so long ago the Ku Klux Klan marched down Main Street at night, all ghost-ly with a fiery cross, an American flag and a drum. It was still the Loyalty League, John Abbott, the organized mob risen from its grave to snoop and tyrannize once more. And it will come up again and again, for ever and ever! If there isn't a good cause like a war, then it will parade for a poor cause. It will always be a cause with ideals so high that no mere law can restrain the execution of its judgments. And it will always be based on hatred and fear. To-morrow it may come again . . . who knows?"

John Abbott moved restlessly in his chair before rising to his feet.

"Time to go over to the 'Y'," he said non-committally.

"I've just tried to explain why you're a fool," remarked Hermann Vogel with a cheerful dismissal of the subject. "They may turn against you too some day, these organizers, these praters, these ex-Loyalty Leaguers. And when they do—God pity you. But go ahead. Give them their money to-night. You even look a little like Napoleon. Your hat's on crooked, and you're not any too tall. To-night will be Ulm.

And then later I'll concede your Austerlitz. But watch out, my friend—be warned against the plains of Leipzig!"

Most of this, John Abbott had decided at the outset, was gibberish. He was willing to concede that the Loyalty League had been a little silly. That was why, in the end, he had resigned from it. And the Klan had split the town and hurt business rather badly for a while. But all of this talk about power and snoopery and Napoleon and unpronounceable names—it was only Hermann Vogel's way of joking, not for a moment to be taken seriously. He bade the school teacher good night, and descended the wooden steps from Mrs. Alloway's veranda to the sidewalk. He was conscious of Hermann Vogel's eyes following him until he reached the corner.

XIII

SUNSET and nightfall were widely separated in Shale City. Long after western mountains had swallowed the sun's fiery mass, a delicate glow lingered on, suffusing the earth with an eerie half-light which was not day and yet not night. Stars appeared abundantly and great yellow moons cut through with treetops loitered in the eastern sky. Yet a tinge of high noon still remained. On summer evenings full darkness did not come until ten or eleven o'clock; and even after that the night was a time of brilliance and splendour.

When John Abbott reached the steps of the Y.M.C.A. he could see the boys on the school grounds across the street as plainly as though it were still daytime. He paused for a moment to watch them. They were playing leap frog with fierce gusto. They shouted, gibed, shrieked; they grunted heavily as they made the leap, and argued excitedly about overstepping after each turn. Their voices rang out clearly, strongly amid the stillness all about them. It was an agreeable sound to John Abbott. Fifty years ago the spot on which they played had echoed to the yelp of coyotes and the melancholy wail of prairie wolves. He had heard a lot of vague talk about spiritual progress, but the happy tumult from the school grounds was something more definite—something by which progress could be measured. Although the admission came with reluctance, John Abbott was quite certain that he was a materialist.

He turned toward the 'Y' stairs, but paused at the landing, listening again. From a distance of at least two or three blocks came a little girl's voice in the shrill concession of hide-and-go-seek—"Allie allie out's in free-ee!" He smiled reminiscently. In his boyhood it had been work until bedtime. The world was a pleasanter place for youngsters now. Other sounds came to his ears from the basement of the building he was about to enter—laughter and dank shouts muffled by thick cement walls and the water. Down there in the swimming pool Hermann Vogel's little savages were releasing all their pent-up energies. In the hush of evening, in the cool restfulness of twilight, these sounds soothed and restored him, filled him with a tranquillity which nourished the deepest roots of his existence.

He walked through the lobby of the building. The banquet he was going to attend carried with it the fate of the Y.M.C.A. For ten days the town had rocked beneath a drive to clear the institution of its seventeen-thousand-dollar indebtedness. John Abbott had contributed a thousand. Committees of business men had called upon every person of importance in Shale City seeking similar—though smaller—contributions. Today the campaign had ended. They were to gather in the banquet hall and receive the final report of its success or failure.

John Abbott was keenly interested in the matter. He discounted the moral aims of the organization, as he was apt to discount most shadowy considerations. He was interested in the Y.M.C.A. primarily for its material advantages. He wasn't concerned about the purity of Shale City, but he was deeply engrossed in its physical welfare. Whatever might be said for or against the Y.M.C.A.—and he had heard much on either side—the fact remained that it was a stout building with deep foundations, offering showers for heated young bodies, a gymnasium for physical diversion, and the only swimming pool in Shale City. Its ideals were high and its locker rooms smelly, but midway between the two John Abbott recognized something of definite value.

He descended a flight of stairs, followed a bare corridor, and found himself in the basement banquet hall. Thirty-five or forty men already were seated at the long table. The rumble of their conversation filled the barren room and echoed flatly from its cement walls. Every eye was on him as he walked to his chair, which, of course, was beside the secretary at the head of the table. He nodded an indiscriminate return to the greetings of the assemblage.

Looming in front of him was Henry Wilhelm, secretary of the institution—an enormous, pink-cheeked Turnverein German with a voice that shook the earth itself. Henry Wilhelm thrust his great fist in the general direction of John Abbott's stomach, his face beaming with a pleasure that bordered closely upon ecstasy. Out of self-defence the merchant extended his own, although past experience warned him of the exquisite punishment which would reward the gesture. Henry Wilhelm pumped aggressively in what John Abbott considered a serious effort to tear his hand from its wrist.

"Hello, John!" bellowed Henry Wilhelm. "Hello! Hello!"

He was one of the few people in Shale City who presumed to call the owner of the Emporium by his first name. Henry Wilhelm believed in fellowship and informality, providing the two were mixed in a wholesome fashion. He was a whooping, broad-minded fellow who didn't even avoid being seen with Father O'Halloran of St. Thomas's Catholic Church. In fact he courted the opportunity of appearing with Father O'Halloran, looming high over the mild priest, impressing everyone with his camaraderie, his daring in the face of Roman peril.

"We've been waiting for you, John!" he thundered on. "Yes, we have! Sit down and we'll have chow!"

John Abbott sat down abruptly. He had a queer sensation that if he hesitated for a split second, Henry Wilhelm would thrust him forcefully into the chair, spread the napkin over his vest and administer food with his own hands. It was difficult for him to maintain his dignity before such a hulking, hearty fellow as the secretary of the Y.M.C.A.

Upon receiving a curt nod from Henry Wilhelm, the Reverend Slocum addressed a somewhat testy prayer to "Our dearly beloved Father", carefully pointing out various details of the evening's business which would, undoubtedly, require a bit of Divine assistance, hinting broadly that no one had been overwhelmed by the success of the debt-raising campaign, and ending with optimistic gratitude for the food about to be served. The mumbled words "in-the-name-of-Jesus-Christ-our-Lord-and-Saviour-Amen" furnished a cue for the Lady's Aid of the Congregational Church to advance in prim lines bearing food.

Each gourmet received a hard French roll, a thin portion of butter, a Frankfurter, a heap of sauerkraut, a sleek boiled potato and a salad composed of an eighth of a head of lettuce and a half-slice of pickled beet, the whole doused with pink dressing. Conversation died away as the men of Shale City addressed themselves to the serious business of digesting the indigestible. The meal came to a flourishing conclusion with apple pie, soft ice cream and tepid coffee. No one expected more at such banquets, for economy had to be the watchword, and the ladies of the Congregational Church needed whatever scant profit they could eke from their labours.

After coffee, the feasters reached for toothpicks and tobacco—the latter a violation of rules which was permitted only upon rare and important occasions. An ear-splitting uproar shrieked through the room as chairs grated against concrete floors. Presently everyone was in a comfortable position facing the end of the table occupied by Henry Wilhelm and John Abbott. Scorning the use of spoon against glass,

Henry Wilhelm thumped the banquet board with his fist until the dinnerware jumped and jingled.

"Order!"he howled.

The meeting instantly came to order.

"Walter Goode, as chairman of the steering committee, will read the final report of the campaign to clear your 'Y' of debt. All right, Walt! Let 'em have it!"

Walter Goode, who sat at Wilhelm's left, arose severely. He was a tall man with a sharp nose and spectacles. He fumbled through a sheaf of papers, and began to mumble names and figures.

John Abbott sat and observed Walter Goode closely, paying no attention to what he said. He remembered what Mrs. Budd had told him of Goode's visits to Lower Street. Walter Goode had a mild little wife, a bovine daughter, and a secretary who was also his mistress. Every time John Abbott thought of Walter Goode and Miss Weems he felt guilty, for their arrangement was so well known that Miss Weems had no reputation at all. Their affair, John Abbott felt certain, wasn't anything like his love for Donna Long. And yet, if the town knew, would it be able to detect the difference? A little spasm of fear darted through him at the very thought of such a thing. Miss Weems actually had had a baby which Walter had sent to a Denver orphanage. Like a starving man at a feast, John Abbott had heard of the child and its fate. Ever since he had been contemptuous of Walter Goode.

The voice droned impassionately while John Abbott mused about its owner. Walter Goode was a real estate man and a very successful one. Although he had the cream of the business, John Abbott occasionally heard complaints about him. There was the case of old Mrs. Eubanks, against whose house Walter Goode held a small mortgage. She went to live with her son in Long Beach, leaving the care of her house to Goode. John Abbott sent three prospective tenants to the real estate agent, only to discover later that Walter Goode had informed them the place was not for rent. In about a year Mrs. Eubanks' mortgage fell due, and the agent got the house. In the face of all these shortcomings, Walter Goode still maintained his piety in the eyes of the town. Miss Weems was a pariah, but Walter was a respected citizen. He went to church monotonously. He organized boys' clubs. He was a Mason and a Knight Templar. He had been a devout disciple of Ku Klux Klan during its hey-day. John Abbott beheld in Walter Goode most of the qualities he detested, and none which he admired. Yet strangely enough, all of Walter Goode's efforts seemed in the right direction. It was difficult to understand.

"And so, gentlemen, I regret to inform you that we are still forty-seven hundred dollars short of our announced goal." A brief pause. "That is all, I think."

Walter Goode sat down amidst ominous silence. Henry Wilhelm leaped to his feet.

"You have heard the report, fellows," he shouted belligerently. "Now, what are you going to do about it? Are we licked, or are we going to put this thing across? Does the Y.M.C.A. continue to stand for all that is fine and strong and clean and decent in this community, or does it close up? The answer is in your hands. Two theatres in Shale City operate profitably. The cigar stores and pool halls are having no trouble. People still find money to support bootleggers! What, then about the Y.M.C.A.?"

He paused for a moment, surveying them pugnaciously. His voice took on a conciliatory tone.

"In the long run, friends, I'm only your employee here in the 'Y'. I really have nothing to say about this campaign. All that I have done in connection with it, I have done at your request. If the 'Y' closes up, I can find other jobs in other 'Ys' in other towns. But I'm thinking of Shale City. I'm thinking what the Y.M.C.A. means to Shale City. And for this reason I'm going to make a suggestion. I submit that it is our duty to clear this matter up once and for all. We have here thirty-seven of the leading men of Shale City. Leaders financially as well as morally. Between us we can raise this forty-seven hundred dollars. I suggest that we not leave this room until it *has* been raised. In proof of my good faith, I offer ten per cent. of my salary for the next three months as my contribution. Are you with me, fellows, or aren't you?"

It was almost as if the whole thing had been arranged beforehand. A mighty chorus of "Yea! Yea! Yea!" greeted the brave announcement. John Abbott was surprised and a little touched at the enthusiasm. Here were men who already had contributed as much as they could afford, pledging themselves to raise among their own number the considerable sum of forty-seven hundred dollars above their previous donations. A great many of them, he knew, were hard pressed. Their determination exemplified the spirit which had made Shale City spring up out of the desert and become a metropolis. Or almost a metropolis.

Harry Twinge jumped to his feet as though an electric current had passed through him.

"Fifty dollars!" he shouted.

"Fifty dollars from Harry Twinge!" roared Henry Wilhelm.

Walter Goode made a notation on a piece of paper. Then he spoke into Henry Wilhelm's ear.

"Fifty dollars from Walter Goode!" thundered the secretary.

Walter Goode made the notation.

Henry Daniels, owner of one of the cigar stores whose prosperity had offended Henry Wilhelm, announced that he would give twenty-five dollars. Someone else volunteered fifteen, and Henry Wilhelm's face fell a little. Then Stanley Brown, editor of *The Monitor,* came through for fifty, and the secretary smiled again.

John Abbott rose modestly. A hush settled over the room.

"A thousand," he said faintly.

Cheers went up, and a great burst of handclapping.

"A thousand dollars from John Abbott!" howled Henry Wilhelm.

Walter Goode made the notation on his paper.

There were a few more fifties and twenty-fives, and one of a hundred. Then the enthusiasm dwindled sharply. Henry Wilhelm pounded on the table and railed at them, but without result. After a great deal of fervid oratory, he called on Walter Goode to calculate how much still was lacking. Walter Goode announced the figure as thirty-three hundred dollars. Henry Wilhelm shouted at them for a while longer, but received only a hundred and seventy dollars for his trouble.

A discouraged silence settled over the room.

"Am I to understand, gentlemen, that you are through? Are we licked? Or are you willing to stick until we've raised the whole sum? All in favour of sticking say aye! Shout it! Make it good and strong!"

"Aye! Aye! Aye!"

"Then do I hear anything further?"

He did not. The place was heavy with gloom. John Abbott sat staring at his plate—completely unaware that every eye in the room was cocked alertly in his direction—thinking about these men who had contributed so heavily toward the debt. Men who he knew couldn't afford it. He was touched by their tenacity, their determination to remain in their chairs until the Y.M.C.A. was free of debt, even though it stripped them of their last dollar. Suddenly he rose to his feet again.

"Gentlemen," he said, "I am very deeply moved by what I have seen and heard here tonight. It seems to me that a splendid thing has been accomplished. You will pardon me, I hope, if I say that I am frankly familiar with the financial condition of some of you who have made large contributions to-night. Frankly, I know of more than a few who can't really afford to give what they have pledged."

He felt a little confused by the rapt attention he was receiving. Reverend Slocum, sitting beside Walter Goode, mused bitterly that during all his years in the pulpit he had never commanded such feverish interest. John Abbott looked down at the table to find that he was toying nervously with his spoon. He dropped the spoon, and raised his eyes again.

"I hope that you will not consider it bad taste when I say that I am eager to contribute proportionately as much as any of you. I am going to give a little more than is needed according to the figures. Then those of you who have over-pledged will be enabled to go privately to Mr. Goode and withdraw a portion of your offer. It's only fair, I guess, to arrange it this way.

"There is but one condition that I impose. If I give any further money to the Y.M.C.A., it must be understood that no boy in Shale City is to be denied use of the building. There must be no financial, religious or racial discrimination. If this is acceptable to you, then I am happy to contribute an additional four thousand dollars to the clearing of the debt."

He sat down quickly, but not quickly enough to escape having his hand assaulted once more by Henry Wilhelm. The wildest sort of confusion broke out. Men rushed up to him, eyes shining, hands extended. Someone started three cheers, and the response nearly burst the walls. John Abbott sat in his chair, a small, happy, bewildered figure, while they boiled around him. When order was restored, Henry Wilhelm delivered a speech which was unequalled in the experience of his listeners either for volume or sentiment.

He delved into the life history of John Abbott—how he had come to the town in his youth and helped build it; how he had never lost the common touch in the acquisition of wealth; how his benefactions were unnumbered and his good qualities without equal anywhere; how he had just performed a service which would enshrine him for ever in the memory of his fellow townsmen.

John Abbott listened carefully. It was only with an effort that he kept tears from his eyes. The fact that he was abjectly embarrassed, that in certain instances he felt that Henry Wilhelm's fervour overstepped the bounds of precise truth, did not diminish one whit of his exquisite gratification. Honesty and generosity were two qualities which he had sincerely striven to acquire. Henry Wilhelm was simply confirming his possession of them. The enthusiasm of these men, their congratulations, their praise, and now Henry Wilhelm's speech—the whole thing left him a little giddy.

He didn't recognize the glibness of Wilhelm's words. He didn't for an instant perceive that they were much too facile for an extemporaneous endeavour. He had no way of knowing that Henry Wilhelm had carefully rehearsed it for three days; that Walter Goode and the steering committee had told him to prepare it, because they could hope to raise the debt only by snaring John Abbott for at least four or five thousand dollars. He wouldn't have believed the truth if someone had told him, for he was eager to accept such things at their face value.

By the time the last tribute had been paid and the meeting had been adjourned, John Abbott was perilously near to sobbing. He could scarcely remember when he had been happier. Here was the perfect answer to Hermann Vogel's cynical nonsense. Who could see and hear what John Abbott had seen and heard without catching the almost electrical spirit of solidarity and affection which bound him to these men? It was nine o'clock when he stumbled out into the twilight and started home, his head among the stars.

XIV

IT was beginning to grow cooler. A mild breeze rustled through branches overhanging the sidewalk. John Abbott sniffed the air, heavy with the flavour of orchards and growing things. The atmosphere was a little sultry. Donna Long had hoped it would rain. Perhaps there would be a thunderstorm later on. Passing along the sidewalk, he saw smudges of light on front porches, beneath which contented burghers read *The Monitor* or *The Saturday Evening Post,* talked softly, luxuriated in this respite from the heat. On other porches there were only the red dots of cigars stabbing the night. From somewhere near at hand came the hypnotic creak of a garden swing, and then a girl's soft laughter trilled through the summer twilight. The peace which hovered over Shale City was almost like death.

John Abbott was happy. He walked slowly through the night, taking in great breaths of sweet air. Absurd phrases from Henry Wilhelm's speech still danced through his mind. He recognized the egotism which prompted him to gloat over them, but he was content to indulge so pleasant a weakness. This was success. It was the stuff of which all men dreamed, but which so few attained.

He had wealth, honour and security. There was little more to be desired. There was nothing complicated about the way he had achieved it. He didn't credit himself with the possession of genius. No one, he thought, knew his limitations as well as he knew them himself. It had been only a matter of digging in and sticking; of enduring the winter and summer of a new country; of learning to understand people and to recognize the miracle of growth. He had made Shale City, and Shale City had made him: a fair bargain on either side.

There were no stirrings in his soul, no longing for travel or new sights. The devil with adventure! And yet—wasn't there adventure in watching a desert become habitable? Wasn't life itself an adventuresome affair? It was no matter: he was content and secure. This valley of the Colorado was definite, immovable, everlasting. The land beneath his feet would never vanish. It would remain for ever and so long as he lived he would possess a generous portion of it. The town was permanent, too: it had an inner life completely independent of disturbances from the outside. If a man was safe anywhere on this earth, he was safe in Shale City. That was because of the land. He worshipped it: he had his roots deeply into it: it was life.

People coming to Shale City from Denver or Pueblo complained that its existence was dull. John Abbott couldn't understand them. They thought the town uninteresting because its life was simple. It was eating and sleeping and working; watching the seasons melt together; finishing a day and starting another. Was life anywhere else greatly different? He was willing enough to concede the simplicity of the town's routine, but it must be profound and wise, else it would not be so simple. It was very direct and close to the verities. It cut through great swaths of complexity and got down eventually to the earth, to the land. John Abbott had observed that a certain type of person could not cope with simplicity. His mind broke beneath the weight of simple things. He was overpowered and crushed by the pitiless logic of fundamentals.

What more could a man desire than that which John Abbott already had?—the sweet words of Henry Wilhelm's speech, the acclamation of fellow townsmen, the comforting possession of land and wealth. Quite suddenly he answered the question. He wanted someone to talk to. He wanted to share this triumph of his. He wanted to pour Wilhelm's heady tribute into sympathetic ears. He wanted to talk to someone so close to him that he could throw off the mask of modesty behind which he always concealed himself. He wanted to have a woman who would not scorn him. He wanted to tell her all that had happened to-night, and to feel that she was proud of him. He wanted to strut before her, to display his gorgeous feathers, to bask in the warmth of her approbation.

Once he had gone home and told Ann of some similar affair. He should have known better, but the words had slipped through in a moment of unguarded exultance. She had stared oddly at him. Then, with a grim little smile playing about her lips, she had uttered two words:

"The philanthropist!"

That was all.

He had rushed furiously from the house to avoid beating her. He had sworn that he would never expose himself to her again. And he had kept the vow. Ann would receive her first information of this Y.M.C.A. affair from *The Monitor*. Occasionally his silences really embarrassed her. A friend would mention some service her husband had rendered for Shale City, and Ann would know nothing of it. Once or twice he had seen her squirm under these circumstances, beheld the flush of humiliation rise to her colourless face. He took a sadistic pleasure in watching her wriggle out of such predicaments with any remnant of grace left to her.

By now there was no feeling between them at all, no affection. They were, of course, accustomed to each other. They could conduct necessary conversations, but beneath this civilized attitude ran deep passions which they never discussed. At times John Abbott believed that they were hanging on only to spite each other. It was a battle of survival, with each vainly trying to torture the other into submission. But surely it wasn't as bad as that. Love simply had run out on them: they were tolerating each other because they were bound together by law.

He yearned for Donna Long. He even toyed with the idea of dropping round to see her. Something was pulling him toward her to-night, something powerful and almost irresistible. But that was out of the question. She and Miss Septimus, the school teacher, had lived together for years in a house which they owned jointly, yet not even Miss Septimus knew anything of the relations between her dearest friend and John Abbott. No, it was quite impossible to see Donna Long. But he wanted her desperately. He wanted to rush to her with this Y.M.C.A. affair, this petty thing which thrilled him so deeply. Donna Long would understand. Her eyes would glow, and she would be proud of him. He would adore her for being proud of him.

He pondered over his love for Donna Long. Sometimes he thought: "John Abbott, you are sixty. Don't be an old fool. People don't think of love when they are sixty. The emotions have all died." That was logic talking to him, for he did think of love. To-night he didn't feel old; he felt young, as though new life had been poured through his veins, as though some exhilarating presence were very close to him. Middle age was yesterday, and youth only the day before that. A man's emotions changed very little. Give him something to adore, something that would permit itself to be adored, something that would respond to adoration, something that would repay adoration with respect—give him these, and he would be a lover for ever.

He seemed to see Donna Long before him, luminous in the starlight. It was almost weird the way her voice sounded in his ears. "I was made to have children!" Like a wail, filled with anguish and accusation; a wail for the hopelessness of thirty years' devotion. They were too old now to have children. A pair of old people . . . drying up in the desert . . . hadn't she said something like that? A family was out of the question—but Donna Long didn't know that it had been out of the question all along. She didn't know that its impossibility had been his only reason for hesitating to divorce Ann and marry her.

He could see it quite clearly now. He had never voluntarily spoken of marriage to Donna Long. For all she knew, he had never wanted to marry her. The whole meaning of their last conversation rushed in upon his consciousness. In that hour of discovery and humiliation, Donna Long had thought that he deliberately had conspired to possess her and hold her for all these years, with no other object than to have her as his mistress. She had thought he had used her without ever wanting to consummate the bargain by marriage.

What had those thirty years done to her? How could he ever hope to atone for the doubt and torture which must have been present in her mind even when they were happiest? What a hell it must have been for her: what a hell it had been for him, who stood to lose nothing. Donna Long deserved to know. He should have told her years ago. Now he would rectify the injustice. He would tell her to-morrow. Then she would understand why he had been so silent about marriage. She would know what she surely had doubted all these years— that he loved her wholly and completely.

He walked more swiftly, thinking of what he would tell her. Foolish, stupid vanity that had closed his lips for so long! It would be done very simply. They would be sitting in his office. It would be in the morning: the first thing in the morning. He would start out casually enough. He would say to her:

"Donnalong, I've wanted to marry you from the first—from that first night down in the old Emporium. But I'm sterile, and I couldn't do it." (It would embarrass him horribly to say it so bluntly.) "For all I know I have been sterile always. It has won me the contempt of one woman, and you were so precious to me that I couldn't risk losing you too. If I had married you, you would have found me out, for you've always wanted children, Donnalong. You would have expected them. I've gone on all these years, keeping you close to me, keeping my secret—because I was terrified at the thought of losing you. Now we have grown older. We couldn't have children anyhow. I'm able to tell you what I was too cowardly to tell you before. That is the reason I've seemed so content to let things be, Donnalong. I was afraid to change them. I've cheated you, and you deserve to know why. It was because I loved you so very much."

He was a fool for not having told her before. To-morrow he would do it. And then, if Ann should ever die . . . God! He couldn't think of that. He mustn't hope for that, even in the secrecy of his own mind. Thoughts of death were almost like death Himself. One never dared summon death, for fear He would strike down the wrong person.

XV

ANN ABBOTT sat in the great square house on North Fifth Avenue and considered her loneliness. The house belonged to her. John Abbott had deeded it and all its furnishings to her ten years before—at the time of Richard Maesfield's suicide. But though it was Ann Abbott's property, it reflected only her husband. It was such a house as John Abbott might have been expected to build. Its stout concrete foundation was set on piles which in turn were anchored to bed rock thirty feet in the earth. It had eleven rooms—none of them small—including the only sun-parlour in Shale City. Built of the same cream-coloured brick which had been used in the bank, its enormous plate-glass windows looked out upon a porch which ran under wide eaves clear across the front of the house. It was a large, comfortable, unimaginative dwelling, too new for tower rooms and cupolas, too old for period stair railings and Spanish balconies.

Neither the fanciest residence in Shale City, nor even the handsomest, it was far and away the best built. The living-room was panelled with solid oak, the dining-room with black mahogany, and a smaller living-room, which they used more than the large one, with bird's-eye maple. John Abbott loved to tell his guests how the woodwork had been polished. A crew of men had gone over it by hand eighty times to bring out the sheen. The furniture was just as honest as the house, broad, stout and restful. The drapes were of velour and brocade, chosen by Ann on their one visit to New York. In the hallway stood an authentic grandfather's clock, with a dial of inlaid gold and silver. Its soft chime stole through the house every quarter-hour. John Abbott prized it more highly than any of their furnishings.

Ann Abbott sat in the smaller living-room, and stared at her hands on which a microscopic diamond feebly competed with the brilliance of five very large ones. The small stone had been given to her by John Abbott when she had promised to marry him. Often, in these later years, he begged her not to wear her engagement ring. Its tininess humiliated him, now that he could afford larger jewels. But such protests seemed to her only another example of his vanity—his colossal, insuperable vanity—and she clung resolutely to the diminutive stone. He tried to win his point by giving her larger ones, until now she had sixteen flashing rings and two brooches. John Abbott liked to see his wife in diamonds.

Sometimes she gazed at the little stone, and wondered if any remote hint of love for her husband had survived the bitter years of their marriage. One did not live forty-one years in a man's house without finding the shabby spots. She knew him so well. She discerned so many preposterous faults which were hidden from everyone else. Yet, in spite of them, there was an attachment which could not entirely be denied.

She knew that when she had married John Abbott she was not beautiful; but he had thought her beautiful, and that was enough. They had journeyed together into this western country, to spend their lives in a new land where things were quickening, expanding, growing; a fresh place in which they could start on an equal footing with everyone else. If she had been dismayed at the first sight of Shale City, she had hidden her feelings from her husband. The new world which had beckoned them was far worse than she had expected—raw, naked shacks; parched bottom-lands; turbulent mountains frowning over a great expanse of valley, vomiting forth a wild and deceptive river. But she was not disturbed. She had cast her lot unhesitatingly with John Abbott. If he chose to conquer this forbidding empire, she was willing to help him.

Her youth shrivelled under the merciless sun. Her skin, whipped by winter blizzards and spring winds, lost its glowing freshness. The store had to be kept open from early morning until far into the night. They huddled in a little room behind it. They battled together and were happy, because attainment lay ahead of them: four years of that before they were able to build a house. They planted a few hardy shrubs along a cinder path leading to the front stoop, hung bright curtains at the windows, and decided that they could afford a family.

After a period of this, with nothing happening, John Abbott sent his wife to old Dr. Bertrand. The old medico hawed wisely over her, and finally suggested that she go to Denver. Two surgeons in Denver, after profound and incomprehensible mutterings, clapped her into a hospital and operated on her. It had been rather a humiliating affair. It seemed that she was not greatly unlike a sow that didn't farrow, or a mare that stubbornly refused to foal. She was, in fine, a poor investment as a wife unless she bore children.

She had wanted them badly enough, too. But John Abbott hadn't handled her delicately. In effect he had commanded her to have these things done, demanded almost bitterly that she be restored to fertility. She could still remember the pang of those long weeks in Denver, sick and hurt, terrified and aching with loneliness. John Abbott had stayed in Shale City to attend the Emporium. She was desperately sick when she returned home: they couldn't afford too large a bill at the hospital. A full year passed, and still she did not recover. Something about the operation had devitalized her. It not only had wounded her spirit; it had maimed her body. All of her courage seemed to have fled. For whole days she wept bitterly and inconsolably. Even now, so many years later, it was difficult to walk any distance, and completely impossible for her to care for the big square house. That was the price she had paid for fertility.

Almost two years after her return from Denver John Abbott went to Dr. Bertrand himself and learned the truth. There had been nothing the matter with Ann. But John Abbott, in old Bertrand's indelicately frank opinion, was "barren as a gelding." The eternal egotism of the male, never for an instant to doubt his own reproductive ability!

She still remembered him as he had come home that night, pale and brutally crushed. After he told her, he went for a walk, returning in the grey hours of dawn passionately repentant for what she had undergone, begging her to divorce him. He told her that all his dreams, his hopes, his aspirations had centred about the desire for a family. He declared that there was no excuse for the institution of marriage if it did not bring forth a new generation to take up where the old one had left off. He stormed profanely at Dr. Bertrand, and at last fell into an exhausted slumber, huddled across the foot of the bed. It seemed strange and horrible to Ann Abbott, staring down at his tear-stained face. She had never realized the dynastic impulse lay so near to her husband's heart.

Looking back, she could see now that a portion of his shame grew out of self-condemnation for having subjected her needlessly to an ordeal which had ruined her health. When she tried to soothe the hurt, he shied from her as though he suspected her of gloating over his incapacity. Although she lost him definitely on the day he received Dr. Bertrand's diagnosis, she was not fully aware of her loss until later. A shadow had arisen between them to nullify all their gay hopes and their harsh labours. They lived in an emotional void during those years when ecstasy should have been strongest in them.

If anyone should have resented the turn events had taken, it was she, who had paid for his mistake with her youth. But as the years dragged out, she realized the truth: John Abbott was thinking only of himself. He was savagely willing to sacrifice all their happiness on the altar of a disappointed hope. Under Ann's sharp analysis the whole affair was only another proof of his incredible vanity. John Abbott had wanted to found an hereditary house as well as an empire. These men—how highly they valued their glands!

Several years later Donna Long came to the Emporium, and Ann suffered the exquisite agony of beholding her husband slip into infidelity. At first it wounded her cruelly. She redoubled her efforts to keep him, to soothe his shattered pride, to make him unafraid of her. Later, the misery of defeat left her with only the harsh, bitter contempt of a wife for an adulterous husband. It was either that, or permit him to break her spirit. Of all the splendid natural equipment for marriage which she had brought to John Abbott, her pride alone remained unaltered. She had to cherish it, or go down in the wreckage completely.

Until this morning she had kept from him her knowledge of his infidelity. All through the years of loneliness she had treasured his punishment against the time she would administer it. She had listened to his absurd lies, his pitiable artifices, with carefully concealed scorn. Never for one moment had she lost command of the situation. She had beaten him back at each encounter, leaving him puzzled and angry and bewildered. He had no suspicion that she knew about Donna Long. A hundred times the accusation had risen to her lips, but she had held it back.

Considering himself a faithful husband in so far as her knowledge was concerned, he accused her of ingratitude, pointing with an injured air to the luxury in which she lived. He had concealed his infatuation for Donna Long so skillfully that it never entered his mind as a factor in evaluating his relationship with Ann. What she did not know did not exist. In honest bewilderment he asked her how a man could be almost a god in the eyes of his townspeople, yet wholly a contemptible person in the sight of his wife.

He hadn't understood until this morning. In a brief five minutes she had made everything clear to him. She had told him very quietly, very explicitly, taking a grim satisfaction in his stricken silence.

But she could not tell him that she was dying from loneliness. She couldn't let him know how desolately unhappy she was. Far away from anyone close to her, miserable and ill in an alien land, there was no one on the face of the earth to whom she could turn for comfort. Her long sicknesses prevented her from taking any satisfactory part in the town's social life. She was welcome everywhere as John Abbott's wife: nothing more. In the final analysis, he was all she had—her sole hope and her only future. Yet he belonged to another woman.

Occasionally she had mentioned adopting a child, but he had opposed the idea fiercely. He wanted her to devote herself entirely to him, to listen approvingly as he expatiated upon his generosity, to marvel as Shale City marvelled when he responded to the promptings of his amazing vanity with some new benefaction. She would have been willing enough to indulge him on this account, but in view of her knowledge of Donna Long, such a course smacked too much of sycophancy. Her pride could not endure that. She understood the motivation of his grand gestures so clearly that it was difficult to conceal her disgust. Daily his associates profited by his eagerness for flattery. Ann Abbott was a tough-minded woman. How could he expect her to encourage him along a course which in the end could only weaken and destroy him? She was the one person in Shale City who knew that her husband's public spirit grew from the poverty of his own soul.

Sometimes in moments of desperation she felt an impulse to rise against him, to strike him in his Achilles' heel, to cheapen him before the town. But she knew she would never do it. And if she did, the town would discredit her. If she ran through the streets screaming that he had been untrue to her for thirty hideous years, the town would shrug its shoulders and say that she was a crazy, neurotic old woman, weakened by semi-invalidism until she dreamed dreams and saw visions.

For he was impregnable. One had just as well question the omnipotence of God. When she considered her helplessness before this village prophet, as she once had called him, she was steeled with a cold determination to hurt him. He had ruined her youth, destroyed her health, wrecked her life, sought refuge in another woman's arms when his vanity drove him from hers. Now he had progressed so far above her that she could never hope to cross swords with him anywhere but in the privacy of their home. On every hand she was beaten and humiliated, while he advanced on a growing wave of public adulation.

That was why she had declared war this morning on Donna Long. After thirty years of torture, she had declared bitter, unremitting warfare upon John Abbott's mistress. Her club was ready, and she would hold it above him from now on, never using it, but always finding immeasurable satisfaction in possessing it.

"I'll ruin her, John Abbott," she had said calmly. "I have records of detectives who have checked the St. Albans in Denver during every 'buying trip' for the last eight years. Listen to a page of it: 'Subjects left hotel at 10.15 A.M., lunched at Buffalo Grill, returned to hotel at 4.52 P.M. Dined together in room 418, and remained until 3.27 A.M., when woman went to own room, 532, returning in twelve minutes with small travelling bag. Subjects ordered breakfast in room 418 at 9.43 A.M.'"

She would never forget the sight of his face, white with horror, as she read off the cold history of his adultery.

"I've all the rest—eight years of them. Some day I will use them. I haven't decided exactly when, but I thought you'd like to know. You may be able to stand up under the storm, but Donna Long will be disgraced . . . disgraced. . . ."

And yet . . . there were times when he came into the house with an odd expression on his face, and she knew that he, too, felt the sting of defeat. Upon such occasions he seemed a pathetic little peddler who was puzzled by circumstances far beyond his comprehension. She had to fight back an impulse to rush to him and comfort him; to plead with him to forget everything but her—Ann Abbott—his wife. She never yielded to such temptations. She didn't dare to bare herself before him.

He was coming through the front door now. She heard his step. The stride was light and youthful. She could tell from it that he was in high spirits. He walked through the big living-room. Now he stood on the threshold. She turned in her chair to look at him. He mumbled a greeting without having seen her—at least without definitely looking at her. His face was filled with an almost mystical happiness. She was at the point of speaking when the telephone jangled in the room behind him. He turned to answer it. She could hear his conversation.

"Hello . . . This's him . . . Who? . . . Oh, yes, now I understand . . . You say she's——!" She heard a little moan, and then his voice almost whispering: "I—I'll be right over. Right—over!"

Without speaking a word to her he slipped out of the house. She heard the front screen door nestle into the jamb. She went into the room where he had been a moment before. The receiver was still hanging, knocking faintly against the wall.

XVI

JOHN ABBOTT knocked at the door of the house on Harbin Street where Miss Septimus, the Latin teacher, lived with Donna Long. Miss Septimus opened the door. Her eyes were red from weeping. "Oh, it's you, Mr. Abbott," she faltered. "Come in."

He followed her into the neat living-room, in the most remote corner of which a small lamp furnished the only illumination. Miss Septimus dropped into a chair and covered her eyes with an inadequate handkerchief. Her frail little shoulders quivered. John Abbott sat down too.

"She—she's dead?" he finally heard himself ask.

The woman across from him burst into a little torrent of words.

"I'll never love anyone again—ever!" she sobbed. "Everyone I love dies. First——" She broke off abruptly.

John Abbott knew that the ghost of her lover had walked sighing through the room: he knew she had been about to say, "first Lawrence Ring, and now . . ." Miss Septimus had been engaged to marry Lawrence Ring years before. He had been killed on his way to the wedding, and she had lain her bridal bouquet on his grave.

Miss Septimus recovered herself. John Abbott heard the rattling of her voice, as if she felt in some measure responsible for this later death, and wanted to show him that she was blameless.

"She came from the store a little early. Then she went upstairs to lie down. I called her to dinner, but she told me to go ahead. I saved some for her, though. Then later I called her. She didn't answer, so—" Miss Septimus burst into tears. There was a painful silence while she composed herself sufficiently to continue— "so I went up to awaken her. She was lying on the bed. Dr. Hannan said it was heart failure . . . about nine o'clock."

"Did—did she say anything when she came in?"

"Yes." Miss Septimus seemed to be prodding her memory. After what seemed an interminable pause, she continued. "I remember her face as she walked in the front door. It was all white and drawn. She said, 'I'm so tired, Eva. It's been such a long hard day, and so very hot. I'm going upstairs for a good rest'."

"That's—all?"

"Yes. 'A good rest——!' "

"I'm so sorry—so terribly sorry." Why was he apologizing to her? Or was he? He hesitated a moment before going on. "Is she still—here?"

Miss Septimus nodded. "Mr. Karwin was out when I called. They'll send him over just as soon as he comes back."

He nodded mechanically. Karwin was coming to take Donna Long. John Abbott had wanted her, but in the end she belonged to Karwin. This was all unreal. It was utterly fantastic. This wasn't happening at all. It was a dream from which he would awaken in just a moment.

"Could I—would you mind—you see we worked together for so many years—"

Miss Septimus nodded.

"I'd rather not go with you," she said into her handkerchief. "Her bedroom is just to your right after you climb the stairs."

He walked into the hallway and started up the stairs. His legs were tingling. He felt that any moment he might topple into deep slumber. He seemed to be feeling his way. There was absolutely no sensation to this, save the shattering rhythm of his heart. The silence robbed everything of reality. The first door to the left . . . after he climbed the stairs. No, the first door to the right. Right, it was. The first door to the right. It was ajar.

He tip-toed across to her. Miss Septimus had drawn a sheet clear over her—even over her face. His breath faded away. He was so dizzy that he had to place one hand on the bed to support himself. Then with his thumb and forefinger he folded back the sheet.

A dark flood of memories swept into the room—his mother, wasted and severe, slumped over in a rocking chair; his father with a whole half of his shoulder torn away by dynamite; his only sister a chalky image sheltering the nestled form of her first-born. And only yesterday he had seen a bewildered puppy jerking grotesquely towards sidewalk shelter before the final spasm of death stifled its outcry: the unconquerable instinct to delay the end until sanctuary had been reached—the weary homeward struggle of all dazed and death-driven refugees. That was why Donna Long had left the store early.

How tired she looked! How blue her eyelids, with those weary lines at the corners. Poor girl . . . my poor dear child. All alone here in your room, in your safe place: alone, with no one to say, 'Sleep, my bewildered, frightened little puppy. Sleep . . .'

He hung over the bed, staring down at her face, gripping his hat with both hands as though it alone kept him from falling across her body.

Oh Donnalong, why did you go?

You are all that I have.

Why did you leave me? You have left me so alone.

I can't get along without you!

I can't! I can't . . .

He didn't know how long a time passed before he heard Miss Septimus' step on the threshold. The room throbbed to her whisper.

"I'm sorry. Mr. Karwin is downstairs."

She belonged to Karwin now. He wiped his eyes, and followed Miss Septimus downstairs. Karwin was waiting in the living room. John Abbott walked straight to the front door.

"I'll go," he said to Miss Septimus.

"Have you your car?"

He looked at her vaguely.

"No."

"You shouldn't go out in the storm."

"Storm?"

Slowly his senses returned. He heard the roll of thunder, and the rain beating outside on the roof of the front porch. Without answering he opened the door and rushed through it.

Karwin's long black hearse was standing in the drive, its lights blinking crazily through the storm.

XVII

I
T was a wild, terrifying night.

Thunder rocked back and forth over the heavens. Lightning ripped livid fissures in the blackness. Rain and wind tormented the face of the earth. John Abbott walked through the storm, oblivious to the uproar. His hat was gone, and his clothes streamed with water.

Donna Long had been tired of the heat and the blazing, remorseless sun. Well, it was not hot any longer. The heavens were weeping great tears for her. The drought was broken. The earth was sucking up the rain; growing things were spreading eager leaves to receive it. Down by the river there was a spot to which they used to go. Down there the rain was hammering on the river, sending up fine spray over its lonely breast, while the wind was whipping it into little wavelets. Out on Sawtooth Mesa the dry farmers were standing in their doorways with their families beside them, staring at the rain, thanking God for rescue from the sun. Up the valley the orchardists were praying it would stop, fuming at the danger to trees heavy-laden with ripening fruit.

If the storm had come sooner, Donna Long would not have died. If she had borne the heat just a few more hours, she could have bared her face to rain and drunk in its freshness. It was the heart-breaking dryness that had killed her—the glare from the earth and cloudless skies. Where in the midst of this present fury had she found refuge? The wind tore small branches from the trees. The rain came at a slant, cutting against his face. Thunderclaps leaped from one end of the valley to the other. Lightning snapped with cold menace, skipping along telephone wires, twisting brightly down lightning rods.

He found himself wandering along Main Street. Lights at the intersections swung crazily in the storm. Shadows veered into grotesque prominence, and then slunk away. The rain was frothy on the pavement. It rushed through the gutters, and sprawled over the street at overflow points.

He paused in the shelter of a store entrance next to Walter Goode's real estate office, and stared across the street at the Emporium. She had died without ever hearing what he had wanted so badly to tell her. How horrible it was to think she would never know. There was no way he could explain it to her now; no way he could confide how desperately he had loved her. Perhaps she had wanted to die. There wasn't anyone, now that she had left him: no one with whom he could talk. No one left whom he could love.

The tumult suddenly died away; the rain ceased, the wind lost its fury. Lightning far away on the horizon flung a last challenge at the beaten earth. He could hear the last discontented grumble of thunder. A little clearing appeared in the clouds overhead, and in the midst of the clearing, a moon.

The clear blue circle around the moon widened, and stars came into view. The street was transformed to flowing crystal at John Abbott's feet. The air was deliciously sweet and clear. He could feel the change, but he could not see it. His eyes were blurred, his mind still numb.

Walter Goode and Miss Weems had been enjoying a rendezvous in the rear of the real estate office. Taking advantage of the sudden calm, they now hurried into the street. The quiet outside was so great that the sound of Walter Goode's key in the door was like the clatter of a chain. As they turned out of the entrance, they were startled to see John Abbott standing awkwardly in front of the adjoining store, staring upward and across the street at the Emporium. Walter Goode's first impulse was to hoist his coat collar and rush Miss Weems past the merchant. But then, in sudden defiance, he tipped his hat.

"Good evening, Mr. Abbott."

John Abbott acted as if he hadn't heard the greeting. He only stared oafishly across at his store, his face dead white in the moonlight. Walter Goode hesitated an instant, puzzled at the merchant's behaviour; then a little tug from Miss Weems overcame his curiosity. He took her arm and they hurried along the slippery sidewalk, their heels clicking loudly as they went. Walter Goode wondered if the owner of the Emporium was drunk. He certainly had a foolish look on his face. What a joke!—the paragon of Shale City virtue, drunk and hatless, staring at his store as if it were a spook.

It was dawn when John Abbott returned home. Mechanically he walked to his desk and opened his diary. "Had a good day and night. Nothing happened. What more could I ask?" He drew a dark, unsteady line across that last entry, and wrote three words below it.

"God forgive me."

He fell asleep in his chair, his cheek resting on the page which contained Donna Long's obituary.

BOOK II

JOHN ABBOTT
AND THE TOWN
1928-1929

I

JOHN ABBOTT went to bed with pneumonia on the day of Donna Long's funeral. For two weeks he wavered uncertainly between life and death. A specialist from Denver moved into the big square house on North Fifth Avenue. Nurses flitted through its darkened rooms, and a strange silence fell over the whole block. Residents of the neighbourhood sent their children elsewhere to play, lest their shouts disturb the stricken man. Motorists slipped by noiselessly, and pedestrians passing the house could not resist quick, curious glances toward the drawn curtains on the second floor behind which John Abbott was fighting for his life.

Each day *The Monitor* printed bedside bulletins which were awaited eagerly by the whole Colorado Valley. Flowers arrived in such profusion that Ann was obliged to have them sent on to the charity ward of the hospital after snipping the cards. Committees-of-one from every organization in town filed solemnly into the big Abbott parlour to pay their respects and offer their services to the sick man's wife.

The specialist declared that while John Abbott possessed a splendid constitution, he lacked a certain spiritual resistance which was almost essential for his ultimate recovery. But the crisis was finally passed. When the town learned John Abbott wasn't going to die, it sighed with relief. After six weeks the convalescent was able to walk about in his room, a wasted stranger accepting the attentions of his nurses with a curiously passive air of resignation. Two months later, still light-headed and weary, he returned to his office at the Emporium.

He called George Boone into the office and gave him a big cigar. George Boone had been with the Emporium for eight years. John Abbott had added him to the store force when Boone's real estate business had failed. For the last six years he had been in charge of ladies' ready-to-wear. He knew how to deal with women, and had brought his department to a high point of efficiency. His eye for style was so shrewd that John Abbott sent him each year on a buying trip to New York. He was a very active member of the Baptist Church. Shale City was always reading in *The Monitor* that Mr. and Mrs. George Boone had entertained the ladies of the church last night, or the men of the church, or the church choir, or the Sunday school.

"I'm going to have to find somebody to fill Miss Long's place," John Abbott said to George Boone. "As you must know, I trusted Miss Long implicitly. Her—her departure leaves a vacancy which will be very difficult to fill. I must have somebody I can depend on. I can't be bothered with details, George. I'm still pretty weak from that sickness. I've got to shunt the responsibility off on to someone, and I've just about decided that you're the man. You've done a pretty good job while I've been gone."

George Boone's face lighted up. "Why Mr. Abbott! I'd be——!"

"As I was saying," interrupted John Abbott wearily, "I have decided on you. I believe you have a fair block of stock in the company by now, haven't you?"

"Yes, sir," said George Boone.

"Miss Long, as vice-president of the organization, owned quite a large amount. I have purchased it from her estate. I mean to put you in charge here. Not as vice-president. We—we'll leave that position vacant. But as general manager—a new office. You'll get a raise of seven-five a month. All of this sum will be applied against the purchase of stock in the corporation. Is that satisfactory to you?"

Emporium stock was very choice. Its earnings were out of all proportion to its par value. It was the best investment in Shale City, available only to those who worked in the store, disposable only to John Abbott.

"Perfectly! And I want you to know——"

"Then you'll start at once," said John Abbott. "Take the place,"—and he made a vague circling gesture—"and see what you can do with it. I'm trusting you. Keep it as good as it is now, and try to make it better. Try to make it," he paused, seeking some fit comparison, "try to make it the best store in the United States—anywhere. See me on anything important. But use your own judgment whenever possible. I'm going to pull out of things for a while—until I feel better. You understand?"

"I do," said George Boone firmly. "And I want you to know, Mr. Abbott, that I——"

"That's all right, George. I'm going home now, I think." He glanced around the office. "I—I feel a little down."

This lasted for two years. All of the zest had gone out of him. People missed him when they shopped at the Emporium. During rush hours it always had been his custom to take a post at the foot of the stairs leading to his office. There he stood with his hands behind his back, smiling at everyone like a genial feudal lord. Farmers came up and spoke to him about crops, credit, crime. Children stared at him in round-eyed respect, as though he were as much a legendary figure as Santa Claus or the Sandman. Young folks went out of their way to wish him a pleasant good day.

But after Donna Long's death they saw him rarely.

He lounged about his office in the mornings. Sometimes he sat for long periods, staring out over the store. People said that he was growing old: and that sickness hadn't done him any good, either. Everyone was very kind to him. It made him vaguely uncomfortable to be regarded with such solicitous eyes. Even Ann had changed.

At first it had been horrible, being around Ann. He was bursting with grief and loneliness which decency compelled him to hide. When he remembered Ann's Denver reports, his pride and his contempt for her made him prefer death itself to any bid, no matter how small, for her sympathies. But Ann was fine about it. She attended him tirelessly during his illness, and afterwards he felt her sympathy flowing out to him, warm and almost forgiving. The bitter words that had flared up between them in the past now died away. Sometimes he wanted madly to talk to her, to tell her how splendid she had been, to shower his sorrow upon her and to let her comfort him. But the brutal pages of detective reports always intervened . . .

He was lost and confused. His mind didn't function as clearly as it had in former times. Petty problems distressed him—problems which customarily had been solved by the simple expedient of turning them over to Donna Long. He was a little startled to discover how greatly he had depended upon her. He was a child in the Emporium: he didn't know anything about the business. Some time when he had regained control of himself he would dig in and familiarize himself with things again. But for the present, he preferred to drift with the seasons, trying to accustom himself to the change.

Two years of it: two years of walking down to the Emporium in the mornings, and being vaguely startled to find that Donna Long was not at her desk across from him; two years of awakening from afternoon siestas with her name on his lips. He found himself straining at the sound of footsteps, hoping they would be hers—waiting with bated breath as a door opened because he could not drive from his mind the stubborn expectation that it might be she who would enter. Going home in the evenings, the intense loneliness of his mood often summoned her into existence; he could see her walking toward him, luminous in the twilight. But she always vanished when he was at the point of taking her into his arms. Each time that the illusion was swept away, each time his fancy was replaced by the brutal emptiness around him, it was as though she had died all over again.

In the summer of 1928 he decided to leave Shale City for a while. Perhaps in some distant place he would find a fresh interest to restore his lagging enthusiasms. He and Ann went to Long Beach, where there was a hotel overlooking the sea in which they had been recurrent guests for years. It was restful and quiet, always filled with people who might have come from Shale City themselves.

John Abbott spent whole afternoons on Point Firmin, staring out at the sea, watching the big boats come and go. The commerce of continents met there in a harbour which had been made by man. It was almost a miracle. He enjoyed trying to identify foreign flags on the ships, sinking into reveries concerning the countries when they came. He found himself for the first time cognizant of the size of the world and the smallness of Shale City. He had, of course, been to New York: but not until now had he considered the outside world as anything more substantial than a rumour. Strange smells floated up the heights to him—hemp and copra and tar. It seemed that he remembered all of this from some long gone past, that the men on ships were his comrades, and the sea his mother.

One afternoon while he sat there gazing over the water, a fantastic notion entered his mind. He rushed back to Long Beach. He could scarcely wait until he found Ann. She was sitting in the lobby, chatting with a pleasant-faced woman from Illinois.

"Ann!" he cried excitedly. "Pack your things. We're going to take a trip. A sea trip. A voyage!"

"When?" she asked breathlessly.

"To-morrow. We can't waste any time. There's a boat leaving. Through the Canal and to New York. Back home by rail. You"—he became a little embarrassed, and then continued more diffidently— "you think you'd like that?"

"Of course I'd like it," declared Ann. "We'll pack right away."

So they sailed on a leisurely voyage through leisurely seas. They stopped at strange ports, approving the scenery and disapproving of the people it produced. They drifted through the Carribean, watching odd lights on the face of the waters of night time, drawing from the endless swell of the sea a portion of its calm vitality.

The night they bade farewell to Cuba, a queer thing happened. The ship was sliding through the bottle neck of Havana Harbour while they leaned against the rail watching lights flicker along the shore. Grim old Morro Castle passed them by and vanished into the mist and darkness. There were young people aboard, young people all about them who seemed to melt together naturally and easily in this other-world of gentle movement and dream-like isolation. John Abbott reached hesitantly for his wife's hand, and pressed it lightly for a moment.

"I'm going to try to be a good husband, Ann," he murmured.

II

JOHN ABBOTT returned to Shale City that fall a new man; a man of action; a prophet. He had perceived clearly for the first time how vast the outer world was and what a very busy place it could be. He was filled with something approaching shame for the complacent ease with which Shale City faced its destiny. This was an era of progress, of speed, of five-minute miracles, and by Heaven, Shale City was going to be a part of it. The town was going to forge ahead even if he had to take it by the heels and drag it into the pulsing tempo of its age.

Several New York manufacturing houses who valued his business had delegated representatives to act as his guides. He had walked through factories which hummed and whirred and threw off blue sparks of efficiency, while a man at his side spoke casually of millions of yards and billions of spools. He had seen great boulevards crowded with automobiles, the property of a new race, a new mass which shared the fruits of its labour. He and Ann had dined in golden restaurants, with someone always close at hand to point out the man who had made ten millions in a week, or a hundred millions in a month.

New York was the banking capital of the world. New York was the Daniel among nations. New York was the roaring, soaring prophet of the new era. Everywhere there was the rush and bustle of a prosperity which was only just beginning. Even on the sidewalks the new spirit was apparent. People moved swiftly, their faces bright with expectancy. And above the people and the tumult he had seen a fantasy of great buildings nudging the heavens, mounting higher and ever higher in a tingling race toward the stars.

At night, high up in a fabulous hotel, he had looked out over the changing flood of lights, and he had grasped something of the significance of these times. He had listened to the mighty music of riveting machines; he had beheld the rhythm of steel skeletons rising out of chasms in the earth, eager to take on the flesh of brick and the blood of commerce, straining to participate in this tremendous up-stirring of a nation.

In Pittsburgh he had seen a town of industrial emperors, of great names and great families, scrawling their imprint upon history with millions of tons of steel. He had beheld great torrents of molten iron, and men working overtime to fill a demand which became ever more insistent. Pittsburgh, squatted on its dirty river, pouring steel into the framework of Utopia!

And onward to Detroit, where the one-car family was being made over into the two-car family: where Henry Ford sat on his haunches and smiled benignly over a principality which he had built just as surely as John Abbott had built Shale City. Detroit—the fastest-growing metropolis on earth; the city of wheels and chassis and horns, with its motor-driven aristocracy thundering at the gates of the future.

Chicago, too, with its smoking miles of railroad yards, its great heart skipping beats to keep up with the rhythm of the times. Chicago, with its Lake Front changing into a spectacle of soaring beauty; Chicago, planning canals which would lead straight to the heart of Europe; Chicago, the world's greatest inland seaport; Chicago, the Moloch into whose eager maw went quivering, screaming sacrifices, and out of which streamed food for half the world. And there were other cities, all of them straining and roaring to answer the frantic cry of "More! More! More automobiles, radios, refrigerators, aeroplanes, school houses, sky-scrapers, tractors—more of everything for this people who have made themselves a nation of princes!"

Between the cities extended a network of highways, railways, airways, passing through vast interludes of fields, green and yellow with the fruit of the earth, and on into mountains with their bellies vomiting iron and gold and coal and silver and lead and copper, while upon their rising breasts roamed slow-moving stains which were herds of cattle, and white clouds which were sheep.

This thing—this country—this America—it was tremendous! Happy the people to live in such an age. Happy the nation to sponsor it.

The scales of conservatism dropped from John Abbott's eyes. All of his life he had been a cautious person, a man prone to slow beginnings and deliberate conclusions. In view of present happenings, he had been little better than a blind fool. There was no limit to progress, just as there was no limit to the imagination. Whatever man could conceive in his mind, he could accomplish. This was only a faint hint of what was going to happen in the future—a future which was being crowded and pushed until it scarcely existed any more. America was going to be a paradise. It had turned its back on the traditions of a decadent Europe and was flying in the face of the sun.

Workers were going to live on beautiful country estates, and fly to their city jobs in jitney planes. Arthur Brisbane said so, and twenty million people swore he was right. Aeroplanes were going to knit this huge industrial and social organization so tightly together that in six hours one could make the trip from Los Angeles to New York. And across the oceans, too, busy aeroplanes would shuttle back and forth, refuelling at floating aerodromes, selling goods to foreign countries, developing vast untapped markets, cutting away the miles which separated races and nations, uniting a whole world peacefully and happily in the tender arms of economic evangelism.

Nor was this an affair in which only the big fellows shared, either. The little man was receiving his portion of the cream, too! He was suckling the sweet nipple of prosperity and growing fat on it. Even the pullman porter out of Kansas City had told John Abbott about his stock investments. He had won six hundred dollars in five weeks, and his shares were still going up. On all hands this was occurring—a whole people growing rich from the increased value of its holdings.

There had been a time when John Abbott would have regarded all of this with a cold and fishy eye. But that time was long past. The greatest financiers on earth filled the air with their trumpeting to confirm the legitimacy of the movement. Economists, college professors, business statisticians, government experts—all of them concurred with the industrial prophets. "Don't sell America short! Don't sell America short!" That was the cry, and mighty throats were baying it.

John Abbott had determined that Shale City should share in this remarkable phenomenon. There was no limit to what the place might become, considering its matchless situation. It was the only town worth mentioning in that great mountain empire which extended from Denver to Salt Lake. There must be more people in the town. The Chamber must get busy. Shale City was bound to double and treble, both in population and wealth. The surrounding country could support thousands, tens of thousands more people. Shale City must become a place of importance. Nobody knew of its existence now; no one recognized it when you mentioned its name. All of that must be changed. It must come to the point where if a man said, "I am from Shale City", the world would sit up and take note of him.

When John Abbott returned to Shale City, he made a speech to the Rotary Club. He told them all about it.

"We are standing on the threshold of the greatest period in history," he told them. "There is not enough of anything. Factories everywhere are working overtime. People are prosperous, and they are going to become more prosperous. The thing is just beginning—it is in its barest infancy. We in Shale City must share it. We have been behind the times. We have been too slow and cautious. All of this must be changed. We are in a world of speed, and Shale City must take its place in the vanguard.

"There are many things we need. We need more paved streets. We need a better water supply. We need more business buildings. We need more factories. We need more homes, and we need more people to use them. We must let the world know about Shale City. We must advertise. Our Chamber of Commerce must lead out in this work, and we must support it generously. We must let the world know that here in Shale City we have the finest climate in the United States. The more people we attract, the more business there will be, the higher living standards we will develop, and the greater will be our total prosperity.

"And in addition to our already rich industrial life, we must have a leader—some one industry which will set the pace. When you think of Pittsburgh, you think of steel. When you think of Detroit, you think of automobiles. When you think of Akron, you think of rubber. When you think of Chicago, you think of meat. That's what we need here in Shale City. Of course we already have agriculture and stock raising, and the beet sugar industry and the flour mill and the coal mines; but we need more than that.

"I have been thinking a lot about this. And I have come to the conclusion that we are sitting on the greatest supply of wealth on the face of the earth. I refer, gentlemen, to the oil industry! All around us—to the north and south and east and west—there are whole mountains of oil shale. It is rich with oil, heavy with it. We all know that. One geologist estimates that there are eight hundred billion barrels of oil soaked up in these mountains. Think of it—*Eight hundred billion barrels of oil*! Think what it means! It means that we have enough fuel right here to run the world for centuries—right under our feet.

"We have been content to allow these riches to lie unused. We have always said, 'Wait until the oil wells run dry—then we will sell our oil shale to the world.' But that is not in keeping with the times, gentlemen. We must get that oil out now. We must not wait until the wells are dry. We must compete with them while they are still flowing. We must enter the markets of the world and capture our fair share of this business.

"Up to this time, there has been no cheap method of extracting oil from shale. That has been our drawback. But this is a scientific age.

This is an age in which miracles are being accomplished. We know that hidden somewhere in the brain of some scientist lies the method by which we can extract oil so cheaply that we can run the wells out of business. It is up to us to discover the method. While I was in the east I talked this over with prominent persons—men who are participating in this tremendous new prosperity. They were all impressed with the possibilities of the idea. So I have decided to act upon it.

"I am able, therefore, to make an announcement which is of considerable importance to us all. I have established the Shale City Oil Foundation. The articles of incorporation are all drawn up. It shall be the purpose of this foundation to discover how we can extract our oil cheaply. I have two scientists who are coming here to conduct the experiments. The Shale City Oil Foundation is going to have a completely equipped laboratory at La Grange—in the heart of the shale mountains. The contract for this laboratory already has been let. These two men—university professors with degrees, both of them!—are going to take over that laboratory. They are going to try every known method of oil extraction. They are going to improve upon these methods. And eventually they are going to hit upon the right one. They are going to stay there until they are successful, even if it takes all their lives. I pledge myself to that, gentlemen! And I ask that you pledge yourselves to the up-building of Shale City, wherein the fruits of these efforts will be centred!"

The applause was thunderous. He had left Shale City a fragile old man, and had returned a roaring, dynamic lion. They gave him a rising vote of thanks for the Shale City Oil Foundation. That evening *The Monitor* ignored the contest between Mr. Hoover and Mr. Smith, to report full details of the Foundation. John Abbott had put fifty thousand dollars into the project. He was prepared to spend even more whenever the present funds ran out. It was the biggest thing that had ever happened in Shale City. It would, undoubtedly, result in the town becoming a vast industrial centre. Shale City, said *The Monitor,* was very fortunate in having a man like John Abbott to prod it along, to open its eyes to its own destiny, to start it upon the path which led to greatness.

John Abbott also went to the Shale City National Bank, and had a long talk with Gerald Abbott.

"We mustn't be so tight-fisted with loans," he told his nephew. "We must release funds generously for constructive enterprise. There will be a lot of building going on. We must finance that building.

There will be new industries springing up. We must supply the credit which will enable them to become successful. We've buried ourselves in a set of books long enough. Now we're going to come alive.

"The Shale City National Bank is going to pump the life blood of progress into this community. It is not alone the duty of a bank to protect its depositors and stockholders. It must also bear a vital share in the commerce of its district. It must never fear to give that push which will further the general prosperity. We must consider the trend of the times, and not hold back. We must consider character as well as the tangible assets which a man offers as collateral for a loan. We must visualize the future, and base our loans upon it, rather than upon the present. We must attract money to Shale City, just as New York attracts money. We must live in the future, for that is what counts in this country of ours. And the future will be great. Never forget that, Gerald. The future is going to be great!"

He spoke with the deadly, remorseless enthusiasm of a missionary.

III

SIX weeks after John Abbott's return, Shale City registered its choice for Herbert Hoover as thirty-first President of the United States, and was extremely pleased when the rest of the country concurred in its selection. Shale City did not vote for Mr. Hoover in the belief that prosperity would topple without him: prosperity was ordained of God, and no man could unhorse it. It did not vote against Mr. Smith because he was a Catholic, despite the notorious fact that Rome was known to be supporting him hook, line and sinker: for, unless specifically aroused, the town was not fanatical in religious matters. The truth of the matter is that Shale City could not bring itself to the point of trusting a man who wore a derby hat.

At the same election, the citizens approved a bond issue of $255,000 for the paving of certain streets and alleys, an act which was greeted with hallelujas by *The Monitor*. In addition, the town cheerfully appropriated $35,000 for a new high school gymnasium. Pleased with this liberal attitude, the city council ordered a trio of Denver engineers to draw up an extensive survey of the water system, with an eye to its ultimate enlargement. If Shale City was to make its bid for new residents, it must have more of the liquid silver which assured its existence in the face of the desert. Progress was in the air that fall. Shale City breathed it and ate it, and took it to bed at night.

Behind the wave of optimism rode John Abbott, a veritable Nero, scourging the backsliders and encouraging the leaders. To prove the virtue of the medicine he prescribed, he revealed through *The Monitor* that a contract had been let for an extensive addition to the Shale City National Bank. The capacity of the building was to be doubled, at a total cost of $75,000. Every young doctor and dentist in town rushed to Gerald Abbott with reservations for office space. The annex was rented before the first brick was laid.

The Shale City Street Railway, which operated its cars in a sweeping figure-eight through the town, decided to replace its rolling stock with two brand new cars. When the shining yellow coaches arrived shortly before Thanksgiving, everyone was thrilled. They were exactly like the ones used in Denver, with smoking compartments and two operators. It was a luxury to ride in them. Shale City was the only town in Western Colorado or Eastern Utah to have a street car system. Business almost doubled for the Shale City Street Railway that fall.

Two chain stores opened branches in Shale City, and three more were scheduled to enter the territory in the spring. Some of the merchants did not look kindly upon this invasion, but John Abbott welcomed the newcomers. It meant employment for more men. It meant that the world was taking notice of Shale City.

The week after John Abbott's speech to the Rotary Club, Walter Goode bought the old Moffett ranch, which adjoined the eastern boundary of the town. He said he was going to subdivide it in the spring, under the pleasant name of Viewpark Addition. It was Shale City's first subdivision. They guyed him a lot about it at the Rotary Club. They said he was trying to make a regular California shark out of himself. Nevertheless, they were very well pleased with the idea, and Walter Goode received many requests for information.

But the greatest piece of news was that of the $60,000 addition to the Emporium. The store was going to expand, taking over the entire second floor of the building in which it already occupied the first floor and the basement. There was to be an elevator running from the basement to the second floor. It was going to be an automatic elevator—the first in Shale City. The basement would be enlarged to accommodate a new stock of furniture. The second floor would be devoted exclusively to ladies' ready-to-wear. The men's shop would be enlarged to feature, in addition to clothing, a special line of sporting goods and equipment. The silk yardage was to be increased greatly, and a special drapery department was being added to care for the large number of Shale City people who would want to build new homes.

George Boone made a buying trip to New York. He arranged for a line of merchandise which could not be equalled anywhere outside of Denver, and which could not be bettered even there. He ordered seven authentic Paris copies, and all the other models for the ladies' ready-to-wear were strictly limited as to duplications. It was his object, John Abbott said, to give Shale City every facility of a metropolitan shopping centre. The new departments would be ready by December 15th, at which time there would be a grand opening.

Work on the bank building and the Emporium started immediately. The irregular putt, putt-putt of gasoline motors sounded cheerfully through Main Street. The rat-tat-tat of hammers continued from morning to night. The grind of cement mixers and the hiss of steam dredges combined with screeching saws and groaning derricks to form a heady symphony of progress. The whole town took a personal interest in the daily growth of the new buildings. People trudged through their boarded skeleton interiors all day long, speculating upon their final appearance, commenting sagely upon the quality of work.

The town, they assured each other jovially, was getting to be a regular city. There was no peace for a body any more, with all this hubbub and activity. Denver itself couldn't be much worse. It was a caution the way things were changing. That lot at Fifth and Main, for example, had been a livery stable in the old days, and everybody had laughed at Frank Packton when he had tried to get $150 for the half-acre adjoining it! Yes sir, if Shale City kept going ahead as it was now, it wouldn't be long before it would rob Colorado Springs of its position as the state's third city.

In so short a space as three months, the atmosphere of the town changed from smug complacency to an almost electrical eagerness. Concrete evidence of growth aroused civic pride to a state bordering upon aggressiveness. Merchants became inclined to puff out their chests at travelling salesmen and make sharp challenging statements about other towns in the state. In what place of equal size, they demanded belligerently, would you find the same amount of money being spent for construction? The building and loan companies reported a sharp increase in deposits, and many inquiries about the financing of homes. Two business men decided that it would be wise to erect new store buildings in the spring. Shale City was entering the biggest boom of its history: and the boom was sound, because John Abbott was sponsoring it.

The opening of the enlarged Emporium on December 15, 1928, was a momentous event. It had snowed the night before as a prelude to Christmas. Shale City wakened to a scene of pristine splendour. All of its scars were covered. There was no house so decrepit but that its burden of snow enabled it to take on grace and beauty. Gaunt poplars and cottonwoods stood like lovely ermine-coated queens above the awkward outlines of woodsheds and backyard fences which had changed overnight into walled castles of fantastic charm. In vacant lots the snow-birds plotted out their intricate patterns, and the sidewalks teemed with children drawing sleds.

Promptly at noon all of Shale City converged upon the business district. Christmas decorations had been installed the whole length of

Main Street, with trees at every light standard, and gay spangles of red and green and silvered tinsel fluttering from store fronts. The Emporium, bedecked like a bride for her wedding, radiated brightness and gaiety. At the Main Street entrance loomed a huge tree loaded with ornaments. Me-catch Me-kill stood beside it. His swart hide was concealed beneath a white Santa mask; his lean belly was puffed out with cotton wadding. To the ladies as they entered Me-catch Me-kill presented a tiny crested vanity case. Upon the gentlemen he bestowed souvenir cigar lighters. To the children he handed bags of candy, never checking to see who came for a second and third gift. And all the while his pleasant voice was pealing out: "Merry Christmas! Merry Christmas! Merry Christmas!"

John Abbott took his position at the foot of the grand staircase which led to the new ladies' ready-to-wear department on the second floor. His face was wreathed with smiles. Everyone who passed received a kind word from him in return for congratulations upon the splendour of his establishment. The staircase was banked solidly with flowers. The Rotary Club had sent an enormous wreath, and another had come from the Chamber of Commerce. Nearly every business house in town was likewise represented in the floral display, while a nearby table held a great stack of telegrams from out-of-town concerns. Even the Governor of Colorado had neglected affairs of state long enough to send his felicitations.

Concealed in the shoe department behind a young forest of pine trees, an orchestra played Christmas carols. Above the violins arose an intoxicating medley of human sounds. John Abbott, bobbing, and smiling, and listening, had but to close his eyes to behold the unpainted shack from which this glittering institution had sprung. He could see the Shale City of four decades ago, and then, aroused from reverie by a familiar voice, sweep his eyes over the vivid animation of the present. Vaguely he understood that the years had been very kind to him.

Everyone was interested in the new automatic elevator. Children thronged around it, begging their parents for just one more ride. The men stood about and declared that you never could tell what they were going to do next with machinery, what with pushing buttons and everything. Some of the women weren't so enthusiastic about it, however. They preferred the kind at the Shale City National, with an attendant. What would happen to you, they asked with little shudders, if the thing should get out of order and stop between floors? Fred Best operated it that first day, demonstrating how one closed the door tightly, pressed a button, and sped quietly to one's destination.

As for the merchandise, it was all John Abbott had said it would be. The silks and yardages were the finest on the market. The new gowns and coats and underthings were authentic in style and fabric. A small art department had been installed, containing importations from France, Italy, Czecho-Slovakia and heaven only knew where else. Mrs. Belmore Hayes, who purchased all of her things in Denver and was inclined, therefore, to sniff at Shale City pretentions, said that the Emporium would make half of the stores in Denver look sick. Such a statement, coming from such a person, carried weight.

If the first floor was a gay place, the second was something even more wonderful. For there, in the midst of almost sybaritic luxury a continuous fashion show was in progress, accompanied by an orchestra playing Viennese waltzes. All of the pretty girls in Shale City, it seemed, were there, mincing across a little stage in the smartest winter ensembles Shale City had ever seen. Three of them, dressed daintily as maids, walked through the crowd serving tea, coffee, and cigarettes. It was very daring, people thought, for John Abbott to have included the cigarettes. Several women who had never smoked before took up the habit that day.

The ladies on the second floor, amidst the fineries of mauve carpet and subdued lights and soft music and living models and tea and coffee and cigarettes, could look from windows and see the mountains. They could behold the white peaks, jostling each other two and a half miles up in the heavens. They could see the river sliding through its icy bed, and the white desolation beyond the river. They could behold these evidences of a wilderness crowding in upon them, and then sink restfully into the warm animation of the ladies' ready-to-wear. Dimly they realized the significance of this place. It represented the final conquest of a new country. It was an unguent to their very souls. They had been hungry for it all through the years. It conferred upon them the same feeling of worldliness, of sophistication, of splendid independence that Versailles had given to their more fortunate sisters of eighteenth-century France. They lived in Shale City, and there was not another such spot within three hundred miles of them.

The men found themselves strangely out of place in the padded elegance of the ladies' ready-to-wear, and quickly sought refuge in the basement, where new furniture was displayed, or in the sports shop where they discussed the relative merits of lake and fly fishing, with interludes of golf . . .

The merchants of Shale City smashed all records for Christmas business that season. The harvest had been bountiful, and the farmers spent freely. The residents of the town, profiting from the farmers' good fortune, likewise made credit arrangements. Men bought their wives new coats that Christmas, and wrist watches and electric refrigerators and vacuum sweepers and living-room suites of handsome overstuffed velour. Everyone looked forward to springtime and the additional improvements it would bring. The holiday business this year wouldn't hold a candle to that of next year, and the year after that would double anything they had known before.

During the week before Christmas the stores remained open until ten o'clock at night. Main Street was a fairyland of lights and decorated trees, with men bearing great bundles under their arms, and housewives bargaining for turkeys and cranberries and oranges and citron and nuts. By Christmas Eve the holiday spirit mounted to a peak of fraternal ecstasy. Sleighbells tinkled through the business districts, and above their happy confusion arose the voices of choristers from the churches singing carols.

> Joy to the world, the Lord is come,
> Let earth receive her King!

As ten o'clock approached everyone prepared to go home.

"Merry Christmas! Merry Christmas! Merry Christmas!"

The greeting pealed joyously back and forth the full length of the street . . .

Every house in Shale City had a candle in its window that Christmas Eve. The stars shone brightly, and the moon lighted up the pale mountains. The carollers were all young people: it was after midnight and an hour into Christmas morning before the last sleigh load of them went home, singing softly now, boys and girls together, as though the carol reserved some sweet and intimate meaning for them alone.

> Silent night, holy night,
> All is calm, all is bright
> Round yon virgin, mother and child,
> Holy infant so tender and mild;
> Sleep in heavenly peace!
> Sleep in heavenly peace. . .

IV

FOR years Stanley Brown, editor of *The Shale City Daily Monitor,* had been the town's only legitimate theatrical entrepreneur. Although he seldom made more than a modest profit from such efforts, he, like John Abbott, burned with the conviction that what was good enough for Denver was none too fine for Shale City.

An artist or a show could play a one-night stand in Shale City and offset its heavy transportation cost between Denver and Salt Lake. As a result of Stanley Brown's enthusiasm and the accident of its geographical position, the town was accustomed to first-rate theatrical fare. Road shows with the advance agent's flamboyant guarantee of a full New York cast travelled from Denver to Shale City, and thence to Salt Lake and the Pacific coast. Symphonies and magicians, touring operas and serious drama, great virtuosos and musical comedies—all had courted the approval of Shale City audiences.

Stanley Brown leased the old Armoury for such events, and advertised them in *The Monitor* for weeks in advance. The Armoury was a great barn-like structure with an eggshell roof, hot in summer, cold in winter, and thoroughly uncomfortable in any other season. Its acoustics left much to be desired, no one could see beyond the fifth row, and the seats were only folding chairs. Nevertheless it attracted fine crowds, and seemed as permanent a feature of the town's life as the Main Street Bridge or the Emporium itself.

It was just after the New Year that Stanley Brown came to John Abbott with his idea of a theatre for Shale City. He wanted a splendid big theatre to seat fifteen hundred people, with a deep stage, modern dressing-rooms and a high-arched foyer. Stanley Brown argued that the town needed such a structure. His experience had proved that the legitimate attractions, by and large, would earn money, while the house could always pay its expenses by showing motion pictures. It didn't require much persuasion to convince John Abbott. That cold afternoon in John Abbott's new Emporium office they worked out the first plans for the Elysium Theatre.

Stanley Brown was a man of action. Within two weeks he had his campaign under way. The Elysium Theatre Corporation was organized.

Stanley Brown and John Abbott each bought fifteen thousand dollars' worth of its stock. The remainder of its hundred thousand dollar capitalization was to be distributed among the people of Shale City. Stanley Brown ran a fine story in *The Monitor* about it, calling attention to the fact that the truly great artists who deemed it a privilege to play before Shale City audiences should have a modern building in which to display their talents.

The money furnished by John Abbott and Stanley Brown enabled the corporation to break ground for the house immediately. An elaborate ceremony was held, with many speeches, and John Abbott shovelling the first spadeful of earth. The people of Shale City, seeing these visible evidences of faith and progress, hastened to purchase stock in the corporation. John Abbott thought of the new Elysium as a cultural triumph. Here the most famous artists in the world would perform for Shale City just as they performed for Broadway. Here the people of an isolated district would be linked with the capitals of the world. Here was the crowning achievement of civilization over the desert and the mountains and the perversity of the elements.

He counselled all his friends to buy Elysium stock. To his occasional callers—women with insurance money to invest, or retired farmers anxious to place their savings where they would be secure and profitable—John Abbott declared that Elysium Theatre stock was the finest investment in the state. Why put your money in eastern securities, when you could invest it at home, realize greater profits from it, share intimately in its management, and at the same time confer a boon upon the entire community? Fall and winter business had been so rushing on Lower Street that Stumpy Telsa came to John Abbott in the early spring instead of the summer, with the request that he purchase four thousand dollars worth of Elysium stock for her. A little later she sold some of her other investments, and sent him five thousand more by special messenger.

Art French was made a salesman for Elysium stock. He travelled through the western half of the state, selling it in lots of a hundred or two or three hundred dollars to farmers and business men. By early March the building began to take shape. It was three storeys in height, with great vaulted interiors and two fascinating balconies. A constant stream of stockholders impeded the progress of the workmen by wandering through the inner scaffolding, peering here and there, speculating upon every nook and alcove, making suggestions, and generally approving the whole affair. Even the workmen were awed when, upon unpacking the toilet seats, they were discovered to be of pink and white marble.

The grand opening of the Elysium was set for April 15th. The contractors had to postpone one or two items of decoration in order to have it ready on time. Ramon Nairdo, the tenor, had been engaged to open the house. The seating capacity of the building was sold out two weeks in advance, and when the great night finally arrived, everyone of any importance—or even of responsibility—attended.

There was a sprinkling of dinner jackets—usually reserved for Elks' balls or country club formals—in the orchestra circle. The men appeared stiff and definitely uncomfortable, while the ladies all wore the latest evening gowns from the Emporium. The more striking the gown, the later its wearer arrived, sweeping down the aisle amid a progressive stir of whispered comment. Because of some difficulty back stage the curtain was delayed almost a half hour, leaving the assembled citizens to chat self-consciously beneath the impressive dome chandeliers. They nodded and waved to friends, fluttered programmes, adjusted coiffures and neckties, stared frankly at neighbours. Everyone was very happy. John Abbott told Ann that it was exactly like the play they had attended in New York. Shale City, he declared, was getting to be a real metropolis. And so it was, for its unschooled reaction to the occasion demonstrated beyond all doubt that first-night etiquette is a matter of instinct rather than tradition.

High in the top gallery, where the seats cost only fifty cents, the unimportant part of the town congregated, as entranced by the spectacle as those who had paid four dollars and forty cents for the privilege of being nearer to the stage. Ramon Nairdo was a Mexican who had advanced to the first ranks of lyric tenors. Every Mexican beet-picker and section-hand in town had managed to find sufficient money to purchase seats for himself and his brood. Now they leaned over the balcony railing, all eyes and ears for the appearance of their famous countryman.

The curtain rose on a stage banked deeply with flowers. Ramon Nairdo came out, very sleek in evening dress, and made a gracious speech. He congratulated Meestair Brown and Meestair Abbott on this magneeficent home of the arts. He expressed his gratitude that he have the great honour to be the very first to sing in it. The audience released its pent-up excitement in a thunderous volley of applause. Nairdo bowed, but the applause continued. It seemed that a contest was imminent: the more frequently the artist dipped the more gustily his audience clamoured. Ramon Nairdo wished they would let him sing. He had to catch the eleven fifty-five for Salt Lake City.

Finally the uproar subsided. A piano tinkled distantly, faintly, and the house was filled with melody. Ramon Nairdo sang operatic selections to demonstrate his skill, popular little melodies to put his audience at ease, and Mexican folk songs for the sheer pleasure of singing them. His voice floated to his countrymen in the second balcony as clearly and sweetly as if they had paid top prices for their seats. He sang, as some noted, without effort, without the neck-puffing so characteristic of Walter Benson, Shale City's leading tenor.

When he finished, the acclaim was so violently persistent that Ramon Nairdo nearly missed his train because of encores. At first he was irritated with the stormy eagerness of his audience, but in the end its spontaneity won him completely. He sang and sang, and didn't care whether he missed his train or not. On the way to the *depôt* in Stanley Brown's car, he told the manager of the Elysium Theatre that he had never before received such an ovation.

"It almost brings tears," he declared, "to hear how hungry they listen for my music!"

After its glorious opening, the Elysium settled down to movies. During the coming winter it would feature a special artists series, but the spring and summer months, with rare exceptions, would be devoted to more plebian entertainment.

No one thought of the old Armoury. It stood, barren and deserted, sighing over the memories and histories which were heavy upon every beam in its roof, every nail in its walls. Governors had spoken from its rostrum, and once a President of the United States. William Jennings Bryan had filled its whole interior with the vibrations of his great voice, and Pavlova had fluttered breathlessly to its splintered floor in the swan dance. Even the teasers and flats backstage still echoed to the rustle of costumes, the muted, twittering chatter of chorus girls now changed into old women—fluent curses issuing from sweet, pouted little mouths.

Here in winter time, with four great stoves flushing red around their middles, had been mass meetings of petitioning farmers and screaming crowds of high school students watching Shale City win immortality on the basket-ball court. Here had been stern hundreds of the Ku Klux Klan saluting the commander of the realm and the fiery cross, and a little later, more hundreds of Knights of Columbus celebrating their annual fall dance. Here on warm spring nights had been grave speeches, solemn graduations, ghostly roll-calls of the G.A.R. Here the government had drafted long lines of Shale City boys into a war which no one understood, and here they had held a great ball when the soldiers returned—trombone blasts and muted cornets, with hundreds of feet keeping time; bunting festoons, hysterical shouts, girls clasped to uniformed breasts; taps through sweaty, perfumed air, and a deathly hush for those who had died strangely in a strange land, far from friends, far from the mountains of home. . . .

Every time John Abbott walked past the Elysium at night, and beheld its sparkling electric sign and the crowds in front of its box-office, John Abbott experienced the delicious thrill of a Messiah whose doctrines are gaining converts.

V

JOHN ABBOTT had been too busy during the slow years of Shale City's growth to pay much attention to its social life. His long-silent matrimonial feud had combined with his interest in other matters to isolate the Abbotts from all except the simplest social intercourse. The winter of 1928-29 with its liveliness and its happy anticipations brought a great many invitations to the big house on North Fifth Avenue. They had always come, but the consistency with which John Abbott and his wife excused themselves had diminished the inflow, until finally they were entertained very rarely, and then only by their oldest and most intimate friends. Now they surprised the town by going wherever they were invited.

After they became habituated to the change, they found that they liked it very well. John Abbott was always the centre of a respectful group of men, while Ann, as his wife and therefore a person of extreme importance, commanded the same homage from the women. They even attended week-end parties at the country club, never dancing, but nevertheless finding a certain exhilaration in the companionship of those who did. Their lives became a glamorous succession of luncheons, receptions, dinners and bridge festivals.

Ann was obliged to conserve her strength in a niggardly way in order to survive the whirl. She arranged her time so that she rested each day against the stress of the night to come. She entered into the new life with the eagerness of a girl. A strange intoxicating vitality flowed through her veins, and there were times when she felt almost young once more. The old pain, the hateful humiliation of knowing that her husband belonged to another woman—all that had vanished. Donna Long's spell was broken, and although the cemetery lay between the town and the country club, John Abbott never seemed to notice.

Society in Shale City was laid out in precise strata. There was, for example, the church society, headed by Mrs. George Boone, quite separate from the reform clique dominated by Mrs. Budd. The church society specialized in lawn socials and good works. More pious than other groups, it was necessarily much duller. No one ever got drunk at its gatherings, although there were occasional whisperings of sentimental coquetries at choir practice.

Shale City, as an important railway junction, had a large number of well-paid, easy-going railroad employees who, with their wives and children, dominated a considerable section of its social life. Attached to them were a few high-stepping merchants and professional men who could find no comfort in more sedate circles. As a rule their gatherings were spicy, amorous and alcoholic, furnishing delicious conversation for the church group. They played poker with expensive zeal, dominated the Elks Lodge and contributed heavily to the success of the New Year's and Easter Monday balls.

The *haute monde* of the town, the downright serious society, flourished under the leadership of the Art Frenches and Mrs. Mildred Wessingham. It held forth at the country club, at smart dinners in the Shale House, at formal receptions and informal bridge tournaments in the more elaborate of the imposing houses on North Fifth Avenue and East Main Street.

Art French was a lazy, witty fellow, reputed to come from old Southern stock, who appeared to remain permanently at the desirable age of thirty-five. He belonged to the country club without paying dues, and to the Rotary Club, in which he was an energetic leader and speech maker. He was a good mixer, *un homme d'esprit* who existed by cadging quarters from acquaintances who loved him too well to see him starve.

His two stoutest friends were Stanley Brown and John Abbott. Stanley Brown tolerated him because, through *The Monitor*, he regularly elected Art French to the lower house of the state legislature. Each winter Art went to Denver, where he haggled brilliantly over affairs of state, always wangling what Stanley Brown considered desirable in the way of legislative tit-bits. John Abbott was interested in him only to the degree in which Art French appealed to the older man's filial nature. He felt genuinely responsible for the amiable legislator, and so loaned him money whenever he came to grief, and carried at the Shale City National a long overdue note on the French residence. Whenever his creditors clamoured too loudly, Art casually turned a real estate deal, but the greater part of his time was dedicated to the simple and sadly neglected art of being pleasant. One could as easily harbour resentment against a Scotch terrier or a saucy boy as against Art French.

Stella French was the only influence which kept him from going thoroughly and happily to the dogs. She was a handsome blonde with large eyes, a mole on her eyelid, and an air of gay gentility. Her family, well off in former days, had exposed her to the intensive refinement of an eastern finishing school, from which she had emerged a better than average musician. She had returned to Shale City a determined lady with a lamp, a successful emissary of culture in the wilderness.

Although her reputation for virtuosity at the piano had assumed almost legendary proportions, she seldom lent to it the reality of practical demonstration. It cheapened an artist, she declared, to play for every Tom, Dick and Harry. Most people in Shale City didn't appreciate or even enjoy good music, and Stella French did not propose to strew her pearls before swine. Her afternoon musicales, however, were levees from which there was no graceful escape. She gave piano lessons to selected students, making it plain that her efforts sprang from no mean commercial impulse, but, quite to the contrary, from sheer love of the work and a desire to fill her idle hours with definite accomplishment. In consequence her rates were precisely double those of the local maestro, Professor Williams, whose existence Stella icily ignored.

Stella French liked to dramatize herself. Although her home was comfortable and very well furnished—thanks to the leniency of the bank and the credit of John Abbott—she found it pleasant to surround herself with an aura of faded fortune, an air of gentle submission to circumstances immeasurably beneath her former station. Her soul lingered in Boston, her heels were in the sticky gumbo of Shale City, and her nostrils quivered for the scent of Denver political salons. She was determined that Art one day would be governor. The financial assistance of John Abbott and the political support of Stanley Brown gave her something more substantial than hope upon which to base her ambition.

Art and Stella French were nearly prostrate with joy when the Abbotts broke away from their isolated routine. *The Monitor* carried many social notices that winter, pointing out that Mrs. Arthur French, wife of the thirteenth district's able representative, had tendered a luncheon to Mrs. John Abbott in the Blue Room of the Shale House; or that Mr. and Mrs. Arthur French of Shale City and Denver had presided at a dinner in their East Main Street home honouring Mr. and Mrs. John Abbott. Such notices buttressed Art French's credit and added cubits to his political stature.

Stella French's parties were very smart affairs, with gold-tipped cigarettes for the ladies, citric cocktails for the men, and civilized entertainment—chiefly bridge—for all. She passed among her guests like Pompadour, stimulating conversation wherever it had died away by condemning the horrid sensationalism of Gershwin or even of Stravinsky, and drawing mysterious comparisons between two gentlemen named Matisse and Picasso. She likened herself by subtle indirection to Carol Kennicott of *Main Street*. One simply could not, she declared, permit Shale City's provincialism to destroy one's sense of humour.

She was a believer in the power of suggestion, too. She hovered about John Abbott as though he were the most fascinating old *causeur* imaginable. Often while she was talking to him over a caviar canape (which he could never learn to like) or a bit of anchovy and cheese (of which he ate only the cheese), she would be concentrating on him. "You're going to renew Art's note," she would think intensely, knitting her eyebrows and trying to conduct a conversation despite so severe a handicap, "you're going to renew Art's note, you're going to renew Art's note!"

And strangely enough, he always did.

Mildred Wessingham, in every way as prominent a *belle mère* as Stella French, was always present at the Frenches' and the Frenches invariably shared Mildred Wessingham's hospitality; but between them there was a feud. It was very subtle. So subtle that neither of them openly admitted its existence. That winter it centred about the John Abbotts. Both the Frenches and Mrs. Wessingham stood in need of John Abbott's financial good will. Jack French would be ready to enter college in the fall, while Arnold Wessingham, two years his junior, also anticipated a formal education. Both boys were instructed to call the owner of the Emporium Uncle John—after Ann's entry into society she became Aunt Ann as well—and each night to pray devoutly that Uncle John and Aunt Ann would see them through the travails of higher learning.

Mildred Wessingham had a keener sense of the long pull than the Frenches where financial matters were concerned. She was a widow possessed of slender means and a social position which had to be maintained. For the present she managed very nicely, but she was obliged to anticipate a future in which her slender reserves would vanish. When that crisis arrived John Abbott would be a most convenient acquaintance. So she bided her time, never mentioning money, although constantly expressing her amazement at his knowledge of the business world, which, as she often told him, was far far beyond the grasp of a silly woman.

Mildred Wessingham's social repartee consisted largely of three words which served to awe and mystify all but Stella French. The words—gauche, macabre and rococo—were powerful ammunition in any company, forcing even Stella to manoeuvre skilfully to avoid being knocked flat by them. A guest in Mildred Wessingham's house always found copies of *Vanity Fair* and *The New Yorker* flung carelessly about, while upon the table, carefully opened at page eighty-six, lay a first American edition of *Swann's Way*. Complementing the three words, the two magazines and the book, Mildred Wessingham likewise possessed the physical appearance of an aristocrat. She flaunted in her neck and face that corded malnutrition, that lofty and astringent placidness which is the unmistakable mark of patrician forebears. To this splendid natural equipment she added languid airs and an easy grace which never failed to infuriate, and therefore to impress, Stella French.

She was, in truth, a farmer's daughter who had married Warren Wessingham when the old man was practically on his death-bed. Shortly thereafter she had inherited his social position and his vastly over-estimated wealth. Arnold Wessingham was born two weeks after his father's demise. At the time there had been a lot of jovial comment to the effect that old Wessingham had died of exertion, but officially it travelled no farther than the barber shop circles. In spite of the difference in their ages, Mildred Wessingham had persisted in furtive matrimonial passes at Gerald Abbott which ceased only when he married a widow from La Grange.

Ann Abbott was too hard-headed a person to attribute the attention she now received to her personal charm. She saw more clearly than anyone suspected the little vendettas which grew out of the struggle for her husband's favour. She was cynical enough to realize that neither she nor John Abbott belonged to this smooth and sophisticated company. Let the Emporium go bankrupt, she thought grimly, and it would be a different story. But so many years of her life had been cankered with impotent jealousy that she found any sort of diversion preferable to her loneliness.

It amused Ann when Stella French, who was a full twenty years her junior, spoke confidingly to her of literature and art and the amenities of social life in Shale City. Ann knew there was not a single interest she entertained in common with Stella French; and for this if for no other reason, she extracted an odd pleasure from the spectacle of Stella cavorting about in an effort to establish one.

As for Mildred Wessingham with her languishing looks and her broad compliments, Ann Abbott was not at all deceived. She knew that Mildred Wessingham devoutly anticipated Ann's death, so that one day she could have a chance at the widower. And (Ann thought to herself) if she ever did succumb—her health was not improving—Mildred Wessingham would stand a very good chance of landing her fish. John Abbott was not equipped to resist such lavish flattery. Ann could regard this prospect with quiet amusement. If John Abbott ever became involved with Mildred Wessingham, she knew he would regret it heartily: Mildred could not possess all of her honey without also having a stinger concealed somewhere.

VI

IN the springtime, the boys of Shale City sought out swimming holes, and stripped naked and lay down on the warm earth between dips to sleep in the sun. They could, of course, go to the Y.M.C.A. pool, but it was enclosed in a dingy basement, and hardly calculated to thrill a healthy boy when May was at hand. For outdoor swimming there were two choices; the big government canal north of town, or the river. The government canal was muddy, and not more than eight feet wide. The river, on the other hand, was dangerous. It seemed placid enough on the surface, but beneath there were cruel whirlpools and treacherous undercurrents which sucked the unwary swimmer down and seldom released him.

On the second warm spring day after the opening of the Elysium, Shale City was rocked by a minor scandal. Five high school boys were discovered swimming in the city reservoir. The caretaker came upon them unawares, confiscated their clothing, and telephoned for the police. They were immediately arraigned before Justice of the Peace Tubbs, where their hastily summoned fathers paid fines of five dollars each. Justice Tubbs read the boys a sonorous lecture on the evils of polluting the municipal water supply.

The Monitor that night published a scolding editorial about the affair, and although the men of the town viewed the incident with tolerant humour, the women shuddered and boiled their water for three days thereafter. The culprits were made to feel very ashamed of themselves. The city council even passed an appropriation for barbed wire entanglements to be placed about the reservoir. Boys would be boys, but who wanted to have somebody he might not even know swimming around in his drinking water?

The third warm day of spring placed a tragic emphasis upon the matter. The same five boys went swimming in the Colorado River down near the Main Street Bridge, and one of them was drowned. It happened about an hour after high school had been dismissed for the day, and *The Monitor* posted a bulletin about it in the window. By six o'clock the whole town was down by the bridge, watching the rescuers in their efforts to find the body.

Shale City felt its tragedies very deeply. It was neither large enough nor old enough to regard misfortune with equanimity. When someone died, the whole town took an interest in his obsequies; and when someone perished under unusual circumstances the entire community ceased functioning until the affair had been cleared up. No matter what form it assumed, death always sent an electrical impulse through the town's nervous system, impressing upon each inhabitant the narrowness of his own escape, shocking him into a closer—almost defensive—relationship with his neighbour.

The Monitor that night featured the story of the drowning and, in addition, carried an editorial about the victim, dwelling upon his fine record at high school. The editorial occupied the exact space which a few days before had sharply deplored the antisocial tendencies of modern youth. The boy's name was Edward Prince. He was a member of the Shale City high school football team, and business manager of the school paper. Everyone thought very highly of him. His arrest for swimming in the reservoir had been the first smudge upon an otherwise perfect record. All the indignation over that escapade died away in the rush of sympathy at this unfortunate sequel.

John Abbott had been especially interested in Edward Prince. For a time the boy had worked at the Emporium running errands. On more than one occasion John Abbott had told himself that when Edward Prince was ready for college, he would finance the matter.

At six o'clock, when the Emporium closed, its owner joined the silent crowd at the Main Street Bridge. Out on the broad breast of the waters four boats slipped back and forth, back and forth, hunting for the body. A little group huddled on the bank about the boy's parents. In brief intervals of silence, those on the bridge could hear the mother's disconsolate weeping. The men in the boats lowered a seine clear across the river. They jabbed down with long hooks, raking the bottom. Those on the bridge watched breathlessly. Someone suggested that they should look farther downstream, because in the spring the current was very swift underneath. Unless the body had lodged against some obstruction, they might not find it for days. There was some discussion about firing a cannon over the water to bring the corpse to the surface. But no one had a cannon, and beside, there existed a difference of opinion as to the efficacy of the method.

A crowd of boys told how it had happened. The five swimmers had started out to the island. Four of them had reached it when, looking back, they had discovered that Edward Prince was in difficulties.

They had started to his aid, but before they reached him, the luckless boy tried to shout, and evidently filled his lungs with water. He went down, and never came up again. One of the boys explained elaborately that if the victim had only retained his presence of mind, he might have come out all right. You never wanted to let your feet get down, said the boy. Always keep them near the surface, and then the undertow won't have anything to grab.

John Abbott listened to the low conversation, and watched the boats plying back and forth, jabbing their spot-lamps over the river, entrapping each boat in an aura of whitish light. The crowd grew thicker, increased by those who had gone home to supper, and now were returning to the vigil. It was a weird, impressive scene . . . the strange hush, the boats, the lights, the placid murmur of the river against the pilings of the bridge . . . the consciousness that somewhere underneath the water lay the corpse of a boy.

It was shortly after nine o'clock when they found him. The boat was almost directly under the point at which John Abbott stood on the bridge. Somebody shouted, and a dozen lights focused on the little craft. They were bringing Edward Prince out of the river, a great hook jabbed clear through his stomach. John Abbott turned his eyes quickly, and walked home.

That night he was tortured by visions. He tossed in bed, and deliberately awakened several times to drive them away; but the instant he closed his eyes they returned. It seemed that in some inexplicable manner the drowned boy had become his own son—the son of his intense desire and his dreams. His throat choked up with grief. Each time he awakened, his eyelids were sealed with dry tears. The taut, stricken face of Edward Prince's father was his own face, and the shuddering sobs of the boy's mother sprang from his own sorrow. His son—the fine clean son for whom he had worked all his life—his son was dead. It was a bitter thing to lose a son.

The next morning he went down to the Emporium and telephoned Charley Fredericks, the contractor. When Fredericks entered his office, John Abbott asked how much it would cost to build a swimming pool.

"What kind of a swimming pool?" asked Charley Fredericks.

"A real one. One with lots of room. Room . . . and bath houses and diving boards. Yes, and wading ponds for the younger children. Everything—a real swimming pool. Just as fine as they have in Denver, or anywhere else."

"I can't tell exactly," said Charley Fredericks. "I can give you an idea, though."

"Well?"

"I'd say off-hand, for a real good pool, with everything like you say, it ought to cost around thirty or thirty-five thousand dollars. Maybe more—maybe less."

"I want you to draw up a set of plans, Charley," said John Abbott. "Don't say anything about it, but rush them through. Get somebody from Denver, if you have to—somebody who knows all about swimming pools. And don't waste any time. We've got to have it up this summer. Were you—down at the bridge last night?"

Charley Fredericks nodded. "Yeh. It made me sick."

"Me too. Let me know just as soon as you can about this."

Charley Fredericks said he would.

VII

A FEW days later John Abbott called Art French over to his office and told him about the plans for the swimming pool. It would be difficult, he explained, for him to make any personal announcement of the matter. It might appear boastful. Yet he had to let it be known in some way, since the city council would have to vote on accepting the gift. In view of this, he thought it best that a forthright announcement be made immediately.

John Abbott wanted Art French to take the matter up at the Rotary Club. He wanted Art to tell the club in simple English what was being done, and to persuade the club to make all the arrangements. John Abbott would furnish the money, but he would have nothing to do with the rest of it. The Rotary Club would have to arrange with the city council, make the announcement to the town, and take charge of whatever ceremonies were necessary for the opening of the pool to the public.

Art French was enthusiastic about the idea. He told John Abbott to leave it to him to release the information. He declared it the finest thing that had ever been done in Shale City. He didn't add that it also was the finest thing that had ever happened to Art French. It meant that Art French was made, politically. Hereafter a vote against Art French for the legislature or even some higher job, would also be a vote against John Abbott. Any way you looked at the matter it was a wholly delightful affair. The owner of the Emporium said that he would stay away from the Rotary luncheon the day Art made the announcement. He would, if he were there, feel rather foolish.

The very next Wednesday Art French broke the news. He didn't carry out John Abbott's instructions to the letter, for he deserted simple English almost immediately, and launched into a soul-stirring elocutionary bravura.

When he subsided, his colleagues were stunned not alone by the great news, but also by Art French's superb oratory. They thundered their approval while half a dozen men leaped to their feet clamouring for the floor. Henry Wilhelm was recognized by the chair.

"This," said Henry Wilhelm, repeating Art French's words, "is the finest thing that ever happened in Shale City. It is one of the finest things I have ever heard of. Because a boy was drowned for lack of proper outdoor swimming facilities, John Abbott has offered to spend a fortune to see that no other boy meets a similar fate. It is the spirit of Rotary, gentlemen, brought to its highest and richest cultivation."

A reverent hush settled over the room. Henry Wilhelm cleared his throat before continuing.

"I think that none of us quite appreciate the sort of man John Abbott really is. We are too close to him to see him in his true proportions. He is an empire builder. He is just as great, if not the greatest figure Colorado has ever seen. We had Tabor in the earlier days— but Tabor was a vain, pompous man. Tabor was a braggart. Witness the contrast—Tabor swaggering through Washington, and John Abbott staying away from this luncheon because of his deep personal modesty. I like to think of John Abbott as a pioneer—a great pioneer of these later days, when men prove their worth to their country, not by a ready gun, but by an open heart.

"He has been a pioneer of construction. There has been nothing sensational about him. But he has built this town, gentlemen. He has built this valley. He has laid the financial foundation for the whole of Western Colorado—half a state. Whatever any of us here have in the way of wealth and security, we owe to the vision and the faith of John Abbott. Naturally, he has become a wealthy man. He has deserved to become wealthy. But every dollar he has made, he has turned back to the town.

"You all know the magnitude of his enterprises in these last few months—how he has quickened the commercial life of the whole community. Consider the bank addition, the enlargement of the Emporium, the vital part he played in the building of the Elysium Theatre. And consider further his splendid work in endowing the Shale City Oil Foundation, thereby laying the cornerstone for an industry which will rank among the world's greatest.

"But in all this, gentlemen, he has only increased the dimensions of his personal fortune. It is inevitable that this should happen. While he has done it all for the benefit of Shale City, he cannot escape making an eventual profit from the investment. But this swimming pool is something different. He cannot hope to profit from it, save as he gains the love of his fellow townsmen. There is no way he can make money from it. It is an example of pure generosity—and of a deep affection for young people, whatever their race or religion.

"This John Abbott, with whom we have sat for all these years in the spirit of Rotary, is no ordinary person. He is a great man, and we haven't learned to appreciate his greatness. He is the sort of man Abraham Lincoln was. He is the sort of man"—here Henry Wilhelm became a little hysterical, and compared John Abbott to Jesus Christ. He paused after this, evidently realizing that he could go no farther in that direction, and attacked the matter from a different angle.

"It seems fitting to me that we should make the dedication of this swimming pool a great tribute to John Abbott. And the only sort of tribute which would be fitting is one which comes from the citizens of Shale City—from all the citizens equally. I think it would be a fine thing if we of the Rotary Club could appoint ourselves as a committee of the whole to organize this tribute. Let us draw up a formal statement, thanking John Abbott for his magnificent gift. And let us have every person in Shale City sign it. Let the Mexican labourers down by the river sign it, and their children, too. Let the housewives of the town sign it, and the business men, and the railroad men, and the high school students and—yes, and even the girls on Lower Street! Let everybody sign, and let the children who can't write scrawl their marks, and let the babies put their fingerprints to it.

"And then let us get the Governor of Colorado to come to Shale City to make the acceptance speech on behalf of us all, and to present the official thanks of the city to John Abbott. We of this Rotary Club have an opportunity—a rare opportunity—to recognize a great man. Let us not fall down!"

Henry Wilhelm's speech was approved so tumultuously that Art French wriggled in his chair with envy. Henry Crooks, the stationer, announced that he would send to Denver for parchment—real parchment—on which the signatures could be inscribed. William Harwood, the jeweller, declared that he would furnish a silver plaque upon which he would emboss in pure gold the statement of thanks. Then the parchment would be attached to the plaque, and a rosewood casket could be made to contain the tribute.

Both of these offers were instantly accepted. The president appointed the various committees on the spot. Art French was made chairman of the group in charge of arranging the ceremony. Stanley Brown was to use his political influence to bring the Governor to Shale City. Henry Crooks, in view of the fact that he was furnishing the parchment, was selected to assign to each member of the club a section of the city from which he would be required to secure the signature of every resident. William Harwood was made chairman of the committee which would take up the matter with the city council, and arrange for acceptance of the gift.

The Monitor that evening carried the story under a banner headline not unlike the sort John Abbott used when he advertised the anniversary sale of the Emporium. It was three points larger than that which had announced Herbert Hoover's election to the presidency. The news feature of the story was handled by Stanley Brown himself, but the human interest version was written by Claudia McQuaid, the immense literary lady of *The Monitor* staff who gathered society news and interviewed visiting celebrities.

Claudia McQuaid was far and away the fanciest writer in Shale City, and she extracted the last drop of sentiment from her account of the Abbott Natatorium. She whipped herself into as fine a state of creative frenzy as the town had ever seen. It amounted almost to a literary kootch dance. She whirled, sparkled, scintillated in a linguistic saturnalia almost indecent considering her dimensions. Time and again she thundered at the portals of infinity only to fall back, bruised and beaten, but not at all disheartened.

After administering the lexicon quite the soundest thrashing it had ever received at the hands of a *Monitor* writer, she launched into the life history of John Abbott. She told how he had come to the city in its infancy, nursed it tenderly, helped its people, stimulated its present prosperity, and finally made this unbelievable gift to its boys and girls. When both her superlatives and her readers were exhausted, she completed the story by quoting long paragraphs from the speech Henry Wilhelm had made at the Rotary Club, emphasizing the part about Jesus Christ with italics. No mention was made of the signatures, for that was to be kept a secret from John Abbott until the presentation ceremonies.

Stanley Brown sent twenty-five copies of *The Monitor* to John Abbott's office in the Emporium. John Abbott read the story very carefully. When he finished it he did not smile. He merely took off his spectacles and wiped his eyes. There were tears in them.

VIII

MILDRED WESSINGHAM and Stella French, along with everyone else in Shale City, discussed Claudia McQuaid's story about the swimming pool.

"A lovely tribute," declared Mildred Wessingham, "although I do think poor Claudia's work becomes a trifle rococo when she's the least bit excited—don't you?"

"I'm not so certain," answered Stella French, irritated at being forced to defend Claudia McQuaid, whom she heartily detested. She would have agreed with Mildred Wessingham under any other circumstances, but that word rococo never failed to infuriate her. "Claudia does quite well, of course. Decidedly in keeping with the town, I think. Her work has the very flavour of Shale City. I'll tell you, when I returned from Boston and took my first look in two years at this town, I knew exactly how Carol Kennicott felt when——"

"But, my dear," purred Mildred Wessingham, "you surely don't think a character like John Abbott can be found in any of Lewis's books, do you? You wouldn't for a minute, would you, compare John Abbott with—for instance, that frightful Babbitt?"

It was a clear score for Mildred Wessingham. Stella French bit her lip in discomfiture.

"No, Mildred dear, of course not. John Abbott is the exception. He isn't typical of small-town men. But I've certainly met some people in Shale City who would put Bab——"

"Of course," interrupted Mildred Wessingham soothingly. She always took the pepper out of Stella French's remarks by cutting them short with agreement. "I know exactly what you mean."

Little pin-points of light danced before Stella French's eyes, but she strove heroically to maintain her calm. As though, she thought, she were speaking in some dialect!

"We're saying practically the same thing," continued Mildred Wessingham's hateful voice. "Claudia McQuaid simply isn't adequate to her subject. John Abbott transcends her powers. That's what we both mean, I'm sure."

"As you wish," said Stella. "I thought I made myself quite clear."

"That clever husband of yours is enjoying himself immensely, isn't he? What with the ceremony and everything to attend to, he positively wriggles with happiness."

"What do you mean?" demanded Stella suspiciously.

"Why, my dear!—I believe you're cross. I mean, of course, that Arthur enjoys this sort of thing. Who wouldn't? Who wouldn't, I ask you, enjoy doing something that will express the town's appreciation for what John Abbott has been accomplishing all these years?"

"Oh, yes," said Stella distantly. "Art is very busy with it. I—I scarcely see him any more. But it isn't at all unusual. It seems that Art is called in to take over anything of importance that happens here." She gave a little laugh. "I suppose you know that the Governor telegraphed last night that he would come. I'm having a few to luncheon to meet his wife on the afternoon of the dedication. You must come, Mildred. She's a charming woman. We meet her type so seldom here in the western part of the state."

It was Mildred Wessingham's turn to be piqued. She found no pleasure in the thought of Stella snatching the Governor's wife. But she smiled gallantly.

"Of course, Stella, I won't fail you. It *is* rather a formidable task entertaining a Governor's wife, isn't it? Oh, by the way, I'm giving a little musicale Friday week. It won't be complete without you. Miss Thornton will play *Afternoon of a Faun*. You'll love it, I'm sure."

"If one must have Debussy," sighed Stella, thoroughly indifferent, "I suppose you've chosen very well. Thank you, Mildred."

Mildred Wessingham was always throwing Miss Thornton in Stella French's face. Miss Thornton had studied in Chicago, and Stella—during unkind moments—maintained that her playing was still faintly reminiscent of the stock yards. No doubt, she always added, it was the modern influence coming to the fore, with naturalism and what not. But, of course, she'd go to Mildred's absurd musicale. A musicale—at Mildred Wessingham's!

Ann Abbott read *The Monitor* with varying emotions. Nora brought it up to her bedroom. When she reached the reference to Jesus Christ, she laughed so heartily that Nora, who was mending in the next room, came in to see if anything was wrong. Later, when John Abbott came home, very sober and reflective, and went into the living-room to write a note of thanks to Claudia McQuaid, Ann marvelled that he could take the matter so seriously. Had the man no sense of humour at all? When he asked her what she thought of it, she said, "I think it's splendid, John. That swimming pool—with your name on it—will furnish happiness for whole generations of kids."

She said "with your name on it" for a purpose. Nowhere in Claudia McQuaid's story was there any mention of Ann Abbott. John Abbott might as well have been a bachelor or a widower. Ann didn't consider herself an extraordinarily vain woman, but this thing went deeper than mere vanity. It revealed clearly how little she occupied the thoughts of her husband. He might, out of the most elementary consideration, have made the announcement in both of their names. But no! It was the swimming pool given to the city by John Abbott.

She was appalled to discover that after all these years he still retained the power to hurt her. Why couldn't a woman's affection die as quickly as a man's? What was there about a woman that made her such a foolish creature, such a miserably affectionate idiot? She knew he hadn't deliberately excluded her from sharing in the gift. Deep in the miasma of his brooding egotism, he simply had not thought of her. The slight was wholly unconscious, which made it all the more inexcusable. The deepest of all wounds, the most brutal of all sins, she now understood, were those of thoughtlessness. He had considered her neither positively nor negatively: he hadn't thought of her at all.

Now that they were going out so frequently, it would be embarrassing before that idiotic Mildred Wessingham, and Stella French. Leave it to them to notice the absence of her name. They would talk about it. It would be worse than Donna Long, for Donna Long at least had been a private skeleton. No one in Shale City had talked because no one had known. But this unforgivable thing. . . .

She resolved to say nothing about it. She would give neither her husband nor the town the satisfaction of discovering her resentment. She would pretend that there was nothing unusual in it. She would give the air of desiring to remain out of the picture entirely. Not—God forbid!—that she had wanted to climb upon his little pedestal: in these later years it was only her pride that mattered.

That, and something more. Ever since his surprising declaration that night steaming out of Havana Harbour, she had been hoping that she and her husband again might approach some basis for mutual affection. She never expected love again: that sort of thing didn't exist. It was something which never happened. It was a trap for the breaking of hearts and the smashing of souls. In its stead she had hoped for a calm, steady companionship: something quiet and fine, with a generous cancellation of all old scores. But even this had been a delusion. That night on the boat, with the lights and the young lovers all about them, he had merely been trying to deal with her justly. What, she wondered suddenly, was so unfeeling, so terribly heartless as simple justice?

"I am married to Jesus Christ!" she thought suddenly; and then rebuked herself for such blasphemy. But the phrase persisted temptingly in her mind. When she saw him she thought: "My little Jesus! How sweet! My very Christly husband." It worried her to discover such ideas running through her mind. They seemed vicious and indecent, yet she was powerless to exclude them. Sometimes she had to battle an impulse to hurl them at him in a loud voice, to watch his astonished expression at hearing them.

The oversight was remedied by Art French. Without mentioning it either to John Abbott or Ann, he began referring to the swimming pool as "the magnificent gift of Mr. and Mrs. Abbott to the children of Shale City". Ann wondered secretly if Stella might not have prompted the change, and felt a warm rush of humiliation at the thought. If John Abbott was aware of the alteration, he made no mention of it. And so, in the end, Ann Abbott's face was saved, although the resentment remained. Later, Art French consulted her about various details of the presentation ceremony, and Harwood, the jeweller, quietly changed the statement of thanks on the silver plaque to read, "Mr. and Mrs. John Abbott".

The city council approved the gift with great celerity, and read into its minutes a florid tribute to the donors. After heated discussion it was decided that the swimming pool should be located in the old Fair Grounds. The ugly board fence surrounding the place was to be torn down, anticipating the time when the city would change it into a recreation park with a concert shell, a municipal golf links and appropriate landscaping. Two or three weeks later the Fair Grounds passed out of existence, replaced by Abbott Park. Harbin Avenue, which led to it, was given new dignity as Shale City's first and only boulevard. It, too, bore the name of the swimming pool's donor.

Walter Goode was chiefly responsible for the selection of the site. His Viewpark Addition adjoined the Fair Grounds. With all of the elaborate plans in view, Viewpark Addition bade fair to overshadow North Fifth Avenue and East Main Street as the town's most exclusive residential district. Walter Goode was so sure of it that he placed a building restriction clause in each deed. No one in Viewpark Addition could build a house costing less than four thousand dollars. Long before the swimming pool was completed he had disposed of three quarters of the tract, and profited, according to rumour, eleven times the cost of the land.

Other firms also were affected by John Abbott's generosity. Deposits in the Shale City National Bank increased sharply. People knew that their money was safe in an institution of which John Abbott was chairman of the board. Most of the new accounts were from the Farmers' State Bank. The shifting of funds became so formidable that Frank Sloan, president of the Farmers', came to John Abbott. He was worried. His bank was in good condition. He had been very conservative about loans. But he didn't see how the institution could remain in existence much longer, with all the money going out and none coming in.

Frank Sloan left the matter squarely in John Abbott's hands: either something had to be done, or the Farmers' Bank would close its doors. That, as Frank Sloan pointed out, wouldn't be a very good thing for the town's reputation, or for its citizens. John Abbott understood. He remembered a run on the Shale City National back in 1907. The horror of those anxious days had never quite left his mind. It had been a living death to watch the resources of a strong, honest institution crumble before his very eyes. Yes . . . he knew how Frank Sloan felt about it.

He transferred the Emporium's account from the Shale City National to the Farmers' State, and told Frank Sloan to pay out every penny his depositors demanded. And there should be no argument about it, he declared, aside from casual remarks that John Abbott didn't seem worried, in view of the fact that he had a big chunk of the Emporium's money in the Farmers' vaults. In a little while he was sure it would all blow over, and then of course the Emporium account would go back to the Shale City National.

Frank Sloan thanked John Abbott with tears in his eyes. He hadn't had a wink of sleep for nearly a week, he said. He'd almost gone crazy watching old accounts slip out of the teller's window and go across the street to the Shale City National. Without wishing John Abbott any bad luck, he hoped one day to have an opportunity to demonstrate his gratitude in some more substantial currency than words.

The saving of the Farmers' State Bank was but one instance of the magic of John Abbott's name. The Emporium's gross receipts skyrocketed higher than they had ever gone before—even higher than during the boom times of the war. The Shale City Building and Loan opened nearly three hundred new accounts, and passed on the building of twenty-seven homes. Elysium stock was selling at a premium. The people of Shale City preferred it to government bonds. Increasing numbers of business men dropped in to consult with the owner of the Emporium. Even the farmers came to his office to learn his opinion of crop conditions, to discover what he thought about uprooting the pear trees in the north five acres (they were old trees anyhow) and planting the land to vegetables or strawberries or wheat.

If John Abbott had been a demi-god before, he now was a full-fledged Olympian. His slightest comment became word from an authentic oracle. It seemed that the presentation of the swimming pool had given every person in Shale City some mysterious claim upon his attention. Old Mrs. Ludlow, who did Ann's washing, brought her son to John Abbott. She explained that he was always threatening to run away. He had come home drunk one night—and him just a high school student yet!—and she wanted John Abbott to give him a good talking to. So he talked to Mrs. Ludlow's boy about studying harder in classes, and maybe landing a fine job on the railroad after he was graduated. Three or four weeks later Mrs. Ludlow declared to Ann that she'd never seen a person change so greatly in so short a time as that boy of hers!

He was spending more time with other people's problems than with his own. He almost never had an opportunity to look into affairs at the Emporium. George Boone handled everything. It was the same with Gerald at the bank. In addition to thinking of others' problems, John Abbott found himself worrying about them also. He couldn't, for example, imagine what mysterious ability qualified him to tell Mrs. Luke Hastings whether or not Harold Johns was a good match for her daughter. He had, as a matter of fact, gone to several persons inquiring about young Johns, and the reports had been uniformly good. Yet it was something of a responsibility to guarantee a happy marriage. In the end he advised Mrs. Hastings that the Johns boy seemed to be a fine chap, and that, insofar as all the evidence was concerned, he should make a good husband. The nuptials were performed that same June.

Each day he was confronted with a succession of puzzled, anxious faces, looking to him for advice or comfort or commendation. Chiefly, they manœuvered for money, although they seldom made forthright requests. They would, for example, ask him the best way to budget in order to pay off certain bills that were harassing them. John Abbott would sit down, itemize income and expense, telephone creditors to arrange for extensions, and spend at least an hour of time and thought upon the problem. Invariably they departed in a silent rage, declaring to themselves and their assembled families at suppertime that John Abbott, regardless of his reputation for generosity, was a damned old skinflint at heart.

He grew a little older during those months of spring and early summer. His visitors were so numerous that he seldom had time for his siesta. He passed the afternoons in leaden fatigue, and on most of the nights he and Ann went out. By the time he reached his bed he was so weary that sound sleep eluded him. He awakened in the mornings with aching temples and smarting eyes.

It was not altogether what he had hoped it would be. He merely had wanted to give a swimming pool to the town, so that no more boys would be drowned. The town had responded by depositing all of its difficulties at his doorstep. Before, he had advised only business men. He had stood on firm ground there, for he knew values and he was a merchant by instinct. But to find himself regarded as an authority upon every subject from marriage to infant psychology—that was more than he had counted upon.

He was gratified, of course, at the confidence reposed in his judgment. Who wouldn't, he asked himself, be somewhat pleased? But confidence and responsibility were twin children. In a sense, he owed the town precisely what it was collecting, for it had made him powerful and rich. His suzerainty over this empire demanded that he fulfill his responsibilities. Yet he realized vaguely that most of those who came to him sought only to evade the task of thinking for themselves. They were, in a sense, asking him to insure each step they took.

When he became very weary, he found it restful to walk at night along the newly-christened Abbott Boulevard, ending at the park where Charley Fredericks was working extra crews during the daytime to have the pool completed before the summer was over. John Abbott sat on a sawbuck, staring dreamily at the concrete shell of the pool and the scaffolding for the bath-houses and administration building. It was very quiet there, with the dusk all about him, and he could consider the complications of his life.

For the first time he was beginning to doubt himself. He didn't know what it was he doubted, but in the back of his mind there was an uncertainty, a cankering dread that would give him no peace. He felt that in some strange fashion he was perpetrating a monstrous fraud upon all these people. If they only could know how tired he became, how little confidence he placed in his own judgment! Looking backward, he could see that he had been amazingly fortunate. Supposing it was, after all, only luck which had enabled him to climb so far—that same luck might easily turn against him. If it was luck, then it was uncertain; and uncertainty was a thing which could drive him mad. He occupied an eminence which he had hardly dared hope to attain. It was all very fine, and the sensation was heady—but what if he should fall? Oh, unthinkable! But what—what if he should fall . . . ?

That June he was asked to make the announcement address before the graduating class of Shale City High School. He sat on the rostrum and looked at the sweet faces of the girls, primly conscious of fluffy white dresses, and the serious faces of the boys, stiff and oddly mature in blue serge. Professor James made a short little speech about him. "I am proud," he concluded, "to present to you a man we all love—John Abbott!"

IX

THREE days before the dedication of the swimming pool, Hermann Vogel paid a visit to John Abbott's office.

"I think I have your case analyzed at last," he said, sinking into a chair on the other side of John Abbott's desk. "After a great deal more consideration than you're worth, I have come to an amazing and unexpected conclusion. You are covering up an illicit love affair, my friend."

John Abbott's eyes snapped from contemplation of George Boone, who was strolling down the middle aisle, to an alarmed inspection of Hermann Vogel's face.

"What on earth gives you that idea?" he demanded uneasily.

"This energy, this furore of beneficence—all this philanthropy," responded Hermann Vogel. "The wonder is I didn't see through it sooner. Sly old devil! Sensual old Sybarite! Come—out with it! Who is she?"

"Sometimes I think you're crazy," said John Abbott bluntly, not at all pleased with the conversation. "You—I don't like you saying such things."

Hermann Vogel leaned upon the desk, a thin, complacent smile playing about his lips. "Listen, John Abbott—a happy man doesn't behave as you do. You're hunting for escape. Trying to throw up a perfumed fog over your conscience. Perfect sublimation of frustrated desire—probably sexual. Letting off steam in public works—swimming pools. Making a perfect ass of yourself. What's the matter—won't the woman have you?"

A little wave of panic engulfed John Abbott, succeeded by sharp, deadly fear. It was just as if Hermann Vogel were shouting some dread secret the full length of Main Street.

"I—I wish you wouldn't say such things," he faltered.

But Hermann Vogel was merciless. "Why not?" he demanded. "They're true. You know it. I know it. I'm your friend. I want to help you. Show me the woman! What the devil ails her? Why is she driving you like this? "

John Abbott knew that somehow he would have to silence the

school teacher. Vaguely he felt that he had been exposed—that Hermann Vogel knew everything, and that his only recourse was to throw himself upon his visitor's mercy. He must, at all costs, keep the man quiet.

"Supposing she's dead?" he asked quietly, surprisingly.

Hermann Vogel stared incredulously for a moment.

"Dead!" he echoed. And then: "Tosh! What you need is relief. Lacking it, you'll go into bankruptcy. Philanthropy's a much more expensive vice than women. I have a friend down at Mycope. Not bad: not good. She has a friend—not even as good as she, but still passable. Supposing we go down some night? Get it out of your system. Amazing how all this tommyrot vanishes the next morning when you awaken satisfied, with the smell of——"

John Abbott towered suddenly above the desk, staring down at Hermann Vogel's diabolic face.

"Damn you!" he cried. "Haven't you ever loved anyone in your rotten life—haven't you ever really loved anyone?"

Hermann Vogel didn't seem to notice the fervour of the outburst. His eyes, suddenly remote, swept the office, and at last attached themselves to the ink-well on John Abbott's desk.

"I?" he inquired. "Yes, of course. She was a little Bohemian, lovely as the dawn against black Tyrolean mountains. But her soul was wrapped in tin foil, and her heart was pea-sized. What a pity!" Hermann Vogel sighed, and then shrugged his shoulders. "She came to a bad end, of course. Married an engineer with a sour name—a fellow whose mind did not venture beyond logarithms and square roots! Can you imagine anything more disgusting? But he had the stuff. He delivered magnificently, although I often wonder whether she considers his greatest achievement a monument to his love for her—as, for example, a poet's sweetheart must view his finest poem. He built the largest sewage canal in Europe."

Hermann Vogel made a polite little gesture with both hands, and smiled at John Abbott, who by now had sunk back into his chair.

"She revealed to me the most serious tactical blunder which a man in love can make, so our association was not entirely without profit. I regarded her as a lady, and no woman on earth is constitutionally equipped to endure such treatment. After all, who can blame them? I never repeated the error. I seduced the next before I married her, and doubtless we would have been quite happy together had I not, by the sheerest luck, discovered what a beast she really was."

"Beast?"

Hermann Vogel nodded solemnly. "Beast. It was during our honeymoon. We were staying at an hotel in Liége. As I turned over in my bed to go to sleep, I emitted a faint groan. You know—the sort one invariably gives when the final bit of ecstasy has been drained off. I lay for a moment in silence, and then the thought struck my mind: 'Why doesn't my wife ask what ails me?' Where upon I groaned again. Absolute silence. The woman might as well have been deaf. When a third groan, loud this time, and horrifying even to my own ears— when this master of groans elicited no response, I perceived that I had a moral battle on my hands. I resolved to groan until I forced her to make some comment. I groaned all night, John Abbott! I shook a whole province with the strength of my outcries. And throughout the ordeal that wretched slut beside me uttered no single word of sympathy. By morning, of course, I was downright ill. I had to rush to Baden-Baden for the cure, and it was six weeks before I was a normal man. Naturally I divorced her. Pity in a way, but I was lucky to find her out so soon."

"I don't think," said John Abbott, unmoved by the tale, "that you have much respect for women."

"Respect?" murmured the school teacher. "All the respect in the world. The same respect I entertain for sound rum or honest cheese. It amounts to downright reverence. But such respect involves the final tribute of consumption. And who am I—Hermann Vogel—to withhold the tribute?" He made a little gesture of repulsion. "As a gentleman there is no course but to offer irrefutable evidence of my respect. Whatever the cost, however strenuous the effort involved—still I will carry on. And they love me for it—especially your American women."

"The trouble with you," said John Abbott slowly, "is that you've never met the right kind of woman. You've never known what it means to have a—virtuous woman."

Hermann Vogel made a little gesture of dismay. "God spare me!" he implored. "You're amazing, John Abbott. A man of sixty talking like a boy of twenty. Praising the most miserable, commercial tradition on the face of the earth. Why are they virtuous? To strike a bargain, my friend. They keep virtue against the day a better price is offered. Horribly misused term. You keep the virtuous women—give me the bitches."

The school teacher paused, and then glanced significantly to an architect's drawing of the new swimming pool which hung on the wall over John Abbott's head.

"Look around and see what these virtuous women have done for us. You're in the clutches of one right now. She's tearing your heart out, so you throw away forty thousand dollars for a swimming pool to regain your self-respect. And they've slaughtered better men than you. Raw nerves, ruined bodies, shattered minds driven in the end to surcease in alcohol or dope—or, in the most tragic cases, even to literature. Make no mistake of it, my brother. The virtuous women are out to smash us, and generally they succeed."

John Abbott had a sudden flash of insight. "Maybe," he said softly, "that little Bohemian sort of put you through the jumps, eh, Vogel?"

For a moment the school teacher's expression changed. The mocking smile vanished, and the grey eyes were fixed intently upon John Abbott.

"Not bad, my friend," said Hermann Vogel softly. "Not at all bad." He threw his head back on his shoulders, and inspected the ceiling. "Strange about that, too. When I think of her, I'm regretful only for one thing—her breasts. For the rest I can find much better substitutes. But her breasts"—Hermann Vogel's voice trailed off reverently, and then returned with the vigour of an organ—"such breasts as you never dreamed of, John Abbott. The texture—the colour—the softness—the hard little nipples! Why, man, I've spent a lifetime trying to duplicate them. I am a walking anthology of literary reference to breasts. No man living has done justice to the subject. But we're wandering. How about this woman from whose clutches I'm trying to rescue you? Seriously—all this insane philanthropy—and if it's a woman——"

"I'm busy," said John Abbott suddenly. "I—there's some things I have to do."

Hermann Vogel arose and made a sweeping bow.

"Very well," he murmured sardonically. "At any rate you're no longer on my conscience. It's your own funeral, and you seem to be a determined corpse." He approached the door. He paused momentarily before closing it after him. "But if you change your mind about going down to Mycope with me some night. . . ."

John Abbott raised his eyes from the desk to make the second angry retort of the afternoon, but Hermann Vogel had gone.

X

CHARLEY FREDERICKS completed the Abbott Natatorium in early August. The day of its dedication was, appropriately, one of the hottest of the summer. By noon the temperature had risen to a hundred and two, and at three o'clock it crept two degrees higher. It seemed even warmer to Shale City, because all its inhabitants were excited.

The Governor of Colorado and his wife arrived at ten o'clock in the morning. The engineer brought their special car to a halt directly in front of the depot. The Shale City High School Band was lined up on the platform, clad in brilliant new uniforms, puffing away so sturdily that none of the musicians had time even to brush the sweat out of his eyes. A huge canvas sign extended clear across the front of the depot (it was a two-storey building, even larger than the one in Colorado Springs which boasted a population three times that of Shale City) carrying the legend: 'Welcome, Governor, to Shale City!'

Mr. and Mrs. Art French, Mr. and Mrs. Stanley Brown, and Mr. and Mrs. Gerald Abbott composed the welcoming committee. Since Stanley Brown was the town's political leader, and both Art French and Gerald Abbott had been in the state legislature, all three men knew the Governor, whose hand they pumped earnestly. Stella French, Mrs. Brown and Mrs. Abbott fluttered ecstatically around his wife. Stella had the edge on her companions in this respect, for—as she often told her friends in Shale City—"she knew the dear lady very well indeed, and often had dined at her home."

Bill Robinson, the Buick dealer, had been awarded the privilege of furnishing transportation for important dignitaries. It was a fine advertisement for him to have the Governor and his wife and two carloads of the welcoming committee riding in big shiny Buicks all the way from the depot to the Shale House. He had provided open cars chauffeured by his mechanics. The cars were heavily swathed with bunting and flags—but Bill Robinson had draped them in such a fashion that no one could fail to see that they were Buicks. The sun beat down upon the notables as they made their unprotected ride, and the streets were filled with cheering spectators.

After the Governor and his wife had washed their faces at the Shale House, they were at the disposal of the committee once more. Claudia McQuaid met them in the lobby, and secured a fine interview. The men pounced upon the Governor and took him for a swift ride through the town and the near-by orchards. Then they returned with him to the Shale House, where he was guest of honour at the Rotary luncheon. He made a splendid talk about the condition of Western Colorado, and paid a glowing tribute to John Abbott, who sat on his right. He was, however, saving his choicest laudations for the dedication.

The Governor's wife was handed over to Stella French, who took her guest to the pleasant home on East Main Street, where the society of Shale City rendered its homage. Mildred Wessingham, of course, was present at the luncheon; and Stella French was severely piqued by the manner in which Mildred monopolized the guest of honour. Stella played two piano selections—a concession no lesser person could have secured from her. The luncheon, as Claudia McQuaid said that night in *The Monitor,* was "quite the smartest affair of the season".

Meanwhile, Shale City was slowly filling. The ceremonies were not to be held until evening, but as early as noon visitors began to arrive from all points up and down the valley. Main Street, bedecked with almost as many flags as on Armistice Day, 1918, was crowded with automobiles.

Most of the stores had window decorations arranged to illustrate some step in the rise of John Abbott from poverty to philanthropy. The merchants had agreed to close their doors at three o'clock. They lost no business by the arrangement. Long before the closing hour they had disposed of more goods than they would have sold in two ordinary days, or even in one full Saturday.

As the day wore on the undercurrent of excitement became almost unbearable. The sun grew hotter and the people it blessed more restive. The younger children had worn nothing but their bathing suits since early morning. Many of them had never been in a body of water larger than that encompassed by a bathtub. Boys and girls played together half-naked in the vacant lots, yearning for the moment later on when they would plunge into cooling waters. Nearly everyone else in Shale City had purchased a bathing suit as well. It was estimated by merchants that more than three thousand of them had been sold.

Many of the farmers who had driven into town for the ceremonies brought their suppers with them. They ate in Abbott Park, sprawled comfortably on the grass with newspapers spread out as tablecloths, a motley collection of children and dogs playing tag right through the potato salad. The important people of the town were enjoying a banquet at the Shale House, where the Governor, still withholding his most deadly fire, offered another tribute to John Abbott, and, by indirection, to the wife who had assisted him in his struggles.

The ceremonies were to start at seven-thirty. By seven o'clock Abbott Park was a solid mass of people. The slanting rays of the sun yellowed their heads until, viewed from the administration building of the pool, they resembled a field of ripened wheat, swaying and billowing in the wind. *The Monitor,* in its special edition commemorating the pool, said that no less than six thousand people were in the park awaiting the arrival of John Abbott.

Promptly at seven-fifteen distant applause and defiant music gave notice that the time was at hand. A few minutes later the cavalcade swept along Abbott Boulevard. The high school band was playing *Pomp and Circumstance* with fine flair. The first six cars were, of course, the open Buicks furnished by Bill Robinson. Bill calculated that having his machines leading the parade was a better advertisement than a full page in *The Monitor.* Everyone was very solemn, although a few of the irreverent made funny remarks to Bill Robinson's mechanics, who appeared uncomfortable in their Sunday clothes and unaccustomed roles. The first car bore John Abbott, with the Governor of Colorado sitting beside him. Ann Abbott rode with the Governor's wife in the second car. Art French and Stanley Brown were in the third, with their wives occupying the fourth. Mr. and Mrs. Gerald Abbott were in the fifth, and the last carried the president of the Rotary Club and his wife. Following these equipages came the procession of private cars, bearing those who had attended the banquet.

The music ceased as the cortège swung into Abbott Park. The drum section beat out an impressive rhythm. A subdued patter of applause ran through the crowd, increasing steadily until it seemed that the whole world was there clapping its hands for John Abbott. There were no yells, no whistles, no huzzahs: just the slap of palm against palm in the open air. It rose and fell, gained volume and then fainted away, like the tireless measures of surf on a smooth beach.

The Governor was perturbed. In all his career he had never been greeted in such a fashion. He was accustomed to noise and enthusiasm and beatings of the breast. The power of this reception seemed almost ominous to him. Slowly he grasped the significance of the applause. Ceasing his genial head-bobbing, he resigned the field entirely to John Abbott, who made quick little motions with his head and hands as though to say, "Thank you! Oh, thank you so much!" The owner of the Emporium was quite as bewildered as the Governor.

With a great bustle the official party drew up in front of the white stucco administration building. Dusk had descended. Yellow light gleamed through arched windows of the edifice. The occupants of the six official cars debouched gravely. With a fine eye for precedence the party made its way through the central hallway. On the right extended the refreshment room, filled with tables and chairs, flanked by a long soda fountain. To the left was the lounge, with deep upholstered chairs and magazine racks. A portrait of Ann Abbott smiled across the lounge to a portrait of John Abbott.

At the end of the hallway they came on to the full beauty of the pool. It seemed very large, with a thousand coloured lights dancing upon its surface. Along each side extended the dressing-rooms, with graceful arches before them. The arches were pure white, but they had taken on the mottled pink and green and orange of the coloured lights. Beyond the dressing-rooms were benches beneath vine-covered trellises. John Abbott had ordered the shrubs full-grown from a Denver nursery.

At the far end of the swimming pool lay a wading pond for the very young children, and still beyond that a section filled with moist sand. A statue divided the deep and shallow water. No one in Shale City ever discovered the sex of the figure, although it was stark naked. Its hands were arranged very modestly, and four concrete turtles spat water upon its belly. Some said that it was a boy, while others pointed to peculiarities which marked it for a slightly under-developed girl.

A dais had been arranged between the administration building and the pool and upon this the company advanced gingerly until all who were to participate in the dedication had been correctly placed. There they sat, exalted above their fellow citizens, smiling and chatting, waiting for the word which would mark the opening of the ceremony.

At a given signal the boys and girls of the town swarmed along the sides of the pool—several hundred of them huddled closely together in their bathing suits, white legs pressed against white legs, awaiting the word which would impel them *en masse* into the tempting waters. At the open end of the pool thronged other spectators. There was not nearly enough room in the enclosure for all to see, but a loud-speaker system had been installed so that everyone in the park could hear what was said.

A little flutter of nods swept through the dais, and Art French arose. He made a very simple speech, which surprised everyone. He said that they all knew why they were present, so no explanation was necessary. It was his privilege to introduce the distinguished gentleman who had deserted important matters of state to come across the mountains to Shale City and pay tribute to Mr. and Mrs. John Abbott—His Excellency, the Governor of Colorado!

The pent-up excitement of the day gave way. The boys and girls howled their approval as the Governor advanced, and clear out in the darkening portions of the park arose an answering cry. The Governor cleared his throat. The sound was carried by the loud-speaker system to the most remote listener, a static aperitif for the verbal feast to follow. Then his voice reached them—a thin tentacle of sound, rising and falling monotonously in the darkness. On the dais John Abbott sat like a man in a trance, listening to the Governor's speech go on and on and on . . .

This splendid man and woman . . . these great pioneers whose hearts are as large as . . . the debt that is owed them, not only by the boys and girls of Shale City . . . but by the parents who are . . . the kindly terms of the deed to the city . . . that no boy or girl shall ever be deprived of the use of this pool . . . for race or age or sex or religion or for want of money . . . that no profit shall be made from the pool . . . and that no moneys in excess of those needed in its actual operation shall be collected . . . what great humanity, my friends, is expressed in those few simple words . . . and here he sits with the woman who has been his loyal helpmate . . . through adversity and prosperity . . . through honour and disappointment . . . such as must come to every man . . . he has never looked backward . . . never retreated . . . but always kept that splendid faith . . . which has made Shale City what it is to-day . . . and which, in a larger sense, has made Colorado . . . a mighty commonwealth among the states . . . and which has inevitably gone into the making of this splendid nation of ours . . . which is founded upon the same loving humanitarian sentiments . . . as John Abbott has set forth in his magnificent gift to the city . . . and there is a little acknowledgment . . . in which you have all participated . . . all of you, in whatever station . . . the babies and children and the young men and women and the housewives and business men and farmers and labourers . . . all have shared in this which is . . . quite the finest tribute I have ever seen offered to one man and woman . . . and instead of devoting myself exclusively to voicing the presentation of this pool to the city . . . I deem it the rarest privilege of my life ... to present this parchment scroll of appreciation . . . signed by eleven thousand grateful citizens of Shale City . . . to that man who is not alone a merchant . . . or a banker . . . or an industrialist ... or a builder ... or a philanthropist . . . but who stands in my estimation . . . as the first citizen of Colorado . . . and you all know that I refer to . . . John Abbott!

The farmers out on Sawtooth Mesa said they could hear the cheering as distinctly as though it came from no greater distance than the barn.

John Abbott could scarcely see. A rosewood box was thrust into his hands, and he found himself opening it. There it was, in all its glory of silver and gold and parchment—the testament of his fellow citizens. He looked at it briefly—beheld the signatures of his friends and his enemies—the scrawl of children and the smudgy fingerprints of babies. He passed it quickly to Ann.

"Look!" His voice was a croaking whisper.

She took it and smiled at him, and closed the lid.

A little girl, not more than three or four years old, was standing at the edge of the pool. Spotlights were focused upon her. She wore a tiny silk bathing suit. She stood facing the dais, looking straight into John Abbott's eyes. Her yellow hair shimmered under the floodlights, and her body was as straight as a stalk of young corn. John Abbott smiled down at her, and she flashed him an open-mouthed response. Then she took a deep breath. Her voice, shrill and childish, brought instant silence.

"I want—to express the—the thanks—the thanks—the thanks of the boys and girls—and children of Shale City—to Mr. and Mrs. Abbott—for this—for this lovely swimming pool they have—have given to us—and I herebylovinglychristenittheAbbottNatatorium!"

She whirled and waved a silver cornucopia over the waters. A shower of rose petals fluttered downward. As the first of them touched the water, a gleeful shout arose from the boys and girls who had waited impatiently for the speeches to be completed. The whole surface was churned into laughing foam, and the spray was like coloured diamond dust entrapped in the lights.

Some of it fell against John Abbott's face. He started, and then it seemed that a chill shuddered through his body. He drooped in his chair. No one noticed. All eyes were fastened upon the spectacle below. It was three years ago . . . in August. It was night time, and the rain was cutting against his face. He was staring across at the Emporium, while Karwin's long black hearse rushed through the storm . . .

Oh, my God!—have I forgotten so quickly, Donnalong?

He turned an ashen face to Ann. "I—I'm going to get away for a little bit," he told her. "Tell the Governor—I'm sorry. I feel—bad. When it's over you go home. I'll be there—directly." He was gasping at the finish. Ann nodded. The confusion everywhere was so great that he escaped without anyone knowing when or where he went.

XI

IT was almost midnight when John Abbott returned to the pool he had built. The calm air gave no hint of the speeches and applause which had troubled it a few hours earlier. The crowd which had done homage to him had melted into the night. He walked slowly along the route he had taken with the Governor. There were perhaps a dozen cars parked in the darkness—no more. Occasionally he passed some pedestrian, but he gazed steadily at the ground and made no pretence of speaking. When he reached the administration building, he saw yellow light still streaming through its windows.

Cautiously he skirted the edifice, until presently he found himself under the vines at the far end of the pool near the sand boxes. It was a pleasant night. The stars were out, and the moon, too. He sank down thankfully upon one of the benches. He had been walking ever since his flight from the dais, and now he was tired. It was dark by the benches, and he was quite alone, for the swimmers clustered about the diving-tower at the opposite end.

Ordinarily the pool would close at ten-thirty, but to-night was an exception. The coloured lights had been switched off, and the place was illumined only by the regular standards which lined its edge. He could hear the splashing of water, the cries, gurgles, shouts which reverberated dankly, hollowly from side to side. They were having a fine time in the pool to-night.

Those who still lingered were boys and girls of high school age—perhaps thirty or forty of them. John Abbott shrank back in his seat, crossed his legs, and watched them. They were very handsome, slipping through the water and running along the banks. Their white legs and necks and arms glistened in the pale electric glow. From his distance the girls were all pretty, with slim hips and firm breasts and sparkling bare feet, and the boys were all strong, with straight backs and hard, smooth arms. The boys were silver flashes from the diving-tower, and little geysers of spray arose when they struck the water. Some of the girls dived, too; but they were timid, and not as graceful as the boys. Most of them stood, shivering slightly, their knees close together and their arms clasped over their breasts, watching the boys.

In one corner of the pool a furious game of tag churned the water. The boys chased the girls, while the girls screamed with delight and tumbled about to avoid their pursuers. The boys seemed always on the verge of pinioning their arms clear around one of the girls, and then the girl miraculously would slip away, her hips and fine legs passing right through the boy's arms. John Abbott saw the hands of the boys always clutching at those dancing white legs, always sliding off lingeringly, with a great pretence of desperation. The girls thought that they were very sly, and were giving the boys a tough time of it. The boys thought they were sly, too.

In shallower water one boy was trying to teach a girl how to swim. He held his hand under her stomach for support, while she threshed about wildly, laughing in a voice which was choked from so much water entering her mouth. John Abbott could hear the boy's low voice: "Easier ... easier." Sometimes the girl would slip back a little, and the boy's hand would be over her breast, and she would come quickly to her feet, and the boy would withdraw slightly, and then they would begin all over again. The boy said to her: "Come on out where it's a little deeper. I will take care of you. I won't let you go under." And finally, after much begging, she went.

Well, thought John Abbott, this is all as it should be. Let the summer nights be filled with boys and girls together, clean and bare in the coolness. Let designs of white legs and strong arms and straight backs and firm breasts take on the magic of starlight, and let them move rhythmically and beautifully. Let their laughter and their advancings and their retreatings and their desolations and their glad reunions tumble one upon the other in the night-time. And let the earth keep pace with their motions, and the stars, too, and the moon, with the trees bending low to caress them, and the waters and the grasses and the sweet air yearning to kiss them, and the whole of creation swaying around and around, back and forth, waving and dancing with their ecstasy, until in the end there is only quietude and utter darkness and something irretrievable fainting away in a sigh.

For in a little while . . .

For in such a very short time . . .

Oh, my God! Oh, my dear God, let us forgive each other!

John Abbott sat in the shadows, and his conscience threw words at him. What have I done, and what right had I to do it? Why am I so empty and so old and so very lonely? Donnalong—see what you have accomplished! Cool water—water you yearned and thirsted for—

water to quench the heat—water in the midst of a desert—and you have given it to them. *You!* For I am nothing. I am nothing multiplied by all the years of my life. I am just learning—only just discovering—how very much you mean to me, Donnalong, and how forsaken I am without you. You would love this place, Donnalong ... it is very cool here, and there are boys and girls laughing in the water. It bears my name——!

I shall be punished for it. I'll suffer for it all right. Thousands of hands clapping—softly, terribly, oppressively—and I took it all for myself. What a blasphemous thing—to set one's self up as God, to nod calmly and receive adulation, to give and to judge and to take away. You put a strong foundation under me, Donnalong. You thrust me higher and higher, until now I am in the clouds, and I am afraid. You have put me in a tight wire, Donnalong, and I am tottering, and coldness is running through me. My picture hangs in the lounge—and *her* picture. My name is over the arched door, and eleven thousand people have set their hand to a testament thanking me.

John Abbott reached into his pocket, and drew forth a pencil and an envelope. Straining to see in the dim light, he scribbled on the envelope:

"And I further stipulate that it remains my privilege, at any time, and under any circumstances, and by whatever means of communication I may choose, to change the name of the swimming pool to any other which, in my judgment, is fitting."

He read it over carefully, and replaced it in his pocket. The legal transfer of the pool would be accomplished to-morrow. He would insert this clause in it. One day Ann would die, and one day John Abbott would die . . . and then Shale City would know whom to thank for the gift to its children. Donnalong had wanted children so badly . . . so badly. . . .

He was very tired. He sank back and allowed his eyelids to droop, so that everything became blurred. It had been a strange, exhausting day. There were so many puzzling questions in his mind . . . He drifted easily into that mid-region between anticipation and realization, between forethought and hind-thought, between a moment passed and a moment immediately to come. There was an overtone of distant laughter and slim bodies and faint light and tinkling water as the four concrete turtles spat upon the belly of the girl-boy statue.

It seemed to him that Donnalong was floating out over the water. He saw her very clearly in a trail of mist. She approached closely to him, so that he could almost take her in his arms. But she slipped away, as the girls in the pool slipped away from the boys. She was neither young nor old nor beautiful nor ugly. At times it seemed that she had no body at all—that she had resolved into white spray—that she had become only a soothing presence. And then, approaching him once more, she wavered wonderfully before his eyes, with the breeze wafting her just beyond his reach. She was with him for a long, long while. . . .

At two o'clock, long after the pool had dimmed its lights and the boys and girls had slipped away into the darkness, Ann Abbott came for him. He was huddled on the bench, so drunk with sleep that she had to shake him roughly.

"John— John! Where have you been all night?"

He started, and peered up at her. She shuddered slightly, looking down into his wizened face. He seemed so old . . . a pitiable little gnome hunched there in the darkness.

"Donnalong!" he whispered. "You—you came. You are always slipping away from me. But I knew you would come . . . Oh!" There was an instant of pure silence, with no sound anywhere in the world. "I— I went to sleep, Ann. I was worn out."

He followed her obediently.

Ann thought: "I am through. I am finished. Living, I could stand up against her. But now I am quite done with it. I cannot fight a ghost."

Aloud, she said to him: "I am leaving you, John Abbott. I am leaving this town, too. And I am never going to come back."

XII

SHALE CITY was filled with sympathy when it learned that Ann Abbott's health required that she go east immediately for an operation which would be followed by a long rest in a sanatorium.

The Frenches and the Browns and the Gerald Abbotts and Mildred Wessingham, and, of course, John Abbott, went with her to the depot. She was leaving on the five-forty afternoon train.

They stood there, waiting and talking; and presently the train, dusty from its long journey, ploughed through a red sunset into the yards from Salt Lake City. Everybody assured Ann that she would return very soon, better and stronger than she ever had been. Ann smiled quietly, and told them that of course she would. They all kissed her as she stood poised to enter the coach. When John Abbott offered his lips, a quick little motion gave him only her cheek. No one noticed. "Good-bye, John," she said softly in his ear. "Maybe I should tell you—" she broke off abruptly, and then he heard her voice again: "Goodbye—my dear."

"Good-bye, Ann," he said soberly.

The conductor chanted through his nose, the bell set up a clangour, and she withdrew into the train. A tug from the engine sent the coaches smashing against each other. A dry creaking arose as iron wheels ground against iron rails, and then the train was in motion. They all stood there, watching the cars click by, until there was nothing to see but the vanishing observation platform. Then they turned around and started back into the depot.

Mildred Wessingham linked her arm in John Abbott's.

"You poor lonely man!" she said. "You are coming to my house for a good dinner . . ."

John Abbott paused. Distantly he heard the scream of the train's whistle. It was rounding the first curve, entering the canyon. The sound came once more, faintly now, like the sob of an hysterical woman echoing bleakly from one canyon wall to the other . . .

Eight days later Ann Abbott lay dead in a Rochester sanatorium.

After the funeral, Gerald Abbott opened her will. It had been placed in her safety deposit box at the bank seven years before. She left the big house on North Fifth Avenue to a distant cousin in Pennsylvania. She gave her diamonds—with the exception of the tiny engagement ring, which she stipulated should be buried with her—to another cousin. She willed all but one piece of the furniture to a niece. The tall grandfather clock which had chimed off so many hours of her life she bequeathed to John Abbott.

The will was probated secretly. John Abbott bought the house from one cousin, and the furniture from the niece. He allowed the diamonds to remain where she had willed them. Then he closed the house, and had shutters attached to its windows, and closed the shutters. He moved into a two-room suite at the Shale House. Shale City treated him kindly, for the sorrow of John Abbott was the sorrow of the whole town.

Later, people said that he never recovered from the shock of his wife's death.

BOOK III

JOHN ABBOTT
AND THE WORLD
1930-1933

I

THERE was a financial dynasty in London which went under the name of Hatry. London was several thousand miles distant from Shale City, and the name of Hatry held no more significance to the town than Smith or Jones or Brown. In the fall of that year the Hatry structure shuddered and fell.

The London Stock Exchange jumped nervously, and there was a little flurry in Paris. Brussels hesitated for just an instant, and Berlin and Vienna and Rome. Far away in Tokyo and Buenos Aires and Rio de Janeiro there was a faint tremor. New York dipped momentarily, and then the affair was dismissed.

London smiled at Paris, and Brussels and Berlin and Vienna and Rome set up a deprecating chatter, like old maids disturbed at teatime. Tokyo hissed blandly at the world, and Buenos Aires and Rio de Janeiro evinced polite disinterest. New York shrugged its shoulders.

"We seem to be a little nervous," the stock exchanges might have been saying one to another. "It is the change of seasons, and we have been working quite hard." There was an international titter, and after the titter the markets of the world seemed to nod pleasantly and say: "How foolish of us! Let us forget all about it."

The first weeks of that fall, even deep into October, were no different from those of any other autumn. The earth whirled, and events tumbled one upon the other in a pleasant kaleidoscope. It seemed a dull enough season, filled with satisfaction and profits. Herr Foreign Minister Stresemann died in Berlin, and Herr President Paul von Hindenburg, strong man of Germany and defender of the Republic, celebrated his eighty-second birthday. Mr. Norman Thomas asked embarrassing questions of Mr. James J. Walker, with the mayoralty of New York as a prize for the best set of answers. A Prime Minister of Great Britain arrived on the *Berengaria* to talk with President Hoover; and photographers found courtesy and mild satisfaction on the faces of both statesmen.

Lindbergh soared over Central America carving out routes for later caravans of the air to follow. On the bottom of the world in Antarctica, Richard Byrd had a radio which sputtered through unnumbered miles of cold thin air telling bedtime stories of Little America. In New York there was talk of a new Waldorf Astoria with door knobs of gold.

People sang a ballad called *I'm a Dreamer, Aren't We All?* They flocked to the movies to see *Two Black Crows* and *The Great Gabbo.* They went to the theatre to see *Strictly Dishonourable* and *Porgy.* They cheered Toscanini and wept over the death of a young woman named Jeanne Eagels. Sun Beau captured the Havre de Grace Cup, and in Colorado the prisoners in Canon City revolted and tossed murdered guards out of a window at regular intervals.

But all of these things had nothing to do with Shale City. The town read about them in *The Monitor,* and went on attending to its business. The world was a large place, of course, and many things were bound to happen in it. But affairs of importance to Shale City could be counted upon to occur in Shale City. To the east loomed an enormous range of mountains cutting off the world, bursting with undiscovered riches. To the west extended great stretches of barren, parched land, almost uninhabited, but needing only water to become as fertile as the Mississippi Valley. Of this vast country Shale City was the centre. There was enough difficulty in administering it without looking to the outside world for trouble. Shale City was close to realities, and the affairs of other communities and nations could affect it but little.

And then something went wrong with the stock exchange in New York. Like a man who has borne a heavy burden too long, the price level cracked. Fortunes shrank, while men violently deplored what was happening. Shale City read about it, and wondered for a moment, and then settled down to regard the spectacle, as a man in the remote bleachers observes a fist fight between baseball players. It was an interesting phenomenon—nothing more.

But the thing kept on and on, with every dispatch from the east recounting some fresh disaster. There was an intricate juggling of Federal Reserve rates, and that affected credit, and that affected money, and that affected loans, and that affected—only slightly at first—Shale City. Where before there had been a nation-wide scarcity of goods, it now seemed that there was a nation-wide scarcity of money with which to purchase the goods. It was uncanny, the thing that was happening.

A great shout went up that now was the time to buy. The industries of America were for sale at bargain prices. Now was the time to invest for the returning cycle. Many people in Shale City who had never purchased securities before, hastened to participate in the easy profits to come. And urging them on were men who pledged millions, tens of millions with which to enter a market and fight back the rush of falling prices.

The financial geniuses of America went to the White House, where the long fingers of oblivion already were settling over a bewildered President, and told him that things would get better, and that they would not cut salaries, and that they would not discharge men, and that there was no justification for the steady drop in values, and that the banks and great corporations had been wisely operated, and that they would support him vigorously. So the President told the country that the whole affair was ridiculous and inexcusable and probably purely technical, and that perhaps in sixty days ...

That winter John Abbott made a speech at the annual banquet of the Shale City Chamber of Commerce.

"We must not be frightened," he told them, "or in any way discouraged. We must go ahead, as we have always gone ahead, building a better city. The finest brains in the country tell us that we have passed the crisis. Things are coming back, and when that happens our prosperity will be greater than ever—far greater than any of us here can imagine. We of Shale City are, fortunately, isolated and insulated from these outside shocks. We are not"—John Abbott's voice rang out defiantly, as though an ogre in the corner had contradicted him—"we are not peasants bound to the fate of an artificially manipulated stock exchange!"

During that winter Shale City said: "There is just as much gold and as many factories and as many potential customers as ever. We have not lost one iota of our wealth. It is all imaginary."

The Monitor said:

"Now is the time to invest in common stocks. Put them away and forget about them, and in a little while you will be rich. It will be very uncomfortable for anyone who tries to sell America short."

Gerald Abbott over at the Shale City National said of a sound proposition:

"It is as safe as the Bank of England."

John Abbott, giving advice to anxious citizens, said of Liberty bonds:

"They are as good as gold."

And then . . .

II

THE Elysium Theatre was in trouble.

Just a year old, its statement to stockholders revealed a loss and the prospect of a greater loss in the future. Almost from the beginning Stanley Brown, who managed it, had watched the deficit mount without being able to do anything to stop it. There was, of course, what people referred to as "the depression". They were clinging to their dollars a little more closely than in former seasons. But something beside the depression was hammering away at the corporate structure of the Elysium.

Stanley Brown and John Abbott, when they discussed the theatre, were baffled at the problem it presented. They were fighting a battle with adversaries who operated under cover and from a great distance. They were bucking up against something bigger than either of them; bigger, in truth, than the whole town of Shale City. It was the first time either of them had been in such a predicament. It was frightening. They were men who had been accustomed to success. Now they found themselves beaten at every turn.

Only two months after the Elysium had opened, Supertone Pictures Inc. announced that it had purchased the dingy little Gem Theatre. The Gem was the only other movie house in Shale City—a box-like affair, poorly ventilated and dirty. A man came over from Denver to manage the Gem. He had been in town only a few days when he revealed that the Gem was to be completely renovated. The Supertone people tore it all down but the walls, refinished it with gorgeous blue and gold plastering, added a small balcony, and sponsored an impressive opening day.

The improvement of the Gem delighted John Abbott. His belief that an increase in the number of Shale City business firms likewise increased the total volume of business, had always justified itself. Stanley Brown wasn't so enthusiastic about the new Gem, although he grudgingly conceded that a little house like that couldn't hurt the Elysium, with its fifteen hundred comfortable seats.

But the Gem did hurt the Elysium. The Supertone Corporation was large and powerful. It controlled a vast selling organization, and held a substantial interest in other producing companies as well. The Gem gradually acquired a reputation for booking better films than the Elysium. People began to take notice of the difference in quality. Stockholders of the Elysium complained to Stanley Brown about it. Why didn't he get pictures as good as the Gem exhibited? How did he expect to make money out of the Elysium and pay dividends to its stockholders when all the best productions went to the opposition house?

Stanley Brown endeavoured to explain matters to them. He tried to tell them that in order to get any pictures at all, he was forced to buy four bad films for every good one. If he attempted to secure an especially fine picture, he might have to contract for six or even eight poor ones. It was very confusing. The Gem didn't seem to have such difficulty. Every picture it exhibited was as good as could be had anywhere.

Stanley Brown went to the releasing offices in Denver. He frankly told them of his difficulties. Here he was with one of the finest theatres in the state, seating fifteen hundred people—and they wouldn't sell him any decent films to show in it. He warned them that he would have to close the theatre soon unless he received better treatment, and then they would lose a customer.

They listened to him politely. When he finished, they told him that their business was to sell pictures, and his to exhibit them. They were selling him what they had, and if he thought he could do better anywhere else, then by all means he should make some sort of change. It wouldn't break them. They'd get along somehow. When Stanley Brown asked how it happened that the Gem had no such difficulty, they smiled and replied that they had never heard of the Gem.

John Abbott even wrote a letter to Herman Schonk in Colorado Springs, asking him if he knew anyone in Denver who might have influence with the releasing company which would help the Elysium to secure a decent product. Herman Schonk replied that there was nothing to be done. He thought—judging by other cases he had observed—that Supertone itself would come around soon with a proposition to buy the Elysium. When that happened, Herman Schonk advised John Abbott to take what was offered.

A few weeks later Stanley Brown had a visitor. He was a representative of Supertone Pictures, and, sure enough, he wanted to buy the Elysium. If he had come earlier, Stanley Brown would have told him the Elysium wasn't for sale to anybody. But now he had some idea of his competition. He asked the gentleman how much Supertone would pay for the theatre. The gentleman said his company would pay fifty thousand dollars. When Stanley Brown refused the offer, the visitor smiled affably and said that he would return in two or three months. He thought Stanley Brown would change his mind by then. When the man left his office, Stanley Brown knew that he was whipped.

But he waged a good fight, nevertheless. He ran long columns of free advertising for the Elysium in *The Monitor*. After the people grew accustomed to such publicity, they refused to part with their quarters on the strength of what *The Monitor* said about a film. Often Stanley Brown would walk past the Gem with its busy entrance, and then back to the Elysium, where the ticket girl was talking with her beau for want of any better occupation. Then he would go over to his office in *The Monitor* building and sit down and swear softly to himself. The investors of Shale City were being deliberately robbed of their property, and there was nothing he could do about it.

In the spring of 1930 the gentleman from Supertone Pictures came back again. Stanley Brown treated him cordially, and they sat down for lunch at the Shale House to thresh things out. Stanley Brown was no fool, and he could dicker closely when the necessity arose. Supertone Pictures finally agreed to pay sixty-five thousand dollars for the Elysium.

An outline of the offer was sent through the mail to all stockholders of the theatre—all the farmers and widows and business men and retired railroad hands who had rushed to John Abbott and Stanley Brown with their dollars, that they might participate in the earnings of an institution which the town really needed. A meeting of the stockholders was called at the old Armoury for the purpose of voting on the question of taking a loss and retiring, or of remaining in possession and paying steep annual assessments.

John Abbott didn't attend the meeting. He couldn't bear to look at the assembled faces of people who had participated in the stock issue solely on the strength of his name. This was the first time, in all the years of his life in Shale City, that failure had attended his efforts. There was a nightmare quality about the affair which terrified him. The odds against the Elysium had been so staggering . . . he was just beginning to feel the force of exterior circumstances, to understand that someone two thousand miles away might reach out with a heavy hand and crush him.

But Stanley Brown went defiantly to the meeting, ready to fight for the sale. He had been through a lot of disagreeable experiences in his newspaper life, and he was not a man to be easily frightened. He talked to the stockholders for a half-hour, and the gentleman from Supertone talked to them for ten or fifteen minutes. When the two men were finished, the stockholders understood fairly well where they stood. Their faces were bewildered and a little angry. Stanley Brown asked if anyone had questions about the transaction.

A fellow stood up in the back of the room—they discovered later that he was drunk—and yelled:

"Sure, there's some questions! Where's John Abbott? I wonder why he didn't come to this meeting?"

There was an instant of deathly silence, followed by a murmur and then a buzz of soft conversation. Stanley Brown ignored the heckler, and called a vote.

But the drunk's barb sank home. As they filed out of the Armoury that night after having sold their theatre at a loss of thirty-five thousand dollars, they asked each other why John Abbott hadn't been there to talk to them. They would have felt a great deal better about the whole affair if he hadn't stayed away. Was there anything fishy about the sale?—but no!—it must have been something important that kept him away.

While they voted at the Armoury, John Abbott sat in his office in the Emporium and pored over figures. There was a certain moral obligation in this matter of Elysium stock. He was a little short of cash, and he couldn't, naturally, make up the loss of all Elysium stockholders. There was no legal reason why he should; hardly any ethical reason, either. But he felt that he should do something for those whom he specifically had urged to purchase the stock. He wondered, as he considered the idea, whether it was prompted by generosity or justice or fear.

He ran his pencil up and down the list of stockholders, and set certain names on a piece of scratch paper: Miss Eva Septimus, $2,500; Mrs. Alvina Woods, $2,000; Mrs. Evelyn Lathrop, $1,000; Roger Hodges, deceased, $1,500; Mrs. Maria Telsa, $9,000; Mrs. Rugh Hicks, $3,000; John Everhardt, $500; Fred Best, $500; George Boone, $3,000—twenty-three thousand dollars! These he personally had advised to buy. His obligation to them was clear. The rest—those who might have purchased stock because of his name, but to whom he had not spoken directly—they would have to take their losses.

He took his cheque book from its drawer and scratched out eight cheques for a total of $8,050. He would dictate a letter in the morning to go out with them. He must let Gerald know about them, too. Gerald would have to transfer a little cash to his account. Collections were slow, and his credits seemed to be jumping. A lot of his money was tied up just now. He might have to sell that block of Liberty Bonds. But things surely would straighten out before that.

He sighed heavily, and sat for a little period staring out of the window at the lights of the town. He seemed terribly isolated, terribly alone here in his office at night time. The store was so large and impersonal in the darkness—so immeasurably removed from the original Emporium. The impressiveness of this later establishment, when there was no one around, made him feel strangely like an intruder. It was no longer a friendly, intimate, struggling little store. For all practical purposes it had outgrown him.

He switched off his desk lamp and started for his rooms at the Shale House. On his way he passed Mr. and Mrs. Harry Twinge, and it seemed to him—although it might have been his imagination—that Twinge's greeting was less cordial than usual.

III

T HE summer heat was unprecedented even for a semi-arid country. The farmers out on Sawtooth Mesa watched their crops burn to the level of the ground, leaving them with no hopes of harvest. Many of them even lacked the money to buy seed for next spring's planting, much less to support themselves and their families through the winter to come.

The orchards north of the river suffered in a different fashion. There was no spring frost to kill the buds. The government canal supplied enough water to keep them well irrigated. Even the pests seemed to have been driven away by the heat, for the fruit was remarkably free of blemishes. It promised to be a bumper crop. The trees groaned beneath the weight of peaches—three and four boxes full on the outermost branches, bending so low that special props were set up to keep the fruit from touching the ground. Ed Bussey brought an Alberta peach to town that weighed two and three-quarter pounds. It was displayed in the window of the Shale City Building and Loan Association. The pears were fine, too, and the apples were large and juicy.

But when the time came to move the fruit out of the valley into eastern markets, a car shortage developed. The railroad (grumbled the farmers) was always complaining that it couldn't earn money because of bus lines competing on free rights of way over the public highways. Yet this matter of a car shortage came up in Shale City at least once in every two or three years. The hard-pressed orchardists pointed out that when the railroad did have a chance to earn money, it was invariably short of rolling stock.

So the farmers watched their fruit grow over-ripe on the trees, while they made daily trips to the Fruit Growers' Association to see how the car situation was shaping up. There would be five cars when ten were needed, and ten when at least a score should have been on hand. What little fruit was shipped brought good prices, for the eastern cities were always hungry for it, especially at the beginning of the season. But not enough was moved to save the farmers from a loss. Later, when there were a few more cars, the eastern market was flooded with produce which had won out in the seasonal race.

Just as the cars began to arrive with encouraging frequency, the ice houses caught fire. Four of them burned in one night, illuminating the whole town. A row of shacks near them went up in flames too. Shale City stayed up all night watching the shower of sparks which catapaulted volcano-like into the dry heavens. In the morning there was nothing left but steaming masses of ice and charred walls and little streams of water trickling off the ice. After that no more refrigerator cars left the yards, and the farmers let the rest of their fruit rot on the ground. It was heart-breaking, because everyone said the winter was going to be a hard one. If they only had got their fruit out . . . .

After the destruction of the ice houses, the railroad decided to move most of its shops to another division point. Operating expenses were too high, declared a manifesto from Denver, and conditions were such that a full force in Shale City resulted in duplication of work. The railroad had the largest payroll in Shale City. It was a heavy blow to the merchants. Again John Abbott beheld a force from the outside interfere with the destiny of Shale City. And again there was nothing he could do about it. He experienced that little spasm of fear which came so frequently in these later days, and then tried resolutely to put the matter out of his mind.

As though this were not enough disaster for one season, the chemical works moved out of town with most of its equipment, leaving only four men to care for its vinegar production. It seemed that there was a greater market in Oregon for the spray which it manufactured. A payroll of twenty-five men left the city. The chemical company frequently had complained of excessive transportation charges, of discrimination against Shale City as a shipping point, but the railroad had done nothing about it. So the railroad lost a customer, and Shale City lost an industry.

Just before Thanksgiving the Shale City Street Railway Company, which only two years before had delighted everyone with the new coaches, announced that it was obliged to discontinue car service. Four buses had been purchased. The street cars would be sent on to another city in which the utility company could use them to better advantage. Buses were cheaper to operate, and their initial cost was much less. They would, said the company, provide better service for the town. But Shale City didn't like them nearly as well as the cars. They were stuffy, and had no smoking compartment, and they lacked that feeling of urban bustle and progress which the rumbling street cars had induced. Things must be getting pretty bad, people thought, if the Shale City Street Railway Company found it necessary to economize.

Business at the Emporium was very bad that fall. The store had a large stock of quality merchandise which it had been forced to mark down to current prices, entailing a considerable loss. Even at the reduced prices there were few people who cared to buy. Those who did have money were spending very cautiously. A great many farmers came to John Abbott explaining that they didn't have any money, but would, of course, be able to pay him next year if he only could arrange to carry them. There was nothing for John Abbott to do but to let them have what they needed.

John Abbott talked to George Boone. They would have to stock a less expensive line of merchandise for the coming season. The chain stores—there were five of them now in Shale City—were cutting in on the business with cheap goods. People patronized them because they could save money. That was reasonable enough. But the Emporium, greatly as he disliked to think of it, would have to enter this cheaper market out of sheer self-defence.

And George Boone must keep a sharp eye out for waste, too. He must cut down wherever possible. Discharge help? Certainly not! That was what ailed the country now—employers forgetting all about their responsibilities to the people who worked for them, cutting down payrolls, destroying purchasing power, speeding the work of demoralization. The Emporium would discharge no one. Besides—where would all of these people go if they lost their jobs? What would they live on? John Abbott was surprised at George Boone for making such a suggestion.

John Abbott did a lot of figuring that year. People commented that he was ageing rapidly. His cheeks lost their healthy colouring. They became grey and a little puffy. When he walked, his pace was slower, and his eyes seemed intent upon the earth. It was the Elysium failure, people said. It hurt the old man's pride. *Old man* . . . the phrase was just beginning to be used in connexion with John Abbott. No one would have considered it a few months before. It would, somehow, have been disrespectful. . . .

John Abbott was going to have to cut down somewhere. He didn't have enough money to go around. It was an odd feeling. But then he had spent a great deal since that trip with Ann through the canal. He had spent an awful lot. There was fifty thousand for the Shale City Oil Foundation, and sixty thousand for the Emporium, and a large portion of the seventy-five thousand for the bank addition, and forty thousand for the swimming pool, and his losses in the Elysium failure, and his boys in college—why, he had spent over a quarter of a million dollars! No wonder he was short of cash. How had he come to throw money about so recklessly? Hadn't Hermann Vogel said something about philanthropy being a vice? He had always been so conservative, too. But he wasn't exactly worried even now. He owned a great deal of property, and his business interests were comfortably large. He was still the biggest man in western Colorado. He didn't owe a dollar, and he had resources which were worth more than the cash he had spent. But, damn it all, he had no reserve. Funny how a person could be caught like that. If he had suspected. . . .

He was going to have to cut down. No doubt about it. He would have to sell that block of Liberty Bonds after all. He hated the idea, too. It had been his policy never to sell a government bond. Keep them, and wait until the government buys them back. That had been his motto. But now there was nothing else to do, unless he wanted to borrow. And he wasn't ready for that.

And he might just as well sell the house on North Fifth Avenue. It was there, all boarded up, doing nobody any good. He might as well have his money out of it, and give someone the pleasure of living in it. He was certainly justified in selling it—he had paid for it twice! It was a fine house. He smiled wistfully, thinking of the pleasure he had taken in building it. That pile foundation—nothing else like it in town. But it was big and lonely, and he much preferred his comfortable rooms at the Shale House. They were very nice to him at the hotel, too. He had assumed the rôle of honoured guest, showered with courtesies that weren't extended to other people. Yes . . . he would sell the bonds and the house.

But even so, he still would have to cut down. In times like these a man should have a little ready cash. He had to cover his large outstanding credits. There was new merchandise to be purchased, and the Emporium hadn't failed to discount a bill in over forty years. And then he should have some money on hand in case the bank needed a little. But where to cut . . . ?

In the back of his mind he had known for months. He couldn't afford to continue with the Shale City Oil Foundation. That would have to go. It had cost more money than he had calculated to keep the project in operation. The fifty thousand was gone already, and the professor in charge of the experimental station said it might require a million before they discovered what they were after. There was expensive equipment which was used once and then discarded for something different. John Abbott knew that all the expenditures were legitimate. They had even extracted some very fine oil out of the rock—and an unusually high grade of oil. They had discovered a lot of by-products, too: dyes and perfume bases, and even a good substitute for asphalt. But the cheap process, the process which would make a roaring industrial centre out of Shale City, still eluded them.

John Abbott quietly notified the man in charge of the station at La Grange to cease operations. When business improved, the project would be resumed where it had left off. But for the present he thought it wise to discontinue the work. A month's extra salary would be forthcoming. He hoped no one would suffer from his decision, and begged the professor to understand that only the most urgent necessity prompted it.

The Monitor made no mention of the matter. The place merely suspended operations, and the men in charge of it vanished, and presently someone driving by noticed that it was deserted, and came back to Shale City to say:

"I didn't know John Abbott's oil station was closed down, did you? Well, it is. I was driving by there just yesterday. Tight as a storm cellar. Say, the old man must be pretty hard hit, eh? He wouldn't let it go without a fight. Things . . . things are getting worse."

IV

FREDDY KILNER was a cub reporter for *The Monitor*. He covered the high school news, and on Saturdays, when there were no classes, he scouted around the town for local items. He was laying the foundations for what he confidently expected to be a brilliant literary career. His ability was widely recognized in high school English classes, although *The Monitor* work offered little outlet for his talents, aside from the composition of items which maintained that R. U. Jenkins of Mycope had spent the afternoon in Shale City on business.

One of Freddy's most pleasant jobs was that of hopping precincts on election nights. He would rush from one polling place to another, imperiously snatch the latest returns from the judges' hands, and then pedal fiercely back to *The Monitor* office, where Stanley Brown and his cronies would be waiting. It thrilled Freddy Kilner to storm right into Stanley Brown's office, conscious that the eyes of half of Shale City's civic leaders were eagerly fastened upon him.

He would walk over to Stanley Brown's desk and hand him the slip of paper. Stanley Brown would read the vote to his friends, making notations on a scratch pad as he read. There would be a chorus of exultant comments—or, if the result were unfavourable, a few of the leaders would declare themselves sons-of-bitches. After this dramatic interval the paper would be handed back to Freddy Kilner. Freddy would rush back to his desk in the outer office, tabulate the returns with a blue crayon on a sheet of newsprint, and paste them on the front window for the edification of an excited audience.

The 1930 fall election found him busy at his usual job. It would be his last election for *The Monitor*. He was to be graduated from high school in June, and then would be off to the glory of college journalism classes. Stanley Brown had hinted that he would recommend Freddy Kilner to John Abbott. That would help a lot.

The polls closed at seven o'clock, and a half hour later Freddy set out on his bicycle for the first reports. They were a little slow on the east side, but by pumping furiously he managed to reach *The Monitor* office with the first returns a little before eight-thirty. He rushed through the outer office and threw open the door of Stanley Brown's sanctum. What he beheld there transfixed him for an instant.

Upon Stanley Brown's desk were three whisky bottles and a flagon of seltzer water, which was not unusual for election night. There were glasses beside the bottles, and the guests who sprawled over the chairs toyed with still other glasses. This wasn't surprising either. Stanley Brown, Art French, Gerald Abbott, Walter Goode, Henry Crooks, William Harwood and one or two others were present, getting quietly drunk against the long night's vigil. And that, too, was quite the ordinary procedure.

The sight which caused Freddy Kilner to stand in the doorway with his eyes popping out of his head was John Abbott, almost lost in the depths of his chair, staring across the room in an alcoholic daze.

After the first swift shock had passed, Freddy Kilner walked over to Stanley Brown's desk. Stanley Brown looked up at him for a moment before he turned to the tabulations which Freddy had given him. Freddy Kilner understood that his boss comprehended the reason for that brief pause in the doorway. Then Stanley Brown focused his eyes on the paper and droned the results. The exclamations were all favourable. While the results were being read, Freddy Kilner, by straining his eyes to one side without moving his head, could obtain a fair view of John Abbott.

The first citizen of Shale City was deep in his cups. His jowls sagged heavily, lending ten years to his appearance. A faint spray of sweat glistened on top of his head. His face, from the midst of which heavy slits of eyes played stupidly over the room, had the appearance of grey decay. Tucked between his legs was a half-filled whisky glass. People in Shale City didn't drink their liquor from jiggers; they drank it from tumblers, and waited a long while before saying when. John Abbott twirled the glass laboriously with both hands, staring at it soberly from time to time, after which he lifted it to his lips and took a tiny sip. When he noted that everyone seemed pleased at the way the election was going, a vapid smile played over his lips; and as Freddy Kilner left the office, the owner of the Emporium was chuckling loudly into his liquor.

Freddy had barely reached his desk when Stanley Brown marched into the outer office. He came over to Freddy and looked gravely down at him for a moment.

"I wouldn't say anything about Mr. Abbott if I were you, Freddy," he cautioned solemnly.

"Of course I won't!" came the hot protest.

Freddie Kilner would as soon have carried tales about his own father. Mr. Brown ought to know that. He looked earnestly up at Stanley Brown, and repeated his words:

"Of course I won't, Mr. Brown."

Stanley Brown nodded kindly, wheeled, and returned to his office.

At hourly intervals until three o'clock in the morning Freddy Kilner snatched surreptitious glimpses of his fallen idol. The last time he entered the office the donor of the swimming pool was fast asleep. His short legs were sprawled grotesquely in front of him, and one hand dangled limply over the arm of his chair, almost touching the rug. He had fallen asleep with a cigar still in his mouth. By now the cigar had unravelled, so that only a leaf, stuck fast to John Abbott's open lips, kept it from falling to the floor. It rested against his vest. It had burned a little hole there; but the smouldering had been extinguished by fine strands of spittle which followed the course of the leaf down the cigar, and ended in a stain around the burn.

There he slept in Stanley Brown's office, with the leaders of the town beholding his degradation, exulting profanely over a victory at the polls, remarking humourously about the merchant's forlorn condition. Freddy Kilner left *The Monitor* office and went home through the first flush of dawn, bitterly disillusioned. Why had they let him do it? Why hadn't they taken him to his rooms at the Shale House and put him to bed when he became too drunk to stay awake? What right had they to titter at him? Freddy Kilner was packed to the ears with ideals. Wasn't there one person among his friends, Freddy asked the vanishing rim of the moon, just one who might have taken a burning cigar from the old man's lips?

V

THE Emporium was in the throes of its fall inventory. Clerks were present in full force, unloading stock from the shelves, counting bolts and yards, numbering dresses and suits and shoes, calculating hairpins and bobbins and tasks. These annual reckonings were always on a Sunday, and although John Abbott wasn't needed for them—George Boone handled practically everything—he made it his invariable habit to be present. He didn't like to demand of his clerks a sacrifice which he himself was unwilling to make.

The merchant always sought refuge from such confusion in his office. There, tightly barricaded against the outer tumult, he went over his accounts. This year things were fairly bad. The farmers who had been going to pay in the fall had been obliged to let their accounts slip over for another year. With sales down, credits up, and expenses undiminished, John Abbott wondered what his position would be at the end of another year. He couldn't quite figure which way the trade winds were shifting. . . .

Glancing up, he saw that Phil Haley had entered the office. The young man was troubled. Fine lines of perplexity wrinkled his forehead, betraying a reluctance to complete the errand which had brought him there.

"What's the trouble, Phil?"

"Something I've got to tell you," responded Phil heavily.

John Abbott had heard those words once before from Phil Haley's lips. Good Lord! He hoped the boy hadn't got himself into another mess. Once was excusable, but twice. . . .

"Sit down," he said grimly.

Phil Haley sat down.

"Now tell me what's on your mind."

"There's something funny going on here," said Phil Haley.

"Funny?"

"What I mean is, we don't do any wholesale business with the Mycope Mercantile Company."

"I haven't the faintest idea what you're talking about."

"I mean, if we're shipping stuff up the valley to the Mycope

Mercantile Company all the time, and aren't doing any business with them on the books, then something's funny."

"Go on." John Abbott felt a queer little vibration dancing along his spine.

"And then, when Mr. Boone bawls me out for finding those packing boxes in the stock-room addressed to the Mycope Mercantile, and won't let me put them on the inventory sheet—why, that's funny too."

"What else?"

"And then when I try to close the books for the fiscal year, and can't wangle a balance out of them, and Mr. Boone says not to bother, just to let him take them home with him, and he'll find where the mistake is—well, I don't know what to do then, Mr. Abbott. I'm not sure just what to do."

"How much are you short?"

"Seven thousand dollars, and I've gone over every entry two or three times. I've been on these books for five years, Mr. Abbott, and I never had this trouble before. If it was something like a hundred or two, I'd know . . ."

"Boone said he'd balance them, eh?"

"Yes, sir. And when I asked Me-catch Me-kill about the Mycope shipment, he said we've been shipping stuff to them right along. Charley Plummer's stage handles the freighting. It doesn't go by rail."

"Phil, are you very certain about this?"

"It's all the truth," said Phil Haley. "I'll bet when we figure the cash shortage and the shipments to Mycope, it'll run over twelve thousand dollars. And Mr. Boone said he could balance up—that I was just to let him take the books home with him."

"How long have you suspected this, Phil?"

"About a week. If I'd known any sooner, I'd sure have told you. But, after all, Mr. Boone is the general manager, and I didn't want to go off half-cocked. But now I'm dead sure, Mr. Abbott. There're no two ways about it. Mr. Boone has been stealing from us—from the store."

John Abbott nodded his head slowly.

"Don't say a word about this, Phil. Just go on with your work. You're in charge of this inventory from now on. Watch everything carefully, and try to find out how much actual stuff has gone out of here, in addition to the cash. I'm depending on you to get the whole works. And send George Boone up to me. I'll tell him that you're to have no interference—and one or two other things besides."

Phil Haley nodded and left the office.

Things had been happening so rapidly the past year that John Abbott could regard this latest development with a grim sort of detachment. He sat huddled in his chair, tapping his pencil against the desk top, waiting for George Boone to come.

When he finally appeared, the manager of the Emporium was very cheerful.

"Want me, Mr. Abbott?" he inquired easily. "Lord, what a mess! Darned glad inventory comes only once a year—but it's much easier in the fall than after the New Years. What's up?"

"Sit down, George."

John Abbott stared for a moment through the window at the full brilliance of a fall afternoon. Then he turned suddenly to George Boone.

"I made you general manager over five years ago, wasn't it, George?"

"Just about."

"Five years ago and better—October 14th, 1926. I remember the date."

"Then that's right, of course."

"Never had to ask for more money, did you, George?"

"No. But I don't understand——"

"Just a minute, please. I gave you four raises, didn't I?"

"That's right."

"And no cuts."

"No cuts."

"You own quite a nice block of Emporium stock, too."

"Yes—a nice block."

"And your home's clear, isn't it?"

"Yes. I paid out on it eighteen months ago."

"Everybody seems to think well of you, too. Since you were made manager you've gone a long way. Very active in church work. Country club, and all that sort of thing."

"I've been fortunate," said George Boone.

"Always treated you pretty fairly, haven't I, George?"

"Always, Mr. Abbott."

"George—how much have you stolen from me?"

George Boone's eyes stared out at John Abbott. He laughed nervously.

"Are you joshing me, Mr. Abbott?"

"I'm not joshing, George. Charley Plummer's been hauling stuff out of here to Mycope for over a year now. And we've been getting no money for it. No—I'm not joshing, George. I'm serious."

George Boone flushed angrily, and jumped out of his chair.

"Say!" he gritted, "I don't have to take that off you! You've got crust, coming at me with something like this! Listening to a lot of gossip! If you don't like the way I've managed this place, why—why—why, suppose you manage it yourself! I'm through." He started to walk out of the office. "Get another manager. Find one you can call a thief and get away with it. If that's the kind of man you want, count me out!"

"Just a minute, George!" snapped John Abbott. "Walk out of that door, and I'll have you in jail before sundown. I think you'd better talk."

George Boone paused for an instant, and then, shrugging his shoulders, returned to the chair he had deserted.

"Well, if you want to be reasonable. . . ."

"Very reasonable, George. As I said, Charley Plummer's been hauling this stuff to the Mycope Mercantile. Me-catch Me-kill has been packing it for you. He thought it was legitimate. There are some boxes in the stock-room now, addressed to the Mycope Mercantile."

"I've just landed them as customers," said George Boone. "Been trying for a long while. It's a first shipment."

"No, George, you're lying. This has been going on for a long while. It's one reason why the Emporium hasn't been able to pay any dividends. You've been bleeding it dry. There's a cash shortage, too. You've even dipped your fingers into the money-boxes. I don't think it's going to do you any good, George, to deny it. You're caught."

George Boone's face set defiantly. "It's a lie!" he said softly. "It's a lie, Mr. Abbott—I didn't steal anything."

"You'd better come through, George. I can't afford to take a loss like this. Three years ago, it would have been different. But now, I'm fighting with my back to the wall. I can't stand the loss, George—I simply can't stand it. . . ."

He broke off and glanced wretchedly around the office. He was almost pleading with this man! That wasn't the way——

"I have enough evidence to send you to the penitentiary, and that is just what I'm going to do. There's evidence for a dozen counts of grand larceny. You're going to prison, George. For a long while. Twenty—maybe twenty-five years. All your life in prison, maybe. For stealing from me when I needed the money so badly."

George Boone turned white and ran his tongue along his lips. Then, like a prizefighter unable to rise for the count, he crumpled.

"I did it, Mr. Abbott!" he howled. "I did it! Don't send me to jail, Abbott! Think of my wife—my boy—they couldn't stand it! Oh-my-God-what-am-I-going-to-do?"

"First you're going to sign a confession, George. Take this pen and some paper . . . there. Now write down just what I say."

John Abbott dictated very slowly, and the sound of George Boone's pen scratching across the paper filled the little intervals of silence.

". . . of my own free will . . . confess . . . to shipments to the Mycope Mercantile Company . . . to thefts of cash amounting to over . . . surrender to John Abbott immediately . . . house at 523 Abbott Boulevard . . . 350 shares of Emporium common stock . . . fully aware that if these assets do not cancel the total sum of my defalcations ... I will be prosecuted to the full extent of the law . . . and hereby swear . . . that this is the truth . . . signed, George Boone."

John Abbott blotted the paper carefully. George Boone watched the operation with sick eyes, all his crispness wilted.

"How much do you figure the total will run, George?"

"About eighteen thousand."

John Abbott started. He hadn't thought it would be so much. Eighteen thousand—what a lot of money! It was going to be more serious than he had thought.

"Your assets won't cover it, George."

"No . . ."

"George, when you came here, you were broke. You were a failure in the real estate business, and you were finished. Remember?"

"Yes."

"I took you on and taught you the business. I advanced you, and finally made you general manager. Every dollar you own, every friend you have came from your association with me. I've made you, George. God knows you weren't promising material. But you were the best at hand. So I made you into a successful man. I"—he paused a moment— "I trusted you, George."

"Yes."

"And now you repay me by stealing—at a time when I'm borrowing money to keep things going! Hear that, George? I'm borrowing money to keep you in a job—*and you stole from me!*"

"Oh, God, Abbott, I'm sorry! If I could only do something to help! You don't know how—how awful I feel."

"I'm all through being a philanthropist, George. I—can't afford it any more. I'm going to take everything you have. If it hadn't been for me, you wouldn't have it anyhow. And if that doesn't cover your theft, then I'll send you to prison just as sure as my name's John Abbott. I've been made a fool of for the last time, George. It'll be hard on your wife and the boy—but you can't expect me to think any more of them than you do. Now you're going home, and you're not going to make a move until you hear from me. Understand? To-morrow you'll transfer your assets to me. Naturally, you're through here. But I warn you, don't make a move until I give you permission. We're going to do a lot of checking here. Understand?"

"Yes," came the whispered reply.

"Now—get out of here!"

George Boone walked out of the office.

John Abbott was still sitting there staring down at George Boone's confession, when Gretchen Boone, George's wife, ran sobbing into the office. She didn't wait for John Abbott to greet her. She rushed over to him and clutched his arm.

"Mr. Abbott! George told me about—about everything. Oh, Mr. Abbott—it was all my fault! I wanted pretty things—all my life I've wanted a house and a car and nice clothes. I never had them—until George started here at the Emporium. We were so happy—and I made such a fool of myself! It was all my fault. I spent too much money, Mr. Abbott! It was because I'd never had any before in my life. I went—I went a little crazy, I guess. I just didn't think. And George couldn't deny me. I didn't know George was—that he was *stealing* it! I forced him to steal, because of my spending. I see it all now. He says if he can't pay it all back, he'll go to the penitentiary. We—we belong to the church, Mr. Abbott—everybody likes George—and there's Junior—don't you see, Mr. Abbott—don't you see that I can't stand it?"

He wished she weren't a woman. He was never able to deal forcefully with them. She was rather a pretty little woman, too. He paused a moment before answering her. He had to be just, and yet——

"He stole the money," he said dully. "I need it. He's a thief. It's too bad you made him do it. But I've got to protect myself."

"I'll kill myself!" she shrieked. "I won't go through with it! That'll be murder, John Abbott! I can't bear to look at people, and have them know!"

She couldn't bear to look at people and have them know. John Abbott had heard that declaration once before: the same words in the same office. She was getting louder. "George Boone is a thief," he kept repeating to himself. "He is a menace to the community.

He has betrayed me. He deserves to be in prison where he can't steal any more. . . ."

"Take everything we've got—but don't send him to jail! I'll work for you here—I'll pay the difference in working. I'll spend the rest of my life here in the Emporium to pay it back—only please don't send George to jail! Please, please, please!"

She fell to the floor and reached out convulsively for the cuff of his trouser leg. He wished she would stop. He withdrew his leg from her embrace. Her supplications pounded grimly away at his conscience.

"Please—please—please—please!"

"Get up. Try to pull yourself together. I—I accept your proposition. You can work out whatever remains to be paid."

In an instant she had regained her feet. Her eyes were fixed greedily upon his face.

"Then—you won't send him to jail?"

"Look."

He was tearing the confession to little scraps. He stacked the bits into an ash tray, and applied a match to them while she gazed at the performance with tear-filled eyes. A thin flame shot up from the tray.

"Mr.—Mr. Abbott—God bless you! Oh, God bless you for ever!"

She kissed him full on the cheek, and ran out of his office, laughing and crying simultaneously.

He remained at his desk for the rest of the afternoon, going over column after column of figures. It was expensive—so frightfully expensive to have God's blessing. He really couldn't afford it much longer. He was stupefied by what had occurred. More money to raise . . . and whom could he trust?

Gretchen Boone never returned to the Emporium. George Boone's assets were eight thousand dollars short of covering his defalcations. The eight thousand meant as much to John Abbott as eighty thousand a year or two or three before. About six months later, George Boone opened a little dress and dry goods store, which he called the Budgette Shoppe. He had, people declared, the nicest line of $12.50 dresses in Shale City. John Abbott understood that some of George's friends in the church had assisted him in his fresh start. George Boone had supported the church generously in his fat years, so it was only Christian that fellow parishioners should come to his rescue during the lean.

VI

MILDRED WESSINGHAM was growing pleasantly, even wistfully retrospective over the strawberry *soufflé*. "It *is* odd—the loneliness of age," she told her guest softly. "One is a little surprised—a little stunned even—to find that the years have advanced so quickly . . . that one has seen so much happen. It is the time of life when companionship becomes more precious than ever before."

John Abbott nodded across the table to her. A candle between them lifted its tiny flame; he was obliged to move his head to one side or the other if he did not want to have Mildred's face bisected by the taper. The strawberry *soufflé* was delicious. As soon as he had swallowed his mouthful, he answered her.

"That's right," he said. "When you see people beginning to say to themselves, 'He isn't what he used to be'— why then a man's bound to appreciate friendship. Somebody, for instance, like you, Mildred. It makes him feel that things—well," he floundered for the exact word, and finished lamely—"that they could be a lot worse."

She had given him a large glass of sherry before dinner, and the glow of the wine persisted through the meal, leaving him in a warm, expansive mood. Mildred Wessingham seemed about the only friend he had left. The only friend, at least, with whom he could spend an evening during the course of which not one word concerning business would be mentioned. Ever since Ann's death she had been kind to him, filling his desperate need for feminine companionship.

Other people invited him out, of course, but he enjoyed himself more at Mildred's. After a hard day at the store wrangling with townspeople over bills they owed to him, writing apologetic letters to wholesalers and manufacturers, it was soothing to come to Mildred Wessingham's, and to know that in her eyes, at least, he was still John Abbott. She had become a necessity to his comfort, a pleasant adjunct to his existence.

There was no selfishness about her, either. She wasn't like the rest—fluttering about him like greedy moths around a financial bonfire. Mildred had never mentioned money to him. Every day someone

came to him for help, and was offended when he had to give a negative answer, and went off muttering that John Abbott had changed,
and that he must be feeling the depression pretty badly. But Mildred
Wessingham liked him just for himself. She hadn't even mentioned
her financial condition when Arnold Wessingham had enrolled in college last fall. She had gone calmly ahead, planning to see the boy
through on her own slender means. He knew they were slender
because he had investigated.

She had actually protested when he insisted on sharing the burden of the boy's education. She declared that she didn't want to be like
the rest of Shale City—indebted to John Abbott for every good thing
she had. It had required a surprising amount of argument to impress
upon her the logic of his viewpoint. If he could help Art French's boy,
then he certainly could help Mildred Wessingham's.

"Do you know, John Abbott," she murmured, snatching him from his
reverie, "you are just about all I have, now that Arnold's gone? Just our
dinners here together—the candlelight—and quietude."

"I can imagine, if I had a son, how I should hate to see him leave,"
agreed John Abbott. "It makes you feel a little . . . empty, doesn't it?"

He paused a moment, and sighed blissfully. The wine, the meal—
he was very content. He could forget things at Mildred Wessingham's.

"How", he demanded abruptly, "was that chicken fixed to-night?"

She flashed him that deprecating smile, indulgent and faintly superior, with which women invariably meet the lovable faults of their men.

"It was roasted," she told him, "and basted with cooking wine. Then
it was stuffed with ripe olives, but I took them out before Emmy served
it. The French way. You liked it?"

"Perfect!" he breathed.

Emmy walked in with a little tray upon which sparkled a bottle and
two goblets.

"A surprise to-night," said Mildred. "Champagne—poor Warren left
five bottles, and this is the first I've opened. Nineteen years . . . and
many of them lonely, too." She turned to the tray, felt the bottle judi-
ciously, popped the cork.

"Lonely!" echoed John Abbott. "Lonely!—why I've been that way all
my life."

He shuddered a little. How could she know what loneliness was—
she with her son? Even Gerald, his own nephew, seemed to avoid him
lately. Gerald always had favoured Ann, anyhow. Sometimes John
Abbott suspected that Ann had told Gerald about Donna Long. How

else to account for some of the things which his nephew occasionally said, and the manner in which he said them? Gerald had received nothing but good at John Abbott's hand. There was no explanation for his slowly changing attitude, aside from the obvious one that Ann had poisoned him against his uncle. Gerald was his only blood relative. No wonder he felt lonely. He had only these dinners at Mildred Wessingham's—and Mildred herself.

"Let's drink," she said, handing him his glass. "Give us a toast, John, and we'll feel gayer."

He hesitated a moment, inhaling the gaseous bubbles from the wine.

"To you, of course!" he declared with a rush of emotion.

They walked into the living-room. Emmy followed with the tray. They sat down in deep cushioned chairs, and Mildred asked him about politics. Hoover, he told her, was certain of the Republican nomination. And Hoover would receive John Abbott's vote in the autumn, too. The Democrats were never certain. You couldn't trust them at any time, under any circumstances. Why they even hated each other! Look at the number of men fighting for the party nomination—two to every state. He thought that Ritchie of Maryland would be nominated. Al Smith would be shut out by the west and mid-west; and when he saw that his cause was lost, he would switch his delegates to Ritchie. That would start the landslide which would carry Ritchie to the nomination. Roosevelt would lose out. He was too anxious, too aggressive. But he might make off with the vice-presidential nomination. John Abbott's personal choice among the Democrats— if, he hastily qualified, one could make a choice among them—was John Garner. There was a man with some common sense in his head. But if the country knew what was healthy, it would stick with the Republicans until this confounded mess was over. It was no time to experiment. . . .

He had another drink, and informed Mildred that it would require something bigger than a donkey to pull this country out of the dumps. The quip seemed extremely funny to him, and he laughed a little about it. Yes sir, nothing less than an elephant could turn the job. He was still chuckling when the door bell rang.

Art and Stella French were calling. John Abbott was surprised to see them. Mildred wasn't in the least surprised. She had invited them and the Boones. "Do come over," she had urged the Frenches and the Boones, "just for a quiet evening."

John Abbott started to rise, but he sat down again, with startling abruptness. His head was whirling. Stella French looked askance at his movements, but Mildred Wessingham quickly explained them.

"Champagne, my dear. Poor John was feeling so blue to-night that I couldn't endure his mood another moment. I dug into my oldest and finest."

"Oldest and finest," confirmed John Abbott floridly, "is right. Not half of it, in fact. Have a drink Stella . . . Art?"

Stella said "No" a little coldly, but Art was glad enough to have one. They all sat down, and John Abbott related what he had been telling Mildred about a donkey—it had become a jackass by now—not being able to pull the country out of the dumps. He laughed at it all over again, and although Stella only smiled in a vague fashion, Art managed a polite chuckle. Mildred looked at Stella and shook her head hopelessly, as though to say, "You see? I have absolutely no control over him. He is just a naughty boy!"

Stella started to tell Mildred Wessingham something new she had heard about Walter Goode and Miss Weems. It seemed that Wendel Burgess had gone into Walter's office quite suddenly and——

The door bell rang again. This time it was George and Gretchen Boone. They both reddened at the sight of John Abbott. The owner of the Emporium stared at them with bewildered incredulity. They had not spoken to each other since that fatal inventory day. Nobody knew, of course, what had impelled George Boone to leave the Emporium. George had let it be tacitly understood, however, that he had resigned because old Abbott's merchandizing methods were obsolete, and he felt he could do better by himself. Whenever George Boone was mentioned to John Abbott, the donor of the swimming pool merely glared and said nothing. He made no attempt now to rise in politeness to the newcomers.

After the first little flurry of confusion, George and Gretchen assumed command of the situation. They spoke very kindly to John Abbott, blandly ignoring his curt response. Mildred opened another bottle of champagne, and filled three glasses.

George Boone refused the wine with a sententious, "I never touch it."

Mildred Wessingham murmured a low apology and set the extra glass on the mantel. Art French and John Abbott began to sip slowly.

"Never drink, eh, George?" asked John Abbott.

"You know I don't," responded George a little sulkily.

"Fine habits," declared John Abbott approvingly. He was enjoying the situation thoroughly, now that he had overcome his first sensation of wanting to go over and twist George Boone's nose. "I always said, George, that you'd go a long way. Lord!—I said that when I first took you in as a clerk. Remember the ribbon counter? Well, I was right, wasn't I?"

"John!" murmured Mildred Wessingham reprovingly.

Gretchen Boone glanced sharply at Mildred. She hadn't known that any woman in Shale City had enough claim on John Abbott to address him in that tone. She was beginning to understand a thing or two.

"Quite right," said George Boone shortly.

"And how is business?" persisted John Abbott. "The $12.50 dresses and the 38-cent yardage and all?"

"Fine," declared George Boone. "Picking up every week."

"Good. Wish you luck, George. You were always such a square shooter. Well"—he gulped the sparkling wine and winked broadly at George Boone—"Well——" He weakened suddenly. It seemed that some inner agony had taken hold of him. "That's fine," he finished in an undertone.

When Mildred came over to take his glass, he held her hand for a moment. He wanted also to chuck her under the chin, but she was too far above him for that. To hell with George Boone! Mildred—she was a friend. She tugged gently with her imprisoned hand, and he chuckled. She pulled again, sharply, and he released it.

"John!" she said, making a little grimace, "it's so very *gauche*—when there are guests." She glanced at Gretchen Boone and added, "I can't do anything with him!" Gretchen Boone's eyes stood out in their sockets. Stella French looked down her nose as though it harboured some infuriating blemish. Art French grinned openly. George Boone's face was a cold mask of disapproval.

Art French related something amusing that a Mexican had said to him that afternoon. John Abbott answered with a story of his own. It was a little off-colour. He had heard it two years ago in Stanley Brown's office—on election night, as he recalled it. He had never thought of repeating it until now. Indeed, he had never remembered it until now. Yet here he was, a trifle astonished at his own derring do, reciting it in loud, defiant tones.

When he had finished, Mildred gasped, Stella French smiled in pained tolerance, and Art French chortled happily. But John Abbott's attention was fastened on George Boone. George's expression hadn't changed. It was as though there had been no joke at all.

"Don't you think it's a good joke, George?"

George cleared his throat. "I haven't any doubt," he said precisely, "that it is a very good one of its kind. But you know, Abbott—I am here with my wife." He stared icily at his tormentor.

"Your wife?" John Abbott jerked his head to a full scrutiny of Gretchen Boone. His eyes swept her from head to foot until she squirmed and flushed richly. "So you are. So you are. Your wife! I haven't seen her for a long while. You must come to see me at the office some time, Mrs. Boone. And you don't like the joke, eh, Boone? Not nice enough for you, hey? Oh dear, oh dear. Not nice enough, eh? Oh my—oh-h-h ha! ha! ha! ha!"

He burst into uncontrollable laughter, patting his stomach hysterically, rolling from side to side in his chair.

"Oh mercy—Oh-h-h—ha-ha-ha! Oh-h—ha-ha-ha! Oh dear—get me—ha-ha!—get me that glass off the mantel, Mildred! You heard him? Oh-h-h—ha-ha-ha-ha-ha! It isn't nice enough for Georgie! Gracious!"

George Boone was standing up, white with anger. Gretchen Boone was standing, too, and Mildred Wessingham was hovering about them, making soft apologetic sounds and turning occasionally to say, "John! John, dear. Stop it, won't you?"

George and Gretchen Boone said they really must be going. They would come over again. And Mildred Wessingham must come to see them. Some time this week, sure. It was so seldom they saw each other.

A little later Art and Stella found that they, too, were obliged to leave. John Abbott managed to get out of his chair to see them to the door. He leaned heavily on Mildred Wessingham's shoulder. They said good night very cordially, and John Abbott winked at Art. He received a round, solemn wink in return.

"We'll leave you two to yourselves," murmured Stella. She didn't dare say anything meaner. After all, John Abbott was still paying Jack French's tuition. "And thanks for a lovely evening."

They were quite alone. They went back into the parlour, and Mildred gave him the other glass from the mantel. He drank it while she sat on the arm of his chair. "Dear Mildred," he sighed, half to her, half to himself. "What a sweet old girl you really are!"

He seized her hand and kissed it, and then he brought her shoulders down, and kissed her lips. His hand stole to the lace-covered sag of her breasts. He wanted suddenly to cry, to laugh, to leap to his feet and damn George Boone. He felt ecstatically wistful, his mind washed of all its troubles, his emotions naked and tender.

"You're right, Mildred. You're all I have, and I'm all you have. The rest of 'em—pouff!—they don't amount. Simply don't, my dear. For another drink—no, kiss me first!—for another drink I'd love you. I'd really love you, sweet old Mildred!"

She brought him the drink, and presently he was very sleepy.

"You can't go home in this condition," she soothed him. "You've had too much, John, dear. Here . . . lean on my shoulder . . . like that. I'll try to get you into the bedroom. Poor boy. Poor little boy. He's so sleepy."

He saw her dimly through tears, and then felt her tugging at his shoulder. Summoning a last reserve of strength, he staggered to his feet. Upstairs in her bedroom she started to undress him. In the early stages of the operation he protested feebly, and swore that she was tickling. Then a fit of giggling seized him, and after it had passed he was so very tired that he fell asleep before she finished. She stripped him down to his underdrawers, rolled him on to his back, and pulled the covers over him. She looked down at him with a little shudder. His face was wrinkled and his mouth was open. Below the collar line his throat was as stringy as old dough, chalky white with blue veins showing through. What an old man he was! Almost as old as Warren Wessingham had been.

She turned off the light, undressed quickly, and climbed into bed beside him. Then she called loudly.

"Emmy! Emmy!"

Emmy came to the bedroom door, peering timidly through the darkness.

"Switch on that light, Emmy. And bring me a glass of water, please. I'm so thirsty."

Emmy switched on the light, and started violently. She left, and returned quickly with the water. Mildred Wessingham raised herself on one elbow and drank it.

"Thank you, Emmy," she said, returning the glass. "If you wish, you may go to your sister's for the night. It doesn't matter. But if you'd rather. . . ."

Emmy made a frightened little motion with her head and said "Yes'm." Then she turned off the light and tiptoed out of the bedroom, leaving John Abbott and Mildred Wessingham undisturbed.

VII

THERE was something about Mildred Wessingham's champagne that made John Abbott sick. When he awakened in the morning it seemed to him that his head was larger than the pillow; and the pains which darted through it were far too agonizing for him to notice anything unusual in the fact that Mildred was in his bed. He awakened her with his moaning, and she got up to take care of him. For over an hour he was in convulsions. When Mildred finally managed to get to the telephone, she called Dr. Lawrence and Gerald Abbott.

Dr. Lawrence pronounced it a case of acute indigestion. He said, profoundly, that either it would pass off quickly, or culminate in death. In any event, it was unthinkable for John Abbott to be moved out of the house in his present condition.

When Gerald Abbott arrived, he didn't inquire how John Abbott happened to have spent the night with Mildred, and Mildred didn't volunteer any information. He told Mildred that if anything developed she was to call him at the bank. He would be around that night to see his uncle again. She went to the front door with him. As he left, he paused an instant to say to her, "You're a very clever woman, Mrs. Wessingham."

There was poison in the remark, but Mildred ignored it. She had almost had Gerald in a bad fix once or twice before he married that disgusting widow. She wasn't at all afraid of him.

The news spread rapidly. Emmy told her sister about seeing John Abbott and Mildred Wessingham undressed right to their night-shirts, in bed together. She related how Mildred had dismissed her for the night, and, encouraged by the rapture with which her sister listened, she added one or two details of her own invention. Her sister told a friend, and the friend told someone else. By noon the town rocked and chuckled and feverishly demanded more. Mildred Wessingham, with her sour face and her high-hat ways!

And John Abbott. Guess the old boy still had a little life left, eh? Poor old devil—all like that. A wonder somebody hadn't thrown a harpoon into him long ago. But there was no reason for him to keep on being so distant from now on. He wasn't kidding them any more. He was a nice old fellow, but he was no angel. You could bet your life on that. And with Mrs. Wessingham—delicious!

Gretchen Boone went to the Baptist Study Circle that afternoon. Most of the meeting was devoted to a study of John Abbott. Gretchen went into lascivious detail. How John Abbott had held Mildred's hand. How he had pawed over her. How disgustingly drunk he had been. How he had told that vile story. Oh no! She wouldn't dare repeat it. No, my dears—it was far too *risqúe* to tell. Oh my, it was a lewd thing. Well . . . she really oughtn't. But if you'll promise not to tell a soul . . . it seems that there was a travelling man going through the country, and . . .

"There is nothing more disgusting," said Gretchen Boone solemnly, "than a lecherous old man. Positively nothing. And he is so old! I'll tell you, I'm certainly glad *I* haven't a daughter working down there at the Emporium. I'd not have a single easy minute! Men are so dangerous when they reach that age—so nasty. Oh, he's done a lot for the town all right. But he's changing. Yes . . . too bad. Tch! Tch! Tch!"

Stella French was indignant. She berated Art fiercely.

"You should have taken him home," she stormed. "I always knew Mildred Wessingham was after him. But no! You would stand there and wink back at the poor old fool. A fine friend you are! Now when he gets out of that house I want you to go right down to the hotel and talk to him. It's a shame—her snatching him like that."

"None of my business," shrugged Art. "But I can't say that I admire the old boy's taste. Mildred Wessingham—ugh! I'd kick her out of bed!"

"I don't think it's anything to become vulgar about," said Stella icily. "If you're not interested, then of course . . ." Her voice trailed off insinuatingly and then returned to the assault with fresh vigour: "I don't imagine that Mildred, once she gets him, will relish John Abbott paying out money for Jack's college. And she'll tell the whole town about how much you owe at the bank. But just go right ahead. It's none of your business. Oh, not at all. My fine broad-minded husband. Go right ahead, and let John Abbott ruin himself. Oh yes. Certainly. And let Mildred Wessingham ruin you, too, when she snags the old man. Yes indeed!"

"Well," said Art, given suddenly to think, "perhaps I may say a word or two if the time seems right, and I can do it without making a damned ass of myself. But I wouldn't get all worked up about it if I were you. What's there to it if a man wants to get a little friendly——"

"Indeed!" Stella had him now. "So *that's* the way you look at it. What's the difference! And whom, may I inquire, do you lie up with when you feel 'a little friendly'?"

"Whew! Talk about me getting vulgar! Leave it to you to work the dirtiest meaning into things. John Abbott isn't married at present. I was talking about him—*him!* And I promise you I'll tell him that Mildred Wessingham is a man-trapper, a loose woman, a whore—anything you say, only please lay off me!"

John Abbott lay ill at Mildred Wessingham's house for three days. On the fourth he was able to return to his rooms at the Shale House, and on the sixth he went down to his office in the Emporium. He was somewhat haggard, but otherwise he appeared as if nothing had happened. If he noticed the twinkle in the eyes of passers-by, he gave no sign of it. He could, people said, put on the most innocent face!

There was a note in his mail from Stella French. He read it once, uncomprehendingly. He read it twice, and felt the blood rushing to his cheeks. The third time he realized its full import.

DEAR MR. ABBOTT,

Mildred just told me the secret, and I want to be the first—the very first—to congratulate you. I think that it is perfectly splendid. And I am so glad that the lonely years since Ann left us are about to come to an end. So again I congratulate you, and wish you the best of luck. You and Mildred must come over to dinner—only you and she and Art and I—on Friday. Will you, please, just for me?

Your friend,
STELLA FRENCH

He reached for his desk telephone and gave the operator a number. It seemed an age before the connexion was made.

"Hello—Mildred? Say, I've got the queerest note from Stella French here. She says—you *told* her! Told her what? . . . But Mildred, I can't understand. I—I don't know anything about it! . . . *I* said that? I'm sure you're mistaken . . . I said *that* too? . . . Well, I can't see what got into me. I was drunk, that's all . . . No, Mildred, I never thought of you in that way at all. Please listen to me. You've made an awful mistake here. I think you're fine. You're a fine friend, but Mildred, I don't want to marry anybody. If I did, of course it would be you . . . Just a minute, please. Somebody's coming into the office."

Phil Haley wanted to know if old man Hardy's account could stand a pair of four-fifty shoes.

"Sure," said John Abbott. "Give him the store. Only don't let anybody in here until I send you word."

Phil Haley said he wouldn't, and tiptoed out of the office. John Abbott turned back to the telephone.

"Hello . . . Your *reputation!* But Mildred, I was sick. Everybody knows that. Nothing unusual about it at all. Not at all . . . I *forced* you! A drunken man that strong? . . . Yes, there *are* a lot of things I don't seem to know . . . Yes . . . Well, I won't do it. I—I hardly know what to say, but I *can* say that. And I'm busy, and you'd better correct that story, and you're . . . I haven't time to talk to you, Mildred. I'm busy. Good—*what?*"

He turned grey, and listened to the flow of words at the other end of the line. They went on and on. By the time they halted the transmitter was quivering against his ear.

"But, Mildred," he said softly, "you can't do that. I haven't got that much money, and besides, a suit would—it would break me. Think of the bank—it'd cause a regular run if you sued for that much! . . . But *Mildred,* please listen to me. I was hasty. I apologize for what I said. I couldn't marry you unless I—cared for you that way—and I haven't got a hundred thousand dollars . . . No, not even if you went into court and sold me out. Everything I have is tied up . . . Oh my God, Mildred, don't do it! *Please* don't do it! . . . No, don't hang up. Listen just a minute. Things are so desperate down here. Can't we forget all about it? Can't we just go on——"

Click!

He sat there with the transmitter in his hand until an angry buzz reminded him to replace it on the hook. The whole thing was preposterous. That anybody in Shale City would do this thing to him—above all, Mildred Wessingham! Why he—he felt as if he were going to die. Everybody would know. He would be haled before a judge who was his friend, and hear the testimony of a maid who had seen him in bed with this woman—in his underwear! The thing was unbelievable. What a fool he had been to believe that she would treat him well for anything but money. To believe that anybody would treat him well!

The whole town would know about it—all the people who came to him for advice—all the people he had helped—all the people who looked up to him—all the kids who went out to the swimming pool. What had Donna Long said? "Like walking down the street, naked and dirty——" He understood well enough what she was driving at. But what was he going to do?

He went over to the bank and told Gerald Abbott about it. He pleaded with Gerald, trying not to notice the faint leer in the younger man's eyes. Finally Gerald said he'd take care of Mildred Wessingham all right. But he didn't spare John Abbott, for as his uncle started to leave, Gerald said:

"You *do* have the faculty of getting mixed up with women, don't you?"

He didn't answer. As he walked out of the Shale City National Bank, his shoulders drooped heavily, and Harry Twinge, who nodded to him, went home to tell his fat wife that John Abbott had death written all over his face. Mrs. Twinge laughed sharply, and said it wasn't death—it was exhaustion. John Abbott was too old for his ideas, that was all.

Gerald Abbott haggled with Mildred Wessingham for a week, while the town boiled with rumours. He even had a lawyer come over from Denver to frighten her. In the end she settled for fifteen thousand dollars. She came down to the bank for it on the appointed day. Gerald had a long statement for her to sign. It declared that she had lured John Abbott into a compromising situation, that she had threatened him with a breach-of-promise suit which amounted to blackmail, and that, for the sum of fifteen thousand dollars, she relinquished all claims against him and agreed to leave Shale City for ever.

She glanced through it casually. She was too much the aristocrat to be awed by typed words. When she had signed it, she looked across at Gerald Abbott.

"The cheque?" she hinted delicately.

He opened his drawer and withdrew the precious paper.

"Before I give this to you," he said grimly, "I should like to give you just a hint of the foul thing you've done. You have taken an old man—a man who has been kind and generous to a whole city—and you've dragged his name so deeply in the mire that nothing can cleanse it. You might have taken all of his money, and he would have come off cheaply. But no—you had to take his reputation—an honest name he laboured forty years and more to build. You've made the whole town laugh at him, Mrs. Wessingham. There is no greater cruelty. You've broken his heart. I—I haven't the words that I need to tell you what a contemptible old strumpet you really are. I simply lack them."

She smiled at him sweetly. "Dear Gerald," she murmured, "always rising splendidly to the occasion. A lovely sense of the dramatic. And still the orator—never forgetting the college debating days. Well, we all have our memories. But if you're quite finished, *I'll* have the cheque."

He was white with anger as he handed it to her.

"And what would you do, dear lady, if I stopped payment on that cheque—and kept this statement for extortion charges? Where would you be then?" He studied her intently.

"You can't do that. If I just filed suit—without a chance of collecting—the publicity would line people up at this bank in rows a block long! And you know it. Don't try to play with me, Gerald Abbott, because if you do, I'll ruin him. You hear me? I'll ruin him!"

He laughed softly.

"Don't bother, Mrs. Wessingham. You've done that."

Mildred Wessingham took her fifteen thousand dollars and moved to Denver, so that she could be with Arnold. She thought that John Abbott probably would stop Arnold's school cheques, and it would be cheaper for her to be where she could keep house for him.

VIII

THE autumn of 1932 was the most tragic in Shale City's history. For two years the town had told itself with each season that the next would usher in the return of prosperity. But instead, each season had been more disastrous than its predecessor. Now the community resigned itself to a dreadful and despairing fear, not at all like the fear of an enemy which could not be located, which could not be fought, which offered no quarter. No one knew where the next blow might fall.

The fruit ripened in the orchards, and no effort was made to pick it. It dropped to the ground and rotted, while little children in Denver—so short a distance as Denver!—almost starved for want of it. A lot of the corn wasn't even harvested, and a great portion of that which was gathered found its way into ranges and heaters during the winter. The sugar factory didn't open. Shale City longed for the evil stench of beet pulp which in previous autumns had lingered over the town, rich and gaseous, inducing wry faces and unpleasant remarks. How sweet that odour now seemed!

The sheep and cattle men were ruined. Although there were plenty of hungry men in the cities, the ranchers couldn't give their animals away. Nor could they afford to feed them during the winter. Many of the cattle were left on the range to die of starvation, or to feed the wolves. Great pits were dug, and the sheep which perished were tossed into the pits to enrich the soil. One by one the old ranchers—men who had held their land for a score of years and more against the elements—turned their holdings over to the terrified bankers. They were weary of paying interest.

A lot of honest men went into bankruptcy that fall. Stores closed their doors, leaving ugly scars along Main Street, which once had been so animated. The county ran short of funds with which to pay its school teachers. The pedagogues received tax anticipation warrants instead. For a while those few who possessed cash bought them. But soon no one had cash, and they were unsalable. The coal mines closed down. The operators couldn't earn enough to pay their workmen.

There were rumours about the banks. The Farmers', people said, was in a fairly bad way. But then the Shale City National scarcely could be much more fortunate, considering all the losses John Abbott had taken. Still, it was a national bank, and John Abbott was behind it. John Abbott remained the only man of any size in Western Colorado who still managed to keep his head above water. Half of Shale City was riding along on his shoulders. And yet—hadn't John Abbott's building and loan long since exercised its privilege of demanding notice for withdrawals? That certainly wasn't very encouraging. If you owned a dollar, where were you going to put it? Where would it be safe? Where would it remain a dollar?

John Abbott closed the basement of the Emporium that fall. All the glistening hardware and gay toys and brightly-painted garden furniture were moved to the main floor. Rather than discharge employees he instituted a short shift, with a day off each week for every clerk. They were not paid for their idle days, but otherwise there had been no salary cut. When a clerk left the Emporium, his place was not filled; but very few quit. John Abbott stubbornly refused to economize at the expense of those who worked for him. He would find some other way.

It nearly broke the old man's heart, people said, to have to close the Emporium basement. That store was the apple of his eye. Yes, he must be having a pretty serious time of it. And if John Abbott was in difficulties, what of everyone else? Who could hope to escape that which threatened to cut down the strongest man in the community? Well . . . there wasn't much hope of anything immediate. Just try to hang on during the winter. Perhaps by spring . . .

John Abbott knew that he was close to insolvency. The thought kept him awake nights in his lonely bedroom at the Shale House, followed him down to the Emporium each morning and rode him all day like a fiend. He spent long hours carefully passing upon all credit purchases, endeavouring to collect a few of the many thousands which were outstanding on his books. He had over two hundred thousand dollars in his ledgers—two hundred thousand dollars which the people of Shale City owed to him. Many a family would have done without warm clothing these last three years if it hadn't been for John Abbott. Many a child would have gone barefoot through the freezing winters. But what was he going to be able to do for John Abbott? And how was he going to maintain the pace? Another winter was approaching, and the same people were back again. If he would only trust them a little further . . . and then when things picked up, they would pay him sure . . . they simply had to have a few things . . .

The chain stores hurt him. They hurt worse than he cared to admit. Every day he could look across the street to Hafley & Flint's gaudy window front, and see old customers of the Emporium passing through those alien doors—people whose parents had purchased their swaddling clothes at the Emporium, now going to Hafley & Flint's! Hafley & Flint had the prices. The merchandise, of course, wasn't as good as that offered by the Emporium. But people had forgotten about quality. They wanted price, price, price. They would go over to Hafley & Flint's to save three cents, even though a similar product at the Emporium would wear for twice as long. John Abbott remembered the time when he had been glad to see the chain stores enter Shale City. Now they were doing half the business of the community. One by one the merchants who had risen with the town, who had shared its misfortunes and extended credit to its citizens, had quietly closed their doors before the glittering invaders. John Abbott, gazing across at Hafley & Flint's, wondered where it would end.

He would muddle through somehow. He had started this institution in a shack—surely he was strong enough to rescue it from its present sinking spell. He had survived 1907, while his fellow merchants and bankers all over Colorado fell like ripened wheat; fair enough, then he would survive 1932. He wasn't too old to get into the swing of things again. He had been intimately acquainted with every detail of the Emporium's management since George Boone's dismissal. He and Phil Haley had worked together grimly to keep the store on an even keel.

He would have to get in and dig. In the old days, he had gone right out after business. He had never been afraid, if necessary, to load a little cart and push it from door to door. By heaven, he would start in all over again. He would get this thing rolling somehow. He would go to large buyers, and prove to them—prove to them that they could save money by dealing with the Emporium, even though the prices were a little higher. There were a lot of places in town . . . he walked over to the accounts receivable journal, and spent a long while looking through it. Then he put on his hat and left the store.

He walked over to the Municipal Building, and entered the city manager's office. The city manager's name was Herbert King. John Abbott didn't know him very well, although he had heard of him as a very efficient and honest man. He had come to Shale City about eighteen months before, a youngish person, with a bald head and sharp grey eyes. John Abbott sat and chatted with him for a while, and then he posed a question:

"By the way, King, where's the city buying towels for the swimming pool now?" He knew they used a lot of towels out there—and the Emporium wasn't getting the business.

Herbert King thought for a moment.

"Why, we're getting them over at Boone's shop," he said. "Have been for a year, I guess. Before that we bought from Hafley & Flint. Boone gave us a better price, so we went over to him."

"Um-m. What are you paying for them, King?"

Herbert King told him.

"Uh-hmm." John Abbot knitted his eyebrows. He was getting into the swing of selling again. It had been years . . . "I can't beat that price, King. But I'll tell you what I can do. I can give you a better towel—a towel that'll last maybe twice as long as the ones you're getting. And I'll guarantee it, too."

Herbert King was politely interested. How much would the towels cost?

"I can figure close on it," said John Abbott, "and give them to you for just seventy cents a dozen more than you're paying now." He hadn't, he mused, gone out after this sort of business for over twenty years. But he'd show them. He'd take this deal away from George Boone on a basis of quality alone. That was the only way to do business—quality. And . . . he needed the order, too.

"Seventy cents is a lot of money, Mr. Abbott. The way things are right now, with everybody hollering about taxes, we've got to cut right down to the bone. You see, that price is about six cents a towel higher than we pay Boone. And we use lots of towels, Mr. Abbott."

"That's just it," put in John Abbott triumphantly. "You'll use less of them if you buy my stuff. You'll cut your annual towel bill by thirty per cent. I can show you figures, if necessary, to——"

"Oh yes, I know, Mr. Abbott. But we haven't much use for really good towels out there. You see, a lot of them are stolen. Then they don't treat towels very gently, these kids. A good towel will tear just about as easy as a cheap one, I guess, with a kid at each end. It would be different, now, if we were getting the right kind of care for 'em."

"But I don't think you see my point, King. It's the washing that wears out a towel. It's the——"

"I see your point perfectly, Abbott," said Herbert King a little crisply. "But you don't see mine. Shale City simply can't afford to pay six cents extra for a towel that some kid is going to swipe or tear up."

"Why, man"—John Abbott felt a strange buzzing in his head—

"man, you're crazy! I tell you, it's washing that ruins a towel—they're not all stolen! I've been selling towels all my life, right here in this town. I can tell you more——"

"Listen, Mr. Abbott," said Henry King softly, "I know all about that. And I know that you gave this pool to the city a few years back. But that——"

"Did I say anything about giving the pool?" John Abbott's face turned an angry red.

"No, of course not. But you're thinking it, all right. And I don't blame you. I'm very sorry. In normal times we would patronize you, of course. For that reason, if for no other. But these aren't normal times. I'm quite sure you don't really want to impose upon the city in this way, and I'm quite certain that I won't permit you to. I've tried to be reasonable about it, but you don't want reason. You force me to tell you that it's my job to buy things for this town as cheaply as possible, and that's precisely what I'll do, no matter——"

But John Abbott had stamped out of the office.

Herbert King shook his head in a puzzled fashion, and then turned to some papers on his desk. Poor old devil! Everybody in town was leaping at the city hall these days. Herbert King was cutting expenses mercilessly. If he had to step on a few sacred toes—well, that was too bad. Later, if things improved, he would transfer the pool account to the Emporium. But he was damned if the old boy could come into his office and tell him he was crazy . . .

John Abbott walked back to the Emporium. That buzzing in his head was growing louder. He couldn't remember when he had been as angry. He was so excited he couldn't think coherently about it. For six cents——! Well, he wouldn't drop the matter. It was false economy. It was the attitude that was ruining legitimate merchants everywhere these days. They were all suffering from it. What sort of towels was George Boone selling at that price? They must be tissue paper! And Boone couldn't possibly figure to make a profit.

He tried not to think of having given the pool to the city. But the thought was there, of course. Herbert King had caught it, too. Well, why shouldn't he think of it? The pool always had paid its expenses. It had never cost the city a cent. Why shouldn't it buy towels from the man who had built it? Particularly when his towels were *better*— much better. And he needed the business. Any little piece of business. Nobody knew how badly he needed it.

He sat down at his desk and picked up the telephone. He called the Y.M.C.A. and got Henry Wilhelm on the wire.

"Hello, Wilhelm. John Abbott speaking . . . Fine, thanks . . . No, I've been keeping pretty close to the store these days . . . Yes, I will . . . Yes . . . Say, Wilhelm, where're you buying your towels now? . . . Hafley & Flint, eh? . . . What price they charging you? . . . Uh-hmm . . . Yes, of course. I understand. But I'll tell you what I can do, Wilhelm. I can give you a real towel—a real towel for only about a nickel more than you're paying Hafley & Flint . . . Oh, absolutely. I'll stand right back of them, Wilhelm. Last you twice as long . . . Surest thing you know . . . Well! That's fine . . . What'd you say? . . . You—you'll take—half—a—dozen————!"

He broke off the conversation without even telling Henry Wilhelm good-bye. He stared straight across the room. The buzzing in his head changed to a hurricane—an incredible confusion of sight and sound which sent the whole office reeling before his eyes. A half dozen! It would have been better to have taken none at all. To order half a dozen towels————! Oh, he'd get to the bottom of this! He'd find out! By God, if it wasn't——

He stiffened suddenly. Some intolerable pressure seemed to be throbbing at the base of his eyes. They were fixed in their sockets, staring through a film of blood. He sat very rigidly in his chair, looking out across the office. His—why—he couldn't move! Nothing on his right side would move. This couldn't be—! No. . . it was quite numb. He couldn't move. A whole half of him couldn't move! Oh, God help him!

He tried to call Phil Haley, but his lips were stiff.

"Thil!" he wheezed. "Thil! Thil! *Thil!*"

They couldn't hear him. He began to beat his left hand against the desk. He pounded it furiously at first, but no one came. Exhaustion gradually diminished the effort. But he didn't dare permit it to stop entirely. It might freeze on him, too. "Thil!" his voice whistled. "Oh, Thil!"

About a half-hour later Phil Haley came into the office and discovered him. John Abbott was sitting bolt upright at his desk, still pounding with his left arm, while his twisted lips whispered over and over again— "Thil! Thil! Thil!"

Phil Haley picked him up in his strong arms, and carried him over to the davenport. He put in a rush call for Dr. Lawrence. Then he went back to the davenport.

"Is there anything I can do?" he asked helplessly. "Isn't there something I can do to help you?"

But the old man only stared up at the ceiling with eyes that jerked rhythmically from side to side, and whispered— "Thil . . . Thil . . ."

IX

THE EMPORIUM
Western Colorado's Finest Store

JOHN ABBOTT   ~~L. GEORGE BOONE~~
President   *General Manager*

THREE FLOORS OF QUALITY
MAIN AT FIFTH, SHALE CITY, COLO.

November 12, 1932.

MR. HERMANN SCHONK,
    Pike's Peak National Bank,
    Colorado Springs, Colo.

DEAR HERMANN,

I have been planning to write you for a long while, and now that I have got around to it, I may as well come to the point quickly. I need money, Hermann, and much as I dislike to do so, I am appealing to you as a last resort.

Things are very bad in this part of the State. Worse, almost, than I can say. We have had more business failures in 1932 than ever before since the town started. It seems that half our people are out of work. The local charities can't meet the situation. The county is practically insolvent. Teachers are receiving warrants, and have been for some time. The city treasure is little better off.

I have outstanding, either in my name or the Emporium's, over a quarter of a million dollars owing me. A good half of it is absolutely no good. The rest, in the course of years, may come back to me. I still have lots of property, but there is no price for it, and nobody to buy; and I've got to be careful how I tie it up— particularly with my own bank. Gerald is working day and night over there. He is flooded with collateral that has shrunk ridiculously. We are getting a lot of sheep and cattle right now—the ranchers can't afford to feed them during the winter, so they say,

'Here we are—come in and foreclose'. It's a problem how to dispose of them, and the loss is terrific.

I need anything up to fifty thousand dollars, Hermann. As I say, I have a lot of clear property for security. I can give you your pick of any one or all of a dozen ranches, houses, business buildings, or whatever you might want. But I know that this is a minor consideration with you. If you haven't the money, why then you haven't it, and that's that.

I wouldn't mind so much if it were just myself. I could do what a lot of others are doing these days: send my creditors to my debtors, and let them fight it out between each other. But I've had that worked on me too often to want to throw it up to someone else. I suppose, by scratching and pulling, I could clear out now with thirty or forty thousand, provided I could find customers for what I am holding, and was willing to sacrifice, and did as mentioned above in relation to what I owe and what is owed me. But I can't do it, Hermann. It would be taking too much out of the town—and God knows, enough has gone already. Without conceit, you know as well as I that it would be knocking the keystone out of the arch. So I'm going to stick.

I think if I can squeeze through this winter, I can come out all right. But I'm not sure I can manage it unassisted. If I go, then the building and loan and the bank and the store and half a dozen other enterprises will go with me. That would affect a lot of people. So I'm really not trying to borrow for myself. (I never thought I'd ever write a letter like this!) It's rather like a nightmare, knowing that if you fail, you'll carry half a State down with you. Anyhow, if you do anything, we can work out the details in another letter. I'm not going to urge you, because I know that if you can, you will.

Some day this town is going to boom. The oil shale industry is coming, Hermann, as sure as you're alive. If we last to see it, it'll make both of us wealthy beyond our wildest dreams. And it will make a real city out of this town, too.

What do you think of Roosevelt's election? I was surprised. Shale City went heavily Democratic. I wasn't feeling well, so I didn't get out to vote. But I think I would have voted for Hoover. I understand, in a very small way, what he has been up against. Things everyone thought impossible. Have you been east lately? Is there any sign of improvement? What do they think of Roosevelt?

I haven't been quite well this fall. I had a stroke—my right side. If you can't read the signature, please excuse it on these grounds. I wish it had been my left side, though. I am on a diet now, and have some exercises to do. Dr. Lawrence—you know him, don't you?—is so cheerful with me that I sometimes think my case must be serious. Anyway, the exercises are doing me good. I feel better than I did. I can't work my fingers very well yet, but I can walk. My right leg drags, but at least I can get around. Let me hear from you as soon as you can.

As ever,
JOHN ABBOTT

HERMANN SCHONK,
17 Beaumont Drive,
Colorado Springs,
Colorado.

November 16, 1932

MY DEAR JOHN,

I've never been so sorry for anything in my life as I am for my inability to do anything in relation to your recent letter. I am skinning by on such a close margin that it makes goose pimples come out every time I think of it. I believe things over here are about as bad as you describe them in the western part of the State. We've had a lot of bank failures, and business, farming, mining and stock-raising are practically at a standstill. I'm only keeping this place here for appearances. If the wolves once suspect, they'll drag you down in a minute. One man takes care of the whole grounds, and things look pretty frowzy.

Our bank is solid enough, I think, but we haven't a red cent extra. People howl about the bankers when they can't get loans. They think we're holding back just to preserve liquidity. They don't know we haven't had it for the last three years. We've so much tied up already that we simply haven't any to loan. If even a small run should start here, then God pity us. I've taken it on the chin for over four millions, and you know I didn't have much more than that. What I have left is frozen—very solidly. There is a newly popular word that I don't like.

I was back east this summer. If we think things are bad here, you should see them back there. People are hungry by the millions, and what they'll do this winter is beyond me. Out here, at least, our people usually can get to a little piece of ground, and raise something to eat.

Everyone in the east is pessimistic. They seem to have lost hope completely. They think we haven't seen the worst by a long shot. I talked with a lot of men who are still up, and they say frankly that they don't understand a thing about what's happening. We may be in for some big changes. Anything may happen. It may be Socialism or Communism or complete financial breakdown, with nationwide starvation and revolution to top it off. Men actually speak of these things, and talk about getting what they have out of the country. We seem to have started something we can't stop. God only knows where it will end.

I voted for Roosevelt. I'm not too sure of him, and he said practically nothing definite in his campaign. He may be just another hack, or again, he may be a miracle. We've got to gamble these days. A lot of people who don't trust the Democrats normally, voted for him out of sheer nervousness. They want a change, no matter what it is. We seem to be in the mood for experimentation, even if it costs us our lives. I'm hoping for the best, but hardly believing what I hope.

You mentioned, John, that you might be able to pull out at this stage of the game with thirty or forty thousand dollars. If I were you, I'd do it. There's an ethical point involved, of course, but people aren't paying any attention to ethics these days. It's every man for himself. You've done a lot for that part of the State, and I see no reason why you shouldn't have a decent little sum left over for yourself. I've had a few examples of human gratitude in my life, and I don't care for it. Don't hold your trump too long, because if you do, and lose, then they'll cuss you just as loud and probably louder than they would have if you had sold out and left them stewing in their own juices.

You knew Charley Laderback, didn't you? He jumped off the eighth floor of his own building last Saturday. A lot of the old birds are going that way. They thought they'd stick it out, too, hoping and praying for an upswing. And it didn't come. Don't hope for one. Go ahead in an honest, decent fashion and liquidate while you still have something. Forget that Colorado Valley for a while and think of yourself. But this, of course, is only my advice. If I could get out, don't think I'd hesitate. I realize that you may have a different viewpoint; probably have.

I was sorry to hear about your health. You must take better care of yourself, John. I suppose it's pretty lonely up there, with Ann gone. But Gerald is a great help and comfort. I am sixty-five, which must make you sixty-seven. Why, we're still a couple of young bucks.

There's a good fifteen years of activity left in us, and after that they'll probably have to take us out and knock us over the heads. I laughed at your comment on Dr. Lawrence's cheerfulness. Tell him hello for me. As I remember it, though, he was never a grouch, so I wouldn't go too heavily on that deduction of yours.

Well, John, let me hear from you again, and tell me what you decide to do. If anything turns up here, I'll let you know in a minute, because you know that it's yours. I'm devilishly sorry I can't do anything now. We both came up with this State, and gave it a hell of a lot more in the long run than it has given us. If we go down with it too, what's the odds? It's all in a lifetime.

Affectionately,
HERMANN SCHONK

JOHN W. ABBOTT, ESQ.,
The Shale House,
Shale City, Colo.

X

THE Emporium passed into receivership shortly before Christmas—almost four years to the day after its triumphant reopening with the addition of the new second floor. The Shale City National Bank was the principal creditor. John Abbott had fought with all the money at his command, and it hadn't been enough. After more than forty years of honourable dealing, of participating intimately in the life of the town, of outfitting its infants and shrouding its dead, the store's treasury was exhausted.

Considering the step in advance, it had seemed to John Abbott a thing of fatal, almost historic consequence. A dozen times he had tried to penetrate the future, to imagine the emotions which would accompany his admission that he was no longer capable of operating the Emporium without assistance. But when the crisis came, he was stunned by the simplicity of his reactions. He merely hobbled over to Gerald's office one fine frosty morning and said:

"I'm washed up. I've done everything I can. You'd better start a friendly receivership action right away, and protect the bank. I can't do anything more."

After that he went to his rooms at the Shale House, and didn't return to the store for two days.

The town buzzed and sighed and chattered resentfully to itself. It was almost as though John Abbott had violated a public trust. If the Emporium was insolvent, what about the bank? What about everything? For nearly half a century the Emporium had been a gauge by which the progress of this western country had been measured. It had been stability. It had been success and prosperity. It had been the symbol of Shale City's cultural existence. And now it was insolvent.

The Monitor published an account of what it termed "the reorganization", explaining that John Abbott had requested the action to protect the store's creditors. The article related how the store had trusted its hard-pressed customers to the extent of well over two hundred thousand dollars. It said that the Emporium was completely solvent, and that there was no need for the people of Shale City to worry.

But they did worry. When John Abbott spent two whole days in his rooms at the Shale House, a flood of shocking rumours quivered through the town. He had fled the country. He had killed himself. He had suffered another stroke, and now was helpless. He had gone insane, and Gerald had committed him to an asylum. He had slipped off to Denver to live with Mildred Wessingham. The collapse of the Emporium was so frightening that these tales seemed quite plausible. A sign from the heavens, an eruption of the earth—anything would be sane and reasonable after this.

With the rumours concerning John Abbott and his store went wild tales about the Shale City National Bank. John Abbott was reported to have stolen from the bank to support the failing Emporium. Gerald Abbott and John Abbott had engaged in a terrific row in which Gerald had forced his uncle to submit to the receivership proceedings. Gerald Abbott had purchased the store at an absurdly low price and was going to operate it with bank funds. There was a flurry of withdrawals from the bank, but Gerald Abbott managed to obtain enough money from the Federal Reserve Bank in Denver to tide his institution over the crisis. And the Shale City Building and Loan——! Oh Lord, what was coming next? And right before Christmas, too!

Two receivers were appointed for the Emporium. One of them was John Abbott. The other was Sol Grunner, who, until that time, had been in charge of the Shale City unit of the Haley & Flint chain. Sol Grunner was a smart merchandiser. He had made a smashing success of Haley & Flint's store, and the Abbotts hoped that he would do the same for the Emporium. Sol had jumped at the chance. He was given blanket authority to make whatever changes he wished. John Abbott's part of the receivership was, in the main, honorary.

Sol Grunner was a handsome fellow with dark wavy hair and the alert eyes of Israel. He was a good mixer, people said, and a very harsh gentleman when a dollar was on the table. At forty he appeared little more than thirty. Anyone who knew Sol Grunner understood that he was a man who would get somewhere before he was through. He had the air.

On the first day of Sol Grunner's management, John Abbott waited until noon to come down to the Emporium. Sol Grunner had announced his intention of spending the morning going over the store from top to bottom, and John Abbott didn't care to watch the inspection. Ever since he had walked into Gerald's office and told the horrid truth, the donor of the swimming pool had been a little hazy about events. The thing was so fantastic that he didn't quite comprehend its full meaning. Now, when he appeared on the street, dragging his leg

E C L I P S E

behind him as he laboured toward the Emporium, he avoided the eyes of his townsmen. He would know that some old friend was passing scarcely two feet away, and he would not look up.

The business men, seeing him pass down the street that day, felt sorry for him even though his collapse had frightened them nearly out of their wits. Yet in their hearts they believed he was still impregnable. Hadn't his bank just resisted a run? Didn't he own more property than any man in the entire Colorado Valley? Wasn't he still a director of every important enterprise in town? Wasn't he owed more money than most of them had ever dreamed of possessing, much less of extending in the form of credit? Yes, although John Abbott might be old and in difficulties right now, it wasn't safe to underestimate him. He was still the biggest man in Shale City. But one could feel sorry for him nevertheless. He had loved that store so dearly . . .

John Abbott clumped through the middle aisle, avoiding the eyes of his clerks, who had assembled covertly as though for some solemn ceremony. He stiffened when he felt their glances, as Napoleon must have stiffened when confronted with the weary, bleeding remnants of his *Grande Armée* straggling home from Moscow. They all looked wretched. They knew that the happy days were over. They had passed beyond John Abbott's protection now. Clump-clump-clump. His eyes were fixed intently on the stairway leading to his office—the stairway which had been covered with flowers four years ago, and before which he had stood like a desert Zeus accepting the town's tribute.

There would be dismissals and pay cuts now. Some of those who stood behind their counters and watched the old man's progress down the aisle and slowly up the stairs, knew that they wouldn't be there to-morrow. Clump-clump-clump. The whole store was filled with fear. There would be no jobs, no money, and hence, no food, no rent, no clothing—what in heaven's name would they do? One or two of the women wept openly as he passed. He might have been on his way to prison.

He sat down at his desk and looked around the office. Over there was the desk which Donna Long had used. He had kept it untouched. And across from it was the safe, in which were lists of all the people who owed him money. In the safe also was a scroll of silver and gold and parchment, confirming the gratitude of the town. There were eleven thousand signatures on it, counting the crosses and fingerprints. Yes . . . the office hadn't changed. Everything was still in its place. He stared about the room curiously. He had half expected it to vanish, to resolve into the nothingness it really represented. But no. Here was his telephone and there his fountain pen . . . everything was quite all right.

He must remember that. Dr. Lawrence had said he shouldn't become excited. He was going to pull out of this mess, and he didn't want to be retarded in his progress by another stroke. He must be calm. Very calm . . .

Sol Grunner entered the office, nodded affably, and began to talk. Sol Grunner wasn't a man to mince words. He came right to the point. That was only business, John Abbott supposed. But he wished Sol Grunner would be a little less positive. After all, there was a chance that he might be wrong at least in one or two details. Sol's smooth voice flowed like oil into John Abbott's ears.

There must be a big reorganization sale. They had too much high-priced stuff on hand. Best to sacrifice it, and replace it with something cheap and catchy—something that would sell fast. Quality was all right, but you must have price these days, if you were going to stay out of the poor house. Why, this place was still as well stocked as lots of stores in Denver. And Shale City wasn't Denver. Not by a long shot. Shale City was a little burg, and getting littler every month. The Emporium would have to come down to Shale City's level, instead of trying to boost Shale City up to its own.

And that ladies' ready-to-wear—it would have to be moved downstairs. Too much room up there not being used. Why, there'd been only three customers in there all morning. Cut out the frills. The shoe department could be shoved over to make room for the ready-to-wear. By getting that stuff downstairs, they could save the expense of operating the elevator—and that was nothing to be sneezed at. And that sporting goods section in the men's department would have to go, too. Nice enough, but there was no money in it.

The window displays would have to be changed. He had spoken to Fred Best about it. People liked to see lots of stuff in the window—not a dress here and a pair of shoes there and some gloves thrown around, with a flower and a panel in back of them. No sir. Merchandise must be displayed—otherwise, how were people to know you had it? It must be stacked in; and they would run sales every week-end. They would buy stuff especially for the sales—something John Abbott had never done—and push it out fast and cheap.

And then the help in this place——! Why, there were twice as many clerks down there as necessary. Far more than the place needed.

That little wop they call Me-catch Me-kill had tried to chase him out of the basement with a clinker-hook, too. What did the little guy do, and was he any good? He would trim the staff at least fifty per cent. And a lot of those women would have to go, too. The place must have been run along the lines of an old ladies' home. Some of them had been there for twenty-five years, he bet, and were so old they couldn't lift a full bolt of woollen yardage! Keep the young ones, and let the old ones go. And salaries would have to be slashed. People were lucky to be working at all, these times. My God, most of the salaries down there were pure charity.

Why, when you stopped to think about it, this place would have been a gold mine, even during the depression, if it had been run right. Take those credits—there would be no more credit. Cash on the line, boy, and see that it's good. Why, he'd never heard of——

Sol Grunner stopped abruptly and peered across at his listener. John Abbott was huddled in his chair, nodding his head mechanically and trying to appear as though he understood and approved everything. But there were tears flowing down his cheeks. Actual tears, running down John Abbott's furrowed cheeks, pelting into his lap. Sol Grunner had never seen anything like it. Why—why the old man must have been nuts about this store. What Sol Grunner saw as an establishment dedicated to the profitable sale of merchandise, the old man across from him must have viewed in another light—in a strange and altogether impractical light. Sol Grunner wasn't a ruthless man, except in business. He was genuinely sorry for John Abbott, and his religion had taught him to respect his elders. In a sudden flash of understanding, he realized that it wouldn't be tactful to apologize. There was nothing he could say to comfort the owner of the Emporium.

"Poor guy," he thought, "he had it once, and he let it get away from him. Never let that happen to you, Sol Grunner. He put his heart in this joint, and he forgot that it owed him something, too. Remember that, Sol Grunner. Poor old guy. Yes . . . he was an earth-shaker once, all right. But he isn't an earth-shaker any more. I'm going to have to go easy with him. He's all shot. No guts. Nothing inside. Why, he doesn't even cry like a man. He's just whimpering . . . snuffling like a nervous old woman."

Sol Grunner walked softly out of the office, and went downstairs, and began to separate the sheep from the goats.

XI

JOHN ABBOTT and Hermann Vogel met one evening as they were entering Mrs. Alloway's Cafeteria. It was John Abbott who suggested that they have dinner together. After the meal was completed they lighted cigars and ordered second cups of coffee.

For a while neither of them spoke, and then John Abbott burst out surprisingly:

"What's the answer, Vogel? You're a school teacher. You think you are pretty smart. You're supposed to know things. All right then, tell me what's the answer?"

"Answer?" murmured Hermann Vogel.

"Sure. What is going to happen? How are we going to pull through? Where are we going to end—you and I and all the rest of us?"

"Oh, I daresay things will iron themselves out in time. They always have. In a way, it's a very good thing."

"Good thing!" echoed John Abbott strangely. "Good—for children to go hungry, for men to be out of work, for honest business men to fail? Good for worry and poverty to drive people crazy?"

Hermann Vogel nodded.

"A splendid thing," he answered. "One mustn't consider it from a personal viewpoint. You and I"—people had commented that Hermann Vogel was living much more modestly of late, although no one knew why—"you and I are merely incidental victims. We will probably go down with the mob. And in a way that is all right. A hundred million or so will go down with us, and that is the important thing—the blessed thing."

"It's your damned European outlook," declared John Abbott, who had asked for bread and felt he was being handed a stone. "You never really became a citizen of this country, Vogel. If you don't like it, you ought to go back."

"I love America," murmured Hermann Vogel. "And I'm not going back. Not now, at least. I wouldn't miss the glory of these times for anything on earth. It's like—taking a clean bath. It's like seeing a dog deloused, with millions of filthy little insects dropping dead after having made him miserable for God knows how long. That's what is happening to America, my friend. The lice are being driven from the body politic. If an occasional ant like you, or a spider such as I, is killed in the process—well, it's a regrettable affair, but a sacrifice we can cheerfully make. I, for one, am almost exhilarated at the thought."

"You're talking nonsense again, Vogel."

"No. I'm telling you truth. My whole reasoning is based upon the immutable law that as soon as a man's thoughts are focused upon his empty belly, he completely forgets about his soul. And that is a very good thing. Hungry men have no leisure in which to annoy their neighbours. A nation that is trying to legislate itself into a square meal has no time to legislate itself into heaven."

Hermann Vogel fixed an eye upon Mrs. Alloway, who stood primly behind the cash register. Mrs. Alloway beheld him with a kind of horrid fascination, and then began to make nervous little movements, like a bird harassed by a skulking cat. When Hermann Vogel returned his glance to John Abbott, Mrs. Alloway grew calm once more.

"The trouble with you, John Abbott, is that you never put two and two together. And when you do, the result invariably runs from twelve to twenty. I'll try to show you what I mean. It's simple addition, I assure you, performed in solitude by a village school teacher. Nothing miraculous about it. Our country—I've been a citizen for a good many years, so I can say what I want—is recovering from the damnedest spiritual jag in history. Let me explain: the profits from the war conferred leisure upon the American peasant. It slapped him right in the face, this leisure, and what did he do? Did he set about to get a little intelligent joy out of living? He did not. The moment his energies were diverted from work, the instant his belly and his backbone were separated by a top sirloin and a piece of apple pie, he began to go key-hole-peeping. Instead of improving his own idle hours, he dedicated himself to the task of purifying the idle hours with which prosperity had blessed his neighbour."

Hermann Vogel snorted with quiet indignation. John Abbott stared moodily at the tablecloth upon which, with his finger-nail, he traced a whole series of little ovals.

"If you doubt me, review the thing for yourself. Ever since the war we have been the battleground of mighty reform movements. Consider the ideals of each group, and contrast them with the practical results. Then you will have arrived at the only fair judgment of their success. Women's suffrage, designed to clean up politics, shot the Ohio Gang into power and presented us with the Teapot Dome.

Prohibition, enacted to eliminate the drunkard, made dipsomaniacs of our children, festered our cities with speakeasies, sponsored the rise of the most vicious criminal class in the history of the world. The schools, successfully raiding the state treasuries upon the assurance that education was the best defence against crime, filled the penitentiaries with their students. The great up-surge of the luncheon clubs, professing to purify business ethics and to exalt the principle of service, swung into power on a wave of commercial dishonesty unparalleled in any country that ever existed. There you have them: the four great reforms in the last decade—the Four Horsemen of Prosperity."

Hermann Vogel spread his hands delicately on the table, palms upward.

"Can't you see, John Abbott? Can't you see the poison with which these swine have permeated the country? We gave them their heads—all these fine reformers of morals, business, politics, azppetites. They sat firmly in the saddle, riding through a sea of gold. They cheerfully accepted the responsibility, and by God, now they are reaping the consequences. Every principle for which they stood was knocked into a cocked hat during the very years of their power—murder, divorce, adultery, robbery, perjury, dope, liquor, illegitimacy, kidnapping, perversion, bribery, theft, forgery—the whole kaboodle flourished, grew stronger, increased. Our self-appointed leaders plunged headlong into a latrine— and, which is worse, they forced us all to wallow there with them.

"And what happened to the fellow who dared question them? What if a man said, 'I doubt this prosperity', or 'I doubt this morality', or 'I doubt this church', or 'I doubt this government'? He was hounded to death by them. He was impaled upon a cross, and all the slobbering sensualists they could muster thrust spears into his side. Well . . . they have taught us a lesson. They have given us a great historical demonstration of the fact that a man cannot believe in anything with his whole heart and his whole soul without becoming an intolerable bigot, and hence a menace to his fellow citizens."

Hermann Vogel rose from his chair and stalked toward the coffee urn. Mrs. Alloway watched him sharply, and when he shot a glance in her direction, dropped a whole handful of dinner checks through which she had been sorting. He returned to the table with a cup of the steaming liquid, took a deep swallow without adding sugar or cream, and continued the dissertation where he had left off.

"Now it will be different. All of our bigots are hungry. Each one is so intent upon obtaining food and clothing that he has no time to interfere with the habits of decent people. As a result, I foresee an era of pleasant, graceful living ahead. It will endure only so long as we keep the moralists hungry. The instant they have a spare hour, they will be on our backs again. Let them, therefore, labour fourteen hours a day at extremely low wages, and they will have little urge to thrust their snouts beyond their own doorsteps. They will have no time to dictate what their neighbour may read, what he may see in the theatre, what he may wear, what he may think, what he may eat, what he may smoke, whom he may love. These filthy little vermin, these nasty millions, crawling over the body of a healthy nation, infesting it, spawning their young in its carcass, spraying their filth over its eyes and nose and mouth, leaving their unspeakable slime wherever they go! Keep them down. Keep them hungry. Let them go back to their hutches, back to their pig-sties. And let us—you and I—pray to God for a depression which will last for ever and ever. It'll be worth whatever sacrifice it entails, for it will give us freedom."

John Abbott reached out with his fork, impaled a crumb of pie crust, and transferred it to his mouth.

"I don't know," he said faintly. "I used to think you were always wrong. I know that you can't be always right. But everything's mixed up. The people you speak of never bothered me. What I'm interested in is getting out—getting back! My God, Vogel—you don't know what all of this means to me. Everybody has a plan. I read plans in magazines and books and newspapers. They're all different. And in spite of the plans things only get worse. Everybody's just as sure as you are—but they're all sure about different things. Me—I'm not sure about—anything."

Hermann Vogel fluttered his fingers in a deprecating little gesture. An expression approaching gravity which had been on his face a moment before now changed to saturnine amusement.

"I have a plan, too," he said. "For a long while I've been buried in figures, and I've come up with a plan that is absolutely foolproof. You see there are but two causes for the depression, according to the experts: over-production or under-consumption. The experts selected over-production as the culprit. Over-production is a positive condition, calling for the negative remedy of under-production—a nostrum involving curtailment and downright destruction. It is un-American, Satanic and probably of Russian conception. It must go.

"A diagnosis of under-consumption would have uncovered a horse of quite another colour. Under-consumption, being negative, would have demanded the obviously positive remedy of increased consumption. And the most direct way to increase consumption is to increase consumers. You follow me?"

John Abbott nodded to denote comprehension but by no means agreement.

"I've been making charts, too. They reveal the catastrophic fact that a hundred and twenty million of the smartest, richest, hardiest people infesting the footstool are reproducing at the niggardly rate of some two million each year—a net gain over the death rate of considerably less than a million. This disgusting total represents the contribution to our population—to our *consuming power,* mind you—of twenty-six million couples.

"Making all reasonable allowances, the charts show that at least five million couples now non-productive, are capable, if properly stimulated, of bringing from their loins some five million children. These children, or consumptive units, represent an immediate market for no less than forty-five million square yards of breech cloth—the rehabilitation of the South in a single stroke. And this is only a beginning. Consider the doctors, nurses, midwives, hospitals. Think of the immediate outcry for toys, perambulators, heating pads, milk, cereals. Nor should the destructive tendencies of young animals be overlooked. As an example, safety-pins; so many will be lost, so many crippled, so many devoured outright by the incoming generation. In all, the safety-pin octopus stands to profit by upwards of sixty million pins!

"By a process of infiltration, the profits of those industries directly affected will be transmitted to all business. Labourers will be recalled, factory wheels will turn, riveting machines will rivet, stocks will leap heavenward, and above the confusion, the wail of a new-born consumptive unit will be sweeter music than the sirens ever dreamed of. Each five million youngsters will mean an advancing tidal wave of business as long as they live. They cannot love, marry, quarrel, conceive or die without profoundly affecting our economic situation. In the broad and enlightened sense, they will represent, not people, but massed economic robots.

"Only an intelligent imagination—one such as yours, for example—can visualize the magnitude of the thing. It is not difficult to picture a Federal department of child culture, with some exalted midwife as secretary, taking as much interest in raising children as the Department of Agriculture now takes in raising pigs. The moment an economic surplus accumulates, the instant a climbing stock market levels, phallic storm warnings will be hoisted from Maine to California, and within ten months new consumers will be popping forth in well-regulated lots of, say, half a million weekly.

"When things are progressing nicely, a baby will be something of a curiosity—an example of carelessness to be held up to reproving view. But when panic threatens, the increase will pyramid furiously. There will be no break in the market because there will be no doubt. Thus we can achieve a phenomenon unique in the annals of trade—a securities market that will continue to rise for ever. If our population reaches the point where the forty-eight states no longer can contain us, we shall crowd all other people from the face of the earth in the final achievement of manifest destiny. Practically speaking, there is no limit.

"Soon I plan to offer this panacea to the public. The logic is inescapable—and much better, I may add modestly, than that offered by the professional plan-makers. A new cause, a brighter crusade than ever before is immediately before us. Let rose-water and pink ribands and sleek thighs greet every man in his nightly homecoming. Let ogling babies inspire him from bill boards. Let the radio, the novel and the cinema glorify the maternal instinct. Let the social position of a family depend upon its fecundity. Let the logical be dazzled by figures and the sentimental with cradle songs. Let bachelors be shamed and spinsters ridiculed. Let there be parades and bands and socials and four-minute speakers. Let awards of merit be conferred and high-sounding titles bestowed. Let the sweet secret be bellowed with throaty pride from every housetop."

John Abbott took a drink of water, glanced at the clock, and stirred in his chair.

"If pacific measures fail," continued Vogel, sensing John Abbott's mood, "the government must take a hand. We grant the authority to forbid murder during peace and to demand it in war. How, since it forbids conception among the single, can it be denied the right to command it of the married? If dissenters appear, we shall hunt them down, cast them into prison, burn them at the stake, disembowel them as public enemies. But I doubt that such strenuous measures will be necessary. The American people, once I divulge my plan, will have at their disposal a system which will relieve them pleasantly of all their woes. Unless they are complete jackdaws, they will see the light and be guided by it. If they turn their backs, God and Hermann Vogel can do no more for them. Let them starve on their thresholds and pitch their dead into the public highways. They have invited their doom."

Hermann Vogel took a long puff at his cigar, perceived that it had burned out, and struck a match. John Abbott speared a final crumb from the pie plate and placed his napkin on the table. As though by mutual agreement, the two men arose, secured their hats, paid Mrs. Alloway at the little stand near the door, and went out into the raw January night.

XII

WINTER began to relax its grip on the Colorado Valley. The sun plunged over the blinding white rim of Shale Mountain a little earlier each morning, and lingered longer in the evenings. The ice at the river's edge broke into jagged islands which swung majestically out into swifter waters. For a week the snow would disappear almost entirely, and the wet earth would send up little columns of steam, and the townspeople would begin to think about spring gardens. The air would carry the balminess of May, and hardy blades of grass would peep out at the reviving world. Then grey clouds would swoop over the valley, and quietness would steal over the earth, and eight or nine inches of fresh, wet snow would obliterate all traces of the awakening. The snow would freeze over, and its crust would be laced with glistening ice particles. Then another thaw, and more talk of gardens, and vague conjectures about the spring as though it were a season which would always linger distantly in the future.

In late February Stumpy Telsa came to see John Abbott. Sitting at his desk, he watched her enter the store and shuffle down the aisle, moving cautiously to permit the full recoil of her wooden leg. He and Stumpy Telsa would make a good pair, he mused. They were both old, and they were both crippled, and their usefulness to the town was about finished. How nice they would look, walking down the street together, dragging their crippled legs behind them, chattering softly to each other of those remote days when they had possessed two legs.

She carried her inevitable satchel with her: more money to be invested. There was a business, he thought heavily. Year in and year out, in good times or bad, they could always sell love on Lower Street, and make a profit on it. They could strike a balance down there at the conclusion of each day's business, and know precisely where they stood. There was no capitalization, no amortization, no outstanding credit; none of the complicated nonsense of legitimate business except, perhaps, depreciation.

Well, he wasn't going to give her any more advice. On the day the Emporium had passed into receivership, he had sworn that he never again would tell his fellow citizens how to invest their money or how to spend it. All of the confidence had gone out of him. What right had he, who couldn't cope with his own difficulties, to advise someone else? People still murmured about the Elysium, still wondered at the Emporium, and now they were whispering about the bank. Let them murmur; let them wonder; let them whisper. Let them make their own decisions, and suffer for their own mistakes. He was through.

He would miss that ten per cent. of Stumpy's money, though. He had been using it these last two years to help pay the expenses of his boys who were in college. He had never quite been able to desert the boys, managing in spite of all disasters to send them something. Strange . . . he couldn't even remember the names of most of them. He had educated seventy-five, maybe a hundred boys. And he couldn't remember a single name, save those who were on his current list. Where were they now—all these boys? Out in the world, he supposed, accomplishing things, raising families, sending down roots in other communities. That was one of Shale City's fatal weaknesses, he decided: its best brains were always deserting it, leaving the town to vegetate in mediocrity. It would be pleasant to have had all the boys he had educated return to Shale City. They wouldn't have deserted him as quickly as the others. They would have formed a foundation upon which a real future might be built. But no. They were all gone.

"Hello," said Stumpy, sitting in the chair across from him with her usual disdain of ceremony, and patting the satchel which she had laid on the desk. "Got any ideas?"

He shook his head slowly.

"I'm all out of ideas, Mrs. Telsa. I—I'm not advising people any longer. I seem to have made such a fizzle——"

A troubled frown wrinkled her forehead.

"But I've got some cash here to invest," she objected strongly. "How am I to know what to do with it unless you help me?"

"I'm sorry," he said. "I'm sure you'll understand. I just can't go on advising people. A lot of them lost heavily by following my suggestions. I—I'm fighting so hard myself that I can't—I just can't accept the responsibility of advising others. Not that I wouldn't like to—but—well, I don't feel qualified any longer."

"Oh, I already know how I want to invest this," she countered. "I just want you to handle the deal for me."

"Well, if you've made up your mind, that's different. I—I'd be glad to help you. Tell me what I can do."

"I want," said Stumpy Telsa, "to invest this money in John Abbott."

For a moment he didn't say anything. The room was very quiet. Feeble sunlight was streaming in through the window: another thaw. Stumpy sat across from him, her eyes twinkling curiously.

"I—I guess I don't understand exactly what you mean."

"I'll explain," said Stumpy softly. "I know—how things are here. Oh, I get around enough to hear about everything. And what I don't get when I'm out comes to me down there. And I think it's a" —she paused, and then continued defiantly— "I think it's a goddam shame! That's what I think. This stinking damned town! Well, anyhow, I've got some money here that I brought for you."

"But—but—I can't take it. I really can't."

"Try and get out of it!" she gritted. "Listen here, John Abbott, it's time for you and me to talk plain English. I came to this rotten town twenty-seven years ago. I was just a chippy, see? That's all I am now. But when I came to you, you helped me. You've been doing it ever since. I was afraid of old age—afraid I'd be like so many old girls in the game. And I wanted to make sure, see? You gave me the best advice you knew. Most of it was good. You treated me just like I was anybody else. I've made money off you. You helping me. I don't have to worry now—ever. I'm fixed as long as I live. I've got maybe a hundred thousand dollars, all told. Nothing to bother me. And why? Because you helped me out. And there's lots of others in this rotten hole that are in the same boat, if they'd only admit it. You carried all of us along with you. Well, now that things are bum, I want you to know that Stumpy Telsa still holds with you. Understand? I want to make more money, too. And if I'm going to make more, I've got to put it in the surest proposition in Shale City. So I want you to take this— as a sort of personal investment. Me—Stumpy Telsa—I'm investing in you. See? No strings. You can't get out of it."

"But—I don't see how I can pay you back," he protested. "I—I couldn't honestly accept it. It's such a gamble—whether or not I'll come out on top. I'm almost—finished, you see. Getting kind of old—and, who knows how things are going to end?"

"You had enough guts to bet everything you own on your come-back, didn't you?" she asked. "Well, then, I've got enough guts, too. If it wasn't for you, I'd never have this dough. I don't care when you pay it back. Sometime, if you can, you will. I don't even care if you pay it back or not. It—it's just something I've got to do." She paused a moment, and then went on eagerly. "I wouldn't tell a soul. I promise. But I'd like to be able to think that I—well, that I paid John Abbott back a little for what he's done for me. I mean it. Why—I won't even let my girls go into any other store but the Emporium. No, sir. The first one I catch anywhere else gets kicked to hell out of town. You bet."

It was very confusing. He sat and looked across at her. She was an old woman. Almost as old as he, it seemed.

"How much have you?" he asked faintly.

"I've got twenty thousand dollars here in this satchel."

He started. Twenty thousand—God, what a lot of money!

"Where—how did you manage to get so much in these times? That's an awful lot, Mrs. Telsa."

"Oh, I've been selling a little here and a little there. A few bonds and such. I got it easy enough. And I won't miss it, neither. Why, I own my own house, and I've got a little income, and I'm never going to have to worry as long as I live. I have you to thank for that."

He stood up suddenly, and began to hobble back and forth across the floor, while Stumpy Telsa watched him intently. He couldn't take this money. It wasn't his. He might never be able to pay it back. He was John Abbott. It was his job in this town to give out money—not to take it. Twenty thousand dollars was a lot of cash. What a load it would be off his mind to have twenty thousand dollars right now! The bank——

But, of course, he wouldn't take it. It wouldn't be right, even though the satchel was right there on the desk, with twenty thousand dollars in it.

She said that if it hadn't been for him she would never have had it. Perhaps she was right. She had enough so that she would never need to worry—all because he had helped her through the years with his advice; because he had given honestly and freely of the best that was in him. She had profited from his knowledge of things. Well, maybe so. He had explained to her that he might never be able to pay it back—that it was a gamble, such a desperate gamble. She seemed to understand that. Oh, God, should he take it or not? Twenty thousand dollars. He needed it so badly. There was the bank——

He sat down finally, and looked across at her.

"I—I'll take it," he said huskily.

She nodded with satisfaction.

"I'll give you my note."

"No—no notes," she said brusquely.

She opened the satchel and withdrew a fat sheaf of banknotes. She pushed it across the desk. Then she arose.

"I—I don't suppose there is any way on earth I can thank you," he said brokenly. "I never thought it would come to—to——"

"Listen, Mr. Abbott," she said gently, "when I got your cheque for the loss on my Elysium stock, I said to myself, 'One day I'll pay John Abbott back for that.' And so I have. And if I hadn't—why, I'd just never have been a.le to live with myself. That—that's all. You're a fine man, John Abbott. It's worth twenty thousand dollars—just to have known a man like you. There aren't—many. That's all . . . ."

She hobbled to the door.

"I—I'll pay you back just as soon as I can," he said, staring at the money. "I—oh, I'll pay you back, Mrs. Telsa. I swear to God I will——"

But she was gone. . . .

He took the money over to Gerald, and told him to use it where it would do the most good. Gerald was surprised, and wanted to know where he had got it. But John Abbott wouldn't tell him. He said just to use it to strengthen the bank. He was worrying a lot about the Shale City National these days.

XIII

LATER in the spring, when the snow had almost melted and the lower reaches of the mountains had changed from sheer white to a clean, intense blue, Violet Budd paid a visit to the donor of the swimming pool. John Abbott spied her before she reached the stairway. He had little else to do these days but to pass the long hours gazing out over the store, observing those who came and went, trying from his exalted position to see what they purchased.

So Violet Budd was after him again, eh? Well, if it was money, she would be disappointed. If it was some donation from the store, he would turn her over to Sol Grunner. Now that he was unable to contribute to Violet Budd's activities, he felt somehow that it wasn't necessary for him to be so elaborately civil to her. As he watched her panting ascent of the stairs, he was amazed to discover that he really detested the woman; that he always had detested her. How had he managed to be so polite all these years when he loathed her so completely? Well, he would be very blunt now. He was no longer the arbiter of good and evil and economic justice in this town. He didn't have to conceal his feelings from anyone.

When she entered his office, Violet Budd wasn't smiling. Her face had a fixed and pious expression, and her nostrils quivered gently as though a bad smell had just assaulted them. A sure sign, thought John Abbott, that she was after money. Why should he sit meekly and listen to her laments? He would cut her off at the outset.

She said "Hello, Mr. Abbott," and he said "Hello" not at all warmly. She took a deep breath, and then, while she was on the verge of speech, John Abbott spoke up in a tone which surprised even himself.

"If it's money, Mrs. Budd," he said, "I'm afraid I can't do a thing. I've been forced to cut down on all my charities."

Violet Budd surveyed him with mild astonishment.

"I'm sure, Mr. Abbott," she quavered resentfully, "that it isn't money I came about. It is something else."

"If it is a donation from the store, you'll have to see Mr. Grunner. He is in charge of that end now."

"No," said Violet Budd grimly, "it isn't a contribution, either."

"Oh!"

She had stolen his fire. He sat submissively and waited for her to speak.

"I am starting," said Violet Budd with a determined up-flip of her bosoms, "a drive against Lower Street. We are going to run those women out of Shale City. I tell you, Mr. Abbott, you don't realize——"

"But I thought you started a drive every year about this time," he interrupted. "Sort of an annual event like spring house-cleaning and—er—measles."

He couldn't believe his ears. That he had said this thing! He was nervous. That was it. He was very very nervous, and in consequence, he was insulting Violet Budd. He felt that he was going to say something even worse if she didn't leave him alone. He found himself these last few weeks doing and saying very peculiar things. It was his nervousness. Nervousness about the bank. That was what Dr. Lawrence had said, anyhow. He was so upset, said Lawrence, that small matters irritated him. He must try to hold his nerves in check. He must laugh or be rude or be anything but angry. That explained things, he supposed. He was being deliberately rude to Mrs. Budd; and if his soul were at stake, he couldn't be otherwise.

After recovering from her astonishment at his outburst, Violet Budd bestowed a grim smile upon him. "I always try, Mr. Abbott," she said, "to be persistent in good works. It is a command too few—too few, I must repeat—obey. I am always warring against Lower Street. But this time it will be a war to the finish. We have discovered the influence which has protected it all these years. And we are going to destroy the influence as well as the houses."

"Fine," he said, awed a little at his previous sarcasm. "Fine, fine, fine, fine!"

She looked across at him curiously. She had never seen him this way before, although she had heard rumours. Yes, he was cracking, all right.

"Before I go any further in the campaign," she continued, ignoring his almost hysterical enthusiasm, "there is one point which must be settled. It is a very serious thing, Mr. Abbott, and I am willing, to give you the benefit of the doubt."

"*Me* the benefit of the doubt?"

That buzzing was filling his head again. Good heavens, how angry he became at trifles! He mustn't become angry. He must laugh. But he couldn't laugh right in her face. What was she giving him the benefit of the doubt for? What on earth had he done to her?

"Yes," said Violet Budd firmly. "There is a strong report, Mr. Abbott, that you are in league with Lower Street—that you finance the houses down there."

She was staring right through him now.

"That I *what?*"

Violet Budd nodded her head vigorously. "Just that. This Telsa woman has been seen in your office on and off for years. She was here no less than two weeks ago. It has got to stop. All these years you have been flaunting the efforts of decent womanhood in Shale City to clean up that rotten condition down there. If you don't withdraw immediately we mean to take some action on the matter. I have been delegated to warn you never to be seen again with Stumpy Telsa. The Christian womanhood of——"

"I'm beginning to see," he said softly. "You think that I am the power behind the throne of prostitution in this city. Is that it?"

"I regret to say that it is, Mr. Abbott. This woman has been seen frequently in your office. And what is more, *she has been seen to pass money to you!*"

So that was it! Some customer had noticed Maria Telsa give him money; some customer, standing there by the half-opened door. Violet Budd knew that he was about finished. She knew that he would never in the future contribute as handsomely to her charities as he had in the past. So she had decided, since he was no longer useful, to make him the victim of her crusade. How could he ever explain Stumpy giving him money? Well, to hell with them! He wouldn't explain. But he mustn't get angry. He must keep his temper. He mustn't let that buzzing get too loud.

"Suppose I told you," he said at length, "that all the money I have contributed to your charities came from Lower Street? That would make it tainted money, wouldn't it? Thousands of dollars of it, over the course of years—all tainted. If you knew this to be the truth, would you return that tainted money?" He paused, and gazed earnestly at her. "Because a proposition like that would interest me very much right now."

She stared at him in bewilderment.

"Do you realize what you're saying, John Abbott?" Her voice was a frenzied hiss. "Do you realize that you're confessing? Oh!—and all these years I have thought that you were a decent man! Wait until the women of this town find out!"

He leaned across the desk toward her, and spoke very softly.

"Dear Mrs. Budd," he said, amazed at the sound of his own words, "I have been wanting to tell you a few things for a long while. For fifteen or twenty years you have been coming up here for advice. And now you are going to get some more. Listen very carefully. You should tidy up a bit, Mrs. Budd. That's the way for you to whip Lower Street. And you should reduce. You are awfully fat—almost greasy. You couldn't arouse the—the beast in any man. I have no passion when I look at you. Your husband has no passion when he looks at you. No one has any passion when he looks at you. That is why your husband goes down on Lower Street when he is in town. He can't stomach you, Mrs. Budd. So he goes down to Stumpy Telsa's place. You are sour and righteous and you sweat too much. Naturally you are jealous of Stumpy Telsa and her girls. They have stolen your husband from you. He prefers one of them to his wife—Clem Budd does. And that doesn't speak at all well of——"

"*Mr Abbott!* I won't listen! This is the most insulting thing I ever heard in my life. I—I'll ruin you for this, John Abbott!"

"I'm trying to insult you, Mrs. Budd." His voice was quivering, but he fought to keep his self-control. For the moment it seemed that all his troubles had come from her, and that all his bitter resentment was centred against her. "I'm glad that I have succeeded."

The words were flowing out of his mouth without the consent of his mind. It wasn't he speaking at all. It was someone else. John Abbott would never have dared.

"I am going to make a confession to you, Mrs. Budd," he continued. "I am the vice baron of Shale City. I own every house in town. Yes, ma'am! I own great strings of them all over Colorado. I've got rich off them. I'm known everywhere for my choice in whores. I always get young, pretty ones—the ones who chase your husband out of their rooms with hair brushes. They are keen smellers, all my girls. They have sharp noses. They catch that awful odour of cologne which smells up you and your house. They smell it on Clem Budd, and they chase him out of their rooms!"

Oh, this was appalling! He seemed to be sitting apart, thinking his own thoughts, while his voice rolled on and on, calmly, dispassionately, uttering words that he never had spoken before in the presence of a woman. He was listening to himself with avid interest, curious to hear every monstrous word of his denunciation. It wasn't natural. Something was wrong with him. And still he kept on talking. ...

"All these years, Mrs. Budd, you've been taking tainted money from me. Think of it! And all these years I have been sitting here behind my desk, watching you when you talked with me. And do you know what I have been thinking? I have been thinking that I should like to kidnap you, and put you in my Denver house—my big one in the basement of the capitol building. I would set you up on a pedestal in the front room—a stout pedestal—and make you stand there while my girls studied you very carefully. Then I would tell them that I wanted them to be everything that you were not, and to be nothing that you were. That's my way of telling you I wouldn't take ten of you for one Stumpy Telsa, and that I want you to get out of my office and stay out for ever and ever and ever. Get out! *Get out, I tell you!*"

She gave a subdued little gurgle, and galloped through the door. He sank back in his chair. He was trembling violently. Sweat stood out all over his face. But he hadn't had the stroke. No—he hadn't had it. He had let off steam, just as Lawrence had told him to. And he had been fairly calm, until the very last.

He was a little frightened. What was coming over him? Why did he say these things?—things he had never thought of before, coming to his lips, tumbling out as though some malignant stranger had entered his body. He had dreams lately, too, and in them he was constantly denouncing people. But to have said such things to Violet Budd! She would rush out and tell the whole town he was crazy.

Well, maybe he was. That bank. . . . Oh, dear God, whatever was going to happen to the bank? That was what made him this way. That was why he acted like a crazy man. How was he ever going to pull out of this mess? Everything led back to it; all his hopes were tied to it; everything converged upon it. What under heaven was to become of the bank?

The telephone jangled. It was Gerald speaking.

"Harry Twinge is over here," said Gerald, talking into the mouthpiece very softly. "He and his two daughters have savings accounts—total of four thousand dollars. He wants to draw it all out, and I'm stalling him. I'm sending him over to you. He always thought the sun rose at your word. Now try every way possible to ease him. He's badly scared. Heard a lot of rumours. You understand?"

Yes, he understood.

The bank!

He tried to forget Violet Budd and to gather his thoughts for Harry Twinge.

XIV

FOR days there had been a gradually increasing drive against the Shale City National Bank. It had started almost before anyone had been aware of what was happening. Someone had entered the bank casually enough to withdraw an account, and no one had given any thought to the matter. A couple of accounts had slipped out the following day, and two or three the next. It had started as simply as that; and now it had reached such devastating proportions that no one knew where it would stop. Old customers, men who had borrowed from the bank for years, who had found the institution eager to back their judgment, to help them through lean seasons—now they entered it with grim, frightened faces and demanded their money.

It was something which the bank could not fight, because it was a condition the bank could not admit. It required only a word, a gesture, a murmur to fan the smouldering embers of distrust into an open conflagration which would run through the whole Colorado Valley, hurling a disorganized mob against the handsome marble entrances of the Shale City National. There was nothing to do but smile, and pass out the money, and wonder how long the bank could withstand the siege before it toppled.

There had been some trouble in Michigan, and then, like a malignant cancer, it had spread out into other states. Great cities and vast stretches of farmland were in a state of total financial paralysis. No one knew where the next blow might come, or, indeed, cared, so long as his own funds were converted into cash. The affair was so intricate that no one pretended to understand it. News of the terror reached Shale City faintly, as a rumour of pestilence to come, as the murmur of an advancing hurricane, as an apparition of death itself sighing and shuddering as it hurried westward.

Gerald Abbott had sent call after call to the Federal Reserve System for cash with which to meet the constantly increasing demand. He had received some assistance, but not nearly enough. Each day's balance totalled less than the day which had gone before. Credits had been called in, securities had been sold, applications for safe and necessary loans had been rejected. And still there was doubt that the Shale City National could survive the crisis.

That was a strange thing, too; for the Shale City seemed to be suffering more withdrawals than the Farmers'. The Shale City had been the progressive bank of the town. It had handled the majority of the business, distributed credit, financed constructive enterprise, loaned its funds whenever it seemed that a loan would benefit the community. Now it was paying the price of its generosity. The Farmers' Bank, on the contrary, had gained a reputation for niggardliness. Even in good times it had clung tenaciously to its funds, playing the game cautiously, demanding what seemed exorbitant security. Now it inspired more faith than its larger and more powerful rival. People liked stingy banks during a panic, and generous ones when prosperity was riding through the streets.

But the Shale City National was sound. John Abbott assured himself of that fact a thousand times a day. The bank was sound. It was sound, sound, sound. Its loans were all fully secured; it had been honestly managed; it had set its eyes steadily upon the future, and it had built for that future. It owned land alone to pull it through the crisis—if it could get anything for the land. It owned ranches, houses, business, sheep, cattle, dry goods, groceries, stocks, bonds— and still people were afraid of it. Still they were undermining it, driving viciously away at its foundations, pulling great blocks out of its masonry—unconscious that if it fell it would bury them all beneath its debris.

John Abbott was thinking about these matters when Harry Twinge loomed nervously in the doorway.

"See here, Mr. Abbott," said Harry Twinge, walking jerkily across the room, "I go over to the Shale City to get some cash, and Gerald won't give it to me. I don't like that. He told me to come over to see you. I don't like that either. I've got some money over there, Abbott, and I want it. I want it right away, too."

It was the first time within his memory, John Abbott mused, that Harry Twinge had failed to say *Mister* Abbott.

"Sit down, Twinge. I want to talk to you."

"Well—I'm in sort of a hurry. What do you want to talk about?"

"Now, sit down, Twinge," persisted John Abbott soothingly. "Don't worry about your money. If you want it, I'll see that you get it. Sit down and let's have a chat."

Harry Twinge sat down reluctantly.

"Now let's think this thing out clearly. Are you afraid of the Shale City Bank?"

"Well...."

"Do you think anyone in the bank is dishonest or likely to steal your money?"

"No, not exactly that. But——"

"Then what troubles you, Twinge?"

"Well, Abbott, it's just that I need the money, you see."

"Got a deal on, Twinge?"

"Well—no. But I just like to have a little money handy, where I can get it if I do need it."

"Um-m. And you think if you leave it in the bank you won't be able to get it, eh?"

"Well," flared Twinge, "judging by this, no. Having to come over here to talk about getting my own money!"

"Twinge, do you trust me?"

"Well, I suppose I do, Abbott. But that's nothing to do——"

"Oh yes, it has. Because I'm going to tell you something. That bank is solid. It is as solid as the rock of Gibraltar. It has the best sort of security for its loans. But like any bank, it cannot be a hundred per cent. liquid. No bank in the United States could pay its depositors, provided they all made their demands at the same time. It would have to close up."

"Oh, I understand all of that, Abbott. But——"

"Just a minute, Twinge. Let us suppose that the Shale City should find that all of its depositors demanded payment at the same time. It would, of course, close its doors. And what would happen then? Why, it would quietly liquidate its holdings—sell all its securities. By the time it had done that, it would still have enough to pay off a hundred per cent. The only harm would be the inconvenience to its depositors. So if the bank were to close to-morrow, there would be no cause for alarm. Don't you understand?"

"I'm not so sure, Abbott. It's my money, and I don't see why——"

Here, thought John Abbott, was the man who came to him twice a year and said "Yes, Mr. Abbott," or "That's what I think, Mr. Abbott," or "You're right, Mr. Abbott."

"Listen, Twinge," he pursued. "Please listen closely. I've given you advice ever since you started in business here. Twice a year regularly you come to me, and I tell you what to do. It has usually been good advice, hasn't it?"

"Well, I suppose it has, all right."

"And that bank has loaned you money year in and year out,

Twinge. It has enabled you to discount your bills when you were hard-pressed. It loaned you the money to put up your new building. Every time you came to it, you got what you needed. Is that right?"

"Oh, yes. But then you knew I was reliable."

"Precisely. And you know, Twinge, that I am reliable. And I tell you this: leave your money in that bank. Don't become frightened at rumours. By leaving your money there you are helping a whole town. I promise you that it's safe. I pledge everything I have that when you really need your money, you can have it instantly. It is safe—absolutely safe."

Harry Twinge thought for a moment. A medley of emotions passed over his face.

"I realize all that you say, Abbott. But I can't afford to think of the town. I can't risk losing that money. I'm sorry you put it the way you have. But—well, I still want my money."

John Abbott sighed.

"Let me put it another way, Twinge. You and I are old friends. We have been friendly competitors for years. We have always trusted each other. I have never violated your confidence, and you have always come to me when you were in trouble. I am going to tell you this confidentially, Twinge. Not to be repeated to a soul. The Shale City is in difficulties. We are solid, but the demand for cash exceeds our supply. Your money is perfectly safe, but it is difficult to make it immediately available to you. Let me ask you, then, as an old friend—and remembering my pledge that you won't lose a dime—to let your money stay where it is until things get better."

Harry Twinge stared down at his vest. "I can't do it, Abbott," he muttered. "If the bank's in bad shape, all the more reason I should get my money out. You—you can't expect me to stick with a proposition like that. I thought all along it was in a fix! Now I know. And I want my money, John Abbott. I want it right away. If you don't let me have it, I'll——"

"Then you refuse—you refuse this first favour I've ever asked of you?"

"Of course I do. It ain't reasonable. You can't expect me to——"

"All right, Twinge." He shrugged his shoulders helplessly. "Go over and get your money. Gerald will give it to you. It—it's almost worth four thousand dollars to know what kind of a rabbit you are. Just to know what a dirty little coward you really are."

He mustn't let go, he told himself. He mustn't act as he had with Violet Budd. He must keep his head. He must speak precisely—very calmly.

"Now get out of here, Twinge, my good friend," he concluded, "and never show your face again. Go on."

Harry Twinge didn't say anything. As he started for the door John Abbott remembered something which until this moment he had forgotten.

"Oh yes, Twinge. Wait a minute. When you get that money, you'd just as well take it home and put it under the mattress for the burglars. Because the Farmers' won't touch it."

Twinge stopped as though someone had tipped him with a bullet. He turned round slowly.

"That's right, Twinge." John Abbott was chuckling now. That was the thing to do—laugh. Lawrence had said so. "That's right, because I'm going to telephone Frank Sloan and tell him not to take it. And he won't, either. You see, I saved the Farmers' from closing here about three or four years back. Didn't know that, did you? They were in a bad way, and I saved them. Frank Sloan is my friend. He'll do what I ask. So go ahead and get your money out of the Shale City. And keep it!" He reached for the telephone. "Want to hear me call Frank?"

Harry Twinge didn't say a word. He stood in the middle of the office like a man hypnotized, and heard John Abbott explaining the whole situation to Frank Sloan. The owner of the Emporium ended by saying: "And so, just as a favour to me, Frank, I'd appreciate it if you'd refuse to do any business with Twinge until I give you the word. O.K.?"

There was a brief silence. Finally John Abbott heard Frank Sloan's voice, low and ingratiating, at the other end of the wire.

"Why, Abbott—I don't hardly see how we can do that. You see, nobody can afford to turn down an account that size these days."

"Oh, I know, Frank." Chillness ran through him. He wished suddenly that Twinge would leave the office. "But I'm asking this just as a temporary favour. A personal favour. You remember I've switched some pretty big stuff your way when you needed it."

"I appreciate that all right, Abbott. But this is different. Times aren't what they were then. You really weren't taking any risk. Now it's every man for himself. I don't mean to sound ungrateful. After all, you did ease things up a bit over here. But nobody knows where this'll end, Abbott. We're taking every dime we can lay our hands on. If

Twinge comes over, naturally we'll take his money too. It's just as I said—every man for himself at this stage of the game. Sorry, but——"

The buzzing in his head was so loud that John Abbott couldn't hear the rest of what Frank Sloan said. He sat there at his desk and chattered helplessly into the transmitter. He talked until he was exhausted—a thin, bitter, vindictive monologue. When he stopped for a moment to listen, he realized that there was no one at the other end of the line. Frank Sloan had hung up. Frank Sloan, who had declared with tears in his eyes that he would sacrifice his last dime to repay the favour John Abbott had done for him—he had hung up the receiver while John Abbott was talking.

He glanced around the office miserably. Twinge was gone. He had heard, and had understood that Frank Sloan had refused. So he had scooted out, and probably was at the Shale City right now clamouring for his money. Oh, God!—this hurt. There was no use pretending any longer that it didn't. It was as humiliating as though Frank Sloan and Harry Twinge had spat in his face. Nothing was to be gained by hating them or swearing at them or fighting back at them. All he could do was to sit here at his desk, impotent and old, and watch them betray him.

What had Dr. Lawrence said? Just to laugh things off. Yes, of course—to laugh it all off. If he could laugh now, it might save him. The whole world was disintegrating before his eyes. His head seemed to swell as though scorching air were being pumped into it, and the buzzing was so loud he couldn't identify any exterior sound. He broke suddenly into such gales of mirth that Phil Haley, passing by, glanced uneasily into the office.

John Abbott told Phil Haley to go on about his business. Nothing was the matter. He was just laughing.

XV

WHEN the strange fit of laughter had passed, John Abbott looked at his watch. It was eleven-thirty. He arose from his desk and walked to the window, from which he could see the Main Street entrance of the bank. Perhaps fifteen people were clustered around its plate-glass doors, giving him a hint of the crowds that clamoured within.

Thank God it was Saturday. Another half-hour—no, another twenty-eight minutes now—and the bank could close its doors until Monday morning. But Monday morning. . . .

Although he was positive that the bank could endure the strain until noon, he stood rigidly by the window, watch in hand, as the deadly minutes passed. He saw old friends across the street—old friends entering the bank, and then leaving it hurriedly. Another thirteen minutes . . . ten . . . six. He had never known time to pass so slowly. If it had maintained this pace through the years of his life, he would now be either a young man strong enough to fight the thing that was threatening him, or an old man wise enough to thwart it. But time had always passed too swiftly and now—three more minutes—it was passing too slowly.

The glass doors swung shut. John Abbott tottered back to his desk. As he sank into his chair a feeling of delicious relief swept over him. He realized suddenly how tired he was. He doffed his spectacles, folded his arms upon the desk, and nestled his head in the little hollow they formed. He went to sleep.

He was awakened by a blare of bugles. For a moment it seemed as if he might still be dreaming. But the sound repeated itself, swelling triumphantly through the thin door that separated his office from Phil Haley's. He glanced at his watch. It was well after one. The bank had been safely closed now for over an hour. Thank God the bank was tight-shut until Monday. But this music. . . .

Then he remembered. It was Inauguration Day. Strange he had forgotten it. They were making Mr. Roosevelt the thirty-second President of the United States. The very thought of a Democrat in the White House made John Abbott shudder. He was willing to concede that things had gone very badly under the Republicans. But if

Herbert Hoover had been unable to stem the tide, what could one expect from the Democrats who were notoriously frivolous and full of bad logic?

The full significance of the event which was occurring crashed down upon him. Regardless of his wishes, Mr. Roosevelt was going to be President. Since John Abbott was very human, and therefore incapable of giving up hope entirely, he toyed with the absurd thought that perhaps Mr. Roosevelt might be able to do something after all. He *had* to believe in some one. . . .

He listened to the stirring strains of band after band as it passed the reviewing stand two thousand miles distant. *Hail to the Chief! Hail to the Chief! Hail to the Chief!* Unconsciously John Abbott thrilled to the thought of marching Americans, of indomitable Americans passing their chosen leader, and still able, out of the depths of their hopeless bewilderment, to summon that stirring salute.

He moved to the door and opened it an inch or two in order that he might hear more clearly.

"And here comes the Governor of New York!" The announcer's, voice was sharp with excitement. "The car is passing the reviewing stand. But wait! Governor Lehmann is not in the car! Governor Lehmann is not in the official car of the State of New York! He is represented by two aides. Governor Lehmann was called back to New York by aeroplane earlier in the day to proclaim a banking moratorium for the nation's financial centre. His two aides salute the President. The President waves his hand to them. He is nodding now—no, he is shaking his head!

"What an impressive sight, ladies and gentlemen! As the official car of the State of New York passed the reviewing stand, Governor Lehmann was represented by two aides, the Governor himself having flown to New York earlier in the day to issue his bank holiday proclamation. When the two aides saluted the chief executive, President Roosevelt merely waved . . . and shook his head. The most dramatic moment of the review, ladies and gentlemen . . . the President shook his head. . . ."

John Abbott closed the door and moved haltingly back to his desk. *The President shook his head.*

He saw it all now: he realized that he was lost: he understood for the first time that everything he cherished was lost with him. The new keeper of his destiny was merely another man, a man like himself, a man who could doubt, a man who could regret, a man who could shake his head.

The President shook his head.

John Abbott fell to chuckling again, just as he had after Harry Twinge's departure. He chuckled all the way to the Shale House that night. He hobbled down Main Street, always waiting for his crippled leg to catch up with him, chuckling to himself.

The President shook his head.

One or two who passed closely enough to hear him, stopped for a moment to stare. What did the old man find so funny? You'd think that with all this bank trouble everywhere it would take a pretty good joke to make him laugh like that. Especially with the Shale City National on his hands. There had been a strong rumour all morning that the bank was in serious trouble. The old man himself was supposed to have told someone. Yet here he was, walking down Main Street, chuckling as he went. It beat all how some people could. . . .

The President shook his head.

John Abbott broke into silent laughter at little intervals all through dinner, and he was smiling broadly when he hobbled upstairs and undressed for bed. But he couldn't go to sleep. He lay for five hours in a coma of despair, and then got up resolutely and put on his clothes again.

The time was three-fifteen. He walked through the Shale House lobby without even awakening the slumbering night clerk. He walked out into the deserted little canyon of Main Street. He walked by the Shale City National, by the Shale City Building and Loan, by the Elysium, by the Emporium. He walked out North Fifth Avenue, and passed the great square house that was no longer his. He walked through Abbott Park and under the white arched walls of the swimming pool. He walked along Abbott Boulevard and lingered in front of the house in which Miss Septimus lived. He could remember the time when she did not live alone, and when the street was not called Abbott Boulevard. . . .

It was after six when he returned to his room and called Dr. Lawrence on the telephone.

"I can't go to sleep," he said to Lawrence. "I can't go to sleep, and I've got to. I can't stand being awake any longer, Lawrence. You've got to come here and give me something that will let me sleep!"

Dr. Lawrence came and brought some powders with him.

"Did you notice, Lawrence, that when Governor Lehmann wasn't in his car, the President shook his head?"

"Yes," said Dr. Lawrence. "Now you take these . . . that's the stuff . . . you'll be asleep in a jiffy."

And so he was. He slept dreamlessly through the most troubled Sunday Shale City had ever known. It was after midnight when he finally awakened. It was very dark, and a strange sentence, almost like the tag end of a dream, was running through his mind:

The President shook his head.

He stared up at the ceiling, up at the circles of heavy blue darkness which curled slowly before his eyes. The circles of darkness became an abyss into which he was sinking, and into which countless millions were sinking with him. That night, in his lonely bedroom in the Shale House, John Abbott realized for the first time that he belonged to a class, and that his class, like himself, was tottering into the outer darkness without an heir.

It was a strange thing to lie in one's bed in the midst of the night, and to have the tangled, tragic events of a year or two or three suddenly resolve into a definite pattern. He belonged to a class, and his class was vanishing. Its business men had resorted to bankruptcy. Its professional men had devoured their assets. Its salaried men were without salary. Its landowners had been dispossesed. A few of its members would survive; but for all practical purposes, it had disappeared.

It was beside the question to consider his own survival. He was finished. He was completely through. There was no chance for him to recover from the blows he had received. Even a return to prosperity could not save him, for the chain organizations would get him in the end, just as already they had taken the Elysium and the gas stations and all but one of the old grocery stores. This country was not the country of his youth, and it never would be. Something had happened. He could chart its course to his own satisfaction, but he couldn't find the reasons for it.

He turned resolutely upon his right side, and tried to go back to sleep. For weeks he had been thinking fiercely, and now he wanted dreadfully to forget. He wanted only to sleep. He was greedy for it.

He had almost accomplished his desire when the sound of distant shouting reached his ears. He raised himself on his elbows to ascertain the source of the cries as they drew steadily nearer.

"Extry! Extry!"

John Abbott strained for the next words. There hadn't been an extra in Shale City since the death of President Harding. The newsboy was in front of the Shale House now. His voice came shrilly through the room in which John Abbott lay half-raised in bed, listening.

"BANK HOLIDAY! BANK HOLIDAY! NATIONAL BANK HOLIDAY!"

For a moment he thought he was going to faint. Then the nausea was replaced by fear, so black and terrible that his whole body seemed paralysed. He lay frozen on one elbow, holding his breath until the newsboy's cry passed the hotel and faded into the distance. He heard his heart beating painfully against his ribs. Slowly he sank back against the pillow.

The impossible, the incredible, the unbelievable had happened. To-morrow not a bank in the entire United States would open its doors. That, and something more: it meant that the examiners would descend upon the Shale City National before it could re-open. It meant—oh, so many things. He wasn't certain the Shale City could pass an examination right now. He and Gerald had been working so desperately to get things straightened out over there. Now the examiners would come to pass inspection upon their work. And if they should find anything questionable about the diminished liquidity of the bank—if they should challenge the judgment which had passed upon this loan and that one—if in the end they should decide that the Shale City National was no longer fit to remain open!

A spasm of trembling seized him, so violent that his knee joints cracked against each other under the covers. He raised himself suddenly in bed and snapped the light on the night stand. For a moment he was blinded by the glare, but it was a relief from the menacing blue circles of darkness, from the visions of tight-lipped examiners searching through the records of the bank. His eyes fell upon a Gideon Bible which had rested untouched on the stand ever since his occupancy of the room. Some desperate inner need impelled him to take the book in his hands and turn it over speculatively. His mind screamed for relief from the horrible, gasping fear which had clutched it. He hadn't touched a Bible for a long, long while. . . .

He opened the book and placed his forefinger upon the centre of the page. As his glance slid along the finger, he noticed for the first time how large its joints were, how paper-thin and shrunken the skin between, how dead the nail, broad and flat, heavily ribbed. Then his eyes rested on the passage to which the finger pointed. He read it hungrily, as a man who has received some harsh and undeserved sentence looks for reprieve:

Howl, ye ships of Tarshish; for your strength is laid waste!

XVI

SO it finally had come to this! And this stricken creature, shivering about the focal point of the Shale City National Bank—this was the town he had built. For the first time John Abbott was able to see it in its true perspective.

There was nothing in the town; it was as hollow as a gourd. Its farmers were impoverished and its business men were bankrupt. Its industries had suspended operations and its banks were closed. Its young men were far away building up other towns and its substantial people were deserting. Each day, it seemed, saw the departure of some old-timer who had staked his fortune with the town when it was small, increased it as the place grew, and now found himself, after a lifetime of work, poorer than when he started. Those who remained went about pale-faced and wretched, despondent in the midst of a fertile empire. The courage had oozed out of them at the first sign of misfortune.

If the process continued, presently there would be no town at all. It was as though the earth had opened and swallowed itself, leaving Shale City suspended tragically in mid-air. What a dry, desolate, hard-bitten land this was: what an unpromising country in which to have one's roots!

The whole town huddled about the radio, listening to news flashes from the cities. There things were being decided; there Shale City's fate would be determined; there lay the power. The cities. And all along Shale City had thought itself sufficient unto its own needs, serene in its isolation, impervious to the silly occurrences which disturbed the outer world. But now . . . what was happening in Washington, New York, Chicago? What was Roosevelt going to do? When would the banks open? When would their money be released? What were all those mysterious college professors in the east going to do about this thing?

At night the people of Shale City solemnly sat down with *The Monitor,* reading every word about the money situation. After they had read, they smoothed the paper on their laps and stared out at the gathering dusk, wondering what it was all about. Querulous, irritable, panicky, they seemed deliberately to avoid John Abbott when he passed along the street: John Abbott, who had told them the future was going to be great. Great . . . yes, it was great all right!

All of his friends were out of town. Art French was in the eastern part of the state building fences for his campaign for the lieutenant-governorship. Stanley Brown was in California on a vacation. No one called to see John Abbott at the Shale House. No one invited him out to dinner, or for an evening of quiet, pleasant conversation. He was a banker. He was one of those fellows who had set themselves up as prophets of the new era. He was one of those go-getters who had misused the economic system until a whole nation was helpless and prostrate. They were quite done with bankers . . . and besides, it would be embarrassing to entertain the old man when the thoughts of both host and guest would be centred on the money down there in the Shale City National Bank.

His principal visitors were brisk, efficient gentlemen from the Federal Reserve System. They routed out the clerical force of the Shale City National and went through the vaults slowly, methodically, as detectives stalk a murderer. They were trying to find out whether or not the bank was safe, whether it should be permitted to continue as guardian of public money, whether it had been managed wisely and honestly. All of this in connection with the Shale City National—it was incredible!

The people of the town stared curiously through the broad windows of the bank as they passed. They were fascinated at the sight of the strangers within, bending over ledgers, sifting through portfolios, prying into the institution's most cherished secrets. The passers-by wished they knew what the examiners knew—they would have an earful all right. But no one knew what the examiners were discovering: not even John Abbott.

He wished the Shale City National were a state bank, because such institutions were being examined by state officials, and a great many political wires were being pulled. Officials in Denver were winking wisely at one another, planning to ignore the President's demand that no unsound bank should open its doors. Colorado had seen thirty-six of its state banks fail during the past three years. There were over a hundred left, and it was an open secret that most of them would resume business. There might be restrictions here and there, but they would open all right. There wasn't, it seemed, a really weak bank in the lot!

But the national banks were not so fortunate. It was no good appealing to a Federal examiner: no use trying to convert him to economic optimism. Federal examiners were a little like God. If the bank wasn't sound, it wouldn't open. All the agonies in the world couldn't alter that. They took no pride in the good name of Colorado. They were after facts, facts, facts. They had never heard of character as collateral. They wanted figures and percentages and statements of assets and totals worked out to the last thin dime. Everyone knew there would be some tightly closed national banks when the holiday was over. But what about the Shale City National? What about it?

John Abbott grew cold when he thought of the Farmers' and the Shale City National. Here was the Farmers', which everyone knew would be open on the appointed day; here it was, not nearly so large or so strong as the Shale City National . . . yet it would open. And if the unthinkable happened—if the Shale City National should be forced to remain closed—the comparison would be ruinous. It would never—even though it resumed business later—have the confidence of the town. And what would people say about John Abbott——?

The whole affair was a hideous injustice. The Shale City *had* to open. The town would never recover if it failed. Business men would be ruined; collateral would be sold; whole families would be impoverished. The Shale City was one of the strongest banks in Colorado, keystone to half a state; a big, fine, honest bank with marble entrances and five storeys of cream-coloured brick. Yet inside it tight-lipped men were going through its vitals, refusing to give even a hint of what they thought. John Abbott could watch them, but he had no way of knowing what conclusions they were reaching.

The day for re-opening approached. The examination of the Farmers' had been completed: it was as sound as a dollar. But no one knew anything about the Shale City National. The town sighed and murmured with rumours. A physical presence seemed to hover over the whole Colorado Valley, gnawing away at its morale. Why didn't they tell about the Shale City National? What was there to be so secretive about? Wasn't it their money? They wanted to know. Was Shale City going to open? And if it wasn't, why not? Who was responsible? Who had done this thing to them? Oh, God . . . .

The last day of the holiday arrived, and still the examiners would not commit themselves. It was the last day of creation for John Abbott. He stood trembling at the brink of chaos. He prayed that day: not consciously or formally; but nevertheless, he prayed. Oh, God, he thought—and that, he knew, was really a prayer—oh, God, let it open. It's got to open. Oh, dear God, please let it open. I can't stand it if it closes. It will hurt so many people. I've been honest—let it open. A lot has happened, and that is all right, but this would be too much. It must open. There is no other way about it. Merciful God, please help the Shale City National . . .

XVII

WHEN the store closed that evening, John Abbott went to Mrs. Alloway's for dinner, and then, after reading *The Monitor,* he limped along Main Street toward the Shale House. The lights in the bank were still burning. It was a terrifying sight—lights burning at night time in the bank, with strangers inside digging away at the books. The whole town knew. The whole town knew that on the very eve of re-opening the examiners were still down there at the Shale City National. Oh, God——

The Salvation Army was holding its service, ranged in a pious little semi-circle facing the kerb in front of Jimmy Garbutt's pool hall. The Army always conducted its meetings there, for it was considered the wickedest spot in town. In the old days it had been a saloon, with the rampant evil of its long bar spewing clear out into the street. Now its sin had lost dignity. Its bawdy years having ended when Violet Budd sent the liquor demon packing, the very worst which presently could happen within its walls was little more than a tedious anticlimax to the salty, sweaty, alcoholic robustiousness of its great days. The loafers who clustered about its entrance, listening good-naturedly to the Salvation Army corps, were a sorry enough lot, ill-dressed and determinedly addicted to the amiable vices of tobacco-chewing and lewd anecdotes.

John Abbott dreaded to pass through the little crowd, but he was tired, and to cross the street would necessitate many extra steps. So he braced himself and began to elbow his way among his smelly fellow citizens. When he was in the thick of it, Half-wit Sue, who lived at the Army Headquarters, accosted him with a demand that he buy a *War Cry.* He wished she had waited until he had passed Jimmy Garbutt's glass-canopied entrance. As it was, there was nothing to do but stand in the midst of the idlers and fish self-consciously for a quarter.

He heard Ralph Simpkins' high-pitched, wheedling voice, and turned for a moment to listen. Ralph Simpkins stood under the flaring gasoline torch with shadows sinking deep into his cheeks and pale promontories standing out above them. "O my friends," he chanted thinly, "Jesus loves yuh! O ye weary and heavy-laden—O ye hungry and tired and despised—can't yuh feel His arms about yuh? Can't yuh hear His voice calling yuh? Can't yuh sense His in-n-nfinite love encircling yuh? Can't yuh——"

There was a sudden flurry, and Ralph Simpkins' voice broke off abruptly. A young man had thrust him aside, usurping his position beneath the torch. The intruder was a burly youngster, no more than twenty, but he stood in his lumpy clothes like a battered old Job, staring with fierce eyes upon Jimmy Garbutt's collection of loafers.

There was a moment of breathless silence. The members of the Salvation Army glanced nervously at each other. They hoped for a testimony, but something told them that this young man was no casual convert. The idlers brightened expectantly, and two or three who had been inside Jimmy Garbutt's threshold stepped out to watch. John Abbott stood motionless, for it seemed to him that the youth was staring directly into his eyes.

"Who was this guy Jesus?"

Ralph Simpkins winced, and threw a sharp glance over his shoulder to his wife, who stood beside the bass drum. His wife, perceiving her husband's agitated eyes upon her, gazed upward into the night sky.

"Who was this guy Jesus?" came the challenge once more. Ralph Simpkins cleared his throat, as though about to answer. But the speaker answered for himself. "Just a bum—just a carpenter—just a guy who got a nutty idea and hoboed his way through the country telling about it! An' who followed him? Bums like you and me—loafers and tramps and down-and-out fishermen—guys who were sunk and knew it, and thought this Jesus had the right idea. Guys who *expected* something from him!"

John Abbott, at the mention of bums and tramps, shrank into the crowd, so that he could peer at the amazing spectacle from behind the back of a much taller man.

"An' what did he give 'em?"

Ralph Simpkins' wife finally comprehended the message in her husband's commanding stare. She lifted her stick and brought it down full force against the bass drum, which bore the red-lettered motto, "Blessed are the meek."

"What did he——" boom— "give 'em?" Boom . . . boom! The voice broke into a shout to overcome the reverberations of the drum. "He gave 'em lies! Lies and cheap tricks and phoney arguments! That's all. The same goddam lies that they've been hollering ever since. Lies to cheat us with—lies to rob us with—lies to starve us with—!"

Boom—boom—boom! "Everything he said they use against us——"

boom ... boom—"kids going hungry——" boom—"men shot like dogs——"
boom-boom— "Sacco and Vanzetti——" *boom*— "Mooney——" BOOM!

The speaker flailed his arms wildly in the air, pausing only long
enough to fling an occasional curse at Ralph Simpkins' wife and the
bass drum. Somebody in the crowd shouted "H'ray!" and from the
stricken cohorts of the Army there arose an answering "Praise Jesus!"
Half-wit Sue returned from her soliciting and threw herself at the trap-
drums in a perfect fury of sound. The cornetist struck up *Rock of Ages,*
but he was trembling so violently that the tune came only in reedy little spasms. "Give 'im a chanst!" howled the fellow behind whom John
Abbott had taken refuge.

The speaker's voice was scarcely audible above the tumult. The
white of his face was accentuated weirdly by the flaring torch. He spat
out his words as though he hated his audience and his helpless hosts
with equal ferocity. John Abbott stared at that grimacing face so
intensely that his eyes ached in their sockets. It seemed impossible that
one so young could have learned to hate as well as this youngster. The
ugly malevolence in the boy's glare sent little quivers of fear through
John Abbott's body. What—what was the fellow saying now . . . ?

"A swimming pool, huh? . . . you dirty cows! Who's got a right to
give you *any*thing? . . . Where'd he get his money?—from you! . . . an'
you go out an' swim in it! . . . well, you oughta have your guts pulled out
for it . . . an' him an' all his kind too . . . if you had any shame, you'd go
out an' spit on it—tear it down, smash it to pieces . . . that any man had
the gall to *give* it to you!"

The uproar from the two drums became almost infectious. The men
in front of Jimmy Garbutt's pool hall moved restlessly, as though they
wanted to escape the sight of that grotesque figure under the gasoline
torch—as though they had been confronted with some old sin, and were
hesitantly eager to deny its existence.

"Dogs!—Pigs—Dirty——"

The tirade broke off as suddenly as it had begun. Denny Shane and
Bill Corbin, policemen comprising the night beat, loomed beside the
youth. For a moment he stared wildly from one to the other. Then, in
a spasm of desperation, he sank his right fist deep into Bill Corbin's
stomach. Denny Shane came to the rescue of his colleague with a left
to the jaw which sent the speaker reeling backwards. He collapsed suddenly, his cheek bone striking against the head of the bass drum to send
out a final boom. When the two officers jerked him to his feet, the words
"Blessed are the meek" were smeared with blood.

Denny Shane and Bill Corbin dragged their prisoner to the sidewalk. As he touched the kerb he stiffened suddenly, like a man confronted with an audience before which he must put up a brave front. He spat two teeth to the sidewalk, and tossed his chin against his shoulder to wipe the blood from it. He was panting heavily, and his eyes darted from one man in the crowd to another. In spite of Bill Corbin's heavy grip, he managed to free one arm and lash out at the sky with a tightly clenched fist. As he made the gesture he raised his voice in a song which John Abbott had never heard before.

Arise, you prisoners of starvation!

It was the cue for which the Salvation Army had striven vainly ever since the intruder had pushed Ralph Simpkins aside. The cornet and trombone blared, the drums roared, and with one triumphant voice the Army answered song for song. By now the creator of the disturbance had started down Main Street with his captors, but his voice rang out with undiminishing vigour, intermingled with the hymn which Ralph Simpkins was leading.

John Abbott edged his way through the crowd and hobbled on toward the Shale House. He wanted to forget what he had seen, but he could not avoid hearing the songs:

Arise, you prisoners of starvation!
>   *. . . See the mighty host advancing,*
Arise, you wretched of the earth,
>   *. . . Satan leading on;*
For justice thunders condemnation,
>   *. . . Mighty men around us falling,*
A better world's in birth . . .
>   *. . . Courage almost gone.*
No more tradition's chains shall bind us,
>   *. . . 'Hold the fort for I am coming',*
Arise, you slaves, no more the thrall;
>   *. . . Jesus answers still;*
We want no condescending saviours,
>   *. . . Wave the answer back to Heaven;*
To rule us from a judgment hall!
>   *. . . 'By Thy grace we will!'*

When he reached the haven of his bedroom, John Abbott sat down weakly and tried to think. His crippled leg was quite motionless, but his good one trembled so violently that his heel against the floor sent out a nervous little tap-tap-tap. He tried to dismiss the whole scene from his mind, but it was no use. He could still hear that voice cursing him because he had given a swimming pool to the children of Shale City. He shook his head in bewilderment. He couldn't understand it. He simply couldn't make it out. That pool—he was prouder of it, now that the Emporium was humbled, than anything else. He went out on summer nights and watched the kids splashing, and felt somehow worthy of living. And the boy had urged them to spit on it!

His nerves were chattering and shrieking for relief. He jumped up suddenly and went into the bathroom to vomit. When he sat down once more, his whole body was sticky. Although his head whirled, he felt much better. And then, in a frenzy of fear, he saw the whole thing. Something must be done! This thing must be put down! It was too dangerous to dismiss. To-morrow he would do something about it. With people worried and hungry, there was no telling what they might do if this continued. He'd telephone Ed Haynes of the American Legion. He'd tell Ed what he had heard. It was a fight now; there was no escaping it. It was a crisis, as bad, maybe, as the War. It *was* war. He'd tell Ed Haynes all about it, because somebody must stamp it out. The American Legion must stop such things. The Legion . . . or the old Loyalty League. . . .

It was eleven o'clock when he heard someone knocking on his door. He hobbled into the tiny front room which adjoined his bedroom. The door opened. Gerald Abbott and one of the examiners walked into the room. Gerald's face was chalk-white.

"The bank will not be permitted to open to-morrow," said the examiner evenly. "We are not at all satisfied with things over there yet. We don't know, of course, whether there are any grounds for criminal prosecution. Perhaps not. Those Emporium notes . . . and others. We are waiting instructions from Denver. Meanwhile, you will not leave Shale City, Mr. Abbott. There—there may be some points you can clear up for us in the next few days."

XVIII

JOHN ABBOTT arose the next morning at dawn. He dressed, put on his great-coat, and walked out of the Shale House into the sunrise. He paused for a moment on the steps, glancing eastward where the first pastels of morning tipped the skyline of Shale City. There was the bank fringed with pink, and the Elysium facade glistening in the sun, and the Emporium flushing like a girl at the touch of her lover. And there were the other buildings, too, all of them sparkling in the dawn. He sniffed the March air. It was cold and bracing. He turned away from Main Street and set out toward the river.

He used to go down to the river frequently. He used to go down there with Donna Long. There was a deserted cabin by the river. An old woman had spent all of her life there, and they had found her dead one day close by it. No one had lived in it since. He was going down to the cabin by the river. He was going to spend the day there. He was going to run away from the angry, puzzled faces of Shale City, and have this day for himself down by the river in the old woman's cabin. To-morrow, perhaps, he would face the town. But to-day he would run away. He needed the rest. He needed the quietude.

It was a long walk, and the chill entered his withered leg. He crossed the railroad tracks. Someone from the cab of a wheezing locomotive waved at him. At length he found himself walking through the rambling little settlement of the river town. There were shacks sprawled all about, with the first hardy weeds defying the melting snow of their front yards. There were networks of clotheslines in back of the shacks, and forlorn outhouses with half moons cut high up in their walls, and slant-roofed chicken coops from which arose a strident crowing. A goat tethered beside its rough shelter and awake with the dawn baa-ed at him inquisitively, lifting its pink nose as he passed. A huge mongrel snarled at him from one of the battered front porches, and a very small dog rushed out ferociously to worry his crippled leg. He didn't pay any attention to them.

The old woman's cabin was somewhat apart from the rest of the shacks, but it was very close to the river. She had been a lover of solitude. Each springtime of her life the town had worried about her being so near to the rising waters. But the old woman had been a hardy soul: she had stayed grimly on. She had discovered the secret of how to live. She had lived down there and she had died down there, with the river and the willows and the cottonwoods and the chant of bullfrogs for companionship. She had fished for suckers in the river: and sometimes she had fished for salmon just below the sewer outlet, where they grew round and fat. The old woman had been dead for a long while. . . .

He came upon her cabin, rising crazily out of a clump of weeping willows. The door hung open on one hinge; the windows long since had been broken out. Now the cabin was a rendezvous for boys, who came there to smoke in solitude: and at night-time, perhaps, they came with girls. The trees about it were bare and naked, but the sap was rising in them. Wet, dirty snow huddled about their trunks; but farther out where the sunlight penetrated, the snow had melted. There the earth was brown and moist, and green things were beginning to nudge through it. Springtime always came to this place a little before it reached the better part of town.

Not forty feet from the old woman's door was the river, slipping along like smooth oil, slipping along like a flood of quiet thoughts, slipping and rustling through the bed it had carved out of the earth. John Abbott squatted in the doorway, his crippled leg stretched out before him, his back resting against the wall, and watched the river. It was beginning to rise a little. In another month or two it would rush by like a demented old man, carrying railroad ties and shingles and horses and cattle west-ward and southward on its angry crest. But now it was gentle, with the slant of morning sunlight sparkling on every ripple.

He sat there on his haunch, with the early sun playing over his chill old body, and watched the river, and thought about it. The old woman had been very wise. She had come down here by this broad river and she had sucked the strength out of it. She had lived a long life and a contented one, and she was as placid as the waters which passed her door. She let the years flow over her as the rocks under-neath permitted the stream to flow over them. And they found her dead one morning very close to the river.

She was a stout, tough, placid old woman because she saw no far-ther than the river. All the years of her life it slipped past her cabin, and she never saw beyond it. Even so, she must have seen a lot. Not alone the green miracles of growth, but the water itself, and the dreams of where it was going. It flowed on into Utah, and intermin-gled with the Green, and then, gaining speed, rushed toward the

Grand Canyon where it slashed its way fiercely through the bowels of the world. Once he and Ann had stood on a great height, and he had stared down into the Canyon, and had been appalled to think that the same waters which slipped through Shale City had achieved such a magnificent destiny.

One should get closer to the river. He would not go away for a while. Here he would spend his last day as John Abbott. To-morrow he would face them back there in the town, but he would not be John Abbott. He would be someone entirely different. He would be a stranger even to himself. He arose jerkily and stepped into the cabin. It had an earth floor, and on one side, built stoutly against the wall, was a bench on which the old woman had slept. There were windows on all sides, and sunlight was streaming through the open door. He would lie here on the earth floor, and follow the sun around, and no one could see him. Shale City would boil and bubble and curse about the bank, but he would be down here by the river in the old woman's cabin, with the sun streaming over him.

His coat was quite heavy. He buttoned it carefully, laid himself down gently upon the earth, and exulted in the faint warmth of the morning. He had been down by the river before . . . yes, he used to come down to the river often. One time he and Donna Long had come down in the summer, when it was hot and dry and the sight of so much water was a blessed relief. They had found a spot not far from this cabin . . . over to the left a bit and closer to the waters, where the willows were drooping heavily, green and luxuriant, bending down to touch the sweet clover and the earth vegetation.

They had lain down on their backs in that spot, and stared through the leafy willows, stared at the sky and the high white clouds, soaking up the warmth from above and the cool damp of the earth beneath . . .

Donnalong, it is warm and we've been walking a long while . . . loosen your dress and you will rest better . . . . How white your shoulders are, and how soft . . . It is pleasant here in the sunlight together . . .

Over thirty years ago. And they both had been quite young . . . so very much younger than now. Everything was young—the town and the valley and even the river it seemed. She lay there weeping in his arms, and he touched her shoulders lightly and comforted her. It was such a very long time ago . . .

Well, Donnalong, I am all finished now. It was too much for me. I fought, but I couldn't fight hard enough. I thought I had sunk the foundations clear to bed-rock, but the whole thing crumbled apart. Things you could never dream of happened, Donnalong, and I was swept down by them. It wasn't just something here in Shale City that finished me. It was something from the outside, creeping in, smashing in, roaring in on me until I was so confused that I lost my head. People I never heard of . . . things I had never suspected . . . because I thought Shale City had its own ways and its own life, and would remain unaffected. It was awful, Donnalong, to have someone thousands of miles away speak a word, and to watch the word travel everywhere carrying destruction with it. It was unthinkable, Donnalong, the thing that happened. You could never conceive it.

Well . . . they got me, Donnalong. All these things—these things which had nothing to do with Shale City—they finished me. The store is gone, Donnalong. I fixed it up so that you wouldn't recognize it, and now they have changed it again so that even I don't recognize it. They have taken it away from me. And the building and loan—it is finished too. It is still running, but it has no money. No one has any money. Even our bank has none. The bank is—closed, Donnalong. They came in and took it, and I didn't have a thing to say about it. And the fine theatre we built, they took that too. Why—they've taken everything.

And they're not through yet, Donnalong. I got mixed up with a woman, and that made them all laugh at me. I tried to sell some towels—just some towels—and got excited, and half of me stopped living. That made them feel sorry for me and pity me. I can only drag along now, Donnalong. But that isn't all. I think they are going to send me to prison. I am quite sure of it. I didn't expect the other things, but they came just the same. This will come too. They will put me in a witness chair . . . then they will have everything, Donnalong. They will have—everything.

O God, my dear, it all comes back to you. If you had stayed with me, this would not have happened. But you were tired, and you wanted a good long rest. All through the years that I've been fighting them, you have been resting. And I shall rest presently too . . . I shall rest. . . .

He fell asleep.

The sun moved out of the doorway, and cascaded through a window, touching only a part of him. The sun nudged the zenith, and the inside of the cabin was shaded and chill. The sun marched toward the western mountains, and drifted again through the windows. He slept all that while on the hard earth. He slept without dreaming. And when the whole sky was flaming over the Utah border, he awakened, and heard the rustle of the river.

He lay for a time, listening, and then he arose painfully. He hobbled to the doorway and looked eastward. White clouds caressed the mountain-tops, with fiery banners heralding their union. He went to a window and peered into the east. The long horizon was ablaze, with naked willows forming a grill in the face of the conflagration. The air was sweet and cool: although his body ached, his mind was young again. Why, he . . . he wasn't whipped yet. He wasn't too old. The river out there was much older.

He was thirsty for coffee. His throat was parched for want of it. In his mind's eye he beheld himself with a great tin can of steaming coffee tipped to his lips, while he threw back his head and drank gluttonishly. Very well . . . he would indulge himself. There was no harm in it. He would scout around and find some coffee. He brushed his coat, and stepped out of the cabin. He walked through the willows until presently he came upon a spongy path with a shack at the end of it. He knocked at the door.

A woman called out, asking who was there. He said it was someone who would like to have some coffee: he would pay for it. She loomed suddenly in the doorway, her face catching the rosy glow from the west, the black hairs of her chin and upper lip standing out like pig bristles. She wore an apron which was tied round her middle in such a fashion that it cut her great belly in half. He couldn't see the belt of her apron at all. It was hidden, buried in soft folds of fat.

She told him to come in. He entered, and followed her through a bare front room into the kitchen. A fire roared in an old wood-burning range. The lamp hadn't been lighted yet. The lids to the stove didn't fit well. They sent out cheerful red rims into the surrounding gloom. The old woman told him to sit down. She set up a great commotion as she walked. The whole kitchen trembled with her mighty footfalls. Soon she had a pot on the stove, and the fumes of coffee filled the air.

"You're John Abbott, ain't you?" she asked suddenly.

He told her he was.

"I thought so. I seen you on the street a couple of times. My name's Studen."

"It's odd I don't know you," he said. "I know everybody in Shale City. Have you lived here long?"

"Thirty-two years—right here."

"I usually know people who live in Shale City that long."

"You wouldn't know me," she said shortly. "I've always been able to get along."

He thought about that for a moment, and then her voice broke in upon his musings.

"I guess that's boiled enough—not very strong, though." She peered into the pot.

"It's all right," he told her.

She went to a cupboard and brought out a cup.

"If you don't mind," he interposed hastily, "I'd rather have it in a can. Have you"—what a crazy request this was!—"have you a large tin can I could drink it from?"

She stared at him for a moment. Then, without commenting, she brought forth a two-pound coffee can.

"This big enough?"

He nodded. She filled it, and handed it to him with a cupful of milk.

"Ain't got no sugar," she said briefly.

He poured the milk into the black liquid, and put the can to his lips. He took long, greedy swallows while she stared at him in bewilderment.

"Well, I never!" she said at length.

He didn't reply. He just kept on drinking the coffee.

"You be a banker, huh?"

"Yes," he said between delicious gulps.

"Well, I don't hold with bankers." She sat down as though for a long altercation, and shifted her stomach into a comfortable position.

"I'm sorry to hear that," he said.

"Strikes me they don't know their business none too well. Your bank's closed, ain't it?"

He nodded soberly. " 'S what I heard."

He sat the can down and looked at her curiously. "What would you suggest that I do—if I quit banking?" he asked.

"Oh," her voice was vague, "don't make a hell of a lot of difference. A body don't need much. Just a few things."

"What are they?"

"Well, you got to have a shack, and something to fill your belly, and somebody to go to bed with now and then. That's about all."

He nodded. "Nothing else?"

"Well, some folks wants more. Now take you. You did. You wanted banks and such-like. I just wanted a shack and some grub and my

old man. You had what you wanted, but you ain't got it now. But me—
I ain't never lost mine. Nobody else wanted to git it off'n me."

"Your husband living?"

"Uh-huh." She jerked her thumb toward the river. "Out there
ketchin' dinner."

"Does he—hold with bankers?"

"He holds with fishin'."

He arose to go. He handed her a half-dollar, and told her that he
was very much obliged. She invited him to come back sometime when
he was by. She would like him to meet Sim. Sim read a powerful lot
about bankers. Maybe John Abbott and Sim could have some right
smart discussions.

He said he was sure they could, and that he would come back
some time. Then he stepped out into the dusk.

He chose sparsely travelled streets, and finally arrived at the side
door of the Emporium. He paused there a moment, glancing up and
down the street. Over there was the bank, tall and pale in the twilight. It seemed just as real as it had been yesterday. There were no
angry crowds milling in front of it. Everything was calm. Everything
was just as it had been a year ago and a year before that, even if the
Shale City National hadn't opened.

Why . . . the town would survive this blow. The town would grow.
This was only a set-back which would endure for a little while, and
then be forgotten. Just as 1907 was forgotten. The shale would come
in some day, and the town would roar with factories and refineries.
This whole place fifty years from now, wouldn't be recognizable. That
was how much Shale City was going to grow. For he had sunk its
foundations deeply.

He stood there in the twilight, with the key in the lock,
and smelled the air. It was damp. A few clouds scudded along the
southern horizon, speeding in over Sawtooth Mesa. A faint wind was
coming up. . . .

XIX

THE fire alarm in Shale City had a piercing note which could be heard for miles up and down the valley. It screamed like a banshee: and whoever was awakened by it in the dark of night, and did not shudder slightly, could consider himself a very courageous person. To anyone within a mile or two of the fire station it seemed that the horrible lament was no more than an arm's length distant. Its piteous half-moan, half-screech could be heard even as far away as La Grange, sobbing off into a bare echo far up the canyon. To the realm of sound it was what a nightmare is to slumber, summoning to mind old fears, ancient tragedies, half-forgotten terrors that spring from the misty beginnings of evil.

At eleven o'clock that March night it emitted a series of sharp, disconsolate shrieks, with little pauses between, indicating that a fire had broken out in the first ward, which comprised the business district.

The people of Shale City sat up in their beds, listening to the desolate sound. And then, as it continued inconsolably, they dressed in whatever was at hand, and set out toward Main Street. A business building ablaze in the night was a sight not to be missed. It would be a relief, a thrilling climax to the bitter day which had faded out. A bank failure, and now a fire! They would not soon forget it.

As they ran toward the increasing glow, they met others who had preceded them, and now were returning to rouse their families so that they would not miss the spectacle.

"It's the Emporium!" they yelled in answer to excited inquiries.

"Oh, my God, you never see such a fire. It's the Emporium, and it's going to burn clear to the ground!"

The news shuddered through the town like a pain.

"The Emporium!"

"It's the Emporium!"

"The Emporium has caught fire, and she's a goner!"

The conflagration must have been smouldering inside a long while, for by the time the fire department and the first panting citizens arrived, the whole roof of the store was belching yellow fire at the moon. Within ten minutes after the first alarm the street was packed so solidly that the fire brigade had difficulty getting at the blaze. Its tumult filled the air, and the crackling and popping sounded like firecrackers when one becomes extravagant and sets off a whole pack at once.

Merchants scrambled to the roofs of their stores and squirted water from lawn hoses over their tar-paper surfaces. The lingering sparks fell as distantly as two or three blocks.

Sometimes it seemed that flames had subsided, and a wave of "ohs" and "ahs" ran through the crowd like a ripple through water; but an instant later, looking high into the air, they could see great sheets of fire leaping above the black smoke mask. Then the smoke would be whisked by the wind, and Main Street for two or three blocks would take on the brightness of day. Detonations thundered through the heart of the building, as though sections of the roof or second floor had fallen in; and after the crashes there came a renewed roar, with the flames leaping higher against the sky, and growing hotter.

Foot by foot the crowd edged away from the blasting heat, until the streets were quite clear, and they were all pressing against the store fronts on the opposite sidewalk. The fire department played three hours over the roof, but the flames had too great a start. The Emporium was a big store, and it was on fire all over. From across the street they could see through its broken windows. They could see the lurid interior, with flames racing from counter to counter and section to section like greedy customers at a sale, eating away brutishly at show cases and shelves, devouring the wood, twisting the metal, melting the glass. It was even a bigger fire than the ice houses. . . .

Everyone in Shale City, it seemed, was there, watching the Emporium writhe and scream like a living creature as the heat seared through its bowels. And no one among them was unaffected by the sight. Each person, as he stared through half-closed eyes at the blazing pile, felt that the moment held some personal significance for him. The Emporium had been an institution as long as Shale City had been a town. Its regular growth had gauged the progress of this whole western country. It was something like the court-house and the city hall. It did not belong wholly to John Abbott: it belonged to Shale City, for it had been the hub, the very heart of this hard-won civilization. And now it was burning. . . .

There would not soon be another store like it. Never, perhaps, would there be a store as honest in its efforts to bring to Shale City anything that could be had even in a place as large as Denver. More than a few of the spectators knew that their baby clothes had come from the store. They had purchased wedding gowns there, and later, toys and books and perhaps a tricycle for their first-born. Many would have been deprived of warm clothing and dry overshoes during these past three years had it not been for the Emporium. And now it was burning. . . .

An epoch of Shale City was drifting with it into smoke against the sky. There would be other stores, but they would not be as friendly as this one had been. They would not be as anxious to employ widows as the Emporium had been, and they would not be as earnest in their endeavours to please the town. The new stores would let Shale City set the pace: but this old store, this dying store, always had snatched the lead from the town, marching sturdily in the vanguard while Shale City struggled and strained to keep up with it. This tortured building had been a part of them all—and the man who had built it . . .

Where was John Abbott?

The wind stirred, the flames leaped, and rumours ran through the crowd. They stood in excited little groups, their faces ghastly in the glare, their eyes fastened on the horrid beauty of the Emporium, and talked about John Abbott.

"It's just like I told my kid. He came home telling me about what John Abbott said in some speech at high school. It was John Abbott this and John Abbott that, and finally I said to him, I says: 'Jake, there ain't no man that's perfect. And John Abbott ain't any exception.' That's just what I told him. And I was right. Here he turns out to be just about the biggest crook in this part of the state. I always did think I was just as good as John Abbott, and now I figure maybe I'm considerable better. I ain't got no busted banks on my hands, anyhow. I don't go much for this gaddin' around and givin' stuff away. Say, where is the old man? Anybody seen him?"

Someone said that he was under arrest for wrecking the Shale City National, and had been smuggled away to Denver for trial. They were afraid, with folks around town feeling so ugly about the bank, that somebody might take the old devil out and string him up if the facts ever became known. Oh, nobody'd ever learn the truth. No, sir. There had been some mighty funny things at that bank. Look at Richard Maesfield killing himself almost twenty years ago. Nobody had ever got to the bottom of that. Oh, they wouldn't dare let people know the cause of this thing. There would be a lot of big bugs hurt, so they were keeping it quiet.

Some said that John Abbott had set fire to the store himself, in order to collect the insurance. He was that hard-put to make up his thefts from the bank! Others declared that he hadn't been seen all day, and that the Federal examiners had wired his description up and down the line so that he could be apprehended and returned.

Somebody revealed that a track walker down by the railroad yards had seen the old man hobbling toward the river. That was just at sunrise. He must have gone down there and drowned himself—and that would make it Gerald Abbott who had set the fire. One man swore that he had looked through the store windows just before the alarm was given, and that he had seen John Abbott running through the aisles with a torch in his hand, yelling like a maniac and setting fire to everything in sight. Then he probably had sneaked out the back way and taken the eleven-fifty for Denver. He could collect the insurance there, and after that, to hell with Shale City and the bank. But there were others who calculated that John Abbott was still in his store, and had been burned to a crisp by this time.

The whole western wall fell inward, rocketing sparks and debris a hundred feet into the sky. The flames leaped thunderously, as though an enormous poker had stirred them. Smoke drifted out over the river, so rosy with reflections that it seemed the river and the sky had been melted together. The farmers out on Sawtooth Mesa beheld the phenomenon clearly, and the orchardists the whole length of the valley, standing perilously on their barns, shouted excitedly to their families as the distant glow rose and fell.

"Yeh!" howled a derisive voice above the sputtering of the flames, "I could give a swimming pool to the town, too, if I had a whole bank to steal from! Sure—he was a swell guy! He stole our dough, an' give us a swimming pool with it!"

"Where's John Abbott?" came another voice. "That's what we want to know—just tell us where John Abbott is!"

There were answering jeers and cat-calls and profane speculations.

"Burnt to a clinker—that's what! And all the dough he took outa the Shale City National ain't goin' to do him any good where he is now!"

The brutality of the flames entered into the thoughts of the crowd. They were worried, frightened, angry, confused. They had been hurt that day, and some primitive impulse cried out for a victim. It was John Abbott! He had brought them to this pass! He had lied to them and deceived them. He had stolen from them and ruined them! Where was he now? Where had he hidden?

A party of railroad men organized a posse and marched to the Shale House to capture the fallen merchant. They beat down the clerk who tried to hinder them, and forced their way into his rooms. But he was not there. He had not been there all day. He had given them the slip. The return of this expedition gave rise to a rumour that they had taken John Abbott out and strung him up for all the ruin he had brought on Shale City, and that the lynchers, fearing prosecution, had hidden his body.

"Look!" hissed a woman in the crowd to her dishevelled companion. "All the girls from Lower Street are here!"

And sure enough, they were, with grim old Stumpy Telsa at the head of their brigade, staring at the destruction with a harsh and terrible face. Some of her charges were dressed only in the bathrobes of their profession. They were rather pretty, standing there with the firelight playing over them. They were, at least, a more attractive sight than the sleepy-eyed housewives who discussed them.

"You know, of course, my dear, that John Abbott was taking money all his life from Lower Street. Yes, ma'am! That was where he got all the cash to send kids through school and build swimming pools and start oil foundations and such. Right down there on Lower Street!"

"You don't say!" A gasp and a pause. "Well, I always suspected him. It just ain't natural for a man to be as good as he seemed to be. And you know that poor little Effie Birch, who worked at the Emporium? Well, everybody knows she had a baby, and that John Abbott paid her bills when she had it. But I know something else. *It was his own child!* I got it from a woman who knows the Birch girl very well indeed. Oh, you can't watch them kind too close! And taking money from Lower Street——!"

The conflagration diminished; the flames settled to the slow task of devouring the last stick of wreckage. The whole twisted interior could be seen plainly where the wall had fallen in, a mass of molten yellow. The hours of night marched ahead. By three o'clock the flames licked contentedly along the street level, grumbling and popping as they came upon some hitherto undiscovered fuel. At four o'clock only a pleasant red glow remained, and the hissing of the fire hoses could be heard clearly for the first time. By twos and threes and then by scores the distracted townspeople wandered home, chattering drearily about the events of the day and the rumours of the night.

Dawn found a scant dozen who had remained by the smouldering bier of the Emporium. They stood gaunt and dark between the pink flush of sunrise and the glow of the embers. When the town awakened to go to work, nothing remained but crumpled brick, white ashes, little puffs of steamy smoke. The people of Shale City, gazing at the devastation which once had been John Abbott's store, could scarcely realize what had happened.

As for the old man, he was never found. To this day there are people in Shale City who will swear that he escaped with the money from the Shale City National, and now is living luxuriously in Europe. But Phil Haley, who was one of the first to reach the store that tragic night, said that he tried to enter it through the alley, and that while he battered away at the stout iron door, he heard what sounded like John Abbott's voice screaming faintly above the first confusion of the flames. It seemed to him, said Phil Haley, that the voice was chanting some monotonous refrain. He couldn't make any clear sense out of it, but it sounded like: "I'm goin' along! I'm goin' along!"

Hermann Vogel questioned Phil Haley closely about the words, a mirthless smile playing over his lips as though he had found an explanation for something which had troubled him a long while. Nothing more, Phil Haley said; just a thin old voice chanting that senseless litany until finally it gasped away and was lost in the roar of the burning Emporium: "I'm goin' along! I'm goin' along . . ."

XX

W HEN it was decided, about a week later, that John Abbott had perished in the fire, his nephew opened the merchant's will. Drawn up after Ann's death in 1929, it disposed of almost six hundred thousand dollars. No one bothered to probate it, for there was nothing left. Gerald Abbott sat in his office and read it carefully.

To my nephew, Gerald Abbott, the sum of one hundred thousand dollars ($100,000) which, in addition to that which he already has received at my hands, will provide bountifully for him as long as he lives. . .

To a corporation which shall be known as the Shale City Educational Foundation, the sum of one hundred and fifty thousand dollars ($150,000) to be used as a basis for loans to students of any age, sex, race or religion. Notes shall not be required from borrowers; but interest not to exceed four per cent. per year shall be charged for the purpose of enlarging the fund and replacing those small sums which from time to time will be lost. The corporation shall be managed by a board of directors composed of . . .

To the Shale City Oil Foundation, the sum of two hundred thousand dollars ($200,000) which shall be used to advance the researches now being carried on by that group: with the stipulation that the income from all processes developed by the Foundation shall revert in equal shares to the town of Shale City and the county of Shale Mountain. Money thus derived shall be devoted to the lowering of the respective tax rates, with the reasonable expectation that eventually they will be eliminated entirely, thus increasing property values, attracting new residents to Shale City, and assuring present residents a happy measure of protection and permanency for their homes and lands. . .

To all employees of the Emporium who have been with the store not less than one year and not more than three years, the sum of five hundred dollars ($500). To all employees who have been with the store not less than three years and not more than five years, the sum of one thousand dollars ($1,000). To all employees who have been with the store for a period longer than five years, the sum of five hundred dollars ($500) for each year of service, beginning with the first year . . .

To my cousin, Henry Pilcher . . . to my aunt . . . and to my dear friend, Hermann Schonk . . .

And finally, to the Shale City Chamber of Commerce all that remains after the above bequests have been executed and the expenses of administration cleared. This money, which should be considerable, shall be used for the purchase of advertising space in the various national magazines, in which shall be set forth in an attractive and intelligent manner all the manifold advantages of residence in Shale City and western Colorado . . .

Signed by me this twenty-ninth day of August, 1929.

JOHN ABBOTT

Witness, ARTHUR FRENCH

Gerald Abbott, holding the old man's will, could almost see his uncle standing before him in the office—a mild, gentle little man, his normally small body shrinking and shrivelling with the years. Gerald Abbott knew that some tragic secret had motivated John Abbott all the years of his life, but he had never been able to discover it. Ann Abbott, with fierce pride, had kept her counsel to the last. Now an odd speculation flashed through Gerald Abbott's mind.

"If John Abbott had been three inches taller," he thought, "his whole life history might have been different."

He toyed with the idea for a moment, and then dismissed it; and a little later he wondered why it had ever occurred to him.

John Abbott had kept a steel box in the hotel safe at the Shale House. About two weeks after the fire, the night clerk remembered it and brought it to Gerald. It held a few old letters, a snapshot of the Emporium when it had been a shack, and some scratch paper filled with meaningless figures.

There was also a copy of the instrument by which John Abbott had deeded the swimming pool to Shale City; and folded in the document was a little slip of hotel stationery, covered with the old man's faltering script. It was somewhat difficult to decipher, and after he had completed the task, Gerald Abbott frowned and read it over three times very carefully. Then he crumpled it hastily, as though it were something nasty, and threw it into the waste basket. But its message gave him many uncomfortable moments:

The deed by which I transferred the Abbott Natatorium to the people of Shale City empowers me to change its name whenever I desire. I leave one personal obligation which I shall never be able to repay. In recognition of it, I hereby declare, and call upon the city council to confirm, that the municipal swimming pool bearing my name shall be known hereafter as

THE MARIA TELSA NATATORIUM
Signed, JOHN ABBOTT